Gwen Kirkwood's family have always been ~~~~
She was born in South Yorkshire and her brothers
and other relatives still farm there. She went to
Dumfries to work as a dairy inspector in the public
health department of the county council, and though
she didn't enjoy the work she found the countryside
quite beautiful, and she has since settled in Scotland.
She is married to a farmer and has three children.

Fairlyden at War

Gwen Kirkwood

HEADLINE

First published in 1993
by HEADLINE BOOK PUBLISHING PLC

First published in paperback in 1993
by HEADLINE BOOK PUBLISHING

10 9 8 7 6 5 4 3 2 1

ISBN 0 7472 4182 1

Printed and bound in Great Britain by
HarperCollins Manufacturing, Glasgow

HEADLINE BOOK PUBLISHING
A division of Hodder Headline PLC
Headline House
79 Great Titchfield Street
London W1P 7FN

Acknowledgements to my loyal but neglected family and friends, especially my daughter, Marion; to all who have assisted with reminiscences or research, including the staff at the Ewart and Annan libraries, especially Bob on the Mobile Library.

My thanks to Jane Morpeth, my editor, and Yvonne Heather, my agent, for their guidance and encouragement throughout.

THE BANKS OF THE NITH
by Robert Burns

The Thames flows proudly to the sea,
Where royal cities stately stand;
But sweeter flows the Nith to me,
Where Cummins ance had high command:
When shall I see that honoured land,
That winding stream I love so dear!
Must wayward fortune's adverse hand
For ever, ever keep me here?

How lovely, Nith, thy fruitful vales,
Where spreading hawthorns gaily bloom!
How sweetly wind thy sloping dales,
Where lambkins wanton thro' the broom!
Tho' wandering, now, must be my doom,
Far from thy bonnie banks and braes,
May there my latest hours consume,
Amang the friends of early days!

One

Crispin Bradshaw moved towards the window and his resolve crystallised into a firm determination to put his affairs in order. He did not know why he had such a sudden feeling of urgency on a bright April morning. Certainly he was an old man, but he was in good health. It was the letter – the tone of it as much as the actual contents. Ever since he had seen the Yorkshire postmark and recognised the handwriting, he had had a growing sense of unease. When he had read it his heart had thumped, as it often did these days when he allowed himself to be perturbed. He felt angry and indignant – but worst of all was the inexplicable feeling of fear for those nearest and dearest to him.

But as he gazed out of the wide bay window a smile of affection erased some of the lines from his face. He might need his spectacles for reading the newspaper but there was nothing wrong with his sight when it came to recognising the slim figure of his granddaughter, even though she was still two fields away. He was sure no other seventeen-year-old girl would ride a horse as big as the chestnut gelding. The beast was strong, reflecting his distant Clydesdale ancestry, quite capable of carrying a grown man for a full day's hunting, even over rough country. Crispin did not really approve of a young lady, especially his own granddaughter, riding such a mount, and he approved even less of Kirsty sitting astride and wearing that dreadful article of clothing she called jodhpurs. His disapproval on all three subjects had been registered, cheerfully acknowledged – and obviously disregarded.

The rapport which had developed between Kirsty and her ungainly mount was uncanny and Crispin knew there would be trouble for anyone who threatened to separate them, even a well-loved grandfather.

He allowed his gaze to wander over the vista spread before him, while horse and rider were temporarily hidden from view by the knolls and hollows which were a feature of the Long Meadow. It had been a week of brilliant sunshine and sharp,

1

skin-tingling showers but this morning the only clouds in the innocent blue sky were white swansdown powder puffs drifting high in the heavens. Before him the fields were spread out like a freshly painted picture, green, bright, fresh – yes, beautifully fresh, as though the whole world had been newly washed. He drew in a long, satisfying breath. He felt almost young again; surely the hawthorn hedge was greener than it had been yesterday? And the ash trees . . .?

His gaze returned to the meadow. He gasped, sucking in his breath sharply this time. His blue-veined hands clenched the back of a mahogany chair, the knuckles gleamed white. But he could not drag his eyes away from the slim figure bending low over the big gelding's neck, urging him forward, straight at the hedge.

'Why, oh why, doesn't she take time to go round by the Meadow gate?' Crispin breathed tensely.

He could not know the tumult of anger, indignation and dismay which surged in his granddaughter's breast as she gritted her teeth and spurred her mount forward, knowing that Marocco welcomed the challenge just as much as she did herself. He soared effortlessly, clearing the twiggy branches and the narrow ditch beyond with ease. He cantered on, sensing that his young mistress's thought had already returned to whatever had upset her during her brief visit to the Muircumwell Village Store.

Usually Kirsty Fairly enjoyed a chat with Lizzie Whiteley, generally known as Miss Lizzie to a whole generation of Muircumwell children.

'It isna Miss Lizzie's fault that her favourite nephew happens to be James MacFarlane,' she murmured in the gelding's velvety ear, as she leant forward giving his neck a belated pat of encouragement. 'She sounded so proud because he is to dine at Fairlyden with my parents. How dare he invite himself back, especially after he deserted us all for the MacFarlanes of Nithanvale? And after everything my father has done for him. Teaching him all he knows about breeding fine cattle. Sharing his plans and dreams for the future.' Kirsty glanced up at the long Meadow stretching in front of them.

'Come on, boy, we'll cut across towards the track and jump the next hedge as well today. A little healthy exercise is a lot better than wasting time thinking about traitors!'

In her heart Kirsty knew it would take a lot more than exercise to erase the memory of her quarrel with James. She had trusted him implicitly for as long as she could remember. He had been six years old when she was born; he was already settled happily in Fairlyden cottage, with his widowed mother keeping house for her brother, Thomas Whiteley. As she had grown older he had shared so many childhood secrets with her, helped her with her tasks and shared her ploys. They had loved the Fairlyden animals, especially the Ayrshire cows which were her father's pride and joy. 'I shall never understand why he left,' she muttered, as she spurred the big chestnut gelding forward. 'And I shall never forgive him for going to Nithanvale. I wish he'd never discovered that the MacFarlanes are his own distant relations.'

The thrill of a good gallop, and the feeling that she was flying through the air, dispelled some of Kirsty's indignation, at least for the present.

'Och you enjoyed that just as much as I did, didn't you Marocco?' she carolled in exuberant delight, clapping the gleaming coat with true appreciation. Her blue-grey eyes sparkled and her cheeks were flushed with the sheer joy of the moment.

In the dining room at Fairlyside Crispin expelled his breath in a sigh of relief, but he shook his white head several times and his lips pursed.

'It will be Kirsty you're watching, I suppose?' His wife regarded him affectionately but a wry smile curved her lips.

'Yes, but I'm too old to watch with equanimity while our rapscallion of a granddaughter performs such dangerous circus tricks. They jumped the hedge and there's a ditch on this side!'

'We-ell, you know Kirsty. She's always enjoyed a challenge. It's in the breeding of her – though I dinna think she will take any silly risks, for Marocco's sake, if not her own.'

'Mmmm . . .' Crispin was not convinced. He moved to the table, walking easily, his upright bearing belying his eighty-one years. His bushy white brows drew together in a frown. 'I think Logan should warn her to be more careful. After all he is her father.' Sarah did not reply and when Crispin looked up he saw the familiar twinkle in her brown eyes. His gaze softened, taking in the tendrils of white hair which framed her face. 'I know, I know,' he muttered dryly. 'It would be a waste of time. She would look at him with her big grey eyes and blink those ridiculously long lashes . . .'

'Smile sweetly – and take not one scrap of notice.' Sarah finished for him. 'It seems to me the only person she's never managed to wind around her little finger is James MacFarlane. I dinna think she has forgiven him yet for leaving Fairlyden.'

'James would have been foolish not to accept his great-uncle's offer to work at Nithanvale.'

'Mmm, I'm not so sure.'

'Aah, that's because there's never been any place on earth as fine as Fairlyden for you, my dear,' Crispin smiled. 'Kirsty has inherited your love for the farm and she thrives on challenges too!'

'What about that stubborn streak inherited from her grandfather?' Sarah quipped readily.

Before Crispin could respond there was the clatter of hooves on the stony path, followed by light footsteps.

'I've brought you the newspaper from the Store, Grandfather. I thought it would save you walking. Are you—?' Kirsty stopped short as she entered the dining room via the square front hall. 'Don't tell me you two are still eating breakfast at . . .' She cast a teasing glance at the black marble clock on the mantelshelf above the fire. 'At quarter to nine!'

'Life is more leisurely when you get old, lassie,' Sarah smiled.

'You! Old, Granny? Och, you'll never grow old while you come to the milking every morning.'

'It would need something mighty serious to keep your grandmother from the Fairlyden milking,' her grandfather agreed. 'I'm afraid I'm the culprit if we're late finishing breakfast. I must have dropped off to sleep again.'

'And why not indeed.' His wife glanced at him affectionately. 'As I said, lassie, we've all the time in the world. It's a fine thing not to be hurrying from one job to another from dawn to dusk.' Kirsty met her grandfather's eyes and smiled. They both knew Sarah wouldn't know what to do with herself if she wasn't cooking or baking, making jam or chutney, or busy in her garden. Even when she was sitting down to rest she always had some knitting to do.

'I don't like to see a nice young lady dressed in such strange garments, Kirsty . . .' Crispin began.

'Not strange, Grandfather, just comfortable, and very convenient. Anyway, didn't Granny show you the picture of the little Princess Elizabeth riding her pony? She was wearing jodhpurs . . .' She smiled winningly. 'For a man who keeps up to date with all the latest developments in the Yorkshire woollen industry, not to mention the world in general, you

4

have some quaint ideas about young ladies' clothes. You've got to remember this is 1934. Times have changed since the last war. Women did all sorts of things they'd never done before and I'm part of the new generation.'

Sarah watched them fondly, knowing that Crispin was beaten, even before he began. He adored Kirsty. Almost everyone did. There was something so alive, so vital about her. She would never be as beautiful as her mother of course, but she had inherited Beth's fine bone structure, toning down the square jaw which gave her such an air of determination, especially on the rare occasions when she was angry. Then her smiling mouth could set very firmly indeed. Kirsty's eyes are her best feature, Sarah reflected, seeing the golden flecks dancing in their blue-grey depths as she grinned impishly at her grandfather. Her blue open-necked shirt seemed to intensify the colour of her eyes this morning and she had unusually thick dark lashes, even for a girl.

'Are you not cold, lassie? Riding all the way to Muircumwell without even a jacket?' Sarah asked, eyeing her slender waist, the firm young breasts beneath the cotton shirt, the long column of her graceful neck. Kirsty had inherited her own fair complexion, she thought with satisfaction, and the delicate pink colour which emphasised her high cheekbones. Kirsty turned to her, stretching her arms above her head, almost as though she would reach for the sky.

'It's a beautiful morning, Granny, and you know I never feel the cold when I'm riding Marocco. We're there and back almost before we know it.'

'Yes, and no wonder, the way you ride across country, jumping hedges and ditches as though they're no more than matchsticks,' Crispin recalled sternly. 'It's not good for my old heart watching you and that – that circus animal!'

'Oh, Grandfather, you know Marocco is only named after the famous performing horse. He's the trustiest steed in the whole world.' She embraced the air extravagantly. A lot more trustworthy than some of my so-called 'friends', she thought silently. Her smooth brow creased in a frown and her arms fell to her side as she recalled Miss Lizzie's words.

'James says he willna be calling tae see me this Sunday because he has an appointment with your father. An appointment, eh! My, he's fairly come up i' the world now he's at Nithanvale. He says your father asked him tae dine at Fairlyden.'

'James has eaten his meals at Fairlyden often enough before without anyone making a fuss.' Kirsty realised she had spoken irritably, maybe even sullenly, when she saw Miss Lizzie's puzzled glance.

'B-but he was only a laddie then. Your mother and grandmother were very kind tae ma sister Anna and her bairn. James is a man now. A farmer in his ain right,' she had added proudly. 'He said he was going tae discuss business with your father.' Kirsty sighed, remembering. She had had no wish to hurt James's homely little aunt and she admitted to herself that at least part of her pique was because no one had warned her of James's impending visit to her home. Now her young mouth set in an ominous line and she tossed her head, shaking back the thick swathe of wavy brown hair in a gesture of irritation.

'Did your grandmother tell you about the new cooker I am installing for her?' her grandfather asked genially, interrupting her thoughts.

'Cooker?' Kirsty's attention was certainly diverted.

'Yes. It's called an Aga cooker and it never goes out – or at least only once a year, or when someone forgets to fuel it.'

'Never goes out! Granny . . .? Is Grandfather teasing me? This isna the first day of April so it canna be huntegowk.'

'He's not teasing, lassie. I just hope it is as good as he says it will be.' Sarah frowned. She felt she was getting too old for changes and she had grown attached to the big black-leaded range with its shining steel trimmings, and the glow of the fire between the ribs always brought her comfort on a dull winter's day. 'There's no fire, or at least not one you can see . . .' she said slowly, doubtfully.

'No, but it is warm all the time, even first thing in the morning. Think how nice that will be for our old bones on a cold winter morning. And you can cook at any time of the day or night, well, that's what it says. It has four different ovens and we're having a water boiler as well.'

'It sounds wonderful.' Kirsty murmured, marvelling at her grandfather's modern outlook on such things when he could be so very old-fashioned in other ways.

'It ought to be wonderful,' Sarah declared. 'It's costing a pretty penny.'

'Maybe it is,' Crispin's mouth firmed and his bushy white brows drew together in a frown, 'but we've worked hard all our lives to earn our own bit of comfort. We didn't sit back and—'

'Here, here! I agree with Grandfather on that score, Granny, and so will Mother and Father when they hear.'

'Yes, lass, I'm sure they will. They don't expect owt for nowt either – as we say in Yorkshire. Your father has paid the rent for Fairlyden as regularly as clockwork, despite the bad times farming has suffered since nineteen eighteen. I didn't want to take it, but he insisted. Now that nephew of mine – your Uncle Robert – is a different kettle of fish. Half the Bradshaw woollen mill still belongs to me but it's like getting water out of a stone getting any money out of him.'

'Och, Crispin, dinna distress yourself about them, please.' Sarah soothed. It worried her when he got angry and excited. It wasn't good for him at his age. 'Sadie is my own daughter but I have to admit she is just as bad as Robert. She only writes when they have acquired something new to boast about.'

'Yes, I suppose you're right m'dear. They're a well-matched pair.' Crispin turned to Kirsty. 'We had a letter yesterday morning telling us all about their new electric fire and electric cooker, as well as new decorations in their London house.'

Kirsty was surprised. Her grandparents rarely criticised anyone; they were almost invariably tolerant and kind.

'I've only met Aunt Sadie and Uncle Robert once,' she mused. 'I can't remember much about them.'

'Sadie caused your mother a great deal of distress and unhappiness,' Sarah reflected with a sigh. 'Hasn't she ever told you, lassie?'

'Mother never mentions Aunt Sadie now I think about it.' Kirsty frowned. 'She always says if you can't say anything good, don't say anything at all – so maybe that's why.'

'Mmm, your mother is a fine woman,' Crispin nodded. 'Anyway, young lady, we're getting this new cooker put in next week so I expect your grandmother will need a bit of help with the cleaning up afterwards.'

'I'll help, Granny,' Kirsty volunteered instantly.

'Aah, I reckoned you'd say that, lass. You're a grand girl, even if you are a bit wild on that horse.' Crispin's eyes sparkled.

'O-oh, Grandfather!' Kirsty grinned. 'But, speaking of my horse, poor old Marocco will think I've deserted him, and I promised to help Mother and Lucy with the spring-cleaning so I'd better fly.' She gave them both a quick kiss and departed as breezily as she had arrived, but her earlier dismay over James MacFarlane's proposed visit to Fairlyden still lingered.

* * *

Crispin sat in contemplative silence after Kirsty had departed. There was a slight frown on his forehead which told his wife he was pondering a serious matter and she guessed he was thinking about his nephew's laxity over the accounts for the Yorkshire woollen mill. She suspected that Sadie and Robert enjoyed a better lifestyle than the present industrial depression could support. Why, oh why, do people crave for the impossible? she asked herself. She had never had money to waste on luxuries; in fact she had been near to desperation when William Fairly had died and left her a widow with a family to bring up and no money to pay the debts.

Her eyes held a faraway look as she thought of the past. It was seventy-five years since she had been born in the sturdy little farmhouse which overlooked the Fairlyden farmsteading and the surrounding buildings. She had never expected to leave it alive. All her children had been born there . . . Alex, crippled from birth yet with the strength of character to overcome his handicap and prove himself a successful farmer at Mains of Muir with Emma and their three fine sons. Then there was Billy, with his craving for adventure, now living on the other side of the Atlantic; Ellen, gentle, compassionate, a born nurse. She would have been a perfect mother if only her husband, Doctor Brad Leishman, had not died from his war injuries. After Ellen, the twins had almost cost her her life – Sadie and Katie – as different as night and day. Even after all these years, it was impossible to remember Katie's sweet young face without a pang of sorrow. It was still harder for Sarah to accept that she had borne a daughter as jealous and malicious as Sadie.

Ten years later, to everyone's astonishment, including her own, Logan had thrust himself into the world. It was Logan and Beth – sweethearts from childhood – who had kept Fairlyden going through the dark years following the war: even now the shadows of the depression still hung heavily over British farmers and the thousands of hungry men and women who were without work, without money to buy even basic necessities. No wonder there were hunger marches to London. Somehow it didn't make sense that people should go hungry while half the land lay derelict. Sarah sighed heavily as she pondered the anomaly of it all. Yet she herself was more comfortable now, in her old age, than she had ever been.

It was Crispin who had built this house and called it

Fairlyside. It was only a few hundred yards down the track from the farmsteading. She could still see it all from the upstairs windows at the back – the small triangular field, then the tiny cottage where Anna MacFarlane and her brother Thomas lived; a little further on was the byre, the stable, the sturdy farmhouse with the dairy and the bothy attached, the cart sheds and calf houses . . . She brought her attention back to the well-proportioned dining room with its blue and red turkey carpet, the gleaming mahogany furniture, but as always her gaze moved to the wide bay window. It faced south to the fields, the church and the Manse, the village, beyond which she often glimpsed the shining waters of the Solway Firth, the Cumberland hills, the Galloway hills . . . Her eyes were serene and happy as they returned to her husband. Crispin had proved himself a loving and considerate partner in their declining years.

'We've such a lot to be thankful for . . .' she breathed softly. Crispin caught her loving glance and smiled, but his gaze was thoughtful.

'Indeed we have, my dear. We have each other and we've been blessed with good health – better health than Logan,' he added sadly.

'Aah, but it was the effects of the trench gas, and near starvation which made Logan less robust, and he is fortunate too. Beth loves him dearly and no one could give him better care. They're devoted to each other, and to Fairlyden.'

'I agree, my dear. They are still as much in love as they were when they married, and they were only the same age as Kirsty is now.'

'They've had remarkable success too, especially with their pedigree cattle. That's a blessing in itself when the prices for everything else are so low.'

'I have every faith in Logan's ability to win through, at least, as far as it is in his power.' He frowned. 'It's a long time since I made my will. If you remember, we didn't even know Logan was still alive then.'

'I shall never forget.' Sarah shuddered.

'Kirsty was only a toddler. Luke's birth was not even a possibility.' His frown deepened, his expression became grim. 'I must make sure they all get their proper inheritance. Robert and Sadie would be absolutely ruthless if they had any power. I shall pay a visit to the solicitors in Dumfries . . .'

'Carsewell and Donaldson's?' Sarah sat up even straighter,

her tone more than a little concerned. 'You dinna feel ill do you, Crispin?'

'Ill? No, of course not, my dear. But it's spring and I've an urge to set things straight.'

'But I thought the Bradshaw Trust your father made left everything in order.'

'Not quite. Ultimately the Trust was left to my discretion. I know things have not been good since the war, but it is sixteen years since it ended and the profits from the Bradshaw Mills should have been higher by now. I'm not happy with that nephew of mine. I'd like to be sure Robert and Sadie don't get more than their fair share when I'm gone. They've nobody but themselves to consider, no family to inherit the Bradshaw Mills. They're selfish, Sarah, the pair of 'em!' His Yorkshire accent was always more apparent when he was angry. 'They sacked a lot of good workers the minute trade slumped in the nineteen-twenties. I haven't forgotten that. I made Ted Forbes a director so that he might be able to restrain Robert's ideas a bit, but there's a limit to what he can do without real clout. Conditions haven't improved for the workers in the last ten years either, according to his reports. And I can see from the accounts that they haven't replaced any of the machinery or brought it up to date. I expect they think I'm too old to know what they're up to. My father would turn in his grave if he thought he'd pulled himself up from the gutter just to leave his mill to a grandson the likes of Mr Robert Smith! He's just like his father and he'll squander the lot the minute I'm gone.'

'Och, dinna get upset, Crispin. You've been brooding ever since Sadie's letter came.'

'Mmm, well I don't intend to brood any longer. I shall drive to Dumfries first thing on Monday.'

'You're not going in your motorcar?' Sarah's eyes were wide with consternation. 'You know the new doctor said it was not good for you, winding up that handle to start the engine . . .'

'Aagh!' Crispin snorted. 'How can a young chap like Doctor Broombank know what's good for me, lass?'

'I'm scarcely a "lass" anymore,' Sarah observed wryly, 'and you're no chicken either, whether it's spring again or not. I worry about you, Crispin.'

'You shouldn't worry, Sarah.' Crispin looked at her steadily, his grey eyes tender. 'If I died tomorrow, I'd die a happy man, thanks to you. Since you became my wife, these past sixteen years have been a bonus I never expected to have, and I've done nothing to deserve them.'

'Oh, Crispin! They've been happy years for me too – and I dinna want to be left alone – without you. So please take care?'

'I will, lass, I will – but I've no intention of letting either my nephew or your daughter fritter away anything that should belong to Logan and his family.'

'I often wondered whether Sadie guessed our secret and realised that you were Logan's father,' Sarah mused. 'She was always so jealous of him, even when he was a toddler.'

'Well, she might have guessed then, but she would never admit it at this stage – not if it means Logan or his children getting any money she thinks should go to Robert and herself. And Robert's tarred with the same brush. So! It's time I had everything in black and white.'

Two

Kirsty's face had lost some of its usual vibrant glow as she met her mother's eyes across the breakfast table on Sunday morning. 'Why is James MacFarlane coming here to lunch?' she asked. 'Why isn't he having his meal with his mother and his Uncle Thomas as usual? Or is Fairlyden cottage not good enough for Master MacFarlane now that he's found wealthy relations?'

'Kirsty, Kirsty lassie . . . That isna like you,' Beth rebuked, but her voice was calm and soothing as it had always been when Kirsty was a child. It did not have the same reassuring affect now though and Beth realised with a pang that her daughter was no longer a bairn; she was a young woman on the threshold of life and with a mind of her own. Nevertheless, there was no excuse for rudeness or bad manners. Her mouth firmed and became as determined as her daughter's. 'James has some business to discuss with your father. I dinna ken what about, so dinna ask!' she went on, before Kirsty could speak. 'Whatever it is, it's important enough for him to write a letter specially, asking if your father could arrange a convenient time.'

'And did Father remind James that he had forsaken Fairlyden? He didn't consider whether the time was convenient then!' Kirsty bit her lip and frowned. 'Did Father ask him to eat with us?'

'Of course.' Beth's brows rose in surprise. 'You know your father has always enjoyed James's company, even when he was a wee laddie. He went down to Fairlyside specially to telephone him.'

'So the MacFarlanes have a telephone too.'

'Kirsty!' Beth's blue eyes were full of reproach and Kirsty remembered that her mother also had a tender heart where James MacFarlane was concerned. 'There's no need tae be jealous o' the MacFarlanes having a telephone. Your father has decided we should have one as soon as the telegraph poles come further up the glen.'

13

'I'm not jealous of the MacFarlanes! Why I—'

'But you resent the fact that old Mr MacFarlane, or perhaps his granddaughter, persuaded James to leave Fairlyden in favour of Nithanvale?' Beth suggested gently. Kirsty pursed her lips. She was not in the habit of being childish, or unreasonable, and she was not proud of herself, especially regarding her father's invitation. He was hospitable to everyone. They frequently had people to dine since he had become known as a breeder of fine Ayrshire cattle; indeed she usually enjoyed both the company and the conversation at such times, but today she wanted to escape.

'James MacFarlane told me often enough that he and his mother were indebted to the Fairlys, especially Granny, for giving them a home and work after they had to give up the tenancy of Highmuir Farm. He said he would never leave.'

'Och, Kirsty, he was probably too young to ken what his life would hold when he said such things. Anyway it wasna James's fault his father died when he was so young and I'm sure your grandmother never felt Anna MacFarlane owed her a debt. She has certainly repaid us with her loyalty and hard work, especially when things were so difficult after the war – her brother Thomas too.'

'I just canna understand anyone *wanting* to leave Fairlyden.'

'No-o . . . I know how you feel, lassie.' Beth agreed softly and her eyes took on a dreamy quality which told Kirsty her mother was thinking of her own youth, born in the Fairlyden cottage, growing up with the youngest Fairly only a few months older – constant companions from the cradle according to her grandmother. 'I canna imagine wanting to live anywhere else but Fairlyden, but James must have had good reasons of his own for leaving.' A shadow darkened her blue eyes. 'Your father certainly misses him. I just wish Luke would show an interest in the farm and the animals . . .' She loved her delicate, dreamy young son dearly but in her heart she knew he had not the slightest interest in the animals or the farm – or anything else so dear and familiar to herself and Logan. 'James MacFarlane knew the names of all the cows in the byre when he was Luke's age – and so did you.' She met Kirsty's eyes steadily. 'Luke is twelve now but he never goes near the byre if he can help it. It was a shame that old Bess chased him when he was so young. I don't think he'll ever forget his terror.'

'I'm sure he will, Mother, when he grows up.' Kirsty consoled, but in her heart she knew her young brother's mind rarely dwelled on anything except his books or sketching. He could reproduce a likeness in seconds and his bird drawings were remarkable in their detail. Indeed he spent hours lying on his stomach drawing flowers, or by the burn studying the birds and insects which came into his view; but he detested the larger animals – even her own harmless Marocco.

Luke Fairly had always been small for his age, and his fine fair hair flopping over his brow and pale skin gave him a delicate air. Kirsty wondered how he would cope after the summer holidays when he started school at the Dumfries Academy. He was to cycle to the station, three and a half miles away, and catch the train each morning, returning home at night, instead of staying in the school hostel as she had done herself. Her father said the daily exercise would toughen Luke up a little and give him an appetite. Her mother had agreed but Kirsty guessed she was secretly apprehensive for her quiet sensitive son.

Kirsty recalled her own unhappiness in those first dreadful weeks away from home. She was far more resilient than Luke but she knew her initial misery had caused her mother some distress, and she had asked James, already in his final year, to keep an eye on her. He had helped her to accept, and even enjoy, her new life, but she had always looked forward eagerly to the Saturdays when she was allowed to return to Fairlyden. It was the recollection of her own early misery which had prompted her to support the idea of Luke travelling to school each day. He had accepted the arrangements without comment. Indeed he rarely argued over anything. He was a happy, peace-loving boy with their mother's gentle smile and sensitivity. Kirsty loved him dearly, for all he was five years younger than herself and entirely different in nature.

Her mouth tightened suddenly. James MacFarlane had disagreed with her over Luke, believing that her young brother would benefit from the change of company and environment. Since then she had avoided him whenever he returned to the Fairlyden cottage to see his mother and Uncle Thomas. Until today.

'Mother, I've been thinking, maybe I'll stay at Granny's after the kirk.'

'Oh no you will not, Kirsty Fairly.' Beth's tone was firm. 'You will stay in your own home and be as polite to James MacFarlane as you are to any other of your father's guests.' Beth sighed heavily. 'You used to run to James with all your problems – just as if he was your elder brother. He was always patient with you.'

'Well, he's not patient now! He's . . . he's . . .'

'Who isna patient?' Logan Fairly came into the kitchen, his grey eyes sparkling, his warm smile embracing his wife and daughter.

'I'll go and get ready for the kirk,' Kirsty said hastily, flashing her mother a pleading glance. They both knew her father had a high regard for James MacFarlane. Apart from his knowledge of Ayrshire cattle, gleaned during his early years as Logan's constant shadow, he had acquitted himself well, both at school and at the Glasgow Agricultural College. He had won great acclaim and his academic and practical achievements had been applauded in the local newspaper and in the *Scottish Farmer*.

It was this publicity which had brought him and his mother to the attention of his great-uncle, though it had taken George MacFarlane several months before he approached James and several more before he had lured him to Nithanvale. Anna MacFarlane had been suspicious of the old man and his motives, despite his frailty.

'The fine MacFarlanes didna come near me when I was a young widow at Highmuir Farm and in sore need o' a helpin' hand,' she had proclaimed bitterly to her son, to her brother and to Logan and Beth.

'There was a family feud,' James had explained to her parents in Kirsty's hearing. 'Mother found an old journal belonging to my grandfather when she moved from Highmuir. Uncle Thomas read it all ages ago so we know Great-Uncle George is telling the truth. My grandfather was a few years older than him but they had been very close. Two weeks before Great-Uncle George's wedding my grandfather ran away with his bride and married her that very day at Gretna Green.

'Apparently none of the family ever forgave Grandfather for the scandal and bitterness he left behind. He never went back to Nithanvale again, not even for his mother's funeral, nor did he receive any of the MacFarlane money.

'Great-Uncle George married eventually but his wife died in

childbirth, leaving him with a son. His family seems to have been unfortunate. His son married but he and his wife were killed when their carriage overturned. Their only child was thrown clear and she survived. Mary has lived at Nithanvale with her grandfather ever since. She is his only kin – apart from myself, and I dinna feel I'm really kin, although I have the family name.'

Afterwards, Kirsty had listened to her mother and father discussing James's dilemma.

'I'll bet the old man hopes James and his granddaughter will marry. I believe there have been MacFarlanes at Nithanvale for more than a century so a union between them would perpetuate the name for another generation at least.'

'But, Logan, he canna arrange James's life. Or his granddaughter's.' Beth had been shocked at the idea.

'No-o, but it's just the way these proud old families used to arrange things, and old Mr MacFarlane is used to breeding and mating cattle. He probably regards his family in the same way. He will certainly be throwing them into each other's company.'

'B-but he canna arrange human lives.'

'Maybe I'm misjudging him,' Logan conceded. 'I've only met him a couple of times. I understand he engaged a manager at Nithanvale, even before he had his first stroke, so perhaps he merely wants James's help. Anyway it has to be James's decision.'

'Aye. Anna doesna want him to go though. She's very bitter that MacFarlane is only showing an interest in James now he's a grown man and has proved he has some ability.'

'Och, you never ken, he might inherit the cows and take over the tenancy if his great-uncle takes a liking to him.'

'James isna the kind to go to Nithanvale just for his ain gain.' Beth declared firmly. Logan smiled.

'Dinna fret, Beth. I ken James is a fine laddie, but maybe his family should have inherited some o' the MacFarlane money anyway. Maybe the old man is developing a conscience about it now that he's getting closer to facing his Maker.'

So James had gone to Nithanvale and they had all missed him. He had even shown some of the older Nithanvale Ayrshires at the local show a few months later and beaten the Fairlyden animals. So why did he need to talk to her father now, Kirsty wondered, as she brushed her short thick hair vigorously until it shone, curling upwards from her brow before falling in a

17

deep wave which just covered her ears and curved towards the faint hollow beneath her high cheekbones. She saw nothing of the dancing lights in her wide grey eyes, nor the engaging lift at the corners of her mischievous mouth. Usually she donned her clothes with a gay abandon but on this particular morning she stared critically at her reflection in the oval cheval mirror, spoiling the image a little as the well-defined arch of her eyebrows drew together in a disapproving frown. She put her hat on, the blue felt with the fashionably wide brim and pleated crown. Her winter coat was a little heavy for the fine spring morning but it was smart and the double-breasted style and small belt emphasised her slender waist and trim figure, and the brown squirrel collar toned nicely with her leather shoes and gloves. Even so, Kirsty felt dissatisfied with her appearance.

'Are ye ready, lassie?' her mother called. 'Your father says we should hurry or Grandfather Bradshaw will be starting to wind up the engine of his motorcar himself, before we get to Fairlyside.'

Kirsty picked up her bible and handbag and joined her mother on the landing with a rueful smile.

'I think Granny would be happier if Father kept the motorcar here all the time. She doesna like Grandfather driving since the doctor warned him about his heart. Did I tell you he was showing me how to drive the other day?'

'No!' Beth turned to her seventeen-year-old daughter. 'However did ye manage, Kirsty? It might have run away with the both of you.'

'Och, I liked it!' Kirsty grinned at her mother's shocked face. Then suddenly she sobered, remembering James MacFarlane again. 'It's a wonder *he* hasna got a motorcar,' she muttered, speaking her thoughts aloud.

'Who?'

'James MacFarlane, of course.'

'Oh, James is borrowing his great-uncle's. The old man canna drive it himself anyway. Even if he hadna lost the power in one leg, he can scarcely see, so it would be dangerous for him to drive. Apparently James drives him wherever he needs to go now, unless his granddaughter is free to drive him of course.'

'I see.' Kirsty's mouth tightened. So the young lady at Nithanvale could drive, could she? I will take up Grandfather's offer to teach me, she resolved silently. Indeed I will. Anything

18

James MacFarlane, or his half-cousin, can do, then I can do too. I'll show him I'm no longer a wee schoolgirl to be humoured – or overlooked when it suits him.

Three

James was talking to Lucy Kildougan in the kitchen at Fairlyden when Kirsty arrived back from church with Luke and her parents. He did not hear her enter and for a few moments she watched almost enviously as the pair chatted easily. Of course James had known Lucy since he was six years old. She had come to Fairlyden as Kirsty's own nursemaid when she was thirteen so that Beth could help with the field and dairy work while Logan was away fighting in France. Kirsty knew, without conceit, that Lucy was devoted to her mother and herself. She had often told them she had never wanted to work for anyone else in all her thirty years. Five years ago she had met Paddy Kildougan at a dance in the village hall. Paddy had come over from Ireland for the harvest work and had had a job on the other side of Muircumwell. Just as the harvest was almost over Logan Fairly had taken a nasty chill which inevitably settled on his chest, rendering him a very sick man for several weeks. Lucy had volunteered Paddy's help with the milking and he had proved himself invaluable. He was patient with the cows and quite knowledgeable about horses too. He said it was the seventh sense which all good Irishmen possessed – the sixth sense being to recognise the finest woman in the world across a crowded room, even before they had been introduced – a pronouncement which always delighted Lucy and brought the colour to her pretty plump cheeks.

Paddy had made himself comfortable in the bothy. Less than a year after their first meeting he and Lucy were married. There was no spare cottage at Fairlyden but the happy couple had declared that the bothy would be adequate until their bairns were born. This was the only cloud in Lucy and Paddy's little world. So far they had not been blessed with the children they both craved and they had devoted themselves to Fairlyden – Paddy to its cattle and Lucy to its people. Eventually Logan had built an additional room on to the bothy and although it was still very small the pair seemed content.

'Och here ye are, Kirsty, hame frae the kirk already!' Lucy turned from the pot she was stirring over the fire and beamed at the sight of her former charge standing in the doorway. 'My, but ye're looking real bonny today! Indeed ye're a proper smart young lady, d'ye no' think sae, James?'

Kirsty silently cursed the faint colour which mounted her cheeks under James's scrutiny. She saw nothing of the approval in his watchful eyes as he murmured agreement, but she did notice the slight tilt of his angular jaw. Proud he was, and determined too; Kirsty knew, as surely as if he'd told her so, that he was remembering their last stormy encounter.

'Aah, there you are then, James.' Logan unwittingly broke the tension. 'Come awa' into the parlour while the women get the dinner on to the table. I expect ye're hungry but it willna be long.' Kirsty watched them go, James now half a head taller than her father. His legs looked longer than ever in his good tweed suit but he had lost the gangly look he had had for so long. Kirsty noted how his shoulders had broadened.

'A body would think ye hadna seen him before, Miss Kirsty!' Lucy teased. 'Fine young man he's turned out to be, eh?' Without waiting for an answer she hurried on. 'Will ye tell your mother the soup is ready now and the chicken is roasted nicely in the oven. I'll awa' and attend tae Paddy.'

'Thanks Lucy, I'll help Mother. Did you put potatoes in the oven to roast?'

'Indeed I did, lassie. I never forget they're one o' your favourite dishes. Aye and I stuffed the chicken real well tae. Your mother made a big trifle afore she went tae the kirk. She aye minds it's the pudding James likes best. I wonder if Miss MacFarlane cooks the things he likes. I must mind and ask him if she's a guid cook.' Lucy made her exit still chattering and expecting no reply. Kirsty was still shaking her head at her round retreating figure when Beth came into the kitchen, pulling on a white apron over her best wool dress.

'Aren't ye going to take off your coat and help me serve the dinner, Kirsty? Maybe ye'd look and see whether Lucy has set the table properly.'

Kirsty ran upstairs and pulled off her hat and coat but she took time to fluff up her hair. She was glad it had a natural wave and didn't need any of the crimping from the modern permanents which were all the rage. She smoothed her skirt over her flat stomach and hips and glanced in the mirror.

'Vain! That's what you are, Kirsty Fairly,' she told her

reflection sternly. 'But you needn't trouble yourself because James MacFarlane will never notice you have grown out of school tunics!'

The meal went off pleasantly, once Luke had been located and persuaded that it was time to wash his hands and hurry into the dining room. He smiled shyly at James as he took his seat next to Kirsty. He was a slow eater and rarely talked unless asked a direct question, so everyone was surprised when he suddenly looked up from his half-empty plate and announced, 'I did one for ye, James, like ye said.' He glanced sideways at his sister and frowned slightly, studying Kirsty's profile. 'It's not quite right though. Something to do with—'

'It will be fine, Luke. Thank you.' James intervened hastily and Kirsty was surprised to see his heightened colour. He looks almost embarrassed, she thought curiously. Beth, ever sensitive, perceived James's unease. She had seen an excellent sketch of Kirsty in Luke's bedroom and now she wondered if he had done it for James – at James's request perhaps? She diverted the conversation with her usual tact.

'I dinna ken what you're talking about, Luke, but when you go to the Academy you will have to speak better English, isn't that so, James?'

'Mama! How can ye say that! You and Papa dinna say yo-ou and too-oo . . . and things like that – except sometimes when we have visitors who think they're a bit posh.'

'Aah, but your father and I didna go to the Academy to be educated! You will learn to speak like James and Kirsty soon.'

When the meal was over Logan invited James to join him in the little room he had turned into a study. In it he kept the old mahogany desk which had been at Fairlyden since the house was built by the first Earl of Strathtod for his mistress. He also had a glass-fronted cupboard filled with books on the breeding and pedigrees of Ayrshire cows and another lot of brown stud books on Clydesdale horses. It was here he retired when he wanted a little peace, especially when he was troubled with his chest.

'Ye'll not be disturbed in here,' Beth smiled at James and mended the fire with applewood logs and a few pieces of coal. 'I'm just going down to the village hall now to play the piano for the Sunday School but I'll be back before milking time. Will ye stay for supper, laddie?'

'Aah, no thanks, Mrs Fairly. I'd like to get back to Nithanvale for the milking.'

Beth nodded. 'I'll ask Kirsty to bring ye both a cup o' tea before ye leave.' She closed the door quietly behind her. She was not curious about James's affairs. She knew Logan would confide in her if he felt there was anything she needed to know – or indeed if she could offer any help or advice.

James sat in the big brown leather chair on the opposite side of the fire to Logan, but he sat on the edge of his seat, his knees apart, his arms resting on his thighs while his hands twisted and turned as though with a life of their own. Logan took his time lighting up a pipe of tobacco, eyeing James as he did so, noting the angular face – a young face, yet with strength and determination.

'It's aye best tae begin at the beginning, laddie,' he said quietly, removing the stem of his pipe briefly.

'Ye-es, I know. The fact is I badly need to talk to someone who understands my situation . . . someone who will give me an honest opinion.'

'I'll do my best,' Logan promised. He was only thirteen years older than James MacFarlane but as he saw the earnest expression in the grey-green eyes, the rapid pulse jumping in James's cheek, and watched him swallow several times in quick succession, he felt like an ancient sage.

'If—if it was just my business it wouldna be so bad, but I must ask you to – to keep my confidence? Please, Mr Fairly? I need someone I can trust not to spread rumours, or blacken the MacFarlane name.' James looked up anxiously and met Logan's gaze, alert now, though somewhat perplexed.

'I have no secrets from my wife, James.'

'No, I suppose not.' James nodded, but he seemed to relax and sat further back in the deep leather chair. He smiled wistfully. 'It must be wonderful to have someone loyal and understanding, to share problems, to know you can trust them with the most important things in life.'

'Aye,' Logan also relaxed and smiled reassuringly. 'It's the best of all relationships, laddie, if ye're lucky enough tae meet the right marriage partner.'

'Yes, I'm sure it must be. Anyway, I'm not afraid of Mistress Fairly knowing what I have to say. Indeed I think she would understand why . . . why I must try to . . . to do my best for my great-uncle, and for Mary, his granddaughter. Besides I'd like you to understand why I left Fairlyden to go to Nithanvale.'

'I dinna blame ye for that, James.'

'Maybe not, but I know most folks probably think I went there hoping to step into my great-uncle's shoes – to take over his herd and become tenant of a fine farm,' he exclaimed a little bitterly. 'But I didna go easily. It needed a lot o' thought to leave Fairlyden. He really needs me – even more than I realised.' James broke off briefly, his expression deeply troubled. 'He is my own kith and kin, even if the relationship isna very close. He's all I've got of my father's family.'

'Aye, that's true, though I dinna think ye owe him anything,' Logan said warily. 'Your mother had a hard time, long before she came back tae Fairlyden as a young widow. Your father was a fine man, James, from all I've heard, and a hard worker, but he was plagued with tuberculosis even before they married – and none o' the MacFarlanes offered to help him then. It was your mother's family, the Whiteleys who tried.'

'I know. Mother still believes Great-Uncle George only came near when he thought I might be some use to him, but he says he didn't know of my existence until I was featured in that newspaper article when I finished college. Anyway he's an old man now, and growing frail. I feel I ought to protect him if I can.'

'Protect? In what way does he need protection, James?' Logan's eyes held surprise but his expression was grave and a puzzled frown creased his forehead. For a moment James MacFarlane hesitated, then he took a deep breath and began to tell Logan of the disturbing discoveries he had made since he moved to Nithanvale.

'You know my uncle had employed a grieve, even before he had his first seizure? He intended to train him to carry on at Nithanvale, to look after everything for Mary, my half-cousin.'

'Aye . . .' Logan's eyes were hooded. 'Metcalf isn't it? The man's name?' He had seen the man at the shows – narrow faced, thin lipped, close-set eyes – not the sort of man Logan felt any desire to know well. 'How d'ye get along with him, James?'

'I didna.' James's mouth was set, his lean jaw clenched. 'He was a cheat and a liar, Mr Fairly. I'm convinced Great-Uncle George had begun to suspect some of his tricks. I wouldna be surprised it that's what caused him to have a seizure. You knew he'd had another? He's almost blind now. Mary doesna want me to worry him, but if there's any suspicion or doubts about the legitimacy of Nithanvale stock people will blame

George MacFarlane and blacken his character – probably mine too, now that I'm at Nithanvale and known to be his relative. You know yourself, Mr Fairly, people don't have as much success as the MacFarlanes of Nithanvale without making enemies as well as friends in their own sphere.'

'That's true,' Logan agreed wryly, 'especially when a man has judged and shown as many cattle as old Mr MacFarlane. Even those who detest him admit he's a clever man when it comes to breeding cattle. But why should there be . . . suspicion?'

'On account of Metcalf. That's why I needed to talk to you, but I've agreed not to call in the police to please Mary.'

'Police! Was Metcalf a criminal then?'

'He was a cheat. He took advantage of the good name of the Nithanvale herd,' James muttered darkly. 'Almost any animal with Nithanvale blood in its pedigree was guaranteed to fetch a good price – even if it looked like a monkey!'

Logan gave a faint smile and drew on his pipe. 'That's true enough.'

'Metcalf has been selling the genuine Nithanvale stock as calves. Even in a private sale he would get good prices.'

'He certainly would. I thought your uncle usually reared all the Nithanvale calves to sell as full grown heifers or stock bulls? I ken lots o' breeders who would give their right arm for a young Nithanvale calf to rear for their own stockbull.'

'Exactly! Well, Metcalf has been selling calves, pocketing the money and replacing them with ordinary Ayrshire-type calves to keep the numbers up.'

'No! Are ye sure?' Logan stared at James in shocked disbelief.

'He probably thought Uncle George would not know the difference. He may be an old man but he would certainly have known his own stock after breeding them all his life.'

'Of course he would. Surely Metcalf must be a fool if he thought otherwise.'

'Mary thinks Uncle George found out and had a violent quarrel with Metcalf. She found him lying inside the calf sheds when he had his first seizure. Apparently he could not speak at all for several months. His speech is still a little slurred and indistinct. The doctor advised her to keep Metcalf away and make sure her grandfather was not disturbed with business matters.'

'Had she any idea what Metcalf was up to?'

'No, she has never taken any interest in the farm.' A sudden smile softened James's craggy face, dispelling the shadows in his troubled eyes, however temporarily. 'She's a lovely person, Mr Fairly. She finds it hard to accept evil in anyone. But she is intelligent and she sensed that Metcalf's presence upset her grandfather.'

'So that's why they wanted you at Nithanvale?'

'Yes. After her grandfather became ill Mary made a habit of reading to him each day – snippets of interest from the newspaper, especially market reports and farming news. That was how he learned of my existence. She says he brooded over it for ages before he asked her to make enquiries; then he asked her to write and invite me to Nithanvale. As you know I visited them then, but I never considered going to live with them and work at Nithanvale. Great-Uncle George's health improved and he began to get about again. The first thing he wanted to do was inspect his animals . . .'

'Aye, that's natural enough.'

'Metcalf didna like that of course. He told Mary he was a muddled, interfering old man, and causing trouble with the other men. She half believed him too. Metcalf is a plausible wretch and Mary said her grandfather rambled a bit about things she didna understand; she really thought he was confused. Besides she knew she couldn't manage the farm without a grieve, especially since Metcalf had got rid of the herdsman and his family. That was one thing which really troubled her. Adam Alwood had been at Nithanvale for more than twenty years and he was as attached to the Nithanvale cattle as her grandfather. So they decided to come to Fairlyden to see me. Great-Uncle George told me he needed someone he could trust and I was his own kin. Mother was quite angry about that, as you know.'

'Aye, I do that.' Logan exclaimed. 'Not that Beth and I blamed her, mind you, laddie. I thought your great-uncle was using you myself, until I heard he'd offered to take you into partnership with him and his granddaughter.'

'Aah!' James grimaced ruefully. 'That's not so wonderful as it sounds, between ourselves – though I think Great-Uncle George genuinely believed he was offering me a golden opportunity – Mary was too honest to let me leave Fairlyden to go to Nithanvale under false pretences. She told me she had received two letters from the bank demanding to see her grandfather urgently. Nithanvale was in serious trouble. They wanted to know why the decline had happened so rapidly and what he was doing about it.'

'Nithanvale! In trouble!' Logan whistled incredulously.

'Yes, Nithanvale,' James repeated grimly. 'Even then Mary didn't suspect Metcalf. So many farmers have gone bankrupt since the war that she thought Nithanvale was in the same boat as everybody else. Her grandfather never discussed business with her. He doesn't believe women can understand such things.'

'He has never met the Fairly women.' Logan grinned wryly. 'I'm sure my mother still knows as much about farming business as most men. Kirsty is just like her too . . .'

'Yes. I'm afraid Mary MacFarlane is the complete opposite of Kirsty – not that she lacks intelligence,' he added hastily, 'and she is a wonderful nurse.'

Logan nodded and tapped the ash from his pipe, wondering if James was half in love with his distant cousin. 'That was one of the reasons why she refused to bother her grandfather about the letters from the bank,' James went on. 'She knew they would upset him and maybe even cause a fatal seizure. So she told me instead and hoped I would still agree to go to Nithanvale, if only temporarily, to sort things out and reassure him in some way. She seemed to think only another MacFarlane could do that. The more I heard the more I began to wonder whether there was some truth in the old man's muttered hints and ramblings about Metcalf.'

'So it was the challenge that lured ye away from Fairlyden,' Logan mused. 'I often thought there must be more to your move than we knew, laddie. How did Metcalf react to you turning up at Nithanvale?'

'Ugh, he was hostile. He was wary too . . . edgy, sort of sly, and of course the suspicions had been planted in my mind so I suppose I was looking for signs.'

'Aye laddie, but are ye sure of your facts?' Logan asked, with some concern.

'I'm sure. A breeder named Shaw had bought two calves in good faith, believing Metcalf was acting on my uncle's behalf and winding down the herd on account of his age and having no heirs to follow on. When he saw a sale catalogue with an animal with an identical pedigree and records he thought one of his must be a twin, or that there'd been a genuine mistake in the entry. Then he got talking to another breeder at the market. The man had bought four Nithanvale stirks at about the same time. Two of his had the same pedigrees as two which were in the catalogue for sale.'

'Gracious me! Surely Metcalf must have foreseen such a thing?' Logan exclaimed.

'No, I don't think he did. He seemed to think he would be in charge at Nithanvale for as long as Great-Uncle lived. He would have been wise enough not to enter them for a pedigree sale by public auction. He would have kept them at Nithanvale and the standard would have continued to deteriorate as it has been doing since the substitute calves began to take the places of the genuine stock. When I asked him about it he said I'd made a mistake with the entries. Of course the records were all there and the calves even had corresponding ear numbers. Then he blustered and tried to blame Great-Uncle George, said he'd been confused for weeks before the seizure.'

'And had he?'

'No, and the fraud had gone on after his first seizure anyway. As soon as I found out, I withdrew the heifers from the sale catalogue but Metcalf has made the MacFarlanes look dishonest – or at least incompetent.

'Anyway there's more than just the illicit sale of calves. There had been no money paid into the bank for milk for six months. Metcalf said the firm of Donaldson and Simpson had been taking the milk but they had not paid for it. Then the new Milk Board came into operation so of course he couldn't cheat with that any more. I wrote to Donaldson and Simpson. Mr Donaldson himself wrote back to say his firm had dealt with the MacFarlanes of Nithanvale for many years and he had been astounded when the supply of milk had suddenly been stopped without warning.'

'Stopped! You mean Metcalf had changed to another buyer? Was he having the money paid direct to himself?' Logan asked incredulously.

'I believe so. There were also large cash discounts from feeding firms. They were missing without trace and there were several payments to firms that had no connection with Nithanvale, or with farming of any kind.'

'Then Metcalf is a criminal!'

'Yes, but I blame myself for Uncle George's second seizure. Now he's almost blind. And his speech is worse than ever.'

'But ye canna blame yourself for that, James. He's an old man.'

'I know he is. That's why we have never told him about the trouble at the bank. But you see I started taking him round the cattle in the motorcar and sometimes in the pony and trap. He seemed to enjoy it.'

'I can believe that.' Logan agreed fervently. 'His cattle are his life's work.'

'Yes, but I needed help to sort out which were genuine Nithanvale animals and which were substitutes. He seemed eager to discuss them all. He never said anything about Metcalf switching them but sometimes he pointed to one with a look of disgust and shook his head. Then he said, "Sell that one!" or "Get that one out of my sight!" One afternoon we went to one of the most distant fields with fifteen stirks in it. "They're not mine! Not one o' them!" he yelled. He began to tremble and shake his fist. "Metcalf's a rogue and a rotter! Feathering his own nest, ruining my good name. It's your name too. You're the last MacFarlane o' Nithanvale! Do you hear me, laddie! You should have been *my* grandson! You must preserve Nithanvale and the MacFarlane name!" Then suddenly he was sprawled in the bottom o' the trap.' James shuddered at the memory. 'It was awful to see him . . .' he added hoarsely.

'That's when he had the second stroke?' Logan asked quietly.

'Yes.' James bit his lip. 'Mary tackled Metcalf. She has a sort of quiet strength and dignity. She just looked him straight in the eye and told him we knew what he had been up to and that if her grandfather died she would hold him responsible. He must have packed his things and left Nithanvale that night.'

'A sure sign of guilt then.'

'Yes. Mary was glad he had gone though. She doesna want me to go to the police, for all he must have got away with hundreds maybe even thousands of pounds, if you count the value of the pedigree calves he has sold.'

'He doesna deserve to get off so lightly,' Logan growled. 'She must be a saint, this relation o' yours, James.'

'Yes, Mary is a very special person,' he agreed warmly, turning his head to see who had opened the door behind him.

Kirsty stood in silence for a moment, but to her it seemed like an hour. The bright smile she had summoned died; the words she had rehearsed would not come.

'Are you ready for your cup of tea yet?' she asked abruptly.

'Tea,' Logan blinked, returning his attention to his surroundings with an effort. 'Aah, no thanks, Kirsty. Give us half an hour more, will you?' Kirsty nodded and closed the door behind her without so much as a glance at the young man to whom she had run with all her small problems as a child and later as a schoolgirl. Never again would she go to James MacFarlane for help, she vowed proudly. Let him give his support and comfort to his half-cousin since he considered her so special!

Four

'This business with Metcalf has left you with a tricky situation, laddie,' Logan reflected, frowning. 'Especially when he's drained your great-uncle's bank account as well. But it's a lot easier to lose a good name than to make one and from now on ye'll be associated with the MacFarlanes o' Nithanvale whether ye like it or no'. Frankly I think ye've already made up your mind?'

James sighed heavily. 'I suppose so. I couldn't face a scandal if other breeders thought we'd cheated them. Yet it's such a waste of all the years of breeding if we sell all the young heifers as non-pedigree stock, and they'll only be worth a fraction . . .'

'Then why not keep them until they're old enough for ye to see how they turn out; select the ones which seem to be breeding true to the Nithanvale type and conformation? If ye keep them at Nithanvale ye wouldna be cheating anybody else and if they dinna breed as ye expect ye can get rid o' them then.'

'Would you come over to Nithanvale and give me your opinion on the heifers then, Mr Fairly, say in six to nine months?'

'Aye, I'd be pleased to do that, James. In fact there's nothing I'd like better than a look round Nithanvale and the rest o' your great-uncle's herd.'

James nodded. 'I'm sure Great-Uncle George would have been pleased to show you round himself if he had been well. He has a fine respect for your reputation. I only hope I can remember all you've taught me and keep up the Fairlyden standard! But my first priority will be to settle things with the bank.'

'Aye, ye could have done without that sort o' burden as a beginning, James,' Logan agreed. 'Prospects are a wee bit brighter than they've been since the war, but things are far frae rosy. Mr Elliot, the Minister of Agriculture, seems to me to be a good man, but his hands are tied by all the agreements that were made before he came to office. Ye'd have thought the government would have learned a lesson after the war. The whole country was nearly starved into submission once. Now there's this Austrian fellow, Adolf Hitler, or whatever he calls himself. By all accounts he's set on restoring Germany's strength and regaining power. It was bad enough last year when he became Chancellor, but I dinna like the idea o' a man like him being Führer o' the German Reich – him and his so-called Nazis . . .' Logan's thoughts moved away from the cosy little room and he remembered again the hell of the trenches. Surely the Germans had had their fill of war then when the flower of their youth was destroyed, yet reports claimed that this man Hitler was mobilising the new generation – boys, like Luke and James MacFarlane and even girls like Kirsty. He'd read that Hitler was obsessed with creating an ideal nation and even bringing in laws to sterilise Germans who did not conform to his ideas of perfection – the deaf, the blind, the deformed. Dear God, if ever such a man had power in Britain they would sterilise the likes of his own brother, Alex! He thought of his three fine nephews and moved sharply in agitation. He brought his mind back to James's conversation with an effort.

'Surely farming will improve now that the government has passed the Marketing Act? Don't you believe in the idea of Marketing Boards for farmers?' he was asking, eyeing Logan's pale face with concern.

'Oh yes, yes I think . . .' Logan swallowed hard, reassembling his thoughts. 'I think they'll help a lot so long as the government backs them with the right laws. They didna work to begin with, laddie – what with farmers cutting each other's throats, selling milk at threepence farthing a gallon! Those who live near the towns still think they can do better on their own, and some just object to any restriction of their freedom . . .'

'I suppose farmers need a firm hand to make them conform, just like any other men with independent spirits,' James smiled wryly.

'Aye, we need a strong government from top to toe. But ye'll be like us, laddie, depending on the milk and the sale o' breeding stock for your income and there's too big a gap between the price o' milk for drinking and that for cheese and butter. It will stay that way as long as the government allows other countries to dump their butter and cheese on our doorstep, so dinna take any risks if ye can avoid them, until ye're on an

34

even keel again at Nithanvale. Imagine,' he muttered with uncharacteristic anger, 'ten pence a pound for butter here in Britain, and they say it's three shillings a pound in France! Yet we won the war, or so I thought!' He sighed. 'It doesna make sense if ye delve too deeply intae politics, laddie.'

'No . . . I suppose not, yet surely there must be markets for all we could ever produce in our own country? We're importing three hundred million pounds worth o' food and there's two million unemployed men – hungry men or so we're told. So why do they keep telling us we're producing an excess of food when so much o' the land is not producing anything at all?'

'Och, we're not producing more than the people could consume if they were given the chance, but we're producing more than they can afford to buy. Still, ye're right, James, it will help if we can stick together and get our markets organised and make the government see sense.'

'At least we're better off than the arable farmers for once. The potato market has been swamped by potatoes from Germany.'

'Aye, I'm often glad I took my brother's advice when I got back from France,' Logan mused. 'We've concentrated on breeding cattle and producing milk, instead o' relying on promises o' price guarantees for grain. Maybe we havena a fortune in the bank but at least we're fed and clothed and still in business.'

'Yes, Aunt Maggie thinks there's nobody like Mr Alex Fairly from Mains of Muir. My cousin, Ben is proud to be working for him, too.' James gave un unexpected grin. 'They almost have a small war when they get together with my mother and Uncle Thomas arguing over the merits o' yourself at Fairlyden and Mr Alex at the Mains. Poor Aunt Lizzie! She has to act as referee.'

Logan returned his grin. 'The Whiteleys and the Fairlys all began their lives at Fairlyden so Alex and I canna be held responsible. I expect a bit o' friendly rivalry between the Mains and Fairlyden adds a bit o' spice to life though. Certainly your cousin, Ben Donelly, must be a good horseman or Alex wouldna have put him in charge o' his precious Clydesdales. Of course his father, Ewan Donelly was a grand man with the horses, I believe. It was a tragedy for your Aunt Maggie when he and your Grandmother Whiteley both died in the flu epidemic; our own Aunt Beatrice frae the Mains too. It swept the country like a plague, after the war.'

James nodded. 'Let's hope we never have another epidemic like it.' He got to his feet. 'I think I must be going now, but I thank you for your time, Mr Fairly, and for listening to my problems and helping me sort them out.'

'I think ye had them sorted out in your own heart, laddie. Ye were just needing somebody to talk things over. I hope all goes well for ye. Now I'll shout for Kirsty to bring us some tea before you leave.'

'Not for me, thanks.' James smiled and the strain seemed to fall from his craggy features.

'Well, if ye're sure? Then I think I'll just have half an hour to myself before milking. I expect Kirsty will be going to bring in the cows for me so tell her not to bother with the tea. I'll have it with her mother when she comes from the Sunday School.'

Kirsty had the big black kettle already singing on the hob when James put his head round the kitchen door. She had covered a tray with a pristine white linen cloth with a delicate pattern of drawn threadwork in two corners and she was arranging her mother's second-best china. She was determined that Fairlyden hospitality should not lag behind anything the 'very special girl' at Nithanvale presented to James MacFarlane.

Usually Kirsty's eyes danced with golden flecks and laughter was never far away, curving her lips in a ready smile, luring out the tiny dimple which lurked at one corner of her mouth. Today that mouth was set and a small frown was etched across her high, smooth brow.

'Don't bother with tea, Kirsty. Your father is going to wait for your mother to return.'

Kirsty shrugged, striving to assume a nonchalance she did not feel. 'Very well. I'll get on with my work then.' She turned away towards the door on the opposite side of the large flagged kitchen. It led into a long passage and out into the yard.

'Your father said you would be bringing the cows in from the field for milking?'

'Yes.'

'They'll not have been outside for many days, I suppose? They'll be a bit skittish still, eh?'

'A little.'

'I'll come with you then. Maybe I can lend a hand at rounding them up.' He followed her out into the fresh spring afternoon, noting how the sun glinted on her thick wavy hair, turning the front to the same honey gold as her mother's, but there was

36

more than a hint of copper in the rich brown tresses where the sun did not bleach it.

'I can manage the cows fine. Have you forgotten I've been bringing them from the fields since I could walk – almost.' She marched on ahead, her slim shoulders erect, her head high.

'I have not forgotten.' James's long legs brought him level with her without effort and he fell into step beside her. He glanced down at her profile, noting the thrust of her jaw, the delicate structure of her cheekbones and the fair, fine-textured skin, already showing a sprinkling of freckles across the bridge of her small straight nose. She had a generous mouth, too wide for classic beauty, but a mouth made for laughter, as James MacFarlane knew well. Right now he wanted to drive away that buttoned-up expression and watch the smile transform her face – he wanted it very badly and he cursed himself for caring what Kirsty Fairly thought of him, or how badly she had misjudged him. His own mouth set. She had condemned him without a hearing and he was damned if he would tell her the real reason he had left Fairlyden. Either of the reasons in fact. He hoped her father would keep his confidence over the first one and he had told no one of the second.

At the gate into the field Kirsty paused with her hand on the sneck and looked up at him. 'I told you, I can manage.'

'I know how capable you are, Kirsty, but I'd like to walk over the fields again; I'd like to see the cows too. Don't forget I've known Fairlyden's pastures and lanes and burns since I was six years old.' Kirsty flung the gate wide and walked on in silence, her pace quickening instinctively, but James did not seem to notice as he strode easily beside her. She was tall for a girl, almost five feet six inches, but he was at least half a head taller and the way his hair rose in a single crisp brown wave above his forehead made him look taller still.

The cows had only been released from their winter confinement in the byres for a week and they were always reluctant to come back in, even for milking, at the beginning of the season. Normally Kirsty enjoyed wandering over the soft grass to gather them up and shoo them along, especially in such lovely spring weather, but today she felt too tense to pay attention to the little skylark which rose almost from under her feet, or the puffs of cloud drifting slowly in the clear sky. Such things usually made her own spirits soar with youthful happiness.

The West Pasture was a series of rolling hillocks and hollows which provided shelter from sudden spring showers and squally winds so it was always used during the first weeks of turning out until the dairy cows were hardened once more to the changeable weather. Today there was no sign of them and Kirsty sighed, knowing they were probably still grazing contentedly in the furthest hollow.

'You're scarcely dressed for work,' she remarked, casting a critical glance at James's well-polished leather boots and fine tweed suit. In the past they had walked miles together in companionable silence but today silence made Kirsty feel nervous and uneasy. 'Or is that the way you dress for work now that you are Mr James MacFarlane of Nithanvale!' There was more than a hint of mockery in her tone but she couldn't help herself. She saw his mouth firm slightly but he replied evenly enough. 'I'd hardly call this work – either at Fairlyden or at Nithanvale. As I said I am glad of the opportunity to see the Fairlyden herd again. I wondered how the heifers from the Spinneyfields bull are doing. Have they plenty of milk? Has he left them with nice neat udders which will last until they've had six or seven calves?'

'Aah, I see! So you're grasping an opportunity to size up the competition, are you? I should have known you had an ulterior motive!' Why did her wayward tongue insist on being so caustic when she had once considered James MacFarlane her best friend? She knew how genuinely interested he was in breeding cattle. He had followed her father around asking questions even as a small boy, at least according to her mother.

'I know well enough that Fairlyden heifers will provide plenty of competition as far as Nithanvale is concerned, at least for the next couple of years,' he answered coolly. 'But I'm sure your father would show me round his herd any time I asked, and take pleasure in doing so, without jumping to conclusions like a silly schoolgirl writing her first mystery story!'

Kirsty flushed at the scorn in his tone. 'I gave up wearing gym tunics a long time ago, though I suppose you've been too busy planning your glorious future at Nithanvale to notice anything else!'

'Oh, I've noticed that all right!' What man could help but notice, he thought as his gaze skimmed over her slender figure. Even in the yellow cotton blouse and neat worsted skirt she was wholly feminine with her curving hips and trim waist, her young breasts firm and high. James felt the heat in his lower limbs and there was a decided glint in his greeny-grey eyes. Kirsty could not decide whether it was amusement, admiration – or scorn? She felt her cheeks burn at the possibility that he might guess how much he disturbed her – and she didn't even understand herself why she felt so perturbed by him, except that she felt he had deserted her and her family and Fairlyden when he chose to go to Nithanvale – to be with that 'very special person' she had heard him mentioning to her father. Her steps quickened involuntarily and she veered away at an angle over the field.

James made no attempt to follow; he simply kept on walking towards the far end of the pasture, knowing they would both come upon the cows eventually. When they did some were lying contentedly chewing their cud in the afternoon sunshine, others rose at the sight of them and stretched languidly, while a few, more distant than the rest, went on grazing like naughty children, looking up as much as to say, 'We're not ready to come in yet.' Kirsty grimaced wryly and headed for the couple which were furthest away while James headed towards the opposite flank, rousing the dozing animals as he went. How often they had brought in the cows together, Kirsty thought with a sigh. Inevitably they drew closer again as the herd began to head towards the open gate in a straggling line, some swishing their tails at imaginary flies, others butting into the line, claiming their own order of precedence.

'I'm surprised you didn't bring one of the dogs to help you round them up,' James remarked conversationally. Kirsty shot him an astonished glance, then her mouth tightened once more.

'Scott is all right for the sheep but he's too young and fresh for the cows,' she replied shortly.

'Yes but—' Suddenly James clapped a hand to his brow. 'Of course! Mother told me old Bess had died the last time I was at the cottage . . . but so much has happened . . . it slipped my mind for a moment.'

'Of course.' Kirsty's tone was glacial. The old collie had been eleven years old, one of a litter of five born on James's twelfth birthday in the summer of nineteen twenty-two. He had been allowed to choose which of the pups should be kept at Fairlyden to rear as a working collie. The litter was a good one and the rest of the pups were already destined for various shepherds in the area. Kirsty herself had been five and a half at the time and from the beginning she had been devoted to 'James's dog'. He had named her Bess. It was true she had always been a working collie but she had been special to both of them – or so Kirsty had believed.

'I'm sure nothing at Fairlyden is worth remembering compared with Nithanvale,' she muttered and kicked angrily at a tuft of grass.

'For goodness' sake, Kirsty! You know I was deeply attached to old Bess too – but I couldn't take her with me! She belonged at Fairlyden.' Kirsty knew that was true but she refused to meet his eyes and kicked at another tuft of grass instead. 'Don't be so – so childish!' he snapped in exasperation. 'If you must know I—'

'Childish! Don't speak to me as though I'm still twelve years old, hanging on your every word like Luke does!'

'Well, you've been behaving like a deprived twelve-year-old ever since I decided to join my father's family at Nithanvale, instead of staying with your family at Fairlyden . . .'

'Deprived! You couldna deprive me of anything, James MacFarlane!'

'You've been deprived of a good spanking and—'

'Spanking is for children! When will you accept the fact that I'm not the six-year-old you used to give piggy back rides to? Or frighten half to death pretending you'd drop me in the burn whenever I played a trick on you!' For a moment James's mouth quirked with amusement at the memories Kirsty's words conjured up, but there was no answering smiled curving her lips as she turned to face him, hands on hips, twin flags of indignant colour highlighting her cheekbones, and eyes sparking with anger. But it was the rapid rise and fall of her breasts straining against the thin cotton of the yellow blouse which caught and held James's attention.

'No, my God, you're not a bairn any more! Perhaps it is time I stopped treating you as one.' Before Kirsty had guessed his intentions he had taken the pace which separated them and jerked her fiercely against his own hard chest. 'Time too I stopped respecting you because you are your father's daughter!' he breathed angrily. His mouth imprisoned hers in a kiss which shocked Kirsty to the core.

At first she struggled but James held her with ease, just as he had when she had been ten years old. But this was no youthful prank. James MacFarlane was very much a man, with a man's emotions and a man's desire to master. After the first heat of the moment he became aware of the softness of Kirsty's body against his own, the innocence of her mouth. He sensed she had not been kissed before, really kissed – with passion and desire – and more . . . A great joy welled up in him and his own mouth became tender. Kirsty could have broken away from him at that moment, but her brain was confused by the signals her treacherous body was sending to it, and she submitted willingly, almost eagerly, to James's exploring mouth. He had taught her so many things. 'You're beautiful, Kirsty, and desirable . . .' he muttered huskily as his mouth caressed the dimple at the corner of her own. Then suddenly Kirsty heard his voice as it had been in her father's study – warm and tender it had been then too when he had been speaking about the girl at Nithanvale. 'Mary is a very special person.'

'Let me go! Let me go, James MacFarlane!' She broke away with a strength which took James by surprise. Her eyes blazed but her face was pale. James opened his mouth to protest but no sound came as Kirsty stormed, 'Get away from me! Don't ever touch me like that again!' She wanted to burst into tears but tears were a sign of weakness and she held her head high. She, Kirsty Fairly, would never let him see how much he had disturbed her. For a moment James stared at her in silence, the muscle pulsing in his jaw, his face pale, then he gave an odd, stiff little nod. She was once more the daughter of Logan Fairly of Fairlyden, his ex-employer, the man who still employed his own mother and his uncle; how could he have forgotten! He turned on his heel and strode away, skirting the cows, anxious now to put them and everything belonging to Fairlyden behind him.

He had reckoned without Luke Fairly. The boy had slipped a sketch of his sister into the car and James found it, lying face down on the seat. His first reaction was to screw it tightly into a ball, but even as his fingers scrunched the paper he resisted the impulse and smoothed it out again, knowing that Luke had made the drawing specially for him and that it would have been executed with all the boy's usual painstaking care.

Five

Crispin Bradshaw had not forgotten his resolve to make a new will and on the following Monday morning he telephoned Carsewell and Donaldson, the solicitors. The elder Mr Donaldson, whom he knew and respected, was at home with a severe chill and Crispin decided to wait until the man had returned to business.

'I'm very glad you're not going off on your own,' Sarah informed him with relief. 'Are you really intending to teach Kirsty to drive your motorcar.'

'Aah yes, I didn't think she was very interested when I first suggested it but this morning anyone would have thought her very life depended on learning to drive! We're going for our first outing tomorrow afternoon. Are you coming, Sarah my dear?' Crispin's eyes twinkled at his wife.

'You know very well I am not coming. It is quite bad enough riding in that monster with you behind the wheel. I darena think what it would be like with Kirsty wobbling all over the road!'

'I expect she'll soon be an expert chauffeur,' Crispin sighed. 'I confess I'm getting a bit old. I can't help wondering what made her change her mind so suddenly though . . .'

Kirsty was determined she would learn to drive a motorcar. If Miss MacFarlane of Nithanvale could drive one, then so could she! She had found it impossible to forget James's visit and she had lain awake well into the night trying to sort out her emotions. She could not account for the feeling of heat and trembling awareness which seemed to affect her whole body whenever she relived his kisses. No one had ever kissed her like that before, in fact no one except her family had ever kissed her at all . . . But it was not only the memory of James's kisses which troubled her, it was the sound of his voice when she had entered her father's study. In her mind she could still hear the warmth and affection. Why was Mary MacFarlane so very special? she asked herself.

43

Gradually it dawned on Kirsty that she was jealous of the unknown Miss MacFarlane who had already earned so much respect and affection – and maybe love – from her half-cousin, James. She had known him all her life; they had been friends and companions for as long as she could remember, but she had never before heard him speak with such tenderness. But to be jealous? Kirsty had never been jealous of anyone in her life! Apart from anything else she knew how much her own mother abhorred the evil green-eyed monster of envy. How often had she quoted the tenth commandment?

'Thou shalt not covet thy neighbour's wife, nor his servant, nor his maid, nor his ox, nor his ass, nor anything that is his.'

It was not the only commandment her mother quoted for she knew her bible well. Apart from her friendship with Mrs Morrison, the minister's wife, and her duties as a Sunday School teacher, Kirsty knew she tried hard to live according to all the teachings of the scriptures. Yet she had often sensed that jealousy was the one thing which her mother detested above everything; she knew it had something to do with her Aunt Sadie and the terrible unhappiness she had caused when she had lived at Fairlyden before her marriage to Robert Smith.

The following week the men arrived to remove the big black-leaded range at Fairlyside and install the new cream enamelled Aga. Sarah felt bewildered and upset at the upheaval in her kitchen. She was deeply attached to the old range and she had taken great pride in its shining steel and polished black oven doors and ribs. Even now, at seventy-five, she often did the black-leading herself instead of leaving it for Dora Fleming who came up from Muircumwell three days a week to help with the washing and cleaning.

'I pay Dora to do the dirty work and the heavy tasks for you, my dear,' Crispin always remarked if he saw her. Sarah knew his concern sprang from his love and consideration for her and usually she appreciated all his generous gestures but she felt sure she could never learn to love the great cream-coloured invention which seemed to protrude so far into her kitchen: she would miss the blazing fire on a cold winter morning, and the glow of the dying embers when she sipped her last cup of tea before going to bed.

She sighed heavily. She had had another letter from Sadie this morning telling her about the new electric cleaner she had bought – a Hoover she had called it – but imagine paying four pounds nineteen shillings and sixpence for a newfangled sweeping brush! Sarah frowned. Sadie only wrote when she had something new to swank about. She had not shown the letter to Crispin yet. Sadie's and Robert's continual extravagances upset him when there were so many men and women desperate for work in the Yorkshire mill town where they lived.

Despite her misgivings Sarah spent considerable time reading the instructions which had arrived with her new cooker and studying the little recipe book and before the week was out she was turning out enough girdle scones and pancakes to feed half of Muircumwell, as Kirsty laughingly told her mother and father.

'I love Granny's dropped scones!' Luke piped up unexpectedly. 'Maybe I'll call in for some on my way home frae school.'

'You do that, Luke,' Beth smiled lovingly at her young son. 'I know your Granny and Grandfather would be pleased if you called more often, as Kirsty does.'

'I'll bet you'll be so busy daydreaming you'll have passed Fairlyside before you remember about the pancakes,' Kirsty teased gently. Luke smiled back at her.

'I expect Granny would be more pleased to see me if I kenned as much about the cows as you, Kirsty.' The fine fair hair which fell over his brow gave him an oddly vulnerable look and Kirsty wondered if he resented her popularity with her grandparents; but no, Luke had no resentment in him. It was not his nature. Nevertheless Kirsty frowned.

'I could teach you all I know about the cows if you like, Luke?' But her brother shook his head and his blue eyes clouded a little. 'I dinna mind drawing them when they stand in the burn, or graze amongst the buttercups . . . but I dinna think I'll ever want to read all Papa's books about their ancestors. I dinna even ken which one is Queenie and which one is Daisy or Bell like you do . . . and their calves all look the same.'

'It is time ye were learning to milk the cows though, Luke,' Beth reminded him anxiously. 'They are our bread and butter. Fairlyden couldna survive without them. Your father and I were much younger than you are when we had our own cows to milk before we went to school and when we came home at night.' Beth regarded Luke with motherly concern, but his lack of interest in Fairlyden and the animals troubled her.

'Papa always says Aunt Sadie hated milking so maybe I'm like her?'

'Never!' Luke was surprised by his mother's vehemence, she was usually such a gentle person, but Beth pushed back her chair and left the question in his blue eyes. She had tried hard to think of her sister-in-law with kindness and charity, to forgive Sadie's sins as it advocated in the bible, but she could never think of Sadie without remembering the grief and terror of the past. At least I shall never forget the help and understanding I had frae Logan's parents when we all thought Logan had died in that dreadful war, she thought. Even Lucy had proved herself a loyal and kindly little maid in those far-off days when she had found it an almost impossible struggle to take up the threads of her life without Logan.

'Now that I'm getting used to my new cooker I think we should have a family gathering,' Sarah announced a few weeks later, surveying two golden featherlight sponges which she had just removed from the oven.

'You finally agree that it is an improvement?' Crispin asked, his grey-green eyes dancing.

'Mmm . . . well it's grand not having to clean the flues every time I want to bake or cook, and it's even hot first thing in the morning.'

'Ye-es,' Crispin frowned thoughtfully. 'I'm told these cookers last a lifetime.'

'Guaranteed for ten years, the man said.'

'Well, I sometimes wonder what will happen to Fairlyside when we're gone. In fact I've thought a lot about my affairs lately, Sarah. Whatever happens I know you are provided for, my dear . . .'

'Oh Crispin, dinna talk about such things. Anyway there's more than enough put by to see us through, what with Logan insisting on paying the rent for Fairlyden and you still having a share in the woollen mill.'

'Aagh, small profit *that* has yielded these past years!' Crispin snorted disdainfully.

'Well, even your foreman, Ted Forbes, says things have been bad and still are.'

'No worse than farming. Logan has paid us more in rent

than Robert has paid from the woollen mill. It's all down to management and he's taken too much out for his own share, if you ask me. Well I shall never leave it all to him! As for Logan . . .' Crispin frowned again and this time Sarah thought he suddenly looked his age and there were wistful shadows in his eyes. 'I don't think Logan has ever accepted the fact that I'm his real father, Sarah.'

'Well, he believed himself to be a Fairly for so long . . . and at the time we did tell him the truth he was probably too weak and ill to take it in . . . Anyway, what makes you say that, Crispin?'

'It's the way he insists on paying the rent – as though I'm his landlord.'

'Well, so you are, even if you are his father. I know he has always respected you, even before he knew he was not William Fairly's son, and I've always thought he had a great affection for you, but he is very independent, Crispin.'

'Yes, just like his mother! I remember you always insisted on paying the rent however hard times were for you, Sarah. It almost broke my heart sometimes.'

'And you saved the money – all those years. Now you spoil me with it.' Sarah smiled warmly and moved to his side, reaching up to smooth the lines on his wrinkled cheek. 'You're the best husband in the world, dear Crispin, and I'm sorry we wasted so many years when we might have been together – but life has been kind to us in the end.'

'Yes, you're right – as always, Sarah. Even so I must see Mr Donaldson as soon as he returns. Logan will inherit Fairlyden of course and I expect Luke will inherit it in due course as his only son, so I was wondering whether to leave this house to Kirsty when we're gone. She has always loved it.'

'It is not just the house she loves,' Sarah said warmly. 'We couldna have wished for a better lassie for our only granddaughter.'

'Yes, that's why I'd like to leave her something besides money. You know I built this house with you in mind, Sarah, all those years ago? Even though I couldn't persuade you to marry me then; I knew you would always be deeply attached to the farm, but I never wanted to live in the house you had shared with William, you know. Fairlyside was a compromise – near enough for you to stay at Fairlyden, but in my home. I'd always thought it would make an excellent farmhouse some day.'

'But what about the old house?'

'I had ideas about that too.' He proceeded to explain.

'Well!' Sarah was astonished. 'You've been planning all these things for Fairlyden's future prosperity, and you're not even a farmer, Crispin?'

'I'm a businessman, my dear, even if I'm not a spring chicken any longer, as you keep reminding me. At least I'm not six feet under – which is where Robert and Sadie think I ought to be, I believe!'

'Crispin! Surely neither of them ever?'

'Oh, not in so many words, but I suspect they can't wait for the day when I'm gone. They are in for a shock though, the pair of them. I'll see to that!' Crispin spoke with a stubborn resolve and Sarah eyed him dubiously. 'Anyway, my dear, when I listen to Logan and Beth, and Alex and Emma, all discussing their respective farms, I can't help but admire their spirit and it makes me want to help them, and I wish I could live a whole lot longer to see all their plans flourish . . .'

'If British farming ever flourishes again!' Sarah reflected glumly. 'It's a terrible thing if our efforts can only be appreciated when there's a war, but heaven forbid that we should ever go through anything like that again, even if it means there isna a farmer left in the whole o' the British Isles!'

'I agree, my dear. I truly hope Mr Wells does not seriously believe the things he has written in his book *The shape of things to come*.'

Six

Sarah looked around the long oval dining table with quiet pride. She had been preparing for this little gathering of her family for days and nothing would make her admit that the preparations had exhausted her. She caught Crispin's eye on her, saw the concern in his face.

'Dora will see to everything in the kitchen now,' she smiled reassuringly. She had not wanted to ask Dora to help but Crispin had insisted and now she was glad. Dora was not much of a cook but with the new Aga cooker and all her preparations nothing could go wrong and at least the woman was clean and willing.

'I just don't want you to be overtired, Sarah, and neither will your children . . .'

'Children, eh?' Sarah chuckled warmly. 'Alex will be fifty-one this year!'

Crispin's mouth quirked with amusement. A sense of humour was one of the things which had kept them both younger than their years, kept them going through the clouds of life as well as the sunshine. 'All the more reason for you to take things easy yourself.'

'Still it does look nice, doesn't it, with the white damask cloth and the best silver all gleaming and the furniture polished to that lovely rich red. I've always liked mahogany. I must tell Dora she made a good job of that. She's not so happy in the kitchen though. She's watching over the roast ducklings as though they might sprout wings and take flight again. They've cooked beautifully – twenty minutes in the top oven to start them off and then into the bottom one. I've got the broth simmering on one of the huge hotplates and potatoes boiling on the other and the orange sauce is ready. Even the gravy keeps well in a covered bowl in the simmering oven. Imagine having four ovens, and all at different heats! I know I was not very enthusiastic at first, but I confess you really have spoiled me this time, Crispin. I'm sure even Sadie would be envious . . .'

'Oh, Robert and Sadie are sure to have something better!'

Crispin grunted with a bitterness which was foreign to his nature. 'But they will not be here so it doesn't matter. I can't say I'm sorry.'

'No-o, neither can I, I'm afraid. At least I asked them. It's a pity Ellen couldna come though. She works too hard looking after all her patients in that convalescent home.'

'I agree.' Crispin's grey eyes softened. Sarah knew he was as fond of her eldest daughter as she was herself. 'We have to respect her wishes though. I think she would have worked just as hard as a doctor's wife if Brad had been alive. As it is she has done her best to fill the void with her work for other people.'

'Yes. All those poor laddies, crippled in that dreadful war.' Sarah could not suppress a shudder.

'They're here, Mistress! Your family are here!' Dora squeaked excitedly from the doorway, then disappeared once more to the kitchen to stand over the pans as though she expected them to run away.

Sarah and Crispin moved to the front steps. Usually everyone, except perhaps the minister and the doctor, came in at the back door, just as they had at Fairlyden, but the drive was not wide enough for a motorcar and Alex usually pulled up at the front steps. As Sarah watched him alight she thought what a boon the motorcar had been to her eldest son with his twisted feet. Sadly she acknowledged that they had not improved as the years passed and now that he was older she often thought he was more lame than ever, especially when he was tired.

'Hello, Mother!' He was at her side, smiling down at her in no time, as though contradicting her unspoken thoughts. 'You're looking very flushed and pretty . . .'

'Now when did you get such a silken tongue, Alex? It used to be Billy who went in for flattery!' Sarah beamed up at her eldest son with all her old love and affection. Beside him Emma smiled, and her homely face was transformed as always.

'I expect you have been slaving over a hot stove to feed us all, but Alex wouldna ken about such things.' She nudged her husband playfully in the ribs and he grinned at her. Sarah felt a warm glow at the sight of their happiness. It had taken the pair of them a long time to get their lives together, but once they had overcome their earlier inhibitions they had brought true joy to each other and to her family circle. She looked to where Crispin was greeting Alex's three sons. Alexander, the eldest, would not be seventeen until November, but already he was as tall as his father, though his slender limbs were like those of a young colt and his hair and features were more like his mother's. Cameron, two years younger, was the image of his father and Uncle Billy, with his laughing dark eyes and unruly black curls, but he had not inherited his volatile temperament from either of his parents, Sarah reflected, watching him as he regaled Crispin with some story or other, making him throw back his head in a roar of spontaneous laughter. Sarah smiled involuntarily. Her husband loved all young people.

'Hey, Granny, there's Uncle Logan and Aunt Beth coming down the track! Can I go to meet them?' Without waiting for an answer the youngest of Alex's sons bounded off in the direction of Fairlyden. Paul was a sturdier boy than his brothers, tall for his age but with the same dark hair and big brown eyes as his father and his brother Cameron. He was only a few months older than Luke but as Sarah watched the two boys meet she thought Luke looked at least three years younger than his cousin. His build was slight, and his fine features and the fair hair flopping over his brow gave him a dreamy, delicate air.

Sarah rejoiced in the babble of young voices as her grandchildren greeted each other and slowly drifted towards the dining room.

'You would think these laddies o' mine had never been fed for a week!' Emma exclaimed mildly, shaking her head in mock despair when Cameron declared, 'I'm starving! Granny, the smell o' your broth makes me ravenous!' He grinned infectiously.

'Well, if you will all take your places your grandfather will say grace, then you can tuck in.'

'Lord bless us all and make us able,
To eat the food that's on this table.'

The Yorkshire grace was now familiar to all the younger generation and they had learned that their Grandfather Bradshaw did not treat the words lightly; he had once explained that there were still many men and women too poor to afford a palatable meal, and many who had barely the strength to eat at the end of a hard day's work in the mills and mines.

'Can I help, Granny?' Kirsty asked quietly.

'Yes please, lassie. You'd maybe carry the tureen of soup through? It's a bit heavy.'

'I'll bring the soup plates then,' Emma volunteered with a smile. 'I expect Dora is in a wee bit of a fluster, is she?'

'A wee bit. She thinks we're entertaining the gentry from the Mains, you know!'

'Gentry!' Emma raised her eyes heavenward. 'Dora must have even more imagination than you, young Luke!' She ruffled her nephew's fair hair affectionately as she passed his chair. Sarah felt a warm glow of pride. How fortunate she was in her two daughters-in-law. Indeed they had been closer to her and Crispin than her own daughters in recent years . . .

'You're quiet, Kirsty,' she said suddenly as her glance rested on her eldest grandchild.

'Och, I canna get a word in with all these laddies around! Why couldn't you have had at least one lassie, Uncle Alex?'

Alex returned her smile with a shake of his head. 'We kenned we wouldna get one as good as you, lassie, so we had to make do with the laddies.'

His sons greeted this statement with protesting groans, but Alexander's eyes lit up as they rested speculatively on his Cousin Kirsty.

'Mother says Grandfather Bradshaw has been teaching ye to drive his motorcar, Kirsty?'

'Yes, that's right. I'm driving him into town next week, aren't I, Grandfather?'

'Yes, lass, if Mr Donaldson has recovered.' He turned to Alex and his two eldest sons. 'Kirsty is an apt pupil.'

'Maybe Grandfather would let ye have the car to drive to the Farmers' Dance that's to be held in Dumfries then, Kirsty? I could bike to the station and meet ye there.'

'Aah!' Emma exclaimed, helping Beth pass round the plates, 'I wondered why you were so interested in Kirsty's driving lessons. Well, you're not old enough to be going to dances yet, young man! And when you do go you'll need to bike all the way – or use Shanks's pony – isn't that right, Alex?' She appealed to her husband to back her up.

'Indeed it is! My word, the broth smells good. I hadna realised I was hungry until now.' His wife and son accepted the deliberate change of topic. If there were any arguments they would be pursued in the privacy of their own home and not in public. Alex was a fair man but his word was law as far as his sons were concerned.

'I canna wait until I can leave school and see what's going on in the outside world,' Cameron piped up, his dark eyes sparkling.

'Aah laddie, you're just like your Uncle Billy!' Sarah declared, shaking her head, but only Alex and her husband noticed the wistful shadows in her brown eyes.

'Mmm, Father keeps saying I'm like ma Uncle Billy, but I'm beginning to wonder if I'll ever meet him! I hope he comes to visit soon. I keep telling Father and Alexander, and Ben Donnelly – the day for horses will soon be over but they think I'm talking rubbish!'

'Exactly what your Uncle Billy used to say! It sounds like history repeating itself,' Sarah sighed.

'Your father did not say it was rubbish, Cameron,' Emma reprimanded quietly.

'We-ell, maybe no' exactly rubbish – but ye dinna like machines d'ye, Father?'

'Not while we have plenty of good horses and enough men to work them,' Alex replied placidly, then his face grew grave and a small frown creased his brow. 'I just hope we dinna have another war, or that would certainly make us short o' labour . . .'

'Aah, surely not! Let's be more cheerful,' Sarah declared, aware of Luke's sudden attention and his cousin Paul's restless fidgeting. Emma suggested both of them should be excused from the dining room now they had finished their meal. Paul went eagerly and Luke followed obediently, if with reluctance. Sarah turned to Beth and Emma. 'Have either of you entered butter for the Highland Show competitions?'

They discussed the forthcoming shows until Sarah's attention was suddenly caught by Alex and Logan's conversation.

'So I shall try to buy the Mains . . .' Alex glanced at his wife. 'We've talked it over. I know it willna be easy, but we've never squandered our money and we've a tidy sum frae the stallion fees, and the sale o' the Clydesdales we've bred. There's still a good trade for them frae the brewers and coal merchants and carters up and down the country . . .'

'But there's not as much demand frae farmers as there was, Father!'

'Cameron! Dinna interrupt when your father is speaking or ye'll end up outside with Paul and Luke!' Emma's tone was sharp and her fifteen-year-old son bit his lip, his eyes downcast. Alex eyed him reflectively.

'Unfortunately the laddie is right, but the Mains' Clydesdales have a good name and there'll always be room for the best. At least that's what I told Mr Carruthers at the bank. I believe he thinks I'm crazy to think o' buying land when farming is still in such a state o' depression, but Captain Fothergill has been a good landlord and he spoke for me. He's nearly ninety-four so he canna last much longer and I'd never get as good a landlord again – or a better bargain.'

'Aye, and ye've three sons coming on,' Logan mused. 'And all of them set on farming, it seems.' His eyes held a wistful look. 'I'd want to buy land if I'd three laddies to follow in my footsteps – or even one who showed any real interest, but I dinna think there'll be another generation o' Fairlys at Fairlyden . . .'

'Aah, Logan,' Crispin protested gently. 'The farm will be yours when we're gone. Maybe Luke will begin to look upon it as his inheritance then.'

'The name is irrelevant so long as there is another generation to follow in your footsteps,' Sarah said with unusual sharpness. 'Even your own name . . .' Her voice trailed to a halt. She had almost blurted '. . . should have been Bradshaw instead of Fairly.' She stopped herself in time. Her grandchildren knew nothing of the tangles of the past. No one knew except Alex and Emma, Logan and Beth. Even Ellen, who had once been closer to her than any of them, did not know the truth, though she may have guessed that Crispin was Logan's natural father. Somehow the opportunity had never arisen for them to discuss it freely. As for Sadie, she had never had any intention of confiding the secrets of her past to her younger daughter.

'I understand, Mother,' Logan assured her quietly. 'Anyway the land endures long after generations of men have perished whatever their creed or colour. It is an inheritance from God . . .'

'Yes it is, but it still needs to be cherished. I was a woman – I cared for Fairlyden. You have a daughter as well as a son, Logan . . .' Her eyes softened as they sought her grand-daughter's. Kirsty was more like herself than any of her own children, even Alex.

Kirsty blinked, startled. She had always thought of Fairlyden as her home. She loved every inch of it . . . She had never considered leaving it; she had never thought of a future anywhere else . . . Now, suddenly she realised it was Luke's right to inherit the land. He was the only son. It was tradition . . .

Sarah saw something of her shock reflected in her wide expressive eyes. 'The future is not in our hands, lassie,' she said softly, 'and it is better not to look too far ahead . . .'

Seven

Kirsty and her grandfather did not drive to Dumfries to see the lawyer for some months. Old Mr Donaldson had suffered one illness after another and had kept very few of his appointments. His son-in-law, scarcely a boy any longer at forty-two, eventually persuaded Crispin to transfer the appointment to himself and Kirsty drove him to Dumfries on a mellow morning towards the end of September.

'There must be at least a dozen cars parked in the High Street today!' Crispin exclaimed as Kirsty carefully manoeuvred the Austin Ten past the Midsteeple. 'Now if you park in the High Street, lass, I'll walk to Castle Street. You can look at the shops for half an hour.'

'But I could park outside the office.'

'Aah lass, I'm not that ancient yet! I like a walk and I'll be there in no time.'

Kirsty enjoyed wandering along the street looking in the shop windows, for she rarely had time for such idle pleasure. Today she was free until milking time. The harvest was finished and safely built into little round ricks ready for thrashing. The potatoes and turnips were not yet ready for harvesting and Anna MacFarlane had promised to attend to all the poultry and collect the eggs.

The day was calm and still and remarkably warm for the end of September. Kirsty had made the few purchases which her mother and Anna and Lucy had requested her to bring from the town and now she paused to admire a hat in sky-blue felt. It had a high crown and a neat little brim trimmed with a single rosebud . . . She was barely aware of the people passing by as she visualised herself in that hat some Sunday morning in Muircumwell Kirk. A smile tugged at her mouth and she looked up. Suddenly the blood seemed to freeze in her veins. James MacFarlane was walking along the pavement towards her, his hand beneath the elbow of a young woman. He was smiling down into her face with warmth and affection . . . Kirsty felt a crazy desire to run and hide. James visited his mother and Uncle Thomas regularly at the Fairlyden cottage but Kirsty made sure they did not meet.

They were almost level with her. James looked up and his reddish-brown eyebrows rose in surprise, his smile widened then faded almost at once. Kirsty knew instantly that the memory of their last encounter had flashed through his mind, just as it had with her. She had not seen him since that day in the spring when he visited her father – the day he accompanied her into the field to bring in the cows – the day he had kissed her. She felt her own cheeks burn but she summoned her composure and the good manners her mother had drummed into her at an early age.

'Good morning, James.'

'Good morning to you, Kirsty! Mary, this is Kirsty Fairly from Fairlyden. Kirsty, this is my er . . . this is Mary MacFarlane.'

Kirsty nodded stiffly. 'Good morning, Miss MacFarlane.'

'Good morning – but please, will you not call me Mary? I've heard so much about you and your family I feel I almost know you already . . .' Her voice was low and musical, her smile warm. She seemed small beside James's tall figure but she was almost as tall as Kirsty herself, though more finely built. Her eyes were very dark and her thick brown hair was drawn back from her face in a severe bun instead of the modern bob which was so much easier to manage. Yet Kirsty had to admit the style enhanced the purity of her flawless skin and emphasised her delicate bone structure. How pretty and serene she looks, Kirsty thought almost enviously.

'You have just the sort of face Luke would love to paint . . .' She blurted out her thoughts almost before they had formed properly. Surprisingly she felt James MacFarlane relax a little at her side and realised that he had been just as tense as she was herself. Mary MacFarlane blinked and then laughed softly.

'I can't imagine anyone thinking my face would be worth painting!' There was no false modesty in the words, just a mild surprise in her fine dark eyes. 'Luke is your young brother, I believe? James says he is very talented but also sensitive for a boy.'

'Yes . . .' Kirsty glanced at James MacFarlane, frowning slightly. Had he criticised Luke? Was he still convinced that her brother should be sent away to board in the hostel? 'He has settled very well at the Academy though. In fact he seems to enjoy the lessons. He cycles to Muircumwell station, and travels on the train with my cousin, Paul Fairly from Mains of Muir.'

'Yes, I have heard of Mains of Muir. Your uncle is well known for his fine Clydesdales. James! I've just had a thought—'

'Oh yes?' James smiled teasingly. 'What inspiration have you had that makes this thought so special?'

'The Farmers' Ball? Kirsty would be an ideal partner for you! She must know many of the cattle and horse breeders already, through her father?' She turned to Kirsty eagerly but her smile faded a little at the sight of Kirsty's flushed cheeks. 'Oh, please don't be angry with me. I'm not really bossy – but I think it must be awful to go to these functions without a partner and my grandfather says it is important that James should attend and show his presence as a MacFarlane of Nithanvale. You know how it is?'

'Er . . . no, not really. Why do you not go as James's partner, Miss MacF . . . er Mary? Surely . . .'

'No, I cannot do that.' Mary MacFarlane looked grave. 'I do not dance or attend social functions, you understand, though I do live a normal life in most other respects, at least for the present time . . .' Her smile was gentle but her eyes held a faraway look as though she was seeing something very special – something only she could see . . . Kirsty frowned in bewilderment.

'No,' she repeated. 'I—'

'It's all right, Kirsty.' James's tone was cool, his face stiff. 'I know you would not want to be seen socially with me. Many of the cattle breeders have seen me at Fairlyden. They would recognise me for what I am – or was – a labourer for your father.'

Kirsty gasped. 'Such a thought never entered my head!'

'Then you will go as James's partner?' Mary asked eagerly. She squeezed James's arm and smiled up at him with that warm sweet smile which Kirsty felt any man must find irresistible.

'You dinna understand . . .' Kirsty protested faintly, her accent more pronounced than usual in her agitation. 'I—I . . . The ball wouldna end in time for me to catch the last train home!' she announced with relief at having thought up such an excellent excuse on the spur of the moment.

'That is not a problem. Nithanvale is very close to the town.

You could come back with James after the ball and stay the night with us, if your parents can spare you, that is . . .? James says everyone at Fairlyden works very hard . . .'

'Of course we work hard. It is the only way to survive for ordinary farmers. You would not understand, of course. It must be different at Nithanvale.' As soon as she had spoken so harshly Kirsty wished the words unsaid. She stared at the pavement and missed Mary's swift, surprised glance at James, the eyebrows raised in a silent question, and she missed the quick shake of James's head, the warning in his eyes.

'We work hard at Nithanvale too,' Mary said quietly. 'Today we had to come into town to see the ba . . . to see a b-business associate of my grandfather's.' Mary was not used to prevaricating but she sensed James did not want Kirsty Fairly to know anything about the MacFarlane troubles. She wondered why when he had been so anxious to discuss them with Mr Logan Fairly, to seek his advice. 'I would so like you to come to Nithanvale.' Mary's tone was sincere, almost pleading, and Kirsty was surprised. Why should she want her to visit at Nithanvale? Mary MacFarlane was pretty and intelligent and she seemed very sweet natured too. One day she would inherit her grandfather's wealth while she, Kirsty Fairly, would inherit nothing. She frowned hard. It had never occurred to her to feel jealous of her dreamy, lovable young brother, but now she felt a brief string of resentment that Luke would automatically inherit Fairlyden, not because he wanted it, not because he loved the place and the life of it as she did, but because he was a boy, her father's son and heir. Obviously James must have considered this situation too, and his own position at Fairlyden. No wonder he had chosen to move to Nithanvale. He would probably acquire both a wife and a farm there . . .

Crispin Bradshaw beamed when he saw the group of three young people in conversation just ahead of him. He walked steadily up the street towards them, his walking stick tapping rhythmically.

'Well, well, good morning to you, James, and this is Miss MacFarlane?' James spun round in surprise. 'Why hello, Mr Bradshaw. Yes this is Mary, my half-cousin.'

'How do y'do, m'dear? I hope James is treating you well?'

'Indeed he is. Fairlyden's loss is Nithanvale's gain.'

'Good, good. It seems a long time since I saw you at Fairlyden, lad. How are you?'

60

'I'm often at my mother's on Sundays, and I've seen Mr Fairly both at home and at the market.' His glance skimmed over Kirsty's face as he spoke, then he turned back to her grandfather. 'You look exceedingly well, sir.'

'Yes, yes, I'm fine.' Crispin smiled widely. He felt as though a load had been removed from his shoulders after seeing young Mr Carsewell. 'I've just been attending to a bit of business I should have done years ago. It's a good job I've got Kirsty to chauffeur me though. There's a lot more traffic around in the towns now than when I first got my motorcar.' He looked searchingly at Kirsty. 'And we shall have to come back into Dumfries another day so that I can sign all the documents which lawyers deem so necessary, lass. I hope that's all right? You look a mite pale and strained?' he added frowning.

'I'm all right, Grandfather. You know I enjoy driving you in your motorcar.' She made an effort to sound bright and cheerful.

'So poor old Marocco has been pushed aside by four wheels and an engine, has he?' James commented with a faint note of mockery.

'Indeed he has not! No one could accuse me of disloyalty . . .'

A dull flush mounted James's cheeks and the familiar pulse beat in his lean jaw as Kirsty had seen it do when he had been angry or under strain. Mary looked at them curiously, then turned to Crispin. 'I was just trying to persuade your granddaughter to accompany James to the Farmers' Ball.'

'Oh yes? I believe I heard your mother and father discussing that only yesterday, lass. They've been specially invited this year, haven't they?'

'Have they?' Kirsty was surprised.

'Well . . . I believe they're to be presented with some sort o' special honour. Maybe I shouldna be telling you. You'd better not let on you know, lass, in case they're keeping it a secret. They're very modest.'

'I see. So that's what was in that letter a few days ago!'

'Well, it sounds as though I shall know at least two friendly faces,' James announced coolly, 'even though Kirsty is so reluctant to be seen in my company. I think it is time we were going, Mary, or your grandfather will be fretting for you.' He took Mary MacFarlane's arm and with a curt nod at Kirsty and a smile for her grandfather he hurried away down the street.

Inwardly Kirsty wanted to weep, outwardly she put on a

61

bright smile for her grandfather.

'When do you have to see Mr Carsewell again, Grandfather?'

'He's drafting some documents for me and after I've seen and approved them I have to make another appointment. They will not be ready for a week or so as young Mr Carsewell has a lot on his plate just now, what with taking over his father-in-law's clients and attending to his own. He's going up to Edinburgh to defend a case next week.'

Kirsty was surprised a few days later when her mother suggested she should accompany them to the Farmers' Ball.

'I ken you're young yet, lassie, but your grandfather said James MacFarlane would be there and ye know your father and I dinna really enjoy these occasions much. We shall be glad o' your company.'

'And what about Father's presentation? Or am I not supposed to know about that?' Kirsty teased.

'We-ell . . . ye ken how modest your father is, but he feels very honoured too. Ye share his interest in the cattle so ye'll be proud o' his success. I think your grandfather is right, ye ought to be there.'

So this was Grandfather's suggestion, Kirsty thought, and wondered if he had guessed how much she regretted brushing aside Mary MacFarlane's invitation.

'Oh, Mother, I am proud – very proud of you both.' Kirsty hugged Beth with unexpected fervour and her eyes sparkled. 'Father always says he couldn't have done any of the things he has achieved at Fairlyden without you. I'm glad you've agreed to let me go to the Ball with you.' Beth's cheeks flushed at her daughter's words, but in her heart she knew that she and Logan were indeed two halves of a perfect partnership – and always had been really for as long as either of them could remember. She sighed happily.

'I dinna ken what I'd do without your father, I really dinna, but I worry about him when he gets these dreadful colds. They always settle on his chest. We must dress up warm for the journey home. It will be very late by the time we get back frae Dumfries.'

'Are you borrowing Grandfather's car? Father doesna like driving it, even during the day, does he?'

'No-o,' Beth smiled suddenly. 'Maybe that's another reason why your grandfather thought ye should go with us. He keeps telling us how well ye drive, dear. He's still very shrewd for all he's over eighty!'

Kirsty returned her mother's smile. 'Well, I like driving so I don't mind, if Father is agreeable.'

'I'm sure he will be. He never did like mechanical things very much. He and your Uncle Billy often argued about machines when they were younger – before they went to the war . . .' Beth sighed softly. 'Perhaps it's for the best that Billy decided not to return. They might have disagreed about many things.'

'Did you think Uncle Billy would come back to farm at Fairlyden then – when the war ended?' Kirsty asked curiously. She was often intrigued by the varying accounts of this wandering uncle whom she had never met.

'We weren't sure. That's why we offered for the tenancy o' the Muircumwell land belonging to the Guillyman Estate. It came to let in nineteen eighteen, just before the war ended. It was your grandfather's idea. Now we've more cows I dinna ken how we'd manage without it. Of course your father has ploughed and limed it, drained some of it too when he could afford it. It is in better heart than it was, but it's still not as good as Fairlyden land.'

'No, but it's fine for grazing the young beasts and making hay for the winter.'

'Aye. The Fairlyden Ayrshires weren't so well known then, but your Grandfather Bradshaw believed in looking to the future and seizing each opportunity as it comes – even though he kens nothing about farming.'

Kirsty nodded. 'He seems happier now that he has seen his lawyer. I wonder when I shall have to drive him to Dumfries again?'

'I dinna ken, lassie, but if you're going to the Ball you'll need an evening dress. Did you see anything you liked while you were looking round the shops? Of course it couldna be too expensive,' Beth added regretfully.

'Och, dinna worry about that, Mother,' Kirsty smiled warmly, knowing her mother would buy her the best dress in the whole of the county if she could afford it. She and Luke had never gone short of food or clothes, or anything that was essential to their health and happiness, but there was never any unnecessary extravagance at Fairlyden either; there were always too many things needed on the farm. 'But what about your own gown, Mother? You must have a new one if

63

Father is to be a special guest.'

'Aye,' Beth blushed faintly and Kirsty thought how young she looked. Sometimes she felt they were more like sisters than mother and daughter. 'I'm going to make one for myself. I got some lovely satin material when I was in Annan on Friday. Would ye like to see it?'

'Oh yes, Mother, of course I would! What colour is it?'

'Deep blue – about the same colour as the bluebells in the wood up at Westhill.'

'Oh good, then it will match your eyes and I know Father loves to see you in blue . . .'

'Aye.' Beth smiled softly, reminding Kirsty of her young brother. Luke was far more like their mother than she was.

'I brought a new pattern book too . . . er . . . I dinna suppose ye'd like me to make ye a dress, Kirsty?'

'Oh Mother, could you? I mean will you have time to make one for both of us?' Beth was well known for her skill with a needle. She had won so many prizes at the Women's Rural Institute that they had asked her to judge several competitions. 'I'll help with all your other work if you think it willna be too much for you?'

'Och it willna be too much! Especially now I have the new treadle sewing machine.' Beth smiled reminiscently. 'I remember the first dress I ever made. I had to stitch it by hand and there were so many tucks on the bodice! It seemed to take for ever! I thought your father was going to quarrel with me because of the time I had to spend on it – but he understood when he knew the reason.'

'I can't imagine you and Father ever quarrelling.' Kirsty's voice was soft, almost wistful. A tender smile curved Beth's lips.

'No, we've never had a real quarrel. We've been very lucky . . . But never mind me!' she added, suddenly brisk. 'I'd love to make your first evening gown, lassie. In fact there's a pattern in the book. I visualised it on ye when your grandfather suggested ye might like to go with us. Come on upstairs and I'll show ye before we start the milking.'

Eight

Beth would have chosen material made up of lace flowers in powder blue over a white taffeta underskirt for her daughter. 'Ye've such lovely smoky-blue eyes, lassie, and the blue of the dress would emphasise them.' Kirsty knew this was true but she felt this was her parents' special evening and her mother had already chosen blue for her own gown.

'I think the pink lace over the white taffeta would be pretty too,' she smiled. 'Don't you agree, Mother?'

'Well, I suppose I'm biased, lassie, but I think ye'll look lovely in any colour. Ye're bright and young and your hair shines like silk.'

They had settled for the pink and white and Beth had excelled herself with the cutting of the gently swirling skirt which seemed to flow from the slender fitted bodice; the ruched top was decorated with three pale pink rosebuds. As a surprise she arrived home from Annan market the following Friday with a white fur shoulder cape with a pink satin lining as well as elbow-length gloves and an evening purse.

'Oh Mama! You must have spent most of your precious egg money on me. Y-you spoil me.' Kirsty's voice was a little choked and she had subconsciously reverted to the childhood form of address which she had not used since she started school at Dumfries Academy and considered herself almost grown up.

'I'm proud o' ye, lassie.' Beth's own voice was a little hoarse as she looked at Kirsty's shining eyes framed by the dark sweeping lashes and her thick wavy hair, bleached almost to gold at the front by the summer sun.

'My word! I shall have the two most beautiful young women at the ball this evening!' Logan exclaimed when he saw them. 'By the way, Mother wants to see ye both dressed in your finery so we'd better set off early if we're to call in at Fairlyside. I've put two woollen rugs in the car in case ye feel chilly on the way home . . .'

* * *

Almost the first person Kirsty saw as they arrived at the Assembly Rooms where the function was to be held was James MacFarlane; her heart gave an unfamiliar jolt. He had arrived just ahead of them and he looked very handsome, if slightly uncomfortable, in his dark cut-away evening suit. Kirsty sensed that he was a little ill at ease as he stood alone on the edge of a group who were greeting each other noisily. Suddenly he seemed strangely vulnerable and her contrary heart went out to him, but even as she watched he was greeted in jocular tones by another farmer and introduced to his wife, who immediately introduced him to a younger couple at her side.

'Kirsty, did you not hear me, lassie?' Her father was introducing her to an elderly gentleman with a large moustache and twinkling grey eyes. Kirsty gave him her attention and tried to put James MacFarlane out of her mind. It was not so easy to do since her father soon spotted him and hailed him like a long-lost son, and her mother fussed over him being alone like a broody hen with one chick. Yet it was clear that James MacFarlane reciprocated their warmth. Then his gaze fell on her. She saw his greeny-grey eyes widen in admiration; a little surge of happiness began to fill her heart but it was swiftly quenched when his thick lashes came down and his expression grew wary.

Almost immediately they were drawn into the throng and as people greeted her father Kirsty saw him relax and begin to enjoy the evening. She was glad for him and for her mother, but almost inevitably she was thrown into James's company whether he wanted her or not and she felt sure he did not, although he smiled politely when several elderly gentlemen congratulated him on his pretty partner and he conversed pleasantly enough with younger couples whom they had both met at local agricultural shows or at Fairlyden.

The meal consisted of several courses and Kirsty and James made polite conversation with each other when not chatting to their opposite numbers across the table. Kirsty felt rather more sorry for her father than for herself, however. He was seated next to a plump, wheezy woman who seemed to have some difficulty getting her breath. Before the meal was half over she was proclaiming her own foolishness at coming out at all; her head was throbbing and her throat ached abominably. At length her husband, seated on the other side, placated her by promising to take her home as soon as the meal was over but both Beth and Kirsty feared she had probably passed on her germs to her table companions by then.

Eventually the formalities and presentations came to an end and the dancing began. Kirsty did not lack partners. As Logan Fairly's daughter she found herself in demand; she was young and pretty and the older men enjoyed her knowledgeable conversation, for Kirsty was well informed on the pedigrees of the Ayrshire cattle from her conversations with her father. She also demonstrated a refreshing wit for one so young. As for the younger men, they were delighted to partner her whenever an opportunity arose. Consequently the evening was almost over before James MacFarlane asked her to dance and even then it was because he had little alternative. Beth had found herself sitting next to her daughter for a brief spell and when James approached to ask her to dance she had laughingly fanned her face and declared herself exhausted and would he please be gallant enough to excuse her and take her daughter instead. Kirsty's cheeks felt as though they were on fire with humiliation as she met his cool glance and watched him extend a polite hand – very reluctantly – or so she thought.

Yet despite the constraint they both enjoyed dancing and they were soon carried away in the lively rhythm of the Dashing White Sergeant. James was strong and light on his feet and Kirsty forgot to feel awkward and humiliated. When the dance was over their little group was all breathless and laughing but not at all inclined to resume their seats.

'Give me a good old Scottish rhythm anytime and you can keep Fred Astaire and his fancy steps!' one young woman gasped, referring to the popular dancing star of the silver screen.

'Aye, but I wouldna mind an hour or twae with Ginger Rogers!' her partner riposted loudly. James smiled but he drew Kirsty aside.

'That was your mother's dance, now how about the next one for us, Kirsty?' His eyes were still wary, but his hand on her arm was firm. Kirsty was flushed and filled with the lilt of the music. She had not inherited her mother's musical talent but she had a passably good singing voice and a fine sense of rhythm, and above all she loved dancing. The band began to play the haunting melody for the Pride of Erin Waltz and she went unresisting into James's arms.

As they circled the floor in perfect harmony she wondered briefly why Mary MacFarlane had not accompanied James, but then she gave herself up to the pleasure of dancing and refused to think of anything else. James also seemed content not to talk and when she stole a look at him she saw there was a tender smile lifting the corners of his mouth and his eyes seemed to have lost their cool wariness. Kirsty gave a little sigh of contentment and she thought his arms tightened slightly.

As the last strains of the dance died away James slid his arm beneath her elbow instead of relinquishing his hold altogether.

'I would like to talk to you, Kirsty?' He said quietly. 'There's a smaller room through that door where it is quieter. Will you join me?'

Kirsty nodded and allowed him to lead her further down the long ballroom. They were just passing a group of noisy middle-aged men when one of them stepped into their path and leered at Kirsty.

'Dinna trust him,' he drawled. 'Can't trust these MacFarlanes! Give their mother's pedigree tae a bloody cow if it wad earn them a pound or twae extra! Rotters . . .' One of his companions pulled him back into the group and flashed an apologetic smile at Kirsty and then at James.

'He's had a dram or twae, laddie. Ye canna be rethponthi-sible . . . res-pon-sible – see I said it! I did!'

James kept on walking steadily but his fingers had tightened on Kirsty's arm and she wondered if he knew he was hurting her with his iron grip. She looked at his face and saw his clenched jaw and the muscle pulsing in his cheek as it did when he was tense and disturbed. He was so pale too . . . A few yards further along he stopped abruptly and turned to look down at her.

'Maybe you've changed your mind? Maybe you'd rather not be seen with a MacFarlane after all?' His voice was harsh and there was a bitterness in him that Kirsty had never seen in the James she used to know.

'You wanted to talk to me.' Her voice was quiet but determined. She moved forward again towards the alcove leading into a small room with several chairs.

'Will you be warm enough without your cape?'

'Yes.' But as the cooler air swept over her Kirsty could not suppress a shiver and James moved closer instinctively. She could feel the hardness of his chest against her back and his breath fanning her cheek. She half turned, but he did not step back, instead he laid his arm lightly, very lightly, around her shoulders. She could sense the tension in him but this time she guessed it had as much to do with the comments in the ballroom as with herself.

'What's wrong, Jamie?' She saw one eyebrow rise in that quizzical way she remembered and the ghost of a smile erased some of the grimness from his set expression.

'I wondered whether you would ever get around to calling me Jamie again! You only used to call me James when you were displeased . . .'

'We-ell, I was disappointed in you, I suppose. You always said you wouldna leave Fairlyden and I felt you'd broken your promise . . . Now I understand the reason why. There was nothing to keep you at Fairlyden.' Maybe there'll be nothing for me either, she thought bleakly, when Luke grows up and takes a wife. Maybe I shall be like James and seize the first opportunity to leave . . .

'Nothing to keep me!' James was looking at her incredulously. He opened his mouth, closed it again, then said quietly. 'I had good reason for my decision, Kirsty. Two good reasons in fact. I wanted to tell you . . . but you gave me no chance.' And you're not ready to hear the second, he thought, maybe you'll never be ready. 'You condemned me like so many other folk!' He jerked his head backwards towards the ballroom and his tone was bitter.

Kirsty frowned. What had the man meant about cheating? 'I've told your father everything, but I asked him not to tell you.'

'You said I—I condemned you. I didna make you go to Nithanvale!' Kirsty felt indignant and bewildered. 'It was your own decision and even your own mother is still not happy about it.'

'I know, and I canna tell her everything yet either. She would be even more anxious. She wouldna understand, especially when she has such a low opinion of the MacFarlanes anyway. My great-uncle said he didna know of my existence until he read about me in the paper and I believe him, but that has nothing to do with my decision to move to Nithanvale. Great-Uncle George needs me, Kirsty . . .' He looked searchingly into her face and saw the disbelief and doubt. 'He really does!

The grieve he had was robbing him! Cheating in every way he could – and worst of all he has cast doubts on the integrity of the MacFarlanes – and on the accuracy of the Nithanvale pedigrees!'

'Is that what that man meant?' Kirsty gasped.

'Yes it is. We've tried to keep things quiet but bad news always leaks out and rumours spread. There will always be some who believe George MacFarlane was as involved as his grieve – and others only too ready to believe I'm tarred with the same brush now I'm connected with Nithanvale,' he muttered gloomily. 'At least your father knows the truth. I was glad of his support tonight.' Kirsty's heart suddenly went cold. Was that why he had brought her out here – to make people think he had her support too. She frowned at him. But no, James was not like that – was he?

'Is that why you wanted to talk to me – to tell me about your great-uncle? What was the other reason you went to Nithanvale – you said you had two reasons for leaving Fairlyden . . .'

'Aah,' James smiled, 'I can't tell you the other reason, not yet, Kirsty. But I didn't bring you out here to talk about Nithanvale or my relations and their troubles. I wanted to apologise for the way I treated you the last time I saw you at Fairlyden.' He watched the delicate blush colour her clear skin and he knew she remembered their first kiss just as clearly as he did himself. He groaned softly. 'I'm sorry I lost control – but I canna honestly say I'm sorry I kissed you, Kirsty – even though you are Logan Fairly's daughter.' And quite beyond my reach – at least for now, he thought silently. Aloud he added, 'You would drive any man to distraction.'

'Oh James! How can you say that when you're . . . now that you're involved with M . . . involved at Nithanvale?'

'I can say it because I've known you all your life, because I hope we are friends again, as we have always been – you and I – and because you're a very beautiful young woman,' he finished huskily. This time there was no anger in him. 'Now we must return to the ballroom before I repeat my mistake. Anyway, I think they must be playing the final selection and your parents will wonder where you are . . .'

As soon as they entered the ballroom James turned to her. He did not ask her to dance. He simply opened his arms and smiled in a way that made Kirsty's legs feel quite weak. She went into his arms, glad of his strength and support. They did not speak as they moved together to the strains of *Love is the*

70

sweetest thing, but Kirsty could not quite forget that he had described Mary MacFarlane as 'a very special person' with such warmth and affection.

Nine

Less than a week later Logan developed a fever with an aching throat and throbbing head. Beth was worried. She suspected he had probably caught an infection from his table companion at the Farmers' Ball and she was only too aware of the effects such illnesses had on his weak chest. She obeyed Doctor Broombank's stern instructions and summoned him immediately. Logan was confined to bed, but apart from an initial protest he seemed glad to stay beneath the blankets with a hot stone pig at his feet and another at his back, instead of having to make the effort to dress and go to the byre for milking. A few days later Beth and Kirsty were stricken too, though not to the same degree as Logan. They continued to struggle through the essential tasks and tried to insist that Sarah should stay away from the milking until they were clear of infection.

'Och, I've never been one for taking colds and such,' she chuckled cheerfully. 'In fact I've been disgustingly healthy all my life when I think about it.' Her eyes clouded. 'I only wish Logan could have retained his own good health. He was such a sturdy bairn. Crispin is insisting on coming up to see him, Beth. I hope you dinna mind?'

'Of course not, if you think he should?' Beth looked doubtfully at her mother-in-law, before she croaked and began to cough. 'It does seem a rather bad sort of illness. I confess I havena felt so awful myself for a long time, and it's taking its toll on Kirsty, and she's usually so strong.'

'I noticed she was dragging one foot after the other like an old woman this morning, and her face as white as the milk in her luggie. Crispin has an appointment with the lawyer this afternoon but he is going to cancel it until she's better. I confess I hated that telephone when we first had it installed but there's one thing about it, you can do things in a minute. It's not like a letter where you have to make an arrangement the day before.'

Beth nodded. 'Well, I think Kirsty will be quite relieved not to have to do anything more than the milking for a day or two. Thank goodness Lucy is so willing to help in any emergency. She made a big pot of broth this morning and an egg custard for Logan. It's about all he can swallow and I must admit I havena much appetite either.'

'I'll try to persuade Crispin to wait a day or two then, but you know how he worries about Logan . . .' she lowered her voice, 'especially since Doctor Broombank said the breathlessness had put a strain on his heart. I expect he'll feel happier if he just sees him for a wee while.'

'I know.' Beth smiled wanly. 'You're both so very good to us.'

'No better then you deserve, lassie.' Sarah smiled warmly and patted Beth's hand as she had when she was a child. 'Now you go and have a rest yourself. The washing and ironing will wait until another day, or I could ask Dora Fleming to lend a hand?'

'I think I shall be better tomorrow, but thanks anyway.'

Crispin cancelled his appointment with young Mr Carsewell but nothing could keep him from paying a short visit to Logan.

'I know you wouldn't keep anything from me, Sarah – not if he was really bad . . . but I always have a fear that one more bout of wheezing might be more than his heart can stand. I'll not stay and tire him, but I shall feel happier when I've seen him.'

Beth and Kirsty had almost recovered and even Logan was getting up for an hour or two each afternoon. They were all dismayed when Sarah hurried up to the house looking pale and strained in the middle of the morning.

'I've sent for Doctor Broombank. Crispin was still sleeping when I came up for the milking early this morning but I knew he wasna well as soon as I returned. He didna want me to send for the doctor of course but I shall be happier when he's been. He's sleeping again just now and Dora is still at the house so I thought I'd let you know. I shall not be up for the milking until he is better.'

'No, no of course not! You must not think about the milking!' Beth's eyes were wide with concern. She knew Logan's mother was not a woman who panicked and she did not send for the doctor either unless she had a very good reason.

'I'll walk back with you, Granny,' Kirsty offered, her young face registering concern. She had never seen her grandmother look so strained and worried; she felt a sickly pang as she

74

looked at the face which seemed to have aged ten years since the milking a few hour earlier. Sarah made no protest as Kirsty fell into step beside her and that in itself was a measure of her deep anxiety, Beth thought, watching them walk down the track back to Fairlyside.

'I'm afraid your husband is a very sick man, Mrs Bradshaw,' Doctor Broombank declared gravely after he had examined Crispin thoroughly. 'The infection is a severe one and it is already having a serious affect on his breathing, and consequently on his heart.'

'B-but he will be all right, Doctor?' Sarah's face was suddenly lined and deathly white. Her own heart felt cold with fear.

'Please, Granny, won't you sit down,' Kirsty pleaded anxiously, but her eyes were fixed on the doctor's face, searching for signs of hope and reassurance. She found none and her own knees quivered.

'A cup of tea, perhaps,' Doctor Broombank suggested gently, meeting her wide-eyed gaze steadily, willing her to be strong for the sake of her grandmother. She swallowed convulsively but she pulled herself together and went to push the kettle on to the hot plate of the Aga, warming the teapot, spooning in the leaves, her actions automatic.

A little while later the doctor took his leave. 'I will leave this medicine,' he said quietly. 'It is very bitter, but it will help the fever and it may ease his breathing a little. I shall return this evening. Try not to worry, Mistress Bradshaw . . .'

Sarah smiled wanly. 'I'll see you out, Doctor,' she murmured with a dignity which earned her the young man's deepest respect. She returned to the kitchen with dragging footsteps and Kirsty poured her another cup of tea from the big brown teapot and added milk and sugar. Silently she put it in front of her grandmother. Sarah cradled it in her hands as though finding comfort in its warmth, but she did not drink it. Over the rim of the cup she met Kirsty's anxious eyes.

'I'll be all right, lassie, in a minute. He's an old man, your grandfather, I know that. He wouldna want us to grieve, you know . . .'

'Oh, Granny!' Kirsty's voice choked with tears and she struggled to hold them back. 'Maybe the medicine will help.'

Sarah shook her head. 'I'll try to give him some when he wakens, lassie, but the doctor was just offering me a wee bit of comfort. I saw it in his eyes . . .' She stared unseeingly into the gently swirling tea. She took a sip, then another. She set the cup on the table and stood up. 'I'll go up and sit with him now. I'll be all right, you know.' She summoned a smile, but Kirsty could see it was a big effort. 'You go away back home. Your mother and father will be wondering what Doctor Broombank had to say. And they'll need you for the milking later.' Sarah sighed. She felt unutterably weary as though the spirit of her life was draining away. 'You can come back later, if you've a mind, Kirsty. I expect I'll be glad o' company . . . tonight.'

Kirsty nodded, frowning uncertainly. 'If you're sure that's what you want, Granny?'

'It is, lassie, it is – and Dora will be here for a wee while. I'll send her up to the house if I need anything. Your grandfather had another appointment with Mr Carsewell tomorrow, but I doubt it's too late. Remind me to cancel it, will you? He couldna keep the last one because you werena fit to drive him – and this time he isna fit himself.' Kirsty stared at her grandmother. She seemed to be talking to herself.

'I didn't know Grandfather had cancelled an appointment! I would have taken him. It seemed important to him.'

'You couldna go, lassie. You weren't fit.' Sarah shook her head slowly then murmured softly, almost to herself. 'Maybe it's the way things were meant to be. It's God's will.'

Kirsty bit her lip and looked at her grandmother uncertainly but Sarah was staring into space, apparently lost in thought and Kirsty crept towards the door. She had almost reached it when Sarah spoke again in the same half-bewildered tone. 'We've been lucky to have so long together. We wasted so much time . . . Pride, that's what it was. Pride and independence – both thinking we had a duty to do.' She looked up suddenly, straight into Kirsty's troubled eyes. 'Never let pride stand in the way o' happiness, lassie. It's too fleeting . . . far too precious.' She lowered her eyes, almost as though in prayer. Kirsty closed the door softly behind her, sensing her grandmother's need to be alone to have this little time to commune with the past, perhaps to prepare herself for the ordeal she sensed must lie ahead.

In the early evening, when the milking was over and the supper dishes cleared from the table Kirsty said, 'I promised to go back down to Granny's.'

Beth nodded. 'You're a good lassie, Kirsty. I know your grandmother has always enjoyed your company. You're very like her.' She sighed softly. 'But I think I'll come down myself in a wee while and maybe I'll spend the night at Fairlyside.

You'll keep an eye on your father for me?'

'Och, I'm no' needing anyone to keep an eye on me!' Logan exclaimed, coming through to the kitchen. 'I'm going down to Fairlyside with you.'

'But, Logan, you havena been outside yet!' Beth protested anxiously. 'And it's such a chill air now. The autumn evenings are drawing in.'

'I have to see him, Beth.' He looked down into his wife's anxious blue eyes and his gaze was tender. 'If Mother's intuition is right – and it usually is – this may be my last chance to talk ... to my own father.' Logan's voice was unusually husky and Beth looked at him sharply. Kirsty blinked, bewildered by her father's sudden emotion, but he seemed to have forgotten her presence. 'I never really called him Father, you know. I believed I was a Fairly for so long that when I learned the truth – that Fairly was only my name, that Crispin Bradshaw was my natural father, that I was the son of a mill owner, I – I think I shut my mind to it. I rebelled against the idea.'

'I'm sure that's not true. Anyway you were so very weak and ill when you learned the truth. And you always got on well together,' Beth protested in bewilderment.

'Well, maybe it was subconscious,' Logan conceded. 'But I'm sure he sensed it. Now – just once – I'd like him to hear me call him "Father". I want to thank him for bringing me home frae that rotten war ... and for helping you to survive too, dearest, Beth.'

'I'm sure he knows how you feel – that you're grateful to him, Logie, as I am.' Beth's own voice was hoarse.

'I will bring the car from the cart-shed,' Kirsty said quietly into the sudden silence. 'We can all drive down, even if it is only a few hundred yards. Father will be warmer then and we can drive back ...' Up the slope, her expressive eyes told Beth silently. Her mother nodded agreement.

Crispin seemed a little better when they arrived at Fairlyside and Sarah was persuaded to eat a light meal in the company of Beth and Kirsty, whilst Logan took the opportunity to be alone with his father. Later when the women joined them in the firelit bedroom Crispin had a look of infinite peace on his lined face and he greeted them all with a faint smile. They talked quietly as he dozed but an hour later he opened his eyes and held out his hand. Sarah went to him at once and clasped his hand in both of hers, dropping to her knees beside the bed. Their eyes met and held, silently loving. Then Crispin

77

turned his head weakly to look at Kirsty.

'Everything will be all right, lass. I know you'll look after them.' His gaze moved to the other three faces watching him with such love. 'And Luke,' he murmured. 'You and Luke – another generation . . .' He was silent, his breathing shallow.

'Sarah . . . My dearest love.'

Ten

Crispin's death had been peaceful, almost happy, surrounded as he was by the four people dearest to him. Although he had not belonged to the inner circle of those born and bred in the parish of Muircumwell he had long been accepted as a valuable and respected member of the small, close-knit community; he had benefited many in his own quiet way. Consequently the funeral was a large one with mourners overflowing from the large sitting room at Fairlyside, where the Reverend Morrison stood behind the coffin, into the hall and through the open front door into the drive and garden.

Among those squeezed into the room were Crispin's nephew, Robert Smith, with his wife, Sarah's own daughter. Ted Forbes, the man Crispin himself had chosen and trained as manager of the Bradshaw Mill was with them too. Apart from a perfunctory kiss on their arrival from the station just before midday, Sadie had offered no word of comfort to her mother, nor had Sarah expected any.

'The funeral should have been held in Church, as they are in England!' she hissed contemptuously at her eldest brother, Alex Fairly.

'This is Scotland.' Alex's voice was quiet, but it held an authority which forbade further comment. Sadie was taken aback. She had a habit of remembering her family as they had been when they were young, all living together at Fairlyden. Alex had not been so confident then with his twisted feet. She had always thought of him as a cripple – as had their father, William Fairly. She was not pleased to be set so firmly in her place. Her lips compressed tightly and her thin face beneath the fashionable black cloche hat was screwed into a disapproving frown. Luke Fairly, standing next to Kirsty with his head bowed, raised only his eyes to scan those within his immediate line of vision. He did not like the look of the woman who was his aunt. She resembled a witch, he thought, subconsciously taking in every detail of her scrawny legs and pointed black shoes, the straight black coat, cut in the latest

79

low-waisted fashion but doing little for Sadie's gaunt, shapeless figure.

The day was calm and dry, but Sarah felt the chill of autumn – or was it the inner chill of her own immense loss? No one seeing her quiet dignity, the pale composed face beneath the black veiled hat, could guess at the desolation within her heart. It was a tremendous relief when the service was over and the mourners followed the coffin to the horse-drawn hearse. The men would follow it on foot to its last resting place in Muircumwell Kirkyard – all except Robert Smith who had only one leg. He was manoeuvring himself and his crutches awkwardly into Alex's car to be driven to the graveside. According to tradition the women gathered with Sarah on the front steps. Ellen, her eldest daughter, ever loving and caring, gently supported her; Beth, Kirsty and Emma moved to her other side offering silent comfort with their presence. Other women, friends and neighbours, stood a little apart, some ready to help with refreshments when the men returned. Only Sadie stood aloof, barely waiting until the sad procession was lost to sight by the bend in the track.

'You would have thought even Muircumwell could have had a proper hearse instead of a horse and cart in this day and age!' she muttered the moment the rear bumper of Alex's car moved slowly down the track. No one answered. Sarah thought of the care Dick Anderson and his grandson must have taken to groom the two black horses to gleaming perfection and polish the harness. He had asked diffidently whether he should hire the motor hearse from Annan for Master Bradshaw but Crispin had never been a man for pomp and ceremony . . . 'Alex should have made sure Robert was at the head of the procession. He's chief mourner. He will have to have the first cord – at the head . . .' Sarah trembled slightly. At her side she felt Ellen and Beth stiffen, move imperceptibly closer. She was grateful to them both.

'I think you should come into the house now, Mother?' Ellen suggested gently. 'Maybe you could sit down a while until they return?' Sarah nodded but she did not move. She was thinking of the formality of issuing the cords at the graveside. The nearest and closest male relative was always given the cord at the head of the coffin, the next one the foot, and so on in order of precedence. She knew Crispin would have been pleased and proud to know Logan was at his head today. Alex had been quietly approving of his youngest brother's decision. Ellen, who had arrived at Fairlyside the morning after Crispin's death, had been a tower of strength. She had simply nodded acceptance when she learned at last that Logan was Crispin's son. Robert Smith would get a shock – if he was familiar with the Scottish tradition. There would be other onlookers too who would speculate. There was always a keen observance of who had been given precedence over whom and whether honour had been bestowed or withheld in this ritual with the cords. Sarah straightened her shoulders subconsciously and turned towards the sitting room. It seemed strangely bare and empty with the mourners gone and the furniture all pushed back against the walls.

Ellen and Emma followed her, pulling the chairs closer to the fire, seating her comfortably, bringing more coals and a log to make a cheery blaze.

'Kirsty and I will see if there's anything needed in the dining room before the men return,' Beth murmured. Sarah looked up then, summoning a faint smile.

'Everything's ready, Beth. Ellen was up early to supervise Dora, and Lucy and Anna are here to help too. Come and sit down.' She waved Beth to a chair beside Ellen. She looked at her granddaughter's tall slim figure; her grey eyes seemed too big for her pale young face, especially with her bright hair hidden beneath her black hat. Kirsty would miss her grandfather too . . . She held out a hand. 'Sit here, lassie, beside me. Everything will be all right, you know – in the end. In the end,' she repeated softly with a sigh.

'Oh Granny . . .' Kirsty's voice was choked with suppressed tears. Simultaneously they both became aware of Sadie's cool gaze fixed upon them. She frowned as she met their eyes and addressed herself rather hurriedly to her elder sister.

'When are you going back to your mansion house and all your old men, Ellen?'

'Most of my patients are no older than Robert – or Logan,' Ellen reminded her mildly. 'As for Willowman Home, it's far frae being a mansion any longer.'

'All right, all right! Spare me the details. When are you going back there?'

'I'm afraid I must leave tomorrow.' Ellen cast a sorrowful glance at her mother. 'But Kirsty has offered to move in with Mother for company when you and Robert go home.'

'I shall be all right on my own,' Sarah assured them hastily, in case Sadie and Robert decided it was their duty to stay with her. 'But Kirsty knows she's always welcome; don't you, lassie?' She patted her granddaughter's hand.

'Well, Robert and I can't stay more than a night or two. We have so many engagements . . .' Sadie paused but when no one commented on her busy social life she went on sullenly, 'I expect Mother will move back to Fairlyden so she'll have plenty of company there. I—'

'Dinna speak as though I'm not here!' Sarah interrupted with unfamiliar sharpness. 'And I'm not planning on moving anywhere. It takes time to adjust and I shall have to get used to being on my own.'

'Well yes, but you know we already have the London house and the apartment in France, as well as our house in Yorkshire.' Sadie allowed herself another theatrical pause. 'I'm not sure what Robert plans to do with this house, you see . . .' She looked around the comfortable sitting room with critical eyes. 'He will probably sell it as soon as you can make other arrangements, Mother.'

Beth gasped at her sister-in-law's callousness.

'Sadie!' Ellen's voice was bitingly cold. 'How can you even think—'

'Dinna fret, lassie,' Sarah interrupted wearily. 'Sadie hasna changed much it seems.' Her tone was dry, but Kirsty, perched close beside her on the arm of the big easy chair, felt a tremor run through her. She laid her own arm protectively around Sarah's drooping shoulders and glared reproachfully at this Aunt Sadie whom she scarcely knew and felt she would rather not have had as a relation had there been any choice in such matters. No wonder Anna MacFarlane remembered her with such venom.

The thought of Anna brought her son to Kirsty's mind. James had been at the funeral and despite her own grief she had felt strangely comforted by his presence. She had seen the sympathy in his greeny-grey eyes when they had met and fleetingly held her own, across the crowded sitting room. The memory of that look filled her with a warmth which seemed to drive away some of the chill of grief – then she felt guilty. How could she think of James MacFarlane when her grandmother was the one who should be receiving all the sympathy and kindness.

Everyone had been fed at last and Sarah felt a great sweep of relief as she bid the mourners a dignified goodbye. Apart from her immediate family, only Ted Forbes, foreman of the Bradshaw mill, and Mr Carsewell, the lawyer, remained. Sarah felt the tension building up inside her every time she looked at Sadie and Robert. She had seen them talking rapidly together soon after Robert returned from the graveyard. She had seen her daughter's mouth open and snap shut; twin patches of indignant colour had stained her sallow face. She guessed Robert was telling her he had been relegated to the foot of his uncle's coffin instead of taking his place at the head. She could almost hear his pompous words, knowing he had reverted to his former snobbish ways since his marriage to Sadie.

'I think Mr Carsewell is ready to read the will, Mother,' Alex interrupted her thoughts. 'Emma thinks we ought to be going home now – get our laddies out of your way – unless there's anything we can do for you?' Sarah looked into his concerned face and his kindly dark eyes.

'Your laddies could wait in the kitchen with Luke – help themselves to more food maybe? I'd like you to wait, Alex – even though Crispin's affairs dinna concern you. I—I might need your support.'

'With Sadie and Robert you mean?'

'I'm not sure what Crispin had in his will. He meant to change it you know, but he never got round to it – so I suppose they'll come out of it better than they might have done. I do know they're expecting to get this house and I'm afraid they're going to be disappointed about that.'

Alex nodded. 'We'll wait in the other room then until Mr Carsewell is finished.'

'Can you come through, Mrs Bradshaw? Miss Fairly? You too, Mr Forbes.'

'Me? Are you sure you mean me?' Ted Forbes had been sitting in a corner of the dining room waiting patiently for someone to tell him where he was to sleep later that night. Sarah had almost forgotten about him. She apologised hurriedly. He smiled at her, an easy reassuring smile.

'I understand, Mrs Bradshaw. There's many a one will miss him you know, back 'ome in Yorkshire – an' me more than most. Can't think what yon gen'leman wants wi' me, but best get it over wi'. After you . . .' He ushered Sarah gently into the room. She was aware of several pairs of eyes fixed on her, but it was Kirsty's enormous grey eyes looking so bewildered and anxious which drew her to the settee. It was so easy to forget

Kirsty was still only seventeen, she thought. She had always been mature for her age – and capable – but this was a new experience . . . She glanced at Beth, who looked equally troubled, and Logan clasping her hand firmly in his. Her own heartache eased a little. Their love for each other seemed to warm everyone whose lives touched theirs.

Her gaze moved to Sadie and Robert. How smug they look! She frowned, unconsciously wringing her hands as she had a habit of doing when she was agitated. There was sure to be trouble with Sadie, even without the new will Crispin had intended . . .

Mr Carsewell cleared his throat and rustled his papers, drawing her attention back to the business in hand. He began by explaining that Mr Crispin Bradshaw had made a recent will but as he had not managed to sign it, it was now invalid.

'So the old will must stand. However Mr Bradshaw insisted on adding a codicil. This was signed and witnessed on the day he first called at my office in Dumfries. Perhaps he had some sort of premonition . . .' Mr Carsewell looked directly at Sarah.

'He was perfectly well at the time, but . . .' Her words trailed away. In her heart she felt it was God's will.

'At the time the first will was made Mr Logan Fairly was missing, presumed dead, I understand. It was Mr Bradshaw's intention to leave the farm and lands of Fairlyden to you in his new will, Mr Fairly, and I can only say how sorry I am that this cannot be done. However, I suspect it will make little difference to your life in practice for I understand you are a very united family.' Across the room Sarah saw Sadie frown and sit up straighter, watchful now. She wished the lawyer would get it over with.

'So I shall proceed with the original will, then I shall read the codicil at the end. Since this has far-reaching effects I must ask you to bear with me.

'To you, Mrs Bradshaw, your husband left five hundred pounds and an income of three hundred pounds per annum. This is to be drawn from his personal bank account. Also the house of Fairlyside remains yours throughout your lifetime, Mrs Bradshaw, but on your death it will pass to your granddaughter, Miss Kirsty Fairly—'

'What! There must be some mistake!' Sadie exclaimed out loud before she collected herself and nudged Robert. 'Tell him, there must be some mistake!' Robert nodded.

'There is no mistake.' Mr Carsewell's voice grew stern. 'May

I remind you I shall read out the codicil last.'

'To Mr Robert Smith is bequeathed the Bradshaw family home in Yorkshire, the Bradshaw Mills and all the property belonging to the late Mr Cuthbert Bradshaw, also the house of the mill manager occupied by Mr Edward Forbes, also the houses and cottages presently belonging to the Bradshaw Trust and occupied by workers at the mill.'

Out of the corner of her eye Sarah saw the smirk of satisfaction and triumph on Sadie's thin face, and a similar expression on that of her husband. They sat back in their comfortable chairs now. Dear Crispin, she thought sadly, I know this is not the fate you intended for your loyal workers. Mr Carsewell was continuing.

'Miss Kirsty Fairly was an infant at the time this will was drawn up. Therefore her inheritance was put into the hands of trustees until she attains the age of twenty-one years. This inheritance includes the aforementioned house of Fairlyside on the death of her grandmother.'

Kirsty trembled. Sarah reached out a hand and covered the girl's tightly clasped fingers, squeezing them gently. Kirsty looked up at her with wide unhappy eyes. Sarah tried to smile encouragingly but her own mouth trembled dangerously.

'Also bequeathed to Miss Kirsty Fairly are the farm and lands of Fairlyden extending to one hundred and twenty-five acres.'

Kirsty gasped aloud and her face paled visibly. She stared at her father in consternation but Logan smiled back at her with his dear, loving smile. She bit her lip and tried to relax the unbearable tension but she glimpsed a look of near hatred on her Aunt Sadie's face. The lawyer was proceeding with the conditions of her inheritance and she made a valiant effort to concentrate.

'. . . mother, Mrs Elizabeth Fairly, as main trustee, along with her father, Mr Logan Fairly, if he is still alive.' The lawyer looked up and smiled at Logan, relaxing his stern expression a little. 'I am pleased to know that miracles do still occur, Mr Fairly. The other trustee was my father-in-law, who was Mr Bradshaw's legal adviser at that time. This duty now falls to myself, at the late Mr Crispin Bradshaw's request.' He fixed a gimlet eye on Sadie's and Robert's dismayed and disapproving faces. He cleared his throat again and frowned.

'There are one or two minor bequests but the main business remaining is from the codicil. Mr Crispin Bradshaw seemed

85

extremely concerned for the future welfare of the workers at the Bradshaw Mills. He was so concerned in fact that he insisted on the codicil . . .'

Sadie and Robert sat up straight suddenly, leaning forward in their chairs, their faces set. 'These are the main changes and they affect the inheritance of Mr Robert Smith.

'Forty-five per cent of the Bradshaw Trust will now pass into the hands of the said Mr Robert Smith. There is a firm condition on Mr Smith's acceptance of this share. It is this: a new trust will be created with the remaining fifty-five per cent and, should you decide to sell your share, Mr Smith, you are duty bound to give the new Bradshaw Trust the first option to purchase your share at a fair market price.'

Robert Smith gaped at the lawyer. Sadie hissed through her new false teeth, but no words came and the lawyer proceeded.

'Mr Edward Forbes is to be appointed chief trustee of the new trust, he will receive ten per cent of the profits and he will have the use of the mill manager's house for the rest of his life . . .'

'That's ridiculous! The house is far too big for a man like him. Robert meant to sell it and . . .' Sadie's words failed as she caught the lawyer's eye.

'Exactly as my late client feared, Mrs Smith. He also feared for his workers and their homes and there are several conditions relating to their protection, help for their education, their health and so on . . . These must be incorporated into the trust which is to be drawn up. The late Mr Bradshaw suggested the names of three fellow Yorkshiremen as trustees along with Mr Edward Forbes. They had earned his respect in their various fields. They are a fellow mill owner named Eli Jarvis, the senior partner in the firm of lawyers who dealt with the Bradshaw Mill affairs and an accountant by the name of Joseph Felixstone who—'

'No!' Robert Smith ejaculated angrily at the same moment that Ted Forbes heaved a sigh of relief. 'No! No, he can't do this. My uncle had no right. I am the only heir to the Bradshaw money. My grandfather set up the trust for me.'

'Your uncle had every right to act as he did, Mr Smith.'

'I shall contest it!'

'You may try.' Mr Carsewell's tone was cold. His expression remained bland but contempt flickered in his shrewd blue eyes.

Kirsty looked at Ted Forbes. She had seen amazement, dismay, anxiety and relief chase each other over his leathery brown face. He caught her eye and to her surprise and delight he gave a wink and a little nod – as much as to say 'Mr Crispin knew what he was doing all right.' Incredibly her heart lightened a little, despite her sadness and bewilderment.

'He can't do this!' Robert Smith reiterated angrily. 'It should all have come to me. This house as well and the farm! It's mine I tell you, bought with Bradshaw money when the Fairlys were destitute . . .' he added with a sneer and glared venomously at Kirsty. His wife's face paled then turned a blotchy red. After all she was a Fairly by birth and she had been proud of that fact once. Robert's own father had had no money of his own at all; they had lived off an allowance from old Mr Bradshaw . . . But why should her niece inherit so much? It was Beth Jamieson's doing – currying favour with everyone at Fairlyden . . .

Mr Carsewell looked directly at Logan and lifted an eyebrow in a silent question. Logan bit his lip, then he gave an imperceptible nod. He felt the increased pressure of Beth's fingers; he turned his head and smiled reassuringly into her anxious blue eyes. Nevertheless he hated quarrels and he would be glad when Sadie and Robert had returned to Yorkshire.

'I think I should make the situation plain to you, Mr Smith,' Mr Carsewell stated clearly.

'The situation is plain!' Robert exclaimed, incensed. 'These – these scoundrels are trying to cheat me out of my inheritance! They've taken advantage of an old man who had lost his senses!'

Sarah moved sharply in protest.

'That is enough, Mr Smith! You will remember the time and place, if you please. You have no claim to anything except the two houses left to you by your parents. Mr Bradshaw has been exceedingly generous to you in the circumstances and—'

'What circumstances!' Robert sneered furiously.

'The late Crispin Bradshaw had a son of his own. The terms of the trust set up by your grandfather made it very clear that in such circumstances all the Bradshaw wealth . . .'

'A son! How could he have a son?' Robert Smith glared venomously at Sarah. 'He was too old when she married him!' All trace of the polite façade was now stripped from his petulant face. Crispin had never been deceived by that façade though.

Sarah remembered sadly. How right he had been! She gathered herself together and stood up.

'Crispin was Logan's father,' she announced with quiet dignity. How easy it is after all, she thought. Why didn't I tell the world before? How happy he would have been . . .

Suddenly the strain of it all was too much. The tears which she had suppressed since Crispin's death welled up and overflowed. Beth and Logan were at her side in a flash but it was Kirsty's strong young arms which supported her and led her from the room.

Eleven

It was several days after the funeral, and the reading of the will, before Kirsty had an opportunity to speak to her mother and father alone. Sadie and Robert had not even stayed the night, but no one seemed sorry to see their hasty departure. Ellen had returned to England and her patients at Willowman House Convalescent Home and Kirsty had volunteered to stay with her grandmother until she tired of her company.

'Och, I shall never tire o' your company, lassie,' Sarah had assured her, 'but I wouldna like to grow too dependent on you either. I must get used to being alone.' She had stared around the familiar kitchen with shadowed eyes. 'The house seems so empty without your grandfather . . .' she ended in a choked whisper, and Kirsty had known she was both welcome and needed, at least for the time being.

Now Kirsty stared across the well-scrubbed table back in the kitchen at Fairlyden.

'I dinna want Fairlyden to belong to me, Father! Really I do not!' she repeated for the third time, and her voice wobbled dangerously. 'Mr Carsewell could change the will, couldn't he? We know Grandfather intended to leave it to you.'

'Now listen to me, lassie,' Logan insisted. 'What does it matter whose name is on the deeds? We're all the same family, aren't we? Fairlyden provides a living for all of us, and it will continue long after I'm gone. Indeed it may all be for the best. Skipping a generation saves death duties, even with such small landowners as ourselves. They're crippling succeeding generations on large estates.' His voice was cheerful, rallying. 'You are the next generation, Kirsty, and I believe, yes I truly believe, Fairlyden's future will depend on you. Your mother and I are content with the present. Each day . . .' His voice lowered huskily and a smile erased many of the premature lines from his face. 'Each day we have together is a gift more precious than land or money. Isn't that so, Beth?'

'It is.' Beth smiled and moved to his side, laying a gentle hand on his shoulder.

'So, you see, lassie? It doesna matter who Fairlyden belongs to – unless ye're thinking o' turning into a tyrant landlord and turning us all out on to the road!' Logan's eyes glinted with humour.

'How can you make light of it? You know it could never, never make any difference, but it is not what Grandfather intended!' Kirsty exclaimed vehemently, feeling strangely near to tears.

'I know it will not make any difference, lassie, or I wouldna be joking,' Logan murmured soothingly. He reached across the table and put his calloused hand firmly over her own tightly clenched fists. 'Ye're a good lassie, Kirsty, and ye must not worry about this business. Just think how awful it might have been if Robert Smith and your Aunt Sadie had inherited Fairlyden.' He grimaced. 'There wouldna have been another generation frae this family living here, I can tell ye that! Now, how are ye getting on living at Fairlyside? Is it too much of a strain being alone with your grandmother? Ye seem very tense, doesn't she, Beth?'

'Yes, ye dinna seem like yourself at all, Kirsty.' Beth looked at her daughter with anxious eyes. 'Ye'll tell me if it is too much of a strain? I could sleep at Fairlyside for a week or two.'

Kirsty smiled at that. As far back as she could remember her parents had never been apart since her father had returned from France like a ghost from another world.

'Granny is coping wonderfully. In fact I enjoy listening to her stories about the past and Fairlyden, and how it was once part o' the Strathtod Estate. She said there was a terrible family feud too. It does make me realise how deeply our roots are entrenched here; the work and sacrifices each generation seems to have made for the benefit of the next . . . One day Luke may feel this way too. Supposing he thinks Grandfather favoured me and forgot about him?'

'Och, Kirsty! Kirsty!' Beth shook her head reprovingly. 'I dinna think Luke has given it a thought! I dinna ken what he does think in that dreamy mind o' his,' she added with an affectionate smile, 'but there's no jealousy there, I'm sure o' that.'

'I dinna think there's many thoughts o' farming either,' Logan commented wryly. 'But if he ever does want to farm, Kirsty, we have the rented land frae Westhill at the north end and the Muircumwell land frae the Guillyman Trustees at the south. That's a hundred and twenty acres

90

altogether – almost as much as Fairlyden itself.'

'But the land isna as good as Fairlyden, Father, and it's rented.'

'The Muircumwell land has improved a lot with the lime I've put on it and it could be almost as good as Fairlyden if the Trustees would spend a bit o' money on draining. Whoever the real owners are they dinna spend a penny; they dinna even maintain the boundary fences, let alone improve anything. Even Avary Hall itself could do with some repairs, and the old mill and the buildings are all but derelict. If it depended on our absent landlords our cattle would be wandering by the Solway by now.'

'But no one ever troubles us either,' Beth reminded him.

'No, not so long as we pay the rent on time,' he agreed. 'If the Trustees would agree to a long lease when the present one expires, I'd drain some o' the Muircumwell fields myself if I had the money. The present lease ends in nineteen forty. That's only six years – no time at all in farming. Luke will be eighteen by then though and he should ken whether he wants to farm or no'. Ye can help us plan in case he does, Kirsty.'

'How can I do that?' Kirsty asked eagerly.

'Well, draining the Muircumwell land would be a great benefit to future generations. As it is,' he shrugged, 'the lime is washed away in no time; money down the drain. But draining needs money. So we'll need to plan ahead until Luke is eighteen and we can negotiate a long lease. We must make sure your grandmother has all she needs first,' he cautioned seriously, 'but apart frae that, there'll be no rent to pay for Fairlyden frae now on. I've been thinking we could use the money to make room for more cows.'

'More cows, Logan? But what about the extra milk to sell?' Beth asked anxiously. 'We canna sell butter and it's scarcely worth making.'

'James MacFarlane seems to think the new Marketing Boards are here to stay this time,' Logan spoke reassuringly. 'And I think he's right, young as he is. If they keep going as they intend, it will be a grand thing tae ken we have a steady market for our milk and a guarantee o' getting the money for it regularly every month. Producing milk is one thing we can do well at Fairlyden. We have the right cows and we can grow grass, and it's a thing Kirsty understands as well as I do myself.'

'That's true,' Beth agreed, remembering how often she found

her husband and daughter with their heads together studying the milk records every month as soon as the milk recorder drove away in her pony and trap when all the tests were finished.

'And I wouldna feel so bad about Luke if I thought we were doing something for him too,' Kirsty nodded, though in her heart she knew Luke was more devoted to studying his books than he would ever be to farming.

'Did ye tell Kirsty ye may be able to buy the young bull frae Mr Grayson in Ayrshire, Logan?' Kirsty's eyes widened at her mother's words. 'The bull calf out of Grayson Mistress Morn, Father?' she asked incredulously. 'Mr Grayson said he would never sell it!'

'Mmm . . . well he does want a good price – a hundred and fifty-five guineas.'

'Oh dear . . .' Kirsty's eyes clouded. She knew how much her father wanted that particular bloodline for their next stockbull.

'Well, I shall have to make up my mind. The letter came this morning offering me the wee beastie. Grayson wants to know as soon as possible, so maybe I'll come down to Fairlyside and use your grandmother's telephone. Perhaps I can get him to knock a guinea or two off the price if I speak to him . . .' Logan's eyes twinkled.

'You do mean to buy him then!'

Logan nodded. 'We canna let young James MacFarlane get all the prizes now he's with the opposition at Nithanvale!' Kirsty knew her father was teasing. He would never grudge anyone success if it was fairly earned, and especially James MacFarlane whom he regarded as his own special protégé. She remembered the sympathy she had seen in James's eyes at her grandfather's funeral, and the comfort she had felt. Somehow it didn't seem so important any more that he had deserted Fairlyden – so long as they were still friends. She sighed. If only she knew how attached he was to Miss Mary MacFarlane of Nithanvale.

Anna Whiteley had seen Kirsty going into the kitchen at Fairlyden while she was working in the dairy. Now she watched her walk across the yard, deep in thought.

'Kirsty isna her usual bright self yet,' she remarked to Beth when she carried in a large basket of eggs. 'In fact she looked as though she had all the troubles in the world on her young shoulders when she came back frae Fairlyside after breakfast.

D'ye think it's too much for her – staying with her grandmother? If there's anything I can do to help . . .?'

'Och, it's not that, Anna . . .' Beth frowned thoughtfully. Her relationship with Anna went back a long time, even before she was married. Anna had always been sympathetic and discreet. Beth sighed. 'As a matter of fact she's feeling guilty because her grandfather didna get his new will made before he died. She was ill and didna take him for the appointment with the lawyer.'

'But she couldna help that.'

'No. But the first will was drawn up when Kirsty was just a toddler. Ye'll remember Logan was missing in France at the time.'

'I remember.' Anna's voice was expressionless, but Beth knew instinctively she was thinking of Sadie Fairly's treachery. 'I remember how ill ye were too.'

'Yes, well Mr Bradshaw put Fairlyden in trust for Kirsty. He meant to change his will and leave the farm to Logan. Luke wasna born so he didna get a mention either. Logan was just trying to reassure Kirsty.' Beth sighed again, and Anna guessed she was more troubled than she would admit, and she soon knew the real reason as Beth went on, 'It willna make any difference to any o' us at present, and sometimes I believe these things are God's will. Doctor Broombank says Logan's health will never improve . . .' She bit her lip. 'I try to take care o' him, but I canna put him in a glass case. We take each day as it comes.'

'Aye, I see what you mean, Mrs Beth.' This form of address had been Anna's compromise since the young girl she had known as Beth Jamieson had become Mistress Elizabeth Fairly of Fairlyden. 'I pray Master Fairly will live many a long year, but ye'll be thinking o' the taxes if Master Fairly had the land and then passed it on to Master Luke? I dinna really understand these things myself but James said the Carnland family had a lot o' death duties to pay when the old laird died. The new laird is in his sixties already. James reckoned it could spell disaster for Nithanvale and some o' the other tenants if the family had to find two lots o' death duties in a short time.'

Ten days later James MacFarlane was visiting his mother and Uncle Thomas, as had become his habit every second Sunday.

'We're getting a young bull frae Ayrshire on Tuesday,'

Thomas Whiteley informed his nephew. 'Coming on the train he is. I'm tae take the bull cart tae the station tae bring him home.'

'Oh? Where is he coming frae?' James shouted into his uncle's good ear.

'I told ye, young James, the wee beast is coming frae Ayrshire!' Thomas was inclined to be irritable these days.

James nodded patiently. 'I meant which herd? Do you know his name?'

'Name! He's a bull, not a bairn!'

'Let him go to sleep, James,' Anna advised placidly. 'He likes a Sunday afternoon nap these days. He's sixty now, ye ken. Mind ye, we're none o' us getting any younger.' Thomas glowered at them.

'Dinna mumble, woman!' he growled. 'Ye ken I canna hear ye when ye whisper!' He wriggled down in his chair and closed his eyes. Then he opened one to add, 'Miss Kirsty's fair pleased about the wee beast coming tae Fairlyden . . .' There was a glint in Thomas's eye. 'She says he'll get the finest heifers i' Scotland if they're like his mother – then we'll beat yon Nithanvale rubbish!'

'I'm sure Kirsty never said that, Thomas!' Anna chided. Her brother closed his eyes and refused to argue but a wicked little smile tugged at his mouth. Anna shook her head at him in silence. 'He's just teasing ye about Kirsty because he kens the two o' ye enjoy an argument – and there'll never be any place on earth as good as Fairlyden to your Uncle Thomas.'

'Well I suppose neither you nor I would disagree with him on that,' James agreed dryly. 'But we canna all stay at Fairlyden. I expect even Kirsty realises that now. After all, she'll need to leave herself one day – when Luke grows up and takes over.' When she marries . . . he thought dreamily.

'Young Luke will never take over Fairlyden.'

'Och, I know he's not very keen on farming yet, but I expect he'll grow to like it eventually – when he realises it's his bread and butter. He told me he knows he canna make a living drawing pictures.'

'I dinna ken what Luke will do with himself,' Anna frowned, 'but Fairlyden belongs to Kirsty now – or at least it's in some sort o' trust. It will be hers when she's twenty-one.'

'What!' James jerked up in his chair. 'What did you say, Mother?' Anna was surprised by her son's reaction. His dreamy expression had fled. His eyes were like gimlets. 'Fairlyden canna possibly belong to Kirsty! Can it?' he asked sharply, remembering Kirsty driving her grandfather to see his lawyer and striving to control his impatience while his mother assembled her thoughts.

'Her grandfather left Fairlyden to Kirsty.' Anna frowned. 'I'm sure that's what Mrs Beth meant.'

'I don't believe it!' James's face was suddenly pale and Anna regarded him with concern and tried to remember Beth's words exactly, while her son paced restlessly back and forth across the hearth rug, his face tense, his fists clenched. 'Ye should be pleased for her, James,' she finished reproachfully. 'Ye ken as well as anybody how much she loves Fairlyden – just like the old Mistress, she is. Her grandmother worked hard all her life to keep this little farm going.' Still James made no comment. 'Och, James! Master Fairly will be the farmer as long as he lives. It willna make any difference.'

'I pray Mr Fairly will live a long time, Mother, but we both know he canna live forever, even if he had good health.'

'Well in that case Miss Kirsty would make a far better farmer for Fairlyden than her brother – even if she is a lassie!'

'Oh, so it's "Miss" Kirsty now, is it! But I'm sure you're right – there never will be any place in the world for her now to compare with Fairlyden! She'll make it her whole life!' James's voice was harsh, his face pale and strained. Anna looked at him with distress.

He strode to the door and pulled it open.

'Ye're not leaving yet?'

'There's nothing for me here.'

'B-but it's no' even half past one! Ye havena had any tea. Ye never leave before three on a Sunday . . .'

'Goodbye, Mother.' James closed the door with a final little click. Anna stared at it, her eyes filled with dismay.

Twelve

Grayson Masterful, the six-month-old stirk which was to be Fairlyden's future stockbull, arrived as planned. The moment he stepped into the yard he lived up to his name. Finding himself on *terra firma* once more, he began to dance madly. An unexpected jerk pulled the halter from Thomas's grasp. This freedom went to his head and he careered madly round and round the yard.

'Took ye by surprise that time, he did, Thomas,' Paddy Kildougan chortled. He had come out of his little two-roomed bothy to inspect the new addition to Fairlyden.

'I expect he's tired o' being confined, first in the train and then in the cart,' Logan declared, but he viewed his expensive acquisition with some concern. 'We'll give him a minute or two to work the steam out o' his blood then maybe he'll quieten down a bit. Perhaps I should insure him in case he injures himself.'

'Quiet, ye think!' Thomas spluttered indignantly, misinterpreting Logan's words, as he so often did since becoming increasingly deaf.

The young bull eventually came to a standstill some yards away from the little group.

'He's a fine young bull, Father,' Kirsty pronounced, eyeing him critically. 'Don't you agree, Paddy.'

'Ach now, to be sure he looks a handsome young fellow – but handsome is as handsome does, Miss Kirsty. We shall have to be waiting a while yet to be seeing what he leaves behind him, eh?' He began to circle slowly round the panting animal in a wide arc, but Grayson Masterful took to his heels and circled the little Irishman instead, coming to a standstill to paw the ground and billying loudly for a youngster.

'My, and isn't it a cheeky young fellow you are! And the size of him!' Paddy chuckled. The little bull snorted indignantly, and pawed furiously, butting the air with his budding horns. Paddy stood absolutely still. The young bull grew braver and moved closer – and closer. Suddenly Paddy moved like lightning,

97

grabbing the halter before the bull realised what he was about. He struggled wildly. Paddy was tough and wiry but he was short and the bull butted him in the stomach, winding him cruelly. The contest only lasted a minute or two before Grayson Masterful became almost docile and allowed himself to be led away to his new home where a rack of sweet-smelling hay and a trough of clean water soon had him settling down, but the incident was a warning to them all that this bull could not be trusted.

Thomas muttered about the extravagance of buying such a wild young beast when Fairlyden had plenty of fine bulls of its own, then he stalked off across the yard.

'Ach, the bull would have been getting away from any man after his journey. I didn't mean to be upsetting old Thomas . . .' Paddy muttered, still clasping his bruised mid-riff.

'Poor Thomas, he's getting old and he thinks the young bull made a fool of him. He'll get over it.' Logan assured him. He and Beth had known Thomas Whiteley all their lives; they remembered him as a young man who had jumped the gate as sprightly as a young colt, a Thomas who had patiently helped them build a wooden pen for their pet pig, who had shielded them when they were in trouble with Sadie, and helped them with their tasks.

'Are you pleased with him, Father?' Kirsty asked when they were alone, leaning over the gate of Grayson Masterful's pen.

'He's grown well for his age. Certainly he has some good breeding in him or I wouldna have considered him – but as Paddy says – we can only wait and see now. It's a tricky business this breeding. They dinna always pass on the qualities we expect.' The young stirk had eaten and drunk and now he began to gallop round his pen again.

'He's certainly lively enough!' Kirsty grinned.

'Och, we'll put a ring in his nose when he's a bit older. That will make him a bit more manageable but he does seem to have a vicious streak in him.' Logan frowned. 'I wonder if that's the reason Mr Grayson decided to sell him. I was hoping he would be quiet enough to run with the cows in the field.'

'I don't suppose Luke will like him much whether he's quiet or not,' Kirsty said wistfully. Her brother seemed to show less and less interest in the animals and he hated the cows. Later she tried to encourage him to accompany her to see the new bull; she had told him that Fairlyden belonged to him as much as to her, that Grandfather Bradshaw had not meant to leave his affairs as he had.

'Well, I'm glad he's left Fairlyden to you, Kirsty.' Luke had spoken with unusual vehemence. 'I know Father will be disappointed but I'll never be able to earn my living as a farmer. I couldna do it, even to please him.' They had stared at each other. 'Honestly Kirsty, I mean it!' he had repeated.

A few weeks later Logan was proudly showing Grayson Masterful to James MacFarlane. Kirsty joined them. She had not spoken to James since her grandfather's funeral and she had begun to wonder if he was avoiding her, as she had once avoided him. Was he paying her back in her own coin? And if so, why? Had she misread the warmth and sympathy in his eyes at the funeral?

'What do you think of Grayson Masterful?' she asked pleasantly. 'Do you think he'll make Fairlyden's fortune?' Her voice was teasing. The bull could have a great effect on the Fairlyden herd – for good or evil – but they both knew fortunes for ordinary farmers were almost unheard of, except in story books. James did not smile. His greeny-grey eyes seemed to look through her instead of at her.

'He's a fine beast, Miss Kirsty.' Kirsty's eyebrows shot up almost into her hair and even her father looked surprised. James had never called her Miss Kirsty in his life. He had never treated her as anything except a young companion who had pestered him to teach her to ride a bicycle, how to saddle Marocco, even how to learn her French verbs when she started at the Academy . . . Recently of course he had begun to see her as a young woman . . . Suddenly her cheeks burned. Did he think she might pester him for attention now, as she had pestered him then? Kirsty felt cold all over.

'I hope the bull breeds well for you, Mr Fairly. I'd better get off back to the cottage now.'

'But I thought you'd be coming in for . . .'

'No thanks, Mr Fairly.' James's tone was stiff and he did not even look at Kirsty. 'It's time I was getting back.'

'Well! I wonder what's got into James,' Logan exclaimed. 'One minute he was chatting about his plans for Nithanvale and the next he's . . . I don't know what he is.' Logan shrugged. 'Maybe his Uncle Thomas has upset him.'

Kirsty did not reply. She had seen James MacFarlane chatting freely to her father, she had seen the warmth in his smile – until she joined them. So, he did not want her company.

Then so be it, James MacFarlane of Nithanvale.

Unfortunately Kirsty's heart did not echo the words of indignant anger which raced around her mind; she sought for a reason for the change in James's manner towards her.

Christmas came and went and the year of nineteen hundred and thirty-five dawned. Sarah had made a valiant effort to come to terms with Crispin's death, but she knew that a small part of her had died with him despite the cheerful face she showed the world. She no longer helped with the milking – a task she had found soothing and satisfying throughout most of her seventy-five years, but she looked forward to Kirsty's return to Fairlyside each evening and her accounts of the day's events – the progress of the animals, the births and deaths, the joys and disappointments. She was thankful that her granddaughter seemed content to continue living at Fairlyside.

Kirsty went to some of the dances in the village halls with the friends she had known since her schooldays. Sarah enjoyed seeing her dressed in her finery for the Christmas dance.

Occasionally Sarah accompanied Beth and Anna to meetings of the Women's Rural Institute. When the nights were clear and not too cold she still enjoyed the walk to Muircumwell beneath a star-spangled sky. The two younger women were invariably cheerful and considerate companions. Sometimes Logan or Kirsty drove to the village to bring her home afterwards but Sarah always chided them gently for such extravagance on her behalf, especially since petrol had risen to one shilling and sixpence a gallon.

Emma was usually at the Rural meetings too, and Anna's elder sisters – Maggie Donnelly from Mains of Muir and Lizzie Whiteley. Like her brother Thomas, Lizzie had never married. She seemed content looking after the village shop and the adjoining tearoom which she had inherited from the previous owner, a crusty bachelor named Ray Jardine. Sarah always felt better for these meetings with the friendly people she had known all her life, but she thought often of her own childhood friend, Beatrice O'Connor, who had died during the influenza epidemic so soon after the war, and Janet Whiteley too; she had shared many a trouble and many a joy with both of them.

She found it hard to show her usual enthusiasm when the

100

various village committees made plans for the celebration of the King and Queen's Silver Jubilee.

'I'm getting too old for celebrations, lassie,' she confessed to Kirsty. 'But Queen Mary is such a gracious lady. I canna help but wish her well.'

As winter turned to spring the weeks seemed to fly. Kirsty was happy in her work at Fairlyden. Her interest in the farm and breeding cattle, the satisfaction of the changing seasons with seedtime and harvest, left little time to dwell on her own secret yearnings. Only when her thoughts turned to James MacFarlane did her happiness dim; then her moods swung between anger and uncertainty.

She knew her father frequently met James at the markets. She had seen him too – at local shows in the summer, and passing by Fairlyside on his way to visit his mother in the cottage only a few hundred yards further up the lane. Twice she had seen him when riding Marocco in the fields bordering the track to the farmsteading; she could easily have waylaid him, but she restrained her impulsive nature. He knew where to find her but he made no effort to seek her out as he would once have done.

At Christmas she had seen him at a dance. He had been with a group of young men, all strong, healthy, ruggedly handsome, but her eyes had been drawn to James again and again; her heartbeats had quickened beyond her control when his level green-grey gaze had caught and held her own. He had crossed the room towards her, had been only a few yards away when another young man from her own party had asked her to dance. They had no sooner taken to the floor than her partner had declared loudly – too loudly, 'Thought I'd better rescue ye afore that rogue MacFarlane claimed ye, Kirsty. Naebody frae Nithanvale is fit company for a Fairly – or any other decent lassie.'

'Whisht, Edgar.' Kirsty's cheeks had flamed with embarrassment. 'James lived at Fairlyden once you know.'

'Och, I ken that! But he's yin o' the Nithanvale MacFarlanes noo. All tarred wi' the same brush. Cheats they are. Sold my Uncle Jacob a pedigree bull calf – pedigree! It was nae more than a wee scrubber picked up frae a market. The Nithanvale lot gave the beast a number an' a wee bit paper wi' a string o' fancy names. Aye and charged a fancy price – and they did the same for another twae calves out o' the very same cow. Did ye

101

ever hear o' a cow having three calves within a twelvemonth!'
Kirsty frowned and danced in silence. Edgar Walls had always
liked an audience and he was a troublemaker. She knew
James was bound to have overheard at least part of his
remarks. There had been plenty of opportunity for him to
speak to her afterwards but he had not done so.

Luke was still preoccupied with his studies of birds and insects,
and he disappeared with his sketch pad at every opportunity.
His school reports were excellent in almost every subject and
Kirsty suspected their parents scarcely knew whether to be
proud of his achievements or disappointed by his lack of
interest in Fairlyden and their livelihood. He seemed to have
grown several inches in height almost overnight, but he was
as slim and loose-limbed as a young colt. He had never learned
to milk, he hated the hens, especially when they became
broody and were inclined to take vicious pecks at any hand
which sought to take away their precious eggs. He found the
young pigs bearable and the ducks quite funny but it was only
his inherent sense of duty which forced him to carry out the
tasks of feeding allotted to him by their father.

In January of nineteen hundred and thirty-six, just after
Kirsty's nineteenth birthday, the nation mourned the death of
King George V.

'It seemed as though we really knew him after we heard
him speaking in that gruff voice o' his on the wireless,' Sarah
remarked sadly to Beth as another winter's day began to draw
to a close. She had been suffering from a severe cold, more like
influenza. Beth had called in for the second time that day. She
was concerned by her mother-in-law's continuing lethargy.

'I hope King Edward will be as good a king as his father,'
she murmured now. 'Did I tell ye James bought Anna a
wireless at Christmas? She is thrilled at being able to hear
people like the king actually speaking.'

'James is a good lad. I'm pleased he doesna forget that his
mother and Uncle Thomas have done so much for him,' Sarah
nodded. 'A wireless must have cost him most o' three weeks'
wages though.'

'Aye, I suppose it would. Eight pounds Logan paid for ours,
but he got a spare glass accumulator so we can have it charged
while we use the other. Anna says Thomas crouches close up
to the dresser so that he can hear. The first time he listened he
didna catch everything the newsreader was saying so he

shouted "Say that again, will ye?" The man had already gone on to another item, so Thomas banged the dresser with his fist and yelled, "Say it again, can't ye!" Anna had to remind him that the announcer couldna hear him.'

Sarah smiled. 'Poor Thomas, he gets so frustrated when he doesna hear. What have you got in that basket, Beth?'

'I brought a bacon and egg pie and a bowl o' broth. I canna have ye cooking for Kirsty, especially when ye're ill.'

'Aah, Beth, I enjoy her company. I know Dora Fleming would come more often if I asked her, but to tell the truth I don't know what I should do now without Kirsty's company in the evenings – and knowing she's in the next bedroom at night. I'm a selfish old woman.'

'Och, ye could never be that! Anyway Kirsty always liked staying at Fairlyside, even when she was a bairn. And it's no distance for her to come to the byre.' Beth was sincere.

'You were aye unselfish, Beth,' Sarah murmured gratefully. There was a strong bond of friendship and affection between them which had grown and strengthened over the years until it had come full circle. 'You've trained Kirsty well in many spheres. She's a grand cook herself, but she doesna have much time.' Sarah sighed heavily and Beth noticed how drawn she looked. 'I've never heard a word from Sadie and Robert . . .' she went on wearily. 'That's two Christmases that have passed since Crispin died but they didna even send a greeting.'

'Aah I see.' Beth bit her lip. Now she understood something of the reason for Sarah's unusual melancholy. Logan's sister had always caused trouble. Her spite and greed had caused enough unhappiness, and now she was causing even more heartache for her mother by her wounded silence.

'If I didna get a letter frae Ted Forbes every month I wouldna know whether they were alive or dead.' Sarah's tone was a mixture of regret and exasperation.

'I'm so glad Mr Forbes keeps in touch,' Beth said warmly. 'Is he in good health? And how are things at the Mill?'

'Ted seems to be keeping very well. He is planning to buy a wee house for himself, for when he retires. He says there are a lot of houses being built a few miles out of the town and since he came to Fairlyden he quite fancies spending his last years surrounded by green fields. I think he called his house a semi-detached. Anyway it is joined to another house exactly the same. He has paid a five pound deposit and he is going to pay twelve and sixpence a week. I think he really wants my approval now that Crispin is no longer here to advise him. Poor Ted,' Sarah sighed again, 'his life will not be easy with Sadie and Robert. I expect he's afraid I might think he is squandering the money from the Mill but I know he is not the one who will do that!'

'No, I'm sure he seemed a very kindly and conscientious man.'

'He is. He says the men who have work are better off than they have ever been, but there are still such a lot who canna get a job down there, and then there are those who are sick . . . He has started some sort o' savings scheme for the Bradshaw workers but Sadie disapproves. He seems to think I know all about it but I dinna like to admit that I never hear from my own daughter. I think I'll answer his letter tonight, Beth. It's been grand talking to you, lassie. Makes me pull myself together and think about other folks!'

'They say half the bairns in Glasgow had bow legs for want o' milk,' Emma commented during one of her family's frequent visits to Fairlyside. 'So surely the new marketing arrangements must be better for them with milk delivered tae their very door.' She looked at her own three tall sons. 'These laddies dinna ken what it is tae be hungry.'

'Oh we dae!' Paul piped up, bringing an embarrassed flush to his mother's face and a quelling glance to his father's dark eyes. 'Sorry, Granny. I didna mean tae be ill mannered,' he apologised instantly, with a smile which would have charmed the birds from the trees.

'How like his Grandfather Fairly he is!' Sarah remarked involuntarily. Alex raised one dark eyebrow and removed his pipe stem from between his teeth, tapping the bowl absently into his palm.

'I'm sure my father was never as cheeky as that young rascal!' he growled, but there was an affectionate twinkle in his eye; Alex was proud of his three sons, although he was a strict disciplinarian.

'Your father was very charming and handsome when he was young,' Sarah mused, 'but he knew how to get his own way . . .' Now that she was getting older Sarah often thought of the past and the past included William Fairly, her first husband, though she tended to overlook his faults and the problems he had left behind when he sailed away to America to see his late partner's widow, Elsa Guillyman. I wonder if she is still alive? Sarah pondered now, and what happened to her bairn, Simon Guillyman? He would be about the same age as Logan now ... Aloud she said, 'Do you ever hear anything about the trustees for the Guillyman estate, Alex? Logan always pays his rent to a firm of solicitors but they never seem to make any other contact.'

'I've never heard who they are. Logan was telling me that he does all the repairs and improvements himself, but at least no one has ever mentioned putting up the rent.'

'No ... it's a good job they dinna. Kirsty was telling me how much they depend on the Muircumwell land now that Logan is keeping more cows. He's spent quite a lot on lime to improve it but he's hoping to get a long lease when the present one expires in another two years ...'

'Speaking o' leases – they were saying at the market that the Carnland Estate will be tae sell. The laird hasna survived very long after his father.'

'Oh dear, I suppose that means another lot o' death duties to find?' Sarah sympathised. Then she sat up, suddenly alert. 'Surely Nithanvale is on the Carnland Estate?'

'Aye, it's bound to affect young James MacFarlane.'

'Maybe a wealthy man will buy the whole estate ...?'

'According tae Captain Fothergill that isna very likely,' Emma joined the conversation. 'He reckons the landowners are worse off than their tenants now. He says if any of them do manage to make more than two thousand pounds profit they have tae pay an extra rate of tax.'

'Whew, ye mean besides the four and sixpence in the pound that we pay, Mother?' Alexander asked. Sarah looked at her eldest grandson with approval.

'I'm pleased to hear you take an interest in such things, laddie.' Out of the corner of her eye she saw Paul fidget restlessly. 'But maybe you would rather talk about food, eh Paul?' Her eyes twinkled. 'I expect your Uncle Logan and Aunt Beth will be on their way and I hear Kirsty rattling the pans. She insisted I couldna help with the cooking today.'

'Well, it's not everybody that lives tae see seventy-seven harvests safely home, Mother,' Alex smiled.

'But Kirsty is a grand lassie, taking the trouble tae cook for all o' us,' Emma declared warmly. 'And I must admit it makes a lovely change for me.'

'Yes, I'm sure you must have plenty o' cooking with four men to feed, Emma. Kirsty knows how much I like to see all my family together.' Sarah sighed happily. 'It's a pity Ellen couldna come. We could have celebrated her birthday as well, but I'm very fortunate . . . very fortunate indeed.'

When Logan and Beth arrived, with Luke strolling dreamily along behind them, the little gathering was complete and laughter rang out as greetings and quips were exchanged.

'September is the best month o' the year,' Logan declared, 'with the harvest all in and the pace slowing down a bit.'

'Slowing down!' Kirsty echoed, her dark brows rising almost to her wavy hair as she came through from the kitchen. Her cheeks were pink from the heat of the cooker and her cousin Cameron eyed her with appreciation, but she missed his saucy wink. 'When did Father ever slow his pace according to the time of year?' she asked her mother with a smile.

'Never,' Beth chuckled. 'But it does feel good tae ken the harvest is safely in, and it hasna been such a bad year either, compared with the last nine or ten we've had.'

'But the hay was so slow, Aunt Beth!' Alexander protested, 'and Father almost gave away our fat bullocks, the prices were so bad!'

'Well, everything canna be perfect, laddie,' Beth smiled good humouredly.

'And ye canna remember just how bad the last ten years have been either, my lad!' Emma reminded her eldest son darkly.

'Well, come through to the dining room and take your places if you want to eat,' Kirsty announced cheerfully.

'Mmm . . . lovely, ye've been baking fresh bread! I can smell it! What's for soup, Kirsty cook?' Paul asked eagerly.

'Oxtail – and if you dinna eat it, young Paul, I'll not give you any pudding!' Kirsty teased.

'Have ye made a trifle like Granny makes? Ye ken that's my favourite.'

'No, I havena made a trifle. You'll have to wait and see . . .'

'She's made a pyramid o' meringues all stuck together with almond cream,' Luke informed his cousin quietly. 'That's my favourite you see – and Kirsty asked me specially,' he added almost apologetically.

'Oh.' Paul was surprised at his cousin Luke having a preference, and even more at him expressing it.

'I've made a chocolate soufflé and caramel pears as well, Paul,' Kirsty assured him. 'Because I did remember what a large appetite you have!'

Kirsty had put a lot of effort into making the harvest home dinner. She was determined to uphold her grandmother's reputation for hospitality at Fairlyside as well as prove herself a credit to her mother's teaching. The main course was a leg of lamb which she had boned and stuffed before roasting.

'Ye're a fine wee cook, Kirsty,' Alex beamed as he tasted the succulent meat. 'This lamb is delicious and your baked potatoes are as crisp as your Aunt Emma's.'

'Och, that's all due to Granny's Aga cooker,' Kirsty told him modestly.

'Aah, but the cooker canna dae all this by itself, lassie,' Emma assured her. 'Nor can it make mint jelly and this delicious sauce. Mmm . . . your daughter is a credit tae ye, Beth.'

'Aye, ye'll make a good wife for some lucky man, lassie,' Alex teased.

'There's plenty got their eye on her,' Alexander announced and grinned unrepentantly when he saw Kirsty blush.

'Aah weel, there's not many o' the lassies that can tell one end o' a cow frae the other, even less—'

'That isna true, Cameron Fairly!' Kirsty interrupted.

'I was going tae say that *ye* can pick out the best in a byre full o' kie. And ye're no' sae bad tae look at yoursel' either . . .'

'I think that's enough frae you, my lad.' Emma declared firmly. 'Ye're embarrassing Kirsty.'

'Well, she doesna look at any o' them anyway, dae ye, Kirsty?' Cameron's eyes suddenly brightened and he added, 'But ye could be nice to James MacFarlane – the next time there's a dance at Dumfries. Did ye ken he's got a new Vauxhall twelve? Maybe he'd drive us all home in it instead o' us having tae bike frae the station.'

'I forgot to tell ye all that James had a new car,' Luke frowned. 'He's had it a month. I saw him in Dumfries and he gave me a ride to the station after school. He said it cost two hundred pounds but it's more comfortable when he drives his great-uncle to look at the cows, and visit some other farmers.'

It was a long speech for Luke and Kirsty was grateful for his intervention. She wondered if he sensed how much she hated Cousin Cameron's teasing about James.

'Maybe the laddie will be wishing he still had his two hundred pounds and a lot more besides when they get around to selling the Carnland Estate,' Alex reflected with a frown.

'James tries his best tae humour the old man MacFarlane,'

Logan replied a little sharply. 'And nobody can be sure the Estate will be to sell yet.'

'Oh, I'm not criticising the laddie,' Alex declared hurriedly. 'Anyway he wouldna ken the laird was going to die when he bought the car. But I'll guarantee the only way he'll be sure o' staying at Nithanvale will be tae buy the farm now. We've no regrets about buying the Mains, have we lassie?' He looked at his wife. Three pairs of dark eyebrows rose simultaneously; three mouths grimaced. Emma glanced at her sons' faces and laughed aloud.

'Our laddies dinna think their mother is much o' a lassie, Alex!' Then she sobered. 'But there'll be no cars for you three for many a year tae come!'

'Ye really think it was a wise thing to do then, Alex – to buy the Mains?' Logan asked frankly.

'Well, we have a loan frae the bank which we dinna like, but we live carefully and we dinna have as many men to pay now the laddies are fit for work. I reckon it gives them more security – and a challenge if they ken they're working for their ain place. All young folks need a challenge! Keeps them out o' mischief.' His dark eyes rested thoughtfully on his second son, Cameron.

'Mmm, I suppose ye reap the benefit o' any improvements ye make anyway,' Logan mused. 'We're planning on making a few changes at Fairlyden, but we're not as ambitious as you.' He grinned across at Alex. He always enjoyed a good discussion with his eldest brother and he had received many a piece of sound advice over the years. 'We're thinking of improving Anna's cottage. We have been making enquiries about the *Housing of Rural Workers Act* and it seems we could get a third o' the cost o' the improvements if they're approved.'

'Only up to a hundred pounds,' Alex warned.

'Well, that should be more than enough. It willna cost three hundred pounds tae add on a wee kitchen and a bathroom – and lay on piped water. The only problem is we canna dae the same at the bothy cottage for Lucy and Paddy. There isna room . . . and I wouldna like them tae feel neglected. They're grand workers – both o' them.' He turned to Kirsty. 'D'ye still agree with your trustees, lassie?' His eyes twinkled.

'Grandfather always intended you should make the decisions for Fairlyden's future, Father.'

'Aye well, maybe. What dae ye think about our ideas for Anna's cottage, Mother?'

'I dinna think you should improve the cottage,' Sarah stated firmly.

Logan and Beth, Alex and Emma stared at her. This was the decisive mother they remembered, but such a negative reply confounded them.

Thirteen

Even Kirsty blinked when her grandmother swept aside all suggestion of improving the cottage for Anna and Thomas.

'But why, Mother?' Logan demanded in bewilderment. 'We've done better than most breeders with the sale of our pedigree heifers this past year or two, and even the sheep prices have improved a wee bit. We dinna pay a rent now either. Surely ye ken we wouldna think o' spending money we canna afford?'

'No, no, laddie, it isna that.'

'The government are offering to help. I realise it's a cheap way for them tae improve the conditions o' the country folk – but it's surely an advantage, if Anna and Thomas have a better home?' And young James too, he thought privately, if he canna afford to stay at Nithanvale with a new laird. In his heart there was nothing he would like better than James's return to Fairlyden, yet he would be sorry if that meant the end of the young man's dreams and aspirations. He deserves better than a box bed and a tin bath in front o' the fire too.

'It isna the money, Logan.' Sarah interrupted his thoughts. 'You know I always wanted the best we could afford for Fairlyden – be it for workers or animals.' Her brown eyes were faintly troubled now. 'Maybe I'm just an interfering old woman . . .' she said uncertainly. Logan's eyes softened immediately and Beth moved to sit beside her.

'Ye've never interfered – except for our ain guid,' she said gently. 'Tell us what's in your mind?'

'Well, I know Crispin wasna a farmer, but he was a business man – a good business man who always looked ahead. He didna believe there was a surplus o' food in Britain. He said the trouble was that half the population simply couldna afford to buy it and he was convinced all that would have to change one day. He was sure demand would increase, especially for fresh milk. He – he seemed to know you would need more room for extra cows and Kirsty tells me all fifty stalls in the byre are full now?'

'Aye, they are when all the cows are milking, but—'

'Well, your – your father thought it would be sensible, and cheaper, to build on to the end o' the present byre. That would almost join it on to Anna's cottage. He suggested the cottage should be made into a new dairy; under the same roof – almost.'

'Well!' Logan exclaimed. 'Imagine my father thinking o' the future o' Fairlyden to that extent! He was right too. We could do with extra stalls even now.'

'It would be a lot more convenient having the dairy tucked on to the end o' the byre on a cold winter's morning too,' Emma commented wryly. 'Isn't that so, Beth?'

'Indeed it is. It would be cleaner too.'. Beth chewed her lip thoughtfully. 'I think I have a vague recollection that your father mentioned his ideas a long, long time ago, Logan.'

'But what about Anna and Thomas? I couldna turn them out now that Thomas is getting too old to work! The thought o' leaving Fairlyden would kill him. He hates even the smallest change . . .'

'Crispin's idea was that this house should become the farmhouse,' Sarah said simply. 'After all it is not so very far across the garden to Anna's cottage, and if that was the new dairy.'

'That's true,' Logan agreed slowly. 'But . . .'

'The old house could be made into two good cottages.'

'Aye, it could, especially if we can get this money for improvements. We could build another bedroom and a bathroom over the bothy end and add another staircase.'

'Of course it would mean you and Beth and Luke would have to move in here first,' Sarah reminded him quietly. 'It would make me happier to know I wasna depriving Kirsty o' her family, if you were all under the same roof again. But maybe you wouldna want to put up with an old woman like me every day, Beth.'

'Och, dinna say that!' Beth protested gently, and laid her hand on Sarah's wrinkled fingers, stilling their anxious twisting with an affectionate squeeze.

Later, alone in their bedroom Beth and Logan discussed the idea of turning their home into two cottages.

'I'll bet Lucy and Anna would be delighted, and I must say I'd feel happier if we were all under the same roof again,' Beth admitted. 'For your mother's sake as much as for Kirsty's. She is getting frail, Logan; the days must be very long for her while Kirsty is out working, especially in the winter. I thought that in the spring when she was ill for so long. I've never known her spirits so low before.'

'Aye, ye're right, Beth . . . I'll make enquiries about getting official approval for our plans.'

Beth, Logan and Luke moved into Fairlyside at the end of November nineteen hundred and thirty-six.

'I feel like a deserter in a way,' Beth confessed. 'It saddens me to see the old house empty and so forlorn.'

'But ye still agree it'll be better all round once the alterations are complete?' Logan asked urgently.

'Oh yes. I ken nothing can stay the same for ever, and I've always liked Fairlyside too. D'ye remember how we used to call on our way home frae school to see old Mrs Bunnerby when she was your father's housekeeper?' she smiled reminiscently.

'Aye, I do. She always had a treat for us. It's always been part o' Fairlyden really. I'm sure we shall be happy here too, Beth.'

'I shall be happy anywhere, just so long as we have each other,' Beth assured him softly. Logan looked down into her luminous blue eyes and smiled lovingly. He drew her into his arms.

'I'm the most fortunate man on God's earth,' he murmured gruffly as his lips sought hers in a kiss which never failed to fill Beth with the old love and desire they had first discovered when they were seventeen.

Logan arranged for the builders to start work on the main part of the old house first. Lucy and Paddy would then move in there and the bothy end would be extended the following spring for Anna and Thomas.

'That will spread the cost a bit,' Logan declared with satisfaction. 'If all goes well we should be able to afford to build on to the byre and convert the dairy in another year.'

It was no hardship to Beth to move into the same house as her mother-in-law. They had always got on well together. It was Kirsty who found it harder to adjust to living with her family again. She had enjoyed her grandmother's company and her stories of Fairlyden's past. Now she found herself spending more and more time with her father, with the cows and calves, the horses and pigs. She did not care much for the sheep but she was ever anxious to preserve her father's strength and she volunteered to ride to the Westhill fields each morning to inspect them.

'We'll move them to the lower fields before the bad weather sets in,' Logan promised.

'Marocco and I welcome the extra exercise and the sheep are taking no harm yet,' Kirsty assured him.

It was after a Sunday morning ride to the Westhill pasture that Kirsty had an unexpected encounter with James MacFarlane. Her view from the high ground was spectacular and she sat astride her horse enjoying the panorama of shorn fields, rolling meadows and the bronze and gold of a few lingering leaves which still trembled on the trees and hedgerows. The air was crisp and fresh and Kirsty felt exhilarated as she filled her lungs with several long deep breaths. Here and there the rime of the early morning frost still sparkled beneath the hedges as the rays of the winter sun slanted through the gaps, while in the distance the purplish blue outline of the Galloway hills spread long and low across the skyline merging into the horizon. Soon they would be capped with snow.

Afterwards Kirsty wondered if she had been too preoccupied in savouring the beauty of the winter morning to notice the figure in the small field at the back of the Fairlyden steading. Certainly she had no warning of James's presence until she was galloping headlong over the small rise and into the hollow which ran behind Anna's cottage. Just in time she swerved to avoid the young collie which had made a mad dart into Marocco's path.

'Down, Jo! Heel, boy, heel!' There was no mistaking James MacFarlane's urgent command, nor his tall figure. Kirsty brought Marocco to a prancing halt. They stared at each other in silence. Kirsty knew her cheeks were flushed but she hoped James would attribute her heightened colour to her morning's exercise and the excitement of the near catastrophe between the dog and Marocco. The collie now lay obediently at his master's feet, head on his paws. How harmless and gentle he looks, Kirsty thought, until you notice his alert eyes and his pointed ears waiting eagerly for a chance to demonstrate his herding instinct, even on a horse! Her eyes moved from the dog to his master and she noted James's set jaw and the pulse throbbing in his cheek; his greeny-grey eyes were wary, almost hard; Kirsty suppressed a shiver. She summoned all her self-control.

'Good morning, James. Marocco and I did not expect to see anyone in the fields this morning.' She was relieved to know there was not a single tremor in her voice to reflect her sudden nervousness – yet why should she be nervous? She had known James all her life! Unconsciously she squared her slim shoulders as though preparing for battle.

'I suppose you mean I'm trespassing on Fairlyden land,' James replied coldly. 'But you were riding far too fast . . .' Kirsty had opened her mouth to laugh at the idea of anyone trespassing, especially someone who had tramped the fields of Fairlyden until he knew them blindfold. Her mouth snapped shut at his critical words however and the gold flecks in her eyes sparked with anger. She had no idea how beautiful she looked with her thick short hair blown into a tangle of honey-brown curls, the bright flags of pink highlighting her fine cheekbones, and her small square jaw thrust in the air with that familiar proud defiance which James remembered so well from their childhood. As he stood looking up at her he was very much aware of the smooth column of her neck, the skin almost as pale as her white open-necked blouse. Her thick woollen jumper clung to her slender figure and he saw the rapid rise and fall of her firm breasts – as though she had been running. Perhaps Jo had given her a bigger fright than he had realised.

'I'm sorry if Jo startled you and Marocco. He is not trained yet. Uncle Thomas wanted to see him but he was too wild and excited to bide in the cottage after being restrained in the car.'

'Aah yes, I heard you had bought yourself an expensive toy.' She heard his angry gasp. Even to her own ears Kirsty knew her words sounded mocking, almost spiteful, but she could not recall them. James's mouth was grim and his jaw jutted belligerently.

'The car belongs to my great-uncle, as I'm sure you must realise – if you bothered to think!'

'Indeed?' Kirsty was stung by his jeering tone. 'It seems strange that a man who can scarcely see to drive should buy himself a car. Whoever owns it, I heard you had been showing it off in Dumfries the moment you got it.'

'Luke, I suppose!' James almost smiled. 'Perhaps he also told you I was collecting it from the garage the day I saw him and—'

'Oh, I don't ask questions about your new lifestyle, James. I'm simply not interested in your affairs at Nithanvale. I'll bid you goodbye!' But before Kirsty could move Marocco forward, James had grabbed the bridle.

'Not so fast, Miss High-and-Mighty!' Kirsty could see the ice in James's narrowed eyes now. Really she did not understand herself and her wayward tongue. Why did she want to provoke him to anger? Why did she try to hurt him when they met so seldom? Because he had been avoiding her?

'I hear you are not wasting any time in demonstrating your own wealth!'

'What do you mean?' Kirsty stared down into James's upturned face in genuine bewilderment.

'Dinna pretend!' James sneered. 'At least the Kirsty Fairly I remembered was always honest! I'm talking about you having inherited Fairlyden! You! Not your father! Not your brother – but you!' Kirsty stared at James. There was a bitterness in him she could not fathom; it's as though he resents me inheriting Fairlyden . . . 'Well, dinna expect me to thank you for your charity to my family! Mother and Uncle Thomas are perfectly happy in their home, however humble you might consider it. They didna need you with your fine ideas, acting My Lady Bountiful! Demonstrating your power! Showing the world how magnanimous you are! You'll get no thanks frae me!'

Kirsty was too shocked – and too hurt – to defend herself. She closed her eyes as though he had hit her and she did not see the flicker of uncertainty of James's face. Then suddenly her temper flared. Why should she explain anything to James MacFarlane? Anything at all to do with Fairlyden? He had left it! Run away to Nithanvale and his own wealthy relatives. She did not tell him it was her father's idea to provide more convenient and comfortable homes for his mother and for Lucy Kildougan.

'Are you telling me that Nithanvale doesna have water frae a tap? Does your cousin Mary carry water frae a well? Does she still run down the garden to the closet on a cold winter's night, and boil water in a kettle to wash the dishes? Do you, James MacFarlane, still bathe in a tin bath in front o' the fire?' Kirsty's eyes were narrowed and James could not guess that their bright glitter was on account of the tears of hurt and anger which she was struggling to control.

She whirled her horse around, forcing him to release the

bridle. 'I never thought you were such a hypocrite – living like the gentry while your mother—' The young collie had grown impatient of waiting for his master's attention. When the horse moved, he moved too – straight in front of Marocco's front legs.

The gelding was well schooled but he was startled by the sudden yapping, the small body hurtling against his forefeet. He reared. Usually Kirsty would have managed to calm him but her mind had not been on Marocco. She spun through the air like a dandelion puff; she landed like a felled oak. The sky whirled around her head. She had only the faintest recollection of a shadow blotting out the light as James flung himself to his knees beside her, then an enveloping blackness swamped her. She did not see the anxiety in those greeny-grey eyes, or hear the anguish as he called her name, willing her to open her eyes, to move just one muscle of her inert body.

Fourteen

'Lie still, Kirsty dear.' Beth's voice was tender. A faint smile flickered over Kirsty's pale face. For a moment she thought she was a child again. Then she tried to move.

'Oo-h! Wh-what happened? Where am I?' She had lifted her head less than an inch but it throbbed as though a laden iron-wheeled cart had run over it.

'Ye're in my house,' Anna told her softly. 'James carried ye here, lassie. He made sure ye hadna broken any bones first,' she added hastily.

'Poor James,' Beth sympathised, 'his face was as white as your own, lassie. He looked so worried. It's a pity he couldna wait . . .'

'Aye, he hadna been here five minutes – or so it seemed!' Anna muttered exasperatedly. 'He only waited until he heard what the doctor had to say and then he was off back to Nithanvale. I dinna understand him at all. I'd made his favourite fruit pasty for tea. It's the recipe old Mrs Bunnerby gave ye, Mrs Beth, when she was housekeeper for Mr Bradshaw.'

Kirsty winced as her head throbbed. She wondered why Anna was chattering so much. It was not like her.

'I want to go home.' Was that her voice? It sounded croaky and tearful.

'So you shall in an hour or two,' Beth murmured soothingly and wiped her brow with a cooling cloth. 'Doctor Broombank says ye're suffering frae concussion and we've to keep ye quiet, but we can move ye back tae your own bed in an hour or two.'

'Bed?' Kirsty tried to think. 'What time is it? What was I doing?'

'Hush now, lassie, just try to rest. The doctor says ye'll be fine in a few days if ye take things quietly – except for some nasty bruises . . . James was so upset. I reckon it will take him just as long to get over the shock. He blames himself, puir laddie.'

* * *

Two days later Kirsty received a letter from James MacFarlane. She knew he had telephoned Fairlyside later on the evening of her fall and again the following morning. Now he had written her a letter. Her head was still very dizzy and throbbed when she tried to sit up but she was determined to read James's letter herself and she opened it the moment her mother had left her bedroom.

Her spirits plummeted. Yet what was I expecting? she asked herself angrily. The formal phrases were even worse than his stilted goodbye when he left to live at Nithanvale after their first quarrel; she had been angry and hurt and unforgiving.

'It is clear to me now that we must forget the companionship of our youth. It seems we disagree whenever we meet,' he had written. 'I know you condemn me for choosing to live at Nithanvale. One day I had hoped to make you understand my reasons for leaving Fairlyden. Recent events had dispelled such hopes. I admit I came to Nithanvale with the intention of improving my prospects. As a lowly labourer I had nothing to offer the girl I dreamed of marrying.'

'Mary MacFarlane . . .' Kirsty muttered miserably and stared blankly at the wall of her bedroom. Eventually she forced herself to read the rest of James's letter.

'Regarding your plans for the cottage, I humbly apologise for my unjust criticism. Mother and Uncle Thomas do deserve any conveniences which make their lives easier or more comfortable. Perhaps I am jealous that it is you – and not I – who can provide them. I did not intend to seem ungrateful. It seems my family must always be indebted to yours.'

Was there a hint of bitterness behind his words? Kirsty wondered.

'In future I shall do my best not to cause you any further annoyance with my company. Unfortunately I need advice rather badly and your father is the only person to whom I can turn. This will necessitate a visit to Fairlyside but I assure you I would not intrude in your home if the matter was less urgent.'

Kirsty winced at the pride behind James's words. Whatever happened to the youthful friendship we shared? she asked herself. I respected James, aye and trusted him, just as he trusts my father now. She read on.

'I hope you can forgive me for the injuries you have suffered as a result of my negligence. I cannot blame my dog. He is young and knew no better. I trust you will soon return to your usual good health.

'Goodbye, Kirsty, and may fortune smile kindly upon you and your future at Fairlyden.'

How dreadfully final he makes it sound! It is as though he is going on a long journey and might never return. Kirsty shivered involuntarily.

Kirsty's family attributed her unusually low spirits to her painful bruises but everyone's attention was diverted by the shock of the young King's broadcast to the nation.

'I canna believe it!' Sarah repeated over and over again. 'Abdicating! His poor mother! Her son has failed in his duty to his kingdom!'

'Dinna upset yourself, Mother,' Logan protested mildly. 'Ye heard what he said yourself – that he canna carry such a heavy burden without the help and support o' the woman he loves.' He looked across at Beth's troubled face. 'I think I can understand how he feels,' he added softly. Beth met his eyes and her face softened instantly. Kirsty sighed. How wonderful it must be to know that someone loved you beyond everything else in the whole world . . . In her heart she knew her father would have given up Fairlyden rather than sacrifice her mother's happiness, just as King Edward VIII had sacrificed his kingdom for this Mrs Wallis Simpson.

'It must have been a dreadful decision to have to make,' Beth said gently. She knew how greatly Sarah respected the royal family.

'But he's the King!' Sarah sounded bewildered. 'And Mrs Simpson has been divorced . . .' Her voice dropped to a shocked whisper. 'Twice.'

The following morning all the newspapers reported King Edward VIII's departure for France, leaving his younger brother, George, to shoulder the tremendous responsibilities as head of the British Empire.

As the winter turned to spring the alterations at Fairlyden moved ahead rapidly and in May nineteen hundred and thirty-seven Lucy and Paddy Kildougan moved into their new home. Lucy was so proud she showed Willy Taylor, the new postie, all over the house from top to bottom. Jim Braid the old postman had retired and Willy and his wife had moved from a village six miles away so he was only just getting to know the people on his daily round.

'Ye're oor very first caller, Willy!' Lucy announced. 'D'ye no' think it's a braw hoose. Master Fairly had it made specially for us!'

'Aye, my Madge would envy ye if she saw yon bathroom, Mrs Kildougan. So what'll your address be noo?'

'Oh, I dinna ken . . .' Lucy frowned. 'Ye see there'll be twae cottages when the other half o' the hoose is finished. Mistress MacFarlane and her brother will be moving in tae the new end . . .'

'Weel I'll call ye Number One Fairlyden Cottages then, and the MacFarlanes can be Number Two when they move in, eh?'

'That sounds fine tae me. We dinna get many letters anyway,' Lucy added wryly. 'This morning's letter was a real surprise. It's frae James MacFarlane. He was aye a nice laddie. He hopes we'll be happy in our new home. He must have guessed how excited I'd be! He hasna changed for all he's going up i' the world now he's moved tae Nithanvale.'

James MacFarlane did not consider he had gone up in the world. If he carried out his plans to allow his great-uncle to end his days at Nithanvale, the farm which had been home to generations of MacFarlanes for almost a hundred years, he could end up worse off than any labourer. If things went badly he would probably owe more money than his Uncle Thomas had earned in the whole of his sixty-two years. He might even end up in gaol. He shuddered at the thought. Yet what had he to lose now?

He had discussed his problem with Logan, leaving out only the details of his understanding with his half-cousin, Mary MacFarlane.

'Ye want to buy Nithanvale, and in your ain name!' Logan was appalled at the idea. 'It would be a millstone round your neck, laddie, maybe for the rest o' your life. Farming is an uncertain business at the best o' times, but the most fickle weather is nothing compared to the politicians passing their Acts and breaking their promises or changing their minds.'

'But you've managed to survive and times must have been even worse than they are now.'

'Aah, but I only paid a rent for Fairlyden, and a modest one at that,' Logan reminded him. 'It's been hard work and a lot o' penny pinching all round – frae your ain family as well as mine, laddie. We're not so secure yet, even if we are spending a bit on improving the houses. I wouldna do that if we didna have good stock and some cattle to sell as well as the milk.'

'Well, we have good stock at Nithanvale. I think most breeders who fell foul o' Metcalf's swindling realise our animals are sound now. Of course there's a few who dinna want to forget and they like to cause trouble,' James added, his greeny-grey eyes narrowing as he recalled some of the snubs and sly innuendos he had endured, and the remarks of Kirsty's loud-mouthed partner at the Christmas dance. 'I had planned to sell half of the herd and use the money for a deposit on the farm,' he added uncertainly.

'But that will mean ye've less milk to sell and fewer heifers – a big drop in income. Could ye manage, James?'

A pulse beat rapidly in James's lean jaw. 'Things will be tight for a while, but we hope to have two or three young bulls which should fetch a good price . . . like your Grayson Masterful. How is he doing by the way?'

'He's an evil devil!' Logan grimaced. 'I ken none o' the bulls are to be trusted but ye darena turn your back when Masterful is in the field. He'd take a toss at ye for sure. He's sired some nice calves though. I shall have to keep him until we see what sort of heifers they make. That's the trouble with breeding cattle, three years and more is a long time to wait before we ken whether a bull is any good or no'. But tell me more about your ain plans, James?'

'Well, we shall soon build up the numbers in the herd if we keep all the heifer calves – so long as we dinna have any trouble with tuberculosis or foot and mouth.' Disease was every stock farmer's dread. 'I suppose if I'm truly honest, Mr Fairly, I'd like to try and keep Nithanvale for my own sake, as well as Great-Uncle George's.'

'Aah – now that makes all the difference in the world. I'll tell ye what, laddie – I'll arrange for ye to talk to Alex at the Mains. He understands these things better than I do. He would probably advise ye about getting a loan frae the bank. There is one thing I'd advise ye to do though, if ye're thinking o' having a sale of Nithanvale stock. It might help bring in a bit extra money.'

'What's that then?'

'Well, it was Kirsty's suggestion really, but I'm glad I heeded her, young as she is. We've had our ain herd tested for tuberculosis. We are accredited now. That's an advantage when ye're selling.'

'Thanks, Mr Fairly. It would be worth spending money getting the Nithanvale cows tested, so long as we dinna need to postpone the sale too long.'

'What about Miss MacFarlane? Does she understand how hard things will be?' Logan watched James's strained face relax a little and his eyes softened.

'Mary doesna mind hard work or sacrificing her own comforts. She refuses to make any plans for her own future while her grandfather needs her. I know she will not fail him.' There was no doubting the admiration in James's tone. 'I hope I dinna let him down either. I know he needed me after his stroke, but he has given me an opportunity to prove myself too. I shall do my best. I would appreciate Mr Fairly's advice if you think he willna mind me going to the Mains?'

Alex was less wary than Logan had been, but he did not forecast an easy time ahead for James either.

'But you and Miss MacFarlane are both young with all your lives ahead o' ye. Just remember though, when ye dinna have a landlord ye'll need to pay for everything – frae roof tiles to fence posts, drain tiles to chimney pots – if ye mean to maintain the place in good order; ye'll have nothing to spare for improvements, or pleasure, for many a year!'

'The land is in good heart and the buildings are in reasonable repair . . .'

'Well then, if ye can raise a good deposit, the bank will probably arrange a loan for the rest. But ye must remember – if ye canna pay the bank will claim everything. The stock, the carts and horses, even the blankets frae your beds,' Alex said gravely.

'I understand, Mr Fairly. That's why I want to put the land in my name only and protect Mary's share o' the stock. I dinna want her to be responsible if things dinna work out.'

'I wish ye luck,' Alex declared. 'As I've said before – all young men need a challenge, including those three lads o' mine. Cameron now – he's as restless as they come; reminds me too much o' my brother Billy. Of course we canna tell what the future holds and if ye dinna keep good health – or if your cattle get sick.' Alex shrugged. 'Dinna hold me responsible if ye make the wrong decision, laddie!' he smiled grimly.

'I'll not be doing that, Mr Fairly. I thank you for your time though, and your advice.'

'The way things are going with the government talking of supplying every man, woman and child with a gas mask, and

124

making air-raid shelters for the townsfolks – well it makes me wonder whether they're getting ready for another war . . .' Alex looked gravely at his youngest brother. Logan hated the mere thought of war and the memories it conjured up . . .

'If it should come to that our lives are in God's hands and as for money, it'll no' matter whether we have any or not if yon man Hitler takes us over.'

'But if there is a war, surely we should need to grow our own food again?' James mused. 'Even the government would want to encourage British farmers then, surely?'

'Weel ye'd think so, but the way they've allowed imports o' food o' every description to flood the country they must believe we'll never need food grown in Great Britain ever again!' Alex remarked soberly.

'Maybe that's why they're spending such a lot o' money on building up the navy just now,' Logan commented, 'to protect the imports no matter what happens to us!'

'Whatever the reason I wish ye well in your venture, James,' Alex said seriously. 'You and that pretty young cousin o' yours.'

James MacFarlane frowned and opened his mouth to protest, but then he shrugged and changed his mind. What did it matter if they believed his future was irrevocably tied with Mary's?

Fifteen

The last sheaf of corn had been gathered in from the fields and all that remained was to thatch the round ricks in the stackyard at Fairlyden. There was always a sense of relief when the harvest was finished and Kirsty was feeling almost light-hearted when she drew the car to a halt outside the Muircumwell Store one afternoon in late September.

Lizzie Whiteley and her mother had inherited the village store from their former employer and Lizzie had carried on alone since her mother's death during the dreadful influenza outbreak at the end of the war. She was known to a whole generation of Muircumwell children as Miss Lizzie and Kirsty had been one of those children.

'Come to collect the groceries have ye, lassie?' Lizzie smiled at her. 'And how is your grandmother?' Lizzie never failed to ask after Sarah's health. She felt the whole of the Whiteley family, right down to her nephew, James MacFarlane, were indebted to the old Mistress of Fairlyden in one way or another.

'Granny is fine, thanks – or at least she never complains.'

'I had a young man in here asking for her yesterday.' Lizzie's brow puckered as she recalled the incident. 'American, he was.'

'A young man from America? Asking for Granny.' Kirsty echoed incredulously. 'Are you sure, Miss Lizzie?'

'Well . . . older than Jamie. I'd say he was in his thirties, but I'm no good at guessing, Miss Kirsty.'

'Mmm . . . perhaps Uncle Billy asked him to call on her. I believe he's in America.'

'He seemed familiar . . . but I dinna think I have ever seen him before; brown eyes he has and dark wavy hair; very smart – but different.'

'Did he tell you his name?'

'Aye. "Simon F. Guillyman at your service, Ma'am," he said. He has a queer way o' talking.'

'Guillyman!'

'Aye. His father was Sir Simon Guillyman frae Avary Hall,

it seems. Ye'll remember the last tenants moved out o' the Hall a few months ago? It's been empty since, and he's staying there now. He says he has business tae attend, and he wants to see where his ancestors came frae.'

'I see.' Kirsty wondered why she suddenly had such an inexplicable feeling of foreboding.

'My father rents the land which used to belong to Avary Hall.'

'Aye, I ken. Thomas reckons it grows more grass now than it ever grew afore your father had it.'

'Mmm . . .' She frowned. 'I wonder if Mr Guillyman intends to stay? Did he look like a farmer, Miss Lizzie? I hope he doesna want to take over the land frae the Guillyman Trust. We'd never be able to keep all our cows and the young heifers if we couldna rent the Muircumwell fields.'

'He didna mention farming, Miss Kirsty.'

'Anyway, Father's lease doesna run out for another two and a half years,' Kirsty remembered with relief, 'so it canna be that sort o' business.' Or can it, she wondered uneasily as she lifted the box of groceries. Lizzie carefully marked them in the accounts book to be paid for at the end of the month.

'I'm thinking o' buying a wee van to do some deliveries,' she remarked without looking up from the ledger. Her tone was casual but when Kirsty turned back in surprised she realised the older woman was waiting for her reaction.

'Well . . . I must admit this is a surprise, Miss Lizzie, but it seems a good idea. There's a lot o' folk would be glad to have their groceries delivered to the door, I'm sure.' She was wondering who would drive the van. She knew Lizzie Whiteley was younger than her brother, Thomas . . . but she must be nearly sixty, and anyway she was already busy with the shop and her little tearoom.

'It was James's idea really,' Lizzie confessed. 'He says it'll be years before everybody can afford to buy a motorcar. He thinks I'd get extra trade, especially if I send my freshly baked bread and biscuits and such like things?'

'I-I'm sure James is right about that, Miss Lizzie – but who would help you – I mean who will drive the van?'

'There's a young man, name o' Adam Taylor – a brother o' Willy, the new postie. He's wanting to get wed. Willy says he has enough saved to buy half o' the van with me if I could let him and his new wife have rooms to live in. James thinks I should ask your father's advice, Miss Kirsty?'

'My father?' Kirsty echoed. 'I don't think he knows much about vans or shopkeeping.' Indeed her father did not even enjoy driving the car.

'James has a great respect for your father, lassie. Thinks the world o' him in fact, but then I suppose it's because he never kenned his ain father, and Master Logan was aye sae patient with him when he was a wee laddie. And he's kept his ain head above water for a' the terrible times we're having.'

'But so have you, Miss Lizzie!'

'Aye . . .' Lizzie sighed. 'But it hasna been easy whiles. Anyway I dinna like to trouble your father, lassie, but I wondered if ye might mention my wee plan to him? See what he says. I've plenty o' room here ye ken – and well, I'd kind o' like a bit company sometimes . . . I thought Anna and Thomas might have moved in with me when James left Fairlyden but Thomas doesna want to live anywhere else but Fairlyden and Anna couldna leave him tae bide on his ain.'

'No, and we should miss them both at Fairlyden. I'll ask my father, Miss Lizzie. And Granny will be interested in your plans too. I'm sure she thinks all the Whiteleys are an extension of her own family, you know!' Kirsty smiled warmly as she hitched up the box of groceries and made for the door. How fresh and alive she looks, Lizzie thought affectionately as she watched her step lightly into the autumn sunlight.

Simon Guillyman echoed Lizzie's thoughts as he drew up across the street in the Austin Seven for which he had just paid a hundred and forty-nine pounds ten shillings. The smell of the new leather filled his nostrils. They had assured him at the garage in Dumfries that he was getting a de luxe model, with an acceleration from ten to thirty miles in eight seconds, but he had had to pay another six pounds for road tax.

He had wondered, as he drove along the narrow roads back to Muircumwell, whether the owner had tricked him over that. Maybe he would have been wiser to have heeded his mother's last piece of advice to return to America without delay after a brief inspection of the Scottish property. Certainly he would have to issue some explicit instructions to the solicitors to act promptly before things in Europe became any more uncertain. Germany would be sure to win if there was another war, and then where would his inheritance be! He frowned. It was more than a year since his mother's death. She had told him so little about his father's family. Surely it was natural to be curious, even though his father had died before he was born? It was his mother's reticence in talking about him and their life in Scotland which had aroused his interest. She had not wanted him to visit 'the old country'. Her excuse had been that she was an old woman and might die before his return. He sighed. Perhaps she had been sincere in her reasoning, or perhaps she did not want him to be as disappointed as he had certainly felt at his first sight of the lofty old Hall with its large cold rooms, half of them shuttered and gloomy, musty smelling and damp through lack of use. The rooms which had been tenanted were habitable of course, but incredibly shabby. The solicitors had not done a good job of maintaining his inheritance at all. He hoped the land and buildings would be in better condition.

Kirsty swung the starting handle for the fourth time but not a spark of life sounded in the engine. She paused for breath and drew a hand across her perspiring brow. That was the worst of motorcars, she thought crossly, she knew so little about putting them right when they refused to go. Now if she had been on Marocco . . . but then it was almost impossible to balance a large box of groceries on the big gelding's saddle. A reluctant smile lifted the corners of her mouth as she had visions of the thick blue sugar bags spilling to the ground, or perhaps a trail of rice trickling all the way home behind them . . .

'Can I help you?'

Kirsty spun round, her pleated tweed skirt twirling with the sudden movement and giving a tantalising glimpse of her shapely legs. She had been too busy bending over the starting handle, and then catching her breath, to notice the man who had come to her assistance. He was a stranger – and yet he seemed vaguely familiar with his dark hair and twinkling brown eyes. Belatedly she recognised his American drawl.

'You must be Mr Guillyman!'

The dark brows shot up, the firm mouth curved in an ironic smile. 'News travels fast, Miss er . . .?'

'Fairly. Kirsty Fairly.' Kirsty held out her hand and he took it in a firm grasp, but there was no doubting the startled look, the kindling of real interest in his expressive eyes.

'Miss Fairly! Well, this is a surprise. I had hoped to make the acquaintance of Mistress Sarah Fairly, or at least some members of the Fairly family – but I had not dared to hope there would be any of them so – so attractive!'

'Oh!' Kirsty coloured in confusion, but it was more on account

130

of the undisguised admiration in the American's eyes than his flattering words.

'You seemed to be having difficulty starting your car? Maybe I can help?'

'I would certainly be grateful if you could.'

He strode round to the side of the bonnet and folded it back expertly. Kirsty had no idea what he was doing as he fiddled about inside. He was not wearing a hat and she viewed the neatly brushed dark hair on the crown of his well-shaped head, the tanned skin of his neck above his collar and tie.

'There, that should fix her!' he declared with satisfaction and drew a spotless white handkerchief from his jacket pocket and wiped his fingers carefully before moving to the front of the car and swinging the handle effortlessly. The car burst into life.

Kirsty's face relaxed in a relieved smile and Simon Guillyman's attention was arrested by the transformation.

'Thank you, thank you very much!' she called over the top of the noisy engine. He opened the car door and held out a hand to help her into the driving seat.

'You have soiled your handkerchief.'

'No matter.' He shrugged and grinned down at her as she settled herself behind the wheel. It was not easy to carry on a conversation over the noise of the car engine and in any case Kirsty was aware of several pairs of eyes upon them from the cottages which flanked the village street, yet she was strangely reluctant to drive away. Her gallant knight seemed equally reluctant to let her go.

'I shall be staying at Avary Hall for some weeks, Miss Fairly. I intend to call on your grandmother. No doubt we shall meet again.'

Kirsty's earlier foreboding was replaced by a strange feeling of exhilaration.

'The Guillymans who own Avary Hall – and the land belonging to the Home Farm and the mill?' Beth exclaimed incredulously, when Kirsty recounted her meeting with the American visitor to Muircumwell. 'Your father's landlords . . . I wonder what they want?'

'They? There's only one Guillyman, I think,' Kirsty frowned. 'He said he intended visiting Granny, but he didna mention that he had a family.' It had not occurred to her that Mr Simon Guillyman might have a wife and family. Somehow such a prospect was less than pleasing.

Neither of them had noticed Sarah stiffen, or her hands clench on the arms of her chair while her heart began an erratic thumping.

Elsa Guillyman's son was here in Muircumwell – after all these years! She began to tremble. Would he resemble his mother? She was sure he could not resemble Sir Simon Guillyman, the man whose name he bore; she was as sure now as she had been all those years ago when William had sailed away to America, so eager to see his partner's widow again. He had not told her before he sailed that Elsa Guillyman had born a son after years in a childless marriage . . .

'Granny! Granny, are you all right?' Sarah started out of her reverie. She looked up to find Kirsty peering anxiously down at her. 'You're awfully pale.'

'I-I'm fine . . .' Her voice was little more than a thread of sound and to her dismay it sounded as wavery as the autumn leaves rustling in the breeze. She tried to clear her throat. 'I'm fine,' she declared fiercely. 'Why shouldn't I be?'

'I don't know, Granny, but I think I'll make you a cup of tea.'

'Aye, you do that, lassie,' Sarah summoned a smile but her heart was still doing some very funny things and she didn't feel like herself at all.

'I ken ye're upset,' Beth said gravely when Kirsty left them alone. 'I expect the mention o' Mr Guillyman's visit has awakened old memories.'

'Aye. His father and William were partners.'

'I dinna remember the Guillymans ever living at the Hall, but Billy once talked to me about the Fairly and Guillyman's – Agricultural Merchants business being in the old mill premises when he was a laddie.'

'Billy was interested in machinery even then.' Sarah sighed heavily and had to pause while the pain in her chest eased a little.

'He told me how disappointed he was because he couldna take over.'

'It was before you and Logan were born. Billy was too young. The business never prospered! But we owe the Guillymans nothing! Nothing, do you hear me, Beth?'

'Aye, of course . . .' Beth murmured uncertainly. 'Please, please dinna upset yourself, Mama Fairly.'

Sarah smiled faintly then. 'It's a long time since you called me that, Beth – Mama Fairly.'

'Mmm, I suppose it just slips out when I'm worried,' Beth smiled wryly. 'I dinna like to see ye getting distressed – just because some rich young American laddie wants to explore the land o' his fathers!'

'You're right, Beth; silly to get excited. I'm getting old . . .' She closed her eyes, but when she heard the rattle of the tea cups she opened them suddenly. 'I dinna want to see him though! Dinna let him come here, Beth!' she whispered urgently.

'No, no, of course not, if that's your wish.'

Sarah knew she was not herself but she was determined not to complain and Beth and Kirsty went to the milking as usual, leaving her resting in her chair beside the fire.

When they returned a couple of hours later they were dismayed to find her lying prone on her bed.

'I'll bring ye some supper on a tray,' Beth said gently, 'if ye're too tired to come down again.'

'Couldn't eat . . .' Sarah's voice was weak. 'Terrible pain . . .' Her hand fluttered to her chest.

'Just lie still then and rest a wee while,' Beth murmured with a calm she did not feel. She flew down the stairs muttering a prayer of thanks for the telephone which she had hated so much when she first moved to Fairlyside.

'What's wrong, Mother?'

'I'm trying to get the doctor. Aye, aye!' she shouted loudly at Patsy Sharp the local telephone operator. 'I want Doctor Broombank. No, no, never mind who's ill. Get him quick, Patsy! Dinna waste time!'

'Mother!' Kirsty rushed through to the hall in alarm. It was so unlike her mother to shout and even more unlike her to snap at poor Patsy – even if she was a bit nosey and rather naughty at listening in to conversations, but a second or so later Kirsty understood her mother's panic.

'I think it's her heart,' she whispered hoarsely. 'Her lips are blue; she has a terrible pain. Oh, Kirsty, I should have paid more attention. I shouldna have left her alone!'

Luke had also heard and he came through from the dining room where he had been studying. Few things disturbed Luke when he was absorbed in his lessons. It frequently amazed Kirsty that her parents were so tolerant over the time Luke spent with his books, but they seemed to have accepted that he would never be interested in the farm and the animals – even though it was their livelihood – and his too. Luke was fifteen now, the same age as his cousin Paul. Emma had tried to insist that her youngest son should stay at the Academy until he had taken his examinations but Paul couldn't wait to leave and start work with his father and brothers at the Mains.

'It's different for Luke,' he had complained to Kirsty. 'He likes studying and he's brilliant at other things besides his art. He's aye first in German and French, aye and he even likes Latin! Even old Sawbones says he could speak any language he'd a mind to learn. There's hardly any o' the lads frae farms that go to the university but everybody expects Luke will go.'

Strangely Kirsty had never heard her brother discuss his plans, or dreams, for the future. Luke seemed to live in a calm little world of his own, untroubled by ordinary problems; but on this particular occasion his mother's anxiety communicated itself to him. He sensed that Kirsty was torn between a desire to rush up to their grandmother and the need to calm their mother. Luke gently guided Beth to a chair by the kitchen table and made her sit down.

'I'll make Mama a cup of tea, Kirsty, if you want to stay with Granny until the doctor comes.'

Sixteen

The doctor attended Sarah twice a day for the next ten days. He had despatched Kirsty to a chemist in Dumfries for a particular powder. He instructed her carefully, explaining it was a dangerous substance if misused, but he required it urgently to make up his own special tablets in the little dispensary at the top of his house.

Beth and Kirsty took turns to sit with Sarah, with occasional relief from Emma when she could be spared from her own busy household at the Mains.

It did not occur to Kirsty that her grandmother's attack had any connection with Simon Guillyman. She saw him twice in Muircumwell while she was collecting groceries or delivering eggs and butter to Lizzie's shop, but she had little time to linger in those first difficult days. She explained about her grandmother's illness. He seemed extremely perturbed by her news and expressed his wishes for Sarah's full and speedy recovery with a depth of feeling which amazed Kirsty, especially since he was a stranger. This drew her to him as no amount of flattery could have done.

She realised he must be considerably older than herself but there was something about him which intrigued her. He was polite and well mannered, considerate, humorous, extremely attractive in his appearance – but it was none of these things which held such a fatal fascination for Kirsty.

Despite her anxiety over her grandmother, as the weeks went by and Sarah began to make a slow recovery, Kirsty looked forward eagerly to her chance encounters with Simon Guillyman in the village. Soon they were no longer chance encounters but regular meetings in the small tearoom attached to Miss Lizzie's shop. Sometimes Simon took her to lunch in Annan when Beth asked her to attend to the market day business on her behalf. Kirsty looked forward to these Fridays with anticipation and even more to the rare visits to the Lyceum Cinema in Dumfries.

In between these small pleasure outings she worked as

hard as ever. The more cattle they kept the more turnips they needed to grow and these had to be gathered in before the winter frosts damaged them or, even worse, imprisoned them in the iron-hard earth. So they were lifted one by one from the soil, the leaves trimmed and the roots loaded ready for carting to the huge clamps in the yard where they were covered with straw and soil in readiness for the winter feed. As the autumn advanced the November days were cold with a rawness which penetrated to the very bones, but Kirsty never shirked her duties. She worked with Lucy and Paddy, Logan and Thomas, knowing that if she did not do her share they would have to do extra. Sometimes she worried about her father when the constant bending, pulling and shawing set him coughing until he could scarcely get his breath. She knew he had not yet reached his fortieth birthday but sometimes he looked almost as old as Thomas. Her heart ached for him; she longed to protect him from such demanding labours.

'Och, lassie,' he smiled whenever she tried to persuade him to stick to easier tasks. 'I'll be finished as a farmer if I canna manage each job the seasons demand. Besides I used tae enjoy the turnip hoeing and the shawing when your mother and I worked in the fields together. How's that Mr Guillyman?' he asked, changing the subject so suddenly that Kirsty found herself blushing, a reaction which earned her a speculative, if not anxious, stare from her father.

The turnip shawing was finished when Kirsty found herself sharing a cup of tea and one of Lizzie Whiteley's home-baked scones with Simon Guillyman again. He lifted her hand as it lay on the table and gently uncurled her chapped fingers. They were red and sore from the wet and windy weather which had accompanied the last week of the turnip harvest.

'I hate to see you working so hard that your hands are raw, Kirsty,' he said in his deep slow voice. Suddenly he lowered his lashes, which were thick and dark like his hair, and she could not see the expression in his brown eyes as he said softly, 'Come back to America with me, Kirsty? Your life would be easier there and there is so much I want to show you. So many—' Kirsty snatched her hand away and stared wide eyed at Simon.

'You're going back to America? When?'

'Oh yes, I must return, my dear. My home is there.'

'When?' Kirsty asked a little breathlessly.

'When? Well now, Kirsty, maybe that depends on you. I

have grown rather fond of you, you see.' He captured her hand again and began to stroke the roughened palm with an hypnotic touch. 'I have a feeling I ought to meet your family before I make any further plans though . . . Is your grandmother's health improving?'

'Y-yes. Doctor Broombank allows her to sit in her chair in front of her bedroom fire every afternoon now. Luke, my young brother, reads to her every evening when he returns from school . . .'

'Then maybe I shall have the pleasure of talking with her soon?'

'I-I don't know. Mother says we must not upset her and – and . . .'

'And you think my presence would upset her?' Simon Guillyman looked thoughtful. 'I wonder why?' he mused softly.

'I suppose because you remind her o' the past. I understand the Fairlys and the Guillymans were business associates once.'

'Nothing more than business? Surely they were friends? What other reason could my mother have had for giving me the name of Fairly?'

'Fairly! Simon F. Guillyman! The "F" is for Fairly?'

'Indeed it is.' Simon gently mocked her astonished expression. 'So you see, my dear Kirsty, I had hoped to learn something of my family from the Fairlys.'

'Is that the real reason why you came to Scotland – to discover your ancestors?' To Kirsty's surprise Simon avoided her eyes. He looked . . . almost guilty? It was only later that she realised he had never answered her question, and how skilfully he had diverted her attention with his stories of his home in America. She was ready to take her leave when he announced, 'I intend to travel in Europe after Christmas. I believe this man Hitler is bent on war, and if I am right . . .' He grimaced. 'Think of the destruction . . .'

'Don't talk of another war! My father fought in the last one and he is suffering the effects of it still.'

'But we must all face facts. It would appear that Hitler is a very powerful man – and a ruthless one by all accounts. I was serious when I asked you to accompany me back to America. I hope you will consider my proposition while I am away. After all there would be little future for you here.' You or anyone else, he thought morosely.

'I don't need to consider it.' Kirsty's tone was quiet, but there was no doubting its conviction. Simon looked at her searchingly for a moment before his handsome face broke into a smile, erasing many of the lines of maturity.

'You mean you will come with me? I can book your passage? I shall proceed to sell . . .'

'Oh no!' Kirsty flushed and then went pale as the light died in his face. Fleetingly, his dark eyes looked hard, and a shiver passed over Kirsty. 'I could never leave my family – or Fairlyden . . .' she whispered. 'Never.'

For a moment Simon frowned down at her. Then he seemed to make a big effort and he gave her his usual charming smile. 'We shall see, we shall see, my dear Kirsty – but remember the shadows of war are hanging over your country already. What good would Fairlyden be to you and your family then? However,' he shrugged. 'You will have several months to consider before I return from my travels. Now, tell me when I am to accompany you to the Farmers' Dance in Dumfries?'

'You mean you've changed your mind? You will go after all?'

'Yes, my dear. I think I must. Indeed I cannot allow my beautiful young partner to go without me.'

'I did not know you had been seeing Mr Simon Guillyman so often, Kirsty?' There was reproach in Beth's blue eyes. Kirsty bit her lip. She had never deceived her parents in her life, but she had been less than frank about her meetings with Simon Guillyman and she did not know why, except that some instinct warned her they would not be happy about her friendship with the American.

'It was not a secret. We met several times by chance . . .'

'And several times by appointment?'

'Yes, but . . .'

'Your father is anxious about you, Kirsty. You know how deeply he cares for you and he does not want you to be harmed . . .'

'Harmed! How could Simon harm me?'

'Aah, so it is Simon, is it – not Mr Guillyman anymore?'

'Of course, Mother. We are friends. Anyway I think people are not so formal in America as we are. Simon says everyone is more casual in their dress and manners and—'

'And their relationships perhaps? Oh Kirsty, ye're a good lassie and ye work hard, but ye're innocent o' the ways o' men and Simon Guillyman is old enough to be your father! Maybe he has a daughter like you at home.'

'Oh Mother, he is not so old!' Kirsty chuckled. 'Of course he is older than most of the boys I know but they are all so – so immature! I like being with Simon. He is amusing and interesting and considerate.'

'Aye,' Beth said dryly, but her face was unusually pale and strained. She had been too preoccupied with Mama Fairly to pay proper attention to her daughter – but it had never occurred to her that Kirsty might have become involved in an unsuitable friendship – or even worse in a more serious relationship.

'Lizzie Whiteley is worried about you seeing so much of Mr Guillyman. Bless her romantic old heart. I think she always visualised you as a bride for James. He's always been her favourite nephew so I suppose it's a measure o' her regard for ye.'

'I scarcely see James MacFarlane! Anyway he is already attached to Miss MacFarlane of Nithanvale, as I'm sure Miss Lizzie must realise now!'

'Aye, ye may be right.' Beth sighed. 'The Carnland Estate has been sold. The tenants got the chance to buy their farms and James and his half-cousin have bought Nithanvale. He asked your father's advice, but it isna an easy matter to advise anyone. Anyway James still comes to visit his mother and Thomas regularly and your father has seen him several times.'

'Well, I havena seen him.'

'No, he hasna called here since your grandmother has been ill. He was always a considerate laddie, though; he doesna want to trouble us, I suppose.'

Kirsty did not reply. She knew well enough that it was not her grandmother's illness which had kept James away. He was avoiding her as he had vowed to do. So, he and his cousin had bought Nithanvale. They were partners in business then; how long would it be before they were partners in life? The thought did nothing to lift her spirits.

The night of the Dumfries Farmers' Dance was bitterly cold with thickening fog which seemed likely to freeze. Simon came to Fairlyside for the first time and Kirsty introduced him to her parents. Even Beth, prejudiced as she was, had to admit that he was extremely handsome in his dark evening suit, but there was little opportunity to get to know the person behind the charming façade since he did not care to linger on account of the weather.

'I wish ye werena going so far, Kirsty, on such a night,' Beth protested anxiously.

'Please do not worry, Mrs Fairly, I have rugs to keep your daughter warm and I shall drive with the greatest of care,' Simon reassured her confidently.

'What's worrying you, Beth?' Sarah asked kindly when her daughter-in-law brought up her glass of warm milk at bedtime.

'Worrying me?'

'Yes, you've put my milk on the washstand and the ewer on the bedside table. And you have lifted the candle three times and set it down again.' Sarah smiled with something of her old humour and her dark eyes twinkled up at Beth.

'Och, it's just that I wish Kirsty hadna gone all the way to Dumfries on such a night – even if Mr Guillyman has promised to take care o' her . . .' she added unthinkingly.

'Mr Guillyman!' Sarah's face lost some of its colour and Beth remembered too late that it was Simon Guillyman's arrival in Scotland which had triggered her heart attack. 'He's still here? Why has Kirsty gone with him?'

'He-he's taken her to the Farmers' Dance.'

'Taken her? Not – not as her partner, surely?'

'Aye, I'm afraid so.'

'That's impossible! He is old enough to be Kirsty's father!'

Beth smiled gently. 'He's certainly older than Kirsty, but he's not quite as old as that. I did remind her that he'll be more experienced than she is though – and frae America . . .' Beth's unhappiness was evident in her voice. 'She says the laddies she kens are boyish compared with him. He's certainly very handsome, and he has charming manners.'

'He is old enough to be her father!' Sarah insisted vehemently.

'Dinna upset yourself,' Beth pleaded. She felt Logan's mama had probably become a bit confused over the years. It was easy to lose track of time. After all she had never met Simon Guillyman; he had been born in America.

'Dinna humour me, Beth,' Sarah said quietly. 'I know I'm getting old and I know the tablets Doctor Broombank insists on giving me make me sleepy, but I *know* Simon Guillyman is at least a year older than Logan. He was born – he was born before William went to America. I-I don't know when exactly. I-I only found out there was a Guillyman heir by chance, from the pompous wee man who was in charge o' the Trust. I've often wondered if he's still alive and if he knows the Fairlys are still at Fairlyden in spite o' his evil aspersions. Wherever he is I hope he knows it's my son who tenants the Guillyman land!'

'I-I've never kenned ye to be so bitter before,' Beth murmured in amazement.

'No, but he was such an awful lawyer and times were difficult enough. I've always thought that William must have learned Elsa Guillyman had had a son on the night o' the fire when Fairlyden was almost destroyed. He had met a visitor from America at the Jubilee celebrations. He stayed talking to him at the Crown and Thistle and he didna come home at all that night, Beth . . .' Her voice sank to a whisper, and her eyes held a faraway look. 'It was Crispin who came to rescue us. He took me to safety – to Strathtod House. The Estate belonged to his father then. I didna see him again for two years after that night. He-he went to Australia immediately afterwards . . .' Beth could scarcely hear the next words. 'Logan was born the night I learned o' William's death . . . It was nearly nine months after the fire.'

'I-I understand . . .' Beth whispered huskily. She understood many things then which Sarah had left unspoken.

'Aye, lassie, I think you do.' Sarah was weary now, but when she spoke again her voice was firmer. 'It's true what it says in the bible: "The sins o' the fathers shall be visited upon the children." I dinna want Kirsty to suffer, Beth. I said I didna want to see Simon Guillyman. I admit it was a shock to hear he had come to Scotland after all these years. But I shall see him! I have regained my strength now, and my commonsense!' Sarah added with a grimace. 'He canna hurt me, but he could hurt Kirsty, and I couldna bear that! You must invite him here, Beth. Invite him for Christmas. Alex and Emma and their laddies will be here as usual. Kirsty will see them together. Surely she will realise he is too old for her.'

'But she has seen him so often already . . .'

'She has not *really* seen him! Tell me, Beth . . . Does he – what does he look like?' Sarah's voice shook. Beth's heart ached at the strain on her lined face. The heart attack had taken a heavy toll.

'He is tall, with thick dark hair, quite curly I should imagine when it is not greased into immaculate waves. Dark brown eyes . . .'

Sarah sighed. 'Like Alex?'

'Alex?' Beth frowned, then her eyes widened. Suddenly she understood completely. What a tangle!

'Well, Beth? Does Simon Guillyman resemble Alex?'

'He – he looks more like Billy – as I remember him before he went to the war . . .' she said softly. 'A bit like an older version of young Cameron perhaps . . .'

Sarah nodded. 'It is as I feared. They are all Fairlys – all but Logan. Kirsty must see for herself.' She summoned a wavery smile. 'Your daughter has enough of me in her to be stubborn and proud, Beth, and she is young enough to be headstrong. We must handle this carefully. Nothing matters now except Kirsty's happiness.'

'B-but Emma is very observant . . . Alex too. I-I think ye've suffered enough, over the years. Striving alone to save Fairlyden . . .' Beth's tone hardened. 'I willna let ye be humiliated by that man's presence in your own home! If Kirsty notices a resemblance when she sees them all together, then the boys will see it too. Alexander is as observant as his father. It is better that the past should be forgotten. I shall tell Kirsty not to bring that man here again!'

'But Kirsty's happiness is at stake. And maybe more than Kirsty's. Remember he is the owner of Avary Hall and the land in the Guillyman Trust. Logan needs to retain the tenancy, Beth. He needs that land badly now that he has spent good money on extending his byre to keep the extra cows.'

'Aye, more cows need more grass, and more hay . . .' Beth mused anxiously. 'We have a lease though. Even if Mr Guillyman wants to be nasty there is nothing he can do until it expires. Is there?'

'I don't know, Beth. I've never trusted leases and lawyers and such like.'

'I think Logan believed the Guillyman Trustees would just go on renewing the lease . . . After all they wouldna get a better tenant . . .'

'Well, maybe they will renew it, but please, Beth? Will you do as I ask and invite Mr Simon Guillyman to the family party at Christmas? I'm not afraid for myself anymore; I'm too old to worry about past humiliations now.'

'We shall see.' Beth resolved to discuss this whole affair with Logan as soon as possible. He would know what was best for everyone; he would never put his own ambition before his mother's or his daughter's happiness.

Seventeen

Kirsty looked around the assembled crowd in the ballroom. The dancing was just beginning and she recognised several small groups whom she considered the semi-gentry, men and women who spent much of their time hunting and shooting, golfing, fishing, perhaps attending political meetings or doing voluntary work to fill their time. She sensed that Simon probably had more in common with some of them than with ordinary farmers like her own family. She looked down at her hands and was glad of the fine lace evening gloves which hid her rough and reddened knuckles.

She had heard that some of the wealthier young ladies travelled to Edinburgh or Glasgow, and even to London, to buy model gowns for special occasions, but she felt no shame for her own gown of sapphire blue velvet trimmed with tiny covered buttons. Her mother was well known for her dexterity with the needle, even amongst some of the best seamstresses in the county. She felt justifiably proud as she extended her arm a little to steal a glance at the wrist-length sleeves, which were unusual and beautifully tapered. The ankle-length skirt was cut with skill too and sewn to perfection; Beth could not have tolerated a puckered seam or hem. Kirsty felt confident and at ease. She knew the simple flowing lines suited her tall figure far better than fussy frills and flounces, or the clinging tubes which compelled their wearers to walk with knocking knees and revealed the exact shape of hips and bosoms. Her shining brown hair needed no torturing with curling tongs or the newfangled permanent waves. When the band struck up with a lilting waltz her eyes sparkled with anticipation.

'You are the most vital-looking young woman in the whole ballroom tonight,' Simon murmured as he bowed gallantly over her hand before drawing her on to the floor. He was an expert dancer and Kirsty was conscious of many eyes upon them in those first moments before other couples joined them. It was then she saw James MacFarlane and her step faltered slightly, causing Simon to raise a questioning brow. She could not explain that her heart had ached with a pain that was almost physical at the sight of James's unhappy eyes in that fleeting moment before he realised she had seen him. Then she remembered he had vowed not to speak to her; they no longer shared a precious, if youthful friendship. She could no longer kiss his cheek with soft wet lips and stroke his hair as she had when she was nine and he was fifteen and he had cut his leg so badly that Anna had sent for the doctor. Somehow the thought that James was no longer her friend diminished her anticipation of the evening.

He did not need her concern anyway; he was not alone and he certainly looked happy enough now. Indeed he seemed to be with a lively party, although Mary MacFarlane was not in the company and Kirsty wondered why she never accompanied him to such social events. Surely she knew how much James enjoyed music? Anna always maintained it was Beth, her own mother, who had taught him his fine sense of rhythm while he was still a toddler. Anna, her mother, James – they had all spent their childhood in the Fairlyden cottage. Soon it would be the new dairy instead of a happy little house . . .

'Are your thoughts so sad, or is it that you do not enjoy dancing with me?' Simon asked, recalling her attention. Kirsty detected a note of impatience, even pique, in his American drawl and she made an effort to push James MacFarlane out of her mind.

One of the small estate owners, who had bought Fairlyden heifers at several pedigree sales, asked Kirsty for the next dance and proceeded to tell her how well the animals had performed. When the dance finished he insisted on introducing her and Simon to his own party of fellow landowners and their wives and sons and daughters. Simon was an instant success. His American accent was a novelty, his conversation amusing and interesting. Kirsty was not entirely at ease in the company but it was plain that Simon had no desire to leave, especially when a tall, red-headed and very elegant young woman, introduced as Madeleine Marshman, made a very determined effort to attract him. It was not long before the pair had taken to the floor and the red-head's brother immediately seized the opportunity to partner Kirsty. His manner was pleasant enough but his only topics of conversation seemed to revolve around fishing in summer and skiing in winter. Kirsty enjoyed skating and curling when the ice on the local pond permitted but she had never been skiing. She found her attention wandering frequently and she was glad when the dance ended. Simon was still engrossed in conversation with the alluring Miss Marshman when Roderick led her back to their party. Almost immediately another young man asked Kirsty to dance and so it went on as the evening advanced. Eventually the compere announced a polka.

'Good evening, Kirsty . . .' She spun round at the sound of the familiar voice so close to her shoulder. James MacFarlane bowed but not before she had caught a glimmer of amusement in his eyes as the notes of a merry tune filled the ballroom. Her heart soared out of all proportion to the polite greeting. She knew instinctively that he was remembering the first time her mother had tried to teach them to dance the polka together. She had been about twelve and James nearly eighteen. Their long coltish limbs had become hopelessly entangled, their knees had bumped and they had dissolved into helpless laughter. She lifted her face to his and her own eyes danced at the memory.

James held out his hand. She placed her own into it and felt his strong fingers close over hers. Somehow the small formality seemed more significant than the mere acceptance of a dancing partner. It was almost as though James had offered her an olive branch and she had pledged to accept it. Then they were dancing gaily, their steps now in perfect time, earning several admiring glances. Kirsty was breathless but her eyes were sparkling as the music ended. James laid a detaining hand lightly on her arm.

'How is your grandmother, Kirsty?'

'She is recovering slowly, thank you. Shall I tell her you were enquiring for her?'

'Yes, please do. I, er . . . I would have called to see her, but after our last encounter, and your accident. You did not answer my letter. I was not sure whether I would be welcome . . .' There was just the faintest hint of a question in his voice. The amusement over the shared memory of the polka had gone. Kirsty noticed the lines of strain around James's eyes, and the unhappiness lurking in their greeny-grey depths. Again she felt a pang which seemed to tug at her heart.

'Is your great-uncle keeping well? And Miss MacFarlane?' It was not at all what she wanted to say. She wanted to tell James that he was always welcome at Fairlyden. She wanted to ask why he was not happy; why he looked so troubled.

'Great-Uncle George is as well as can be expected at his age, and considering the effects of the two strokes he has suffered, though he gets very frustrated that his eyesight is so poor. Mary is as serene and content as always. Her presence has certainly helped me to cope with the problems I have encountered since we bought Nithanvale,' he added wryly. 'Your father warned me it would not be easy, but of course I did not listen. I have to confess I am enjoying the challenge though, and I have no regrets on that score.'

'You have other regrets?'

'Some.' James frowned, then summoned a smile. 'But at least Great-Uncle George can die happily in the house where he was born. Mary thinks he is more at peace than he has ever been.'

'I'm sure he must be.' Kirsty knew her tone sounded bleak. She was thinking of James and Miss MacFarlane, joined together in so many ways.

'I'm sorry. I suppose I'm boring you with MacFarlane problems. I should have returned you to your friends . . .' But he made no effort to escort her across the room and as soon as the band struck up again he asked, 'May I have another dance, Kirsty?' She nodded, but her thoughts were still revolving around James and his second cousin, and their life together at Nithanvale.

'. . . so we are all very concerned about you, Kirsty.' James's tone was grave and his arm tightened insistently. The music was slow and quieter this time and Kirsty was intensely aware of his lean strength, the muscular power of his arm at her back, despite the light touch of his hand.

'S-sorry, I was not listening. Who . . . is concerned? Why?'

'We are. The Whiteleys – and that includes the MacFarlane branch. I also know your own parents are growing increasingly anxious about your friendship with Mr Guillyman too . . .'

'I see.' Kirsty stiffened. 'Have you been alarming my father, James?' Her tone was sharper, wary.

'No. I would never cause your father any anxiety if I could help it, but I know Aunt Lizzie has been concerned about you and Mr Guillyman for some time. She has mentioned it to my mother several times, and probably to your own mother too by now. We care for you, Kirsty! All of us!' he insisted urgently as Kirsty opened her mouth to protest. 'Aunt Lizzie didna mean to interfere but you know she hears all the village gossip. God knows, I dinna want us to quarrel again!'

he added vehemently.

'No?' Kirsty's tone was dry and her smooth dark brows arched.

'No! Oh, I know we've had plenty of spirited discussions in the past – but we were always good friends . . . It is for the sake of that friendship that I dare to ask you to consider carefully, Kirsty. I mean, if Mr Guillyman should ask you to – to marry him and go back to America . . .'

'He has already asked me to go with him . . .' Kirsty spoke the words involuntarily.

'Oh God!' James uttered a groan which made Kirsty glance up at him in surprise. She never knew what demon prevented her from telling him she had refused to consider Simon's suggestion.

'Maybe you really do care a little what happens to me . . .?' she murmured, enjoying the instinctive tightening of James's arm. 'Or are you merely wondering how my decision might affect Fairlyden and your family?'

'It is not their future which concerns me, Kirsty! It is your own! How can you contemplate leaving your family to go so far – and Fairlyden! I didna believe you would ever leave Fairlyden willingly, even when I believed Luke would inherit everything. When I heard Mr Bradshaw had left Fairlyden to you . . . I confess I was . . . Och, never mind what I felt. I just canna believe you would give up your inheritance so readily.'

'I have not given it up yet, James.' Kirsty met his eyes steadily and her heartbeats quickened at the expression in them. 'Simon is going to travel in Europe for some months before he returns to America.'

'Aah, so you have time to consider his proposal then? At least that is something to be thankful for.' Kirsty felt him relax and gradually he gave himself up to the pleasure of the dance. The music changed to a popular song and they moved together in perfect harmony. James began to hum the words very softly and she felt his breath stirring her hair.

'. . . I will feel a glow just thinking of you
And the way you look tonight . . .'

He smiled down at her and Kirsty felt a delicious sense of well being. James continued to sing the words almost below his breath so that only she could hear them.

'Oh, but you're lovely,
With your smile so warm
And your cheek so soft,
There is nothing for me but to love you,
Just the way you look tonight'

'. . . never, never change,
Keep that breathless charm,
Won't you please arrange it . . .'

Kirsty knew she had not imagined the sudden thickening of
James's voice as he sang the last lines.

'Cause I love you,
Just the way you look tonight.'

Simon Guillyman watched the bemused look on Kirsty's
face through narrowed eyes as James MacFarlane escorted
her back to him. He felt a swift pang of anger and jealousy.
The feel of Madeleine Marshman's voluptuous body so close to
his own had stirred all his inherent passion – passion he had
taken care to control during his growing friendship with Kirsty
Fairly. He had sensed that she was far more innocent than the
women with whom he had generally associated; he had put it
down to her sheltered country background. Now he saw the
slumbering passion in the depths of her lovely eyes and vowed
he would be the one to awaken it. He had waited long enough
– too long! His reaction to Madeleine's obvious advances had
shown him that plainly tonight. He felt the blood pound faster
in his veins.

Simon was still unfamiliar with the full range of British
weather and he was dismayed to find that the earlier swirling
fog, far from dispersing as he had anticipated, had actually
thickened into an impenetrable freezing murk. He was not
disposed to linger but Miss Madeleine Marshman, now wrapped
almost to her ankles in a coat of silver fox fur, called out to
them.

'Don't forget, Simon, Roddy and I leave for Switzerland the
day after tomorrow. You will enjoy the skiing, and everything
else, if you decide to join us.'

'Thank you, I have your address. Good night.' Simon's voice
was smooth, giving away nothing of his thoughts. Kirsty

considered the invitation forward and pushy, but then she had not cared much for Miss Madeleine Marshman and her companions and she suspected the feeling was mutual. They had certainly been condescending once they discovered she actually worked for her living.

Simon muttered several oaths as the car caught the grass verge, bumped and skidded before coming to a halt on the opposite side. He managed to turn and proceed the way they wanted to go but it was impossible to see more than a few feet ahead.

'I believe a Mr Shaw has invented some glass reflectors which are planted in the middle of the roads and glow like cat's eyes; they're supposed to help drivers keep to their own side of the road . . .' Kirsty muttered tensely. She peered through the grimy windscreen while Simon continued driving down the middle of the road.

They stopped three times for him to clear the glass but the moisture from their breath froze against the windscreen almost instantly and it was impossible to see.

'I think you'll have to open the windscreen, Simon, or we shall never get home safely.'

'It will be bitterly cold.' Simon frowned. 'But I fear there's nothing else for it.' He pulled up the collar of his overcoat for the umpteenth time and set his hat more firmly on his head. He was glad of his fur-lined leather gloves but he was wishing himself safely back in the American sunshine. His feet were like blocks of ice in the soft leather dancing shoes. 'Pull the rug up to your chin, Kirsty, you look frozen.'

Kirsty could scarcely answer through her chattering teeth. If she pulled the rug to her chin her legs and feet suffered instead. The wind on their faces was now an icy blast and there was no sign of the fog clearing as they crawled towards the outskirts of Muircumwell.

When Simon drew the car to a halt Kirsty realised they had reached a fork in the road.

'Are you lost? We keep on the main road. It curves to the right.'

Simon turned to face her but it was impossible to see more than a vague outline in the murky darkness. The freezing air had done little to cool the surge of desire which had raged in his veins for the past hour or more. He had observed the mixture of anxiety, anger and yearning in the eyes of Miss Lizzie's nephew, James MacFarlane, as he watched Kirsty circling the floor during the last dance, and his own arms had tightened possessively. He had felt a sense of triumph as he recognised the longing in the younger man's earnest gaze. He had listened to enough of Miss Lizzie's chatter to know she had once hoped he might marry Miss Kirsty Fairly.

He pulled Kirsty into his arms without warning and kissed her with a passion he had never allowed himself to display before. Kirsty was too surprised to protest, even if she had wanted to. The sudden warmth of Simon's arms holding her close was welcome and his lips swiftly lost their icy tingle when they found her own. Simon was encouraged by Kirsty's arms clinging eagerly as she burrowed closer into his topcoat. It was only when his hand moved inside her own coat and sought the swelling softness of her firm young breast that she drew back.

'Relax, my dear . . .' Simon's voice was husky with desire. 'I've been patient too long, I think. You're ready for love.' He silenced her with a long kiss which left Kirsty breathless and bewildered by its searching intensity. A picture of James MacFarlane flashed through her mind: his unhappy eyes . . . his concern for her . . . his deep voice singing softly . . .

'Never, never change,
Keep that breathless charm . . .'

'No! No, please Simon, don't—' She tried to pull away from the persistent fingers fumbling with the long row of tiny buttons down the front of her dress. For a moment she thought he would not heed her wishes, but he gave an exasperated sigh and drew away.

'You're right. This is not the place to teach you about love, but I can scarcely wait, my lovely Kirsty. I think Avary Hall is only a few hundred yards along that fork to the left. I had to halt to make sure in this infernal fog. I think we can get to the east entrance from this side of the village. It's much nearer than Fairlyden. I'm sure your parents would not wish you to risk an accident in the fog.' His voice was confident and assured.

Kirsty felt panic rising in her and making her breathless as Simon's real intentions sank in. She put her hands flat on his broad chest and pushed herself away, although she was still imprisoned in the strong circle of his arms. It was impossible to read his expression but she could see the glitter of his dark eyes.

'Wh-what are you suggesting, S-Simon?'

'Oh, Kirsty, don't pretend! You must know what I want. You are young and beautiful and I have been patient too long . . . Surely even in Scotland young ladies don't choose to remain innocent for ever! Anyway I have promised myself that I shall succeed in taking you back to America with me – one way or another. You are so full of spirit and vitality . . . yet you really are refreshingly innocent. I can scarcely believe it.' His arms tightened swiftly, taking Kirsty off guard; she found herself held closely against his chest while his mouth explored hers with devastating thoroughness. Simon was breathing hard when he lifted his head.

'I don't want to wait, but we should be in a nice warm room, with a glowing fire and a comfortable feather bed and—'

'No! No, Simon. I want to go home. Now!'

'You sound more like a frightened teenager than a grown woman!' There was frustration and impatience in Simon's voice now. 'You will soon change your mind after tonight . . .'

'Simon! Wait.' Kirsty clutched his arm. 'I am not a frightened teenager. I shall be twenty-one in January, but I still have no wish to share your feather bed tonight.' Her voice was cold. 'Maybe you should have taken—'

'Twenty-one! Surely you are older? I thought . . . you are so competent – at least in everything except making love.'

'No doubt that will come with experience – when I am ready for it.' Simon heard the suppressed anger in her voice. He could not help but admire her spirit – a spirit he longed to tame whatever her age. A spirit he fully intended to tame.

Kirsty sensed his frustration, and his impatience. She waited tensely as he released the brake and let in the clutch. He did it clumsily and the car, which had been ticking over steadily all this time, suddenly stalled. Simon swore under his breath and dragged himself out into the night to swing the handle. Try as he would he could not get the engine to fire.

'Well, my dear Kirsty, it looks as thought you have no choice. You will have to spend the night at Avary Hall now.' There was a faint mockery in his tone but Kirsty knew the passion in him was only temporarily subdued. Inexperienced though she was, she guessed Madeleine Marshman was responsible for arousing his desires and revealing this side of his character. She was not at all confident she would be able to control him if they were to spend the night alone together at Avary Hall. Moreover she had no wish to sully her reputation with a sordid affair. She knew only too well how gossip spread in a country parish, how cruel the wagging tongues could be. She cast aside the rug and scrambled out of the car.

'I expect the car will be safe enough here. I will walk back to Fairlyden. Thank you for taking me to the dance but I cannot give you the reward you anticipated. Good night, Simon.'

'My God, Kirsty! So much dignity! So much self-possession! I think I can be excused for believing you must be nearer thirty than twenty. But I will not allow you to walk to Fairlyden on such a night.'

'You have no option. Your car will not start and I refuse to spend the night at Avary Hall.'

'Then I shall accompany you.'

'No. Your company would neither ease nor speed my walk, and you would only have to return alone.'

'You could ask me to spend the night at Fairlyden . . .'

'I could . . .' A picture of her grandmother's face flashed into her mind. 'But I would rather not. Why are you so keen to meet my family?'

'Why? I told you. Our families must have been friends once. Otherwise why should I have Fairly as part of my own name? I know nothing of my father – and I sense . . . yes, I sense a mystery somewhere. I suspect your grandmother could enlighten me, if she chooses.' There was frustration in his voice – and something more . . . confusion? Hurt even? He reminded Kirsty of a thwarted little boy, for all he was such a man of the world. A little boy with an imaginary grievance? Maybe even a touch of spite? She shivered violently and knew it was not just the freezing fog which chilled her.

'You can't blame me for wanting to find out about my roots – my real roots!' Simon muttered and the underlying bitterness was unmistakable. 'Why should I remind Miss Lizzie of your Uncle Billy? Ask yourself that instead of being angry with me,' he called, as she walked away from him.

'I'm not angry,' her voice came back to him eerily through the fog, 'just disenchanted.'

Simon F. Guillyman winced. He had been attracted to Kirsty Fairly from the moment he had watched her trying in vain to start her car – but it was more than the usual attraction which made him want to conquer her proud spirit – and for the first time in his life a woman had rejected him.

Kirsty stepped briskly along the road but her mind was occupied with Simon's last remark. Had Miss Lizzie really thought he resembled her Uncle Billy? She couldn't even remember her wandering uncle so it must be years since Miss Lizzie had seen him. According to her grandmother Uncle Billy had been a mere boy of thirteen or so when Mistress Guillyman left Muircumwell to sail to America. Even if there was some mystery in Simon's family she was sure it could not concern her. Another thought tormented her. Had Simon really found her so appealing or was it only her name which had attracted him from that very first meeting outside Lizzie Whiteley's Store. Had he ever liked her for herself? She shivered. Her dress would be ruined by the time she had walked the four miles or more to Fairlyden, but she knew instinctively that her mother would prefer her to ruin her dress than lose her reputation – and maybe ruin her whole life.

She stopped suddenly. Simon had talked of taking her back to America. Tonight he had demonstrated his desire. But he had never mentioned marriage . . . She remembered James's concern again. However bitterly they might have quarrelled, she knew he would never wish her harm. Did Simon wish her harm beneath his charming manner? She did not know how Simon's mind worked. Maybe he did not know himself. Only one thing was clear – she would never invite him to Fairlyden now.

Eighteen

Kirsty had been numb with cold and exhaustion by the time she stumbled into the house and sought the blessed warmth of the big Aga in the kitchen. The small pan of hot milk which her mother had left on the edge had long since evaporated to a thick yellow skin and she was too exhausted to make any more, or to eat the plate of sandwiches. The kettle was simmering gently and she filled the extra stone pig which Beth had left in readiness.

'Oh Mother, I dinna deserve your love and kindness,' she muttered to herself and her eyes filled with tears of weariness.

It seemed as though she had been in bed no time at all when she heard her mother and then her father going downstairs, ready for the morning milking. It was an effort to drag her aching limbs out of bed and face the cold winter's morning and for the first time since she left school she was the last into the byre. She knew by the expressions on Anna's and Lucy's faces that she must look as terrible as she felt.

As soon as breakfast was finished Logan drew Kirsty into the small room which opened off both the hall and the kitchen and she knew at once that his grave expression meant trouble. The room was usually cosy, used for reading, doing the accounts, writing up the pedigrees, for knitting and sewing beside the fire. This morning there was no fire yet and the freezing fog still hid the view of the hills and fields beyond the garden.

'I heard ye come in frae the dance, Kirsty. It was very late. Too late.' Logan's face registered love and anxiety but his grey eyes were stern. 'Your mother and I are worried about your friendship with Simon Guillyman.'

'I'm sorry, Father . . .'

'You know your mother's happiness means more to me than anything in the world. I will not have—'

'The car broke down and I had a long walk home in the fog. But it is not just last night, is it, Father?'

'No. Mr Guillyman owns the Muircumwell land and ye ken

well enough how much we need it, especially now we're spending so much money extending the byre and making the new dairy. I'm not sure I understand Guillyman's reason for coming to Scotland. I'm no' sure that I trust him.' Logan frowned. He had no real reason to mistrust Simon Guillyman. He did not even know the man. It was purely instinct, but he knew Beth felt the same. 'I dinna want Mr Guillyman using ye as some kind o' pawn, Kirsty. He is too old for you. He's a man o' the world. Above all his home is in America and he'll go back there one day! Aah, Kirsty, lassie – we want ye to be happy! But we dinna want to lose ye . . .'

'I can promise you I have no intention of going to America, Father. I didna understand the real reason for Simon's visit to Scotland either.' She frowned. There was a troubled, almost boyish look in her father's earnest gaze and she remembered he was only in his late thirties himself. He ought to be enjoying himself still instead of worrying about a grown-up daughter and a future for his teenage son. 'I think I should speak to Mother.'

Logan hesitated. 'Aye well . . . I suppose it's aye a good thing to talk things over with your mother, lassie. Just so long as ye dinna make her any more anxious than she is already.'

'I won't, Father, I promise.'

Logan nodded. He found it hard to scold Kirsty and indeed he had seldom had reason to.

Beth listened to Kirsty's account of her evening with Simon Guillyman, and once she understood the reason for her late return her equanimity astonished her daughter.

'I'm only thankful ye had the sense to come home,' Beth muttered fervently. 'I'd make ye a dozen new dresses, but I'd never forgive myself if I let ye ruin your life. As to Simon Guillyman's search for his roots – there is little anyone can tell him for certain if his mother is dead. She is the one he should have pressed for information. And why should it matter to him anyway?' she asked with a trace of anger. 'He inherited the Guillyman money and even the estate is his – though he's neglected it long enough, leaving it in the care o' Trustees who never come near so long as the rent comes in! I dinna see why he needs to pester anyone. Your grandmother can only speculate . . .'

'Granny has reason to speculate then?' Kirsty's eyes widened.

'I think so.' Beth sighed.

'Do you think that is the reason why she was ill? So soon

after she knew of Simon's arrival? Has Granny confided in you, Mother?'

'Yes. She's tougher than we thought now that she's got over the shock o' Mr Guillyman appearing out o' the blue. She seems quite prepared to talk to him now. She's a wise woman and maybe she can help him to sort things out in his own mind – even if she canna give him any facts. I just hope he doesna have any peculiar ideas about seeking revenge for his imaginary wrongs. None o' us can be held responsible if Mr Fairly dallied with his mother.'

'Mr Fairly!'

'I think . . .' Beth's voice sank to a whisper. 'Your Granny thinks it may be possible . . . that Mr William Fairly seduced his partner's widow,' she finished hurriedly, her cheeks pink as she glanced at her daughter. Then she hurried from the room before Kirsty could ask any further questions. Beth hated gossip.

When Kirsty received a letter, specially delivered by a young messenger boy, shortly before midday, she read it with a relief Simon would have found distinctly unflattering.

'Simon has been invited to join a skiing party. He is leaving for Switzerland tomorrow,' she announced when she had read it. Her voice was carefully devoid of expression but she guessed Simon would be travelling with Miss Marshman and her brother. 'When the skiing is over he intends to travel for some months, visiting some of the European cities. He does not expect to return to Scotland until the end of May.'

Willy Taylor, the postman, had recognised Simon's car, abandoned at the foot of the road leading up to Avary Hall, early that morning. He mentioned it to his brother, who in turn mentioned it to Lizzie Whiteley. Lizzie's first concern had been for the occupants.

'Was the car damaged? Miss Kirsty was going to the dancing in Dumfries with Mr Guillyman last night. Could the lassie have been hurt, think ye? It was a terrible night wi' fog!'

'Willie said the car wasna scratched, and there was no sign o' anybody when he went by on his way up to the cottages at the far end o' Muircumwell. I reckon they must hae walked up to the Hall for the night. It would be the nearest house. Anyway the car had gone by the time Willie came back round, so there couldna have been much wrong with it.'

'Surely Miss Kirsty—' Lizzie bit off the rest of her sentence and frowned fiercely. For all Mr Guillyman's charming manners, she thought it was unlikely that he would accompany Kirsty to Fairlyden on foot and then walk all the way back to Avary Hall in freezing fog.

Her curiosity got the better of her when Simon himself called into the shop later that morning with the intention of asking her to suggest a messenger who would take his letter to Fairlyden. A faintly malicious smile appeared on his handsome face when he caught Miss Lizzie's shrewd eyes fixed upon him with more than a hint of condemnation; he recalled Kirsty's unflattering statement that she was disenchanted with him. He might not stoop to telling a downright lie, but he deliberately allowed Lizzie to believe Kirsty had spent the night at Avary Hall. He grinned as he watched the little spinster's mouth tighten with disapproval before the matter was cast aside and his thoughts returned to the arrangements for his trip to Europe. He had much to do.

He left the shop and found a young boy who was only too willing to walk almost four miles to Fairlyden with his letter in return for two pennies.

The Christmas of nineteen hundred and thirty-seven passed happily enough with the usual family gathering at the 'Fairlyden Big Hoose', as Fairlyside has become known since the original farmhouse had been converted into cottages. Anna reported that James and Miss MacFarlane had driven over from Nithanvale with Christmas presents. Kirsty was disappointed she had not seen James, even though he had been in the company of his half-cousin.

Once again Sadie and Robert Smith were the only members of the family who failed to send Christmas greetings. Beth guessed Sarah was saddened by her daughter's continuing jealousy and resentment over Mr Bradshaw's will. Alex and Emma were firmly of the opinion that the household was happier without her.

'It's a pity Aunt Ellen canna come for Christmas,' Kirsty reflected as she helped her mother make mince pies in the big warm kitchen.

'Aye, Ellen is a fine woman, but she cares too much for her patients to leave them at Christmas. As for your Uncle Billy, I dinna think he'll ever come back frae America, especially now he's building up his ain business with a garage and two omnibuses and cars to hire. He always liked mechanical things, even when he was young.'

The harsh winter weather which ended the year caused a great deal of extra work carting feed to the sheep up on the Westhill land, and the hard frosts delayed the completion of the new dairy and the extension to the byre, but by the end of February the byre was finished at last and a short covered passage made carrying the milk to the new dairy a less irksome task, especially when they wakened one morning to find the snow had returned overnight, making every step a mammoth effort. Even Thomas voted the improvements a great success although he invariably criticised anything which changed his daily routine. Anna laughingly reported that he still grumbled about his new home, though they all knew he was privately very proud of it. He had been heard to boast in great detail about the wonders of the newfangled water closet at the Crown and Thistle after consuming a dram or two.

Despite the demanding work Kirsty was restless. She had neglected many of her former friends since Simon Guillyman came into her life. Although her earlier fascination had been dispelled by a feeling of disillusionment she missed the company and the outings they had shared. She supposed Simon was now being just as attentive to Miss Madeleine Marshman – and probably with more satisfactory results. Most of all she wondered why she had never seen James when he visited his mother and Uncle Thomas. He had not called to see her grandmother after all. She had not seen him since the foggy night of the Christmas Dance.

Spring came suddenly. Logan and Thomas completed the working of the land and the sowing of the corn in record time on account of the mild March weather. Paddy grinned happily and talked of getting the cows out to grass almost as early as he would have done in 'dear old Ireland'.

'Kirsty is restless these days,' Anna remarked to Beth one afternoon as they worked together in one of the hen houses. 'I've seen her riding Marocco up to see the sheep on Westhill and ye'd think the devil himself was after them. I dinna like to see her taking such risks.'

'Aye, I know what ye mean, Anna. I heard Lucy telling her too.' Beth's anxious face broke into a smile. 'Poor Lucy, she still thinks o' Kirsty as the wee bairn she used to look after when she came to Fairlyden as nursemaid. It's such a pity she and Paddy couldna have bairns o' their own.'

'Aye, Lucy would have been a grand mother – but at least they have each other.' There was a wistful sadness in Anna's tone and Beth's face softened. Poor Anna had been widowed so young and now even James, her only son, was away at Nithanvale.

'I wish I still had as much energy as Kirsty!' Anna announced suddenly, brushing aside her brief melancholy. 'She makes me feel old just watching her running o'er yon field, hurrying up the brae wi' her buckets o' mash . . . and tending the broody hens. Lizzie says there's still no new tenants up at Avary Hall?' Anna changed the subject, looking at Beth with bright expectant eyes.

'I believe Mr Guillyman intends to return to the Hall himself in four or five weeks, though he doesna seem to have kept in touch with anybody in Muircumwell.'

'Not even Miss Kirsty? James wondered when they . . .'

'Not even Kirsty,' Beth insisted firmly.

'I see . . .' Maybe that's why the lassie is so restless then, Anna thought, but she knew better than to voice her thoughts aloud.

Two evenings later Beth half believed the recent mention of Simon Guillyman must have conjured him out of the air. She answered the door in reply to a loud knocking and found him standing on the doorstep.

'I'm sorry if I startled you, Mrs Fairly.' He smiled charmingly and Beth's heart sank. She could understand how someone as young and untried as Kirsty might fall under his spell, but the glint in his dark eyes was wary, speculative even, and she had an uneasy feeling that Simon Guillyman's visit spelled trouble. Her usual warm smile was absent, her gentle face less than welcoming. Only her inherent courtesy made her invite him into her home.

'I came to see your husband. Is he around?'

'Logan!' Beth stared at her visitor, her heart pounding, her mind reeling. 'If it's about Kirsty . . .'

'It concerns Kirsty, naturally, Mrs Fairly.'

'I see. Logan will be in for his supper in about twenty minutes. The milking was finished before I came back doon to the house. They're just foddering the kie. There's the horses to be seen to, and . . .' Beth knew she was chattering and she took a grip on herself and sighed. 'Maybe ye'd care to wait in here?'

She showed him into the sitting room. Then Beth's natural hospitality got the better of her. 'Would ye like to share our meal . . . Mr Guillyman?'

'I should be delighted to dine with you. Thank you. But please call me Simon . . .' He gave Beth another devastating smile and she scurried back to the kitchen where Sarah was rocking gently in the wooden chair in the corner beside the Aga.

'I must be crazy!' Beth pressed her hands to flushed cheeks.

'Whatever's set you into such a fluster, Beth?'

'Mr Guillyman's back! He wasna due to return for weeks yet! He wants to see Logan..I've asked him to share our meal!'

'Well, that's all right – isn't it?'

'But he willna be used to dining on bread and cheese and jam and scones – even if they are all freshly baked this very day! O-oh . . .' she wailed softly. 'What'll he think o' us, and Kirsty? She'll . . .'

'Be as surprised as we are, I shouldna wonder,' Sarah murmured dryly and rose stiffly to her feet, taking a firm grasp on the walking stick which she had used regularly since her illness. 'Now, lassie, you pour Mr Guillyman a wee dram o' Logan's best whisky and I'll bring the silver tray that belonged to Crispin's father. Dinna panic. He's only a man after all, and I'll wager he doesna get such fine cooking as yours from that gardener's wife up at Avary Hall.'

'Maybe no' but he'll have been dining in all the cities in Europe. We had our dinner at midday but he'll no' be used to that, or having our simple fare of an evening.'

'Well there's good chicken soup, Beth, and you have freshly baked bread and your own butter.'

'Aye . . .' Beth brightened. 'And there's liver frae the pig killing in the larder and the black puddings and white puddings we made. I could cut some slices frae the ham I was saving frae the last pig, if I stand on the stool to reach.'

Sarah smiled at her daughter-in-law's relief. 'And there's an apple pie. I'm sure even Mr Guillyman will consider you've made him a meal fit for a king.'

'I could skim a wee jug o' cream frae the milk . . . or maybe he'd prefer cheese and oatcakes, d'ye think?' she asked uncertainly.

'Offer him a choice, lassie, and dinna worry. Mr Simon Guillyman will see that we have no need to be ashamed o' the way we live at Fairlyden – even if we are just farming folk who work for a living!' There was a grim determination in Sarah's face and the light of battle in her fine brown eyes – something Beth had rarely seen since her husband's death.

'Ye – ye'll not let him upset ye? I-I mean if he asks questions and—'

'Dinna worry, Beth. I shall deal well enough with Mr Guillyman. I may be old but I'm not done yet. Now bring him that whisky, lassie.'

Half an hour later Sarah rose to her feet and crossed the small room to stand at the window, gazing up the short stretch of track from the steading as the bright April day slowly faded. She stood with her back to Simon but her voice was still clear and remarkably steady.

'So, you see, Mr Guillyman, that is all I can tell you – no proof, just circumstantial evidence I believe they call it. I can say this though – whatever your roots, you have no need to be ashamed of either the Guillyman or the Fairly blood. If you are bitter because you believe secrets have been hidden from you, then ask yourself whether your mother did it out of malice or out of kindness. I think you'll find she did it in your own best interests – and maybe . . . maybe even out of kindness to me and my bairns,' she added so softly that her companion only just heard the words. He stared at her silent figure, outlined by the evening light streaming through the window. He had not considered Mrs Fairly's point of view. He had not considered anyone else might have reason to feel resentful. He rose and crossed the firelit room to Sarah's side. He put a tentative hand on her shoulder.

'I'm sorry. I did not mean to distress you. I thought only of myself after I found the letter hidden in my mother's desk. I had had suspicions for a long time that my mother had some sort of secret. The letter was from – from your late husband – Mr William Fairly, that is. He wanted money to expand the business of Fairly and Guillyman. It was not clear exactly what his relationship with my mother had been, but there was . . . something more familiar in the phrases he used than those of a business partner. Please, Mrs Fairly, look at me. Tell me . . .' The pressure of his hand on Sarah's shoulder increased involuntarily and she felt his tension communicating itself to her. She turned her head slowly. 'Look at me and tell me . . . Do *you* think I am William Fairly's son?'

Sarah held the dark eyes which seemed so familiar. For a moment she felt her chest tighten and her heartbeats quicken.

162

She looked back down the years and remembered. Simon Guillyman had been incapable of siring a child in the last months of his life, and probably even before that. She remembered how . . . 'Was William Fairly my father?'

'Yes . . .' Her voice was barely a whisper. 'Yes, I believe you are William's son. You resemble him in many ways – your manner, as well as your fine dark eyes . . .' Her own gaze moved slowly over his face, feature by feature '. . . his mouth too . . . passionate, demanding – not always wise, or even strong I think.' Simon flushed and released his grip on her shoulder. 'William was a good man but he was not a good business man and he had ideas before his time.'

'And Simon Guillyman, was he a good man?'

'I did not know him. The Guillymans moved in different circles to my own family. He was very ill towards the end and your mother nursed him herself. She must have loved him very much, but they both longed for children. I met your mother only once.' Sarah laid her hand on Simon's arm. 'I do not think she was a bad woman. You should remember her without rancour. If she kept a secret locked within her heart, then it was hers – and only hers – to keep.' Sarah turned away from his intent brown eyes and stared out of the window. Suddenly her expression lightened and she smiled warmly. 'See, there's Logan and Kirsty coming across the grass from the steading. The day's work is finished. I expect they'll be hungry.' Simon followed her gaze and Sarah heard his indrawn breath. Kirsty was smiling up at her father, pointing to something in the field. They paused, chatted a moment then both threw back their heads in spontaneous laughter. Sarah found herself smiling too. Kirsty's happiness was always infectious. She made everyone feel younger.

'She has such a blithe spirit,' she murmured softly to her companion. 'I hope you will go back to America now, Mr Guillyman?'

'Simon . . .' he corrected gravely. 'I came here with the best of intentions but—' He broke off as the door opened to admit Beth, with Luke following close behind her. Luke looked pale and tired as he always did after a day's concentrated studying followed by the train journey from Dumfries and the four mile cycle ride from the station.

'Meet my son, Luke, Mr Guillyman.' Beth drew Luke forward, but her anxious glance flew to Sarah in search of any signs of strain. Sarah guessed she had brought Luke in case she needed rescuing from an unwelcome interrogation. She smiled reassuringly. Beth relaxed, her blue eyes reflecting her relief. Sarah turned her attention back to her grandson and Simon Guillyman, surprised to find Luke plying the older man with eager questions about his recent travels in Europe, and Germany in particular.

'Luke's teachers say he is very quick at learning foreign languages, and I suppose he wants to know about the men and women who speak them,' Beth explained with apologetic pride. 'Please excuse him if he asks too many questions. We will be ready to eat soon.'

Nineteen

Kirsty was surprised to find that Simon had returned from his travels already, but she was angered by his intrusion into her home without warning or invitation.

'Is Granny with him? Is she upset?' she asked urgently when her mother informed her of their unexpected visitor. She discarded her outdoor clothes and the clogs she wore for working in the byre and dairy.

'She doesna seem perturbed. Kirsty . . .' Beth frowned. 'Mr Guillyman says he is here to see your father . . . Is he—? Are you still—?'

'There is nothing between us, Mother. Simon probably asked for Father as the head of the house but I suppose he really wanted to talk to Granny. I think that is all he has wanted from the beginning.'

'Maybe ye're right, lassie,' Beth acknowledged with relief.

Kirsty was composed, though wary, when she greeted Simon in person.

The meal started pleasantly enough. Simon was genuine in his praise of Beth's cooking but he soon took over the conversation, describing the food and clothes, buildings and people he had encountered on his travels.

'I have visited one ancient city after another, but in many there is such an air of unease I found myself glancing over my shoulder too. It is worst in the railway stations and other public places. People glance furtively at their fellow passengers and everywhere there seems to be mistrust. Adolf Hitler has been allowed too much power already, or so it seems to me. He was never challenged when he occupied the Rhineland two years ago. Now he has invaded Austria. His influence is felt far and wide. I talked to many who fear he will not stop until he rules the whole of Europe.'

'What d'ye mean by that?' Logan demanded, drawing himself up erectly, his eyes alert.

'It is not only the German Jews who are fleeing.' Simon

looked Logan in the eye. 'I tell you there are many who are afraid of this man, Hitler. The man is greedy for power, or insane – or maybe both. Even German women and children are being drilled in preparation for war and I am convinced the situation cannot be resolved without one.'

'War,' Logan breathed. 'No! No, there can not be another war. There canna be! Man, ye mustna say such things!' Beth glanced at her husband's white face with concern. She knew how clearly he recalled the dreadful years when so many of his fellow men had been slaughtered like animals – and with less dignity than animals even – in the name of war and to save their country. He had come close to death himself and, like millions of others, he still suffered from the effects. No wonder he refused to contemplate the possibility of another war. She did not want him to be upset.

'I think perhaps ye're exaggerating, Mr Guillyman, and it isna kind, or wise.'

'Mistress Fairly! I've seen with my own eyes, heard with my own ears! If you do not believe me, then consider the preparations your own government is making. In London I heard that children are being issued with gas masks. Mr Eden, your foreign secretary, resigned his position, did he not? And why? Because he shares such views as mine. Mr Chamberlain does not appear to see the danger. He is too eager to please Mussolini and Hitler!'

'He will deter Hitler by increasing Britain's strength. That is why the government is building more aeroplanes. And Mr Chamberlain has promised to defend Belgium and France if Hitler should threaten them,' Beth argued desperately.

'But, Mother, he has not made such a promise to Czechoslovakia and . . .'

'Luke?' Beth stared at her son in astonishment and Luke flushed as all eyes centred on him. He rarely joined even the most ordinary conversation. 'I-I . . . We discuss things at school you see, Mother. One of my teachers came frae Germany. He agrees with Mr Guillyman.' He glanced apologetically at his father. 'He is convinced there must be a war . . . He says we should all learn his language, in case the Germans come. He says we shall all need to fight.'

'No, Luke! No! Ye're only sixteen, laddie! Ye're too young to think o' such things. They're filling your head with nonsense!' Beth cried out in real distress. Logan frowned angrily from his son to Simon Guillyman.

'Dinna upset yourself, Beth,' he said quietly. 'Luke, there's no truth in such talk.'

'I'm afraid you're wrong,' Simon interrupted. 'Your own government has already appealed for half a million volunteers in case of air raids over Britain.'

Kirsty bit her lip. She knew this was true. She had heard her cousin Cameron from Mains of Muir talking of joining what he called the 'Air Raid Precaution' volunteers.

Simon Guillyman leaned back in his chair and looked directly across at Logan with his mouth set, his dark eyes slightly narrowed. Watching him, Sarah felt he reminded her more of William than her own sons had ever done – but it was William when he wanted something and did not care to be thwarted. She knew instinctively that Simon Guillyman wanted something now and she felt a sense of foreboding. 'Well, Mr Fairly, I do not intend to take any chances. I intend to dispose of everything that remains of the Guillyman Estate in Britain, including the land which you presently rent from the Guillyman Trust.' His statement was greeted with stunned silence.

'You mean you will sell the land when our lease is finished – in two years time? You do not intend to renew it?' Logan asked at last.

'I intend to sell it now. At once. I shall return to America as soon as I have instructed my lawyers. It was one of my reasons for coming to Scotland anyway, though I had not expected it would be a matter for such haste then . . .' His dark glance seemed drawn to Sarah. She knew the other reason for which he had crossed the Atlantic in person. 'If you have any sense you will sell your own land and emigrate to America yourself, Mr Fairly. I understand you have a brother over there who would no doubt help you settle in a new country. Indeed,' his eyes moved to Kirsty. 'I shall be pleased to offer my own assistance.'

'Emigrate to America!'

'Sell Fairlyden!'

'Leave our home!'

Simon looked at the startled faces, the shocked, accusing eyes.

'If you don't sell now, you'll be left with nothing! When Hitler turns his eyes on Great Britain it will be great no longer. The Nazis will take over everything – not only your land and money, but your women and children – your . . .'

'The Germans will never conquer Britain, I tell you! Never!'

Logan was rigid with anger. '*If* there is a war Britain will fight again – and win again! All those thousands of men cannot have died for their country and be betrayed now!' He pushed a distracted hand through his hair. 'Though I pray to God it will never come to that . . .' he breathed.

'You'll be lucky if you escape with your lives,' Simon almost sneered but his gaze moved to Kirsty, fixed on her face, on the proud jaw, the glinting eyes. 'Come to America while you can.'

'Ye speak like a traitor!' Logan growled. He pushed back his chair and stood up, his face grim and pale. 'I'll ask you to leave this house now, Mister Guillyman!'

'You're a fool!' Simon rose too, his face dark with anger. 'You will lose everything! That includes your precious Fairlyden! I came to give you the benefit of my advice, my first-hand experience! You have—'

'Fairlyden belongs to Kirsty now,' Logan interrupted coldly. He looked at her and Kirsty saw the question in his blue eyes – and the lurking anxiety.

'It belongs to all of us. It is our home. You know I would never sell Fairlyden, Father.'

'This place belongs to you?' Simon stared at her composed face, then turned to Sarah. 'But I thought . . . You said William Fairly . . .'

Sarah looked back at him steadily. She had tried to spare him because she had felt some sympathy towards him, now all her sympathy had vanished.

'When William died there were debts to be paid, many of them from the business of Fairly and Guillyman. I paid those debts, every last farthing, including money to your mother. To do so I had to sell Fairlyden. So if you came here expecting to claim more money, Mr Guillyman—'

'That was not my intention!' Simon denied swiftly, but there was a flicker in his dark eyes and his gaze did not quite meet her own. He frowned and his mouth hardened as he turned once more to Logan. 'As I said, the property belonging to the Guillyman Trust will be sold immediately. If you wish to remain as tenant you will have to negotiate another lease with the new owners.'

'The present lease has two more years to run!'

'Such a burden would reduce the value of the land!' Simon protested indignantly. 'No one else would want it – not with the pittance of a rent you have been paying. The trustees should have increased the rent long ago.'

'Then they would have had to maintain the land,' Logan retorted sharply. 'I've no intention of giving up the lease until it expires so ye'll need to wait two years if ye want to be rid o' me as a "burden", as ye put it!' Despite Logan's forceful assertion he frowned anxiously as he turned aside. Beth had rarely seen him so upset and angry. If they lost the Muircumwell land they would have to reduce the cows by at least a third, instead of expanding to fill the new byre as they had planned. She thought of the money they had spent on the buildings.

'I shall see my lawyers first thing tomorrow,' Simon declared and his tone was almost a threat. Kirsty had also noticed her father's pale set face, his ragged breathing, and clenched fists. He rarely got so excited and she knew it was not good for his heart. 'I will show you out, Simon.' Her eyes were cold as she ushered him into the hall.

At the door he turned to her and she knew he intended to take her in his arms and kiss her, in spite of the strife he had caused in her family in the past hour. She thrust out her hand stiffly and saw him raise one dark brow in that quizzical, charming way he had, but she was immune to his charm and sophistication now. He took her hand, but he held it firmly.

'Goodbye, Simon.'

'I mean it, you know. I shall sell the land.'

'Yes, I know you will, but you may find it is not so easy as you imagine, with or without the burden of a tenant. Most landowners are having too much of a struggle to survive to purchase new land and there are no buildings on the Muircumwell land to attract a farmer wishing to start up. No doubt your own farm in America is prospering at the expense of British farmers. You can't have your bread well buttered on both sides of the Atlantic.'

'I'll take what I can get now, rather than leave it to be taken over by the Nazis. Kirsty . . . I don't think I shall ever return to Scotland.'

'Then I'll wish you a safe journey.'

'My, you're a cool little madam! Still, I can't help wishing I'd been the one to awaken all that dormant passion in you. I suppose you've heard your grandmother believes William Fairly was my father, but I don't feel like your uncle, I can tell you that! I suppose there's no chance of you seeing sense and coming back to America with me?'

'No.'

'Even if the Germans don't take over Great Britain, your father will certainly have to pay a lot more rent to a new landlord. I might agree to let him keep the tenancy indefinitely if you come back with me?'

'That's blackmail! And it will not work with me! Good night, Simon, and goodbye!' She quivered inwardly as his mouth tightened and his dark eyes glittered, but he turned and strode to his car without another word. She knew he would not take kindly to being thwarted. She closed the door quickly.

Kirsty was dismayed by the discussion which was taking place when she returned to the dining room. Her mother had not even begun to clear the table and Beth always liked everything tidy as soon as a meal was finished.

'I just wish I hadna spent good money improving the cottages and extending the byre,' Logan sighed. 'I might have been able tae buy the Muircumwell land myself if I'd kenned what was in Mr Guillyman's mind. We should have got it cheaper as existing tenants, like James MacFarlane at Nithanvale and Alex at the Mains. If we lost sixty-five acres of grassland we shall certainly have tae cut down the number of cows. Paddy and Lucy might have to look for another place.'

'Oh, Logie, surely it willna come to that! Lucy's been with us since Kirsty was born! Anyway Mr Guillyman canna make ye give up the tenancy for another two years, can he?'

'No-o, at least I dinna think so, but a new landlord could make things difficult if he didna want a tenant.'

'Are you serious about buying the land yourself, Logan?' Sarah asked, grasping her walking stick with both hands and hoisting herself to her feet to move nearer the fire.

'Oh, I'd certainly have tried if I hadna spent every penny we had in the bank on improvements.'

'Then I've a suggestion to make.' Kirsty looked at her grandmother's bright alert eyes and determined mouth. It was hard to believe she would be eighty in September.

'I've never needed all the money your grandfather left me, thanks to you all looking after me so well. It would please me to know you were buying the land that used to belong to Avary Hall and the old Muircumwell Mill . . .' Her eyes took on a reminiscent look for a moment, then her voice was brisk again. 'You'd need a loan from the bank to make up the rest, but maybe Mr Sellers would agree if you offer your herd as security . . .?'

'I could certainly ask him,' Logan agreed enthusiastically, 'If ye're sure about us using your money for the deposit on the land, Mother?' His eyes were alight with plans already.

'I'm sure.' Sarah smiled. 'If James MacFarlane can manage to buy two hundred acres at Nithanvale, then you can surely buy the Muircumwell land.'

'James has a struggle to make ends meet though, according to Anna,' Beth said doubtfully. 'We havena seen him for months, have we, Logan?'

Logan shook his head absently, still considering his mother's proposition. He liked the idea of buying the Muircumwell land and being able to improve it over the years as his Grandfather Logan had done with Fairlyden. It would be a challenge and he would be sure his own family would benefit . . .

'If – and I mean if – there is a war,' he frowned, 'then the price o' land will rise.'

'Aye and the price o' milk and eggs and everything else. Our own farmers will be needed then.' Sarah's tone was slightly bitter.

'How can you be so sure, Granny?'

'Because that's what happened in the last war, though Britain was nearly starved into surrender before the government got things sorted out. The ships couldna get through to bring in supplies from other countries you see, lassie.'

'But this will be a different war, Granny.' Luke spoke diffidently but with a peculiar certainty. Because he spoke so seldom they all considered his words seriously. Beth looked worried.

'I dinna like all these thoughts o' war ye have, laddie. Perhaps ye shouldna listen to your teachers, especially the one frae Germany. Maybe he's like Mr Guillyman? Just trying to frighten us for his ain purpose. Maybe he wants to stir up trouble and put fear o' war into our minds and hearts.'

'Oh no, Mother. Mr Spielmann doesna want to return to Germany. He hates what is happening to his country and to his people! He lost most of his money. His son was killed and his wife is dead too.'

'When did he tell ye all this, Luke?' Logan frowned. 'And why? Ye're just one o' his pupils, aren't ye?'

'He – his son was the same age as me. He has no one now. Sometimes he gives me extra lessons – conversation, in German. He – he . . .' Luke flushed hotly. 'He says I'm the best student he ever had. He needs to talk tae somebody!'

'Of course he does, laddie,' Beth said gently. 'Dinna get upset. We're just concerned for ye, that's all.'

'Well, I hope Father is right. I hope there'll never, ever be a war!' Luke declared. 'It all sounds so – so horrible!' He shuddered.

'Are ye sure this teacher o' yours doesna frighten ye?' Logan asked.

'No . . . b-but one day he – he was distressed. He talked a lot. It would have been his son's birthday. He – he's a Jew, Father.' Luke looked anxiously at his parents.

'Well, there are good Jews and bad, I suppose, just the same as in every other religion, laddie.' It was Sarah who spoke and her tone was brisk. 'Only you're too sensitive. Dinna dwell on all the man tells you. He's just unburdening himself because he doesna have anybody else and you're a good listener.'

Luke nodded and smiled at his grandmother. A close bond had grown up between them since her illness and she still liked to have Luke read to her when she was tired. But she did not feel tired now. Crispin had always told her she thrived on challenge and just for a brief spell she felt the blood pulsing through her veins again and secretly she longed for Logan to own the Muircumwell land and even the old derelict mill. It had been the place where her own father had first found work when he and her mother came as penniless strangers to Fairlyden; it was also the place where her greatest friend, Beatrice, had spent her childhood and the place where her husband, William Fairly, had set up in business. To Sarah it seemed fitting that things should come full circle. 'Well, Logan, what do you think? Will you buy the Muircumwell land and the old mill?'

'I shall certainly see the manager at the bank. If he can arrange a loan I'll ask Mr Carsewell for advice about the lease and deeds.' Logan glanced affectionately at his son. 'Maybe ye'll change your mind about studying, Luke, and become a farmer one day. This will be an investment for your future, laddie.'

Luke did not answer. His early terror of cattle had scarcely abated at all and he hated the thought of rearing the young lambs and pigs, only to kill them for their meat! I shall never be a farmer, he thought vehemently, but he would not distress his father by speaking out loud.

One day he would tell his mother that he wanted to be a

minister like the Reverend Morrison. He did not think she would be too disappointed, not like his father. After all she still taught at the Sunday School herself and she had taught him to share her faith. She would break the news gently to his father at the proper time.

Twenty

When Logan kept his appointment with the manager of his bank in Annan he felt the man considered him hopelessly improvident.

'I should be failing in my duty, Mr Fairly, if I aided you in such foolishness in these uncertain times. Indeed the times are not merely uncertain; for small farmers like yourself they are catastrophic. Borrowing money to buy land indeed! Such a scheme would be doomed to failure from the start. No one is buying land, not even the wealthy and well-established landowners.'

His small eyes glinted almost triumphantly behind his steel-rimmed spectacles and even his round bald head seemed to take on an extra gleam as he sat behind his massive oak desk. He glanced down at his clasped hands, studied the stiff white cuffs peeping from his dark pinstriped sleeves, but when Logan did not take the hint that the interview was ended he looked up sharply and reached pointedly for a pen in the ornate brass inkstand.

Logan's jaw set. He had been beset with qualms and uncertainties on his way into town but now this pompous little man's opposition seemed to sweep them all away. He was unaware that he had inherited a streak of stubborn determination from Bert Bradshaw, the grandfather he had never known, but who had succeeded in dragging himself from the gutter unaided in worse times than these.

'Ye've never visited my farm, have ye, Mr Sellers? Maybe ye've never visited any o' the farms in these parts, for all ye have so many farming clients? Ye wouldna know whether I'm a good farmer or no', and—'

'Figures are my business, Mr Fairly! Animals are yours. I know that you had a satisfactory sum in your account last year and this year there is next to nothing. I cannot . . .'

'But I havena squandered the money! We've been saving all we could to pay for improvements. We've finished them now – aye and paid for them.'

'Improvements!' The manager did not even try to hide his disbelief and Logan's eyes flashed angrily.

'We have made the old house into two good cottages for our men, aye and installed running water and water closets,' he said proudly. 'We've extended the byre and built a new dairy. If I'd kenned Mr Guillyman was going to arrive frae America and wind up the Guillyman Trust like this I'd have saved my money and bought the extra land first, but we've been tenants o' that land since it was let and there was never a whisper o' change until now. We need to keep the byre full o' milking cows to justify the changes we've made. I tell ye it's essential I dinna lose that land adjoining Fairlyden. I admit it still needs a lot o' draining to make it as good as our own land, but it's a lot better than when I took it over and I could improve it even more if it was mine.'

'And I'm telling you, Mr Fairly, that there's nothing in your bank account either to improve or buy anything! Therefore you are not a suitable client to be asking for a loan! You do not even have a deposit!'

'My mother, Mistress Bradshaw, had offered me all the money in her account as a deposit. I wouldna take all of it, but I shall ask her to move her account to another bank and I shall do likewise.' He jumped up and was halfway to the door.

'Er . . . don't leave yet, Mr Fairly,' Sellers muttered swiftly. He rubbed his shiny pate. 'Er . . . sit down again, won't you?' Logan stood where he was, his fingers clenched on the rim of his best bowler hat, his square jaw set. Was the man afraid he would lose custom? Maybe business wasn't much better for bankers than it was for farmers and all the other small businessmen in the area.

'Please, sit down again, Mr Fairly? Maybe you could tell me more of your plans, though I still think it would be unwise to borrow money to buy land when so many farmers have already gone bankrupt.'

'I've paid rent for both Fairlyden and the Muircumwell land since I returned frae France and things canna get any worse than they've been for the past fifteen years. I should have no rent to pay if the land was mine.'

'No, you would have the bank to pay instead!' Sellers reminded him triumphantly. 'With interest!'

'Sometimes it's better to swim against the tide – so long as ye think ye can cope with the currents,' Logan insisted stubbornly. 'In nineteen eighteen the government was full o' promises to farmers, telling us they'd guarantee the prices for all the crops we could grow, promising to control imports! Ye must know they've done just the opposite, Mr Sellers. Even biding here inside your ain four walls ye canna be ignorant o' such matters . . .' Logan waved an expressive arm at the offending ochre-coloured walls which seemed to close in on him. 'Well, I didna listen to the promises. I've done the things I kenned I could do best, and the kind o' farming that suited Fairlyden land and our wet climate. It's cows and milk and hard work that have helped us keep our head above water at Fairlyden when so many others have gone under. Ye're right, nobody wants to buy land just now, but surely that should make it cheaper? What's more, I have the lease on the Muircumwell land for another two years and Mr Guillyman is scared up to his eyes that the Germans'll take it away frae him. He canna wait two months to sell, even less two years!'

'You are not afraid the Germans will take it away from you then, Mr Fairly?'

'If there is a war the British will fight again, I'm convinced o' that, aye and win again,' he added in a low voice. 'The government owes that to all the brave laddies that gave life and limb for British freedom the last time.'

Mr Sellers nodded and bowed his head. When he looked up his eyes were no less wary but at least he had lost his earlier contempt. 'So you are determined to buy this land one way or another?'

'I am. I have a good herd o' pedigree Ayrshires I can offer as security to your bank.'

'Cattle die of so many diseases, or so it seems to me. We should require better security than animals.'

'Better?' Logan stared in dismay. 'But they're all I have. My life's work . . .'

'You have the Fairlyden land now surely? Of course even with that I should need to discuss it with my fellow directors, but I think they may be agreeable if we have a bond over the whole area of the land you will own.'

'Aah.' Logan's brow creased anxiously. 'Fairlyden belongs to my daughter now. It was put in trust when she was a bairn. Kirsty is twenty-one now and legally the farm is hers.'

'I see. Well, Mr Fairly, if your daughter has as much faith in you as your mother appears to have, and if you are sure you are doing the wisest thing for all your family, then you will find a solution. I must warn you, your daughter will need to sign an agreement which would give the bank prior claim to the farm of Fairlyden if you get into difficulties. There will be no going back.'

Kirsty was only too eager to sign away her inheritance if it was her parents' wish. Ever since her grandfather's death she felt she had usurped her father's right to Fairlyden and now her guilt was eased. Nothing the bank manager said could shake her faith in her beloved father. In the end the transaction was concluded with remarkable speed. Logan saw Simon Guillyman only once, and that was in the presence of Mr Carsewell, his lawyer. Kirsty did not see him at all. He had moved from Avary Hall two days after his visit to Fairlyden and no one knew where he was staying prior to his return to America. The Hall had not been sold because there were no buyers to be found. The furniture had been removed by strangers.

'It all looks forlorn and sort o' neglected already,' Lizzie Whiteley remarked to Beth when she collected her groceries the following week. 'Thomas and Anna walked up wi' me last Sunday afternoon to take a look. The gardener has moved out but I dinna think he was doing much while Master Guillyman was away abroad anyway. The grounds are overgrown – no' the way they used to be when we were bairns – mind, we only got a wee peek o'er the dyke then.'

'Well, empty houses always look sad and unloved,' Beth agreed. Privately she was relieved that Simon Guillyman had gone. She had harboured a secret dread that he might exercise his charm on Kirsty and persuade her to go with him to America at the last minute. Whether he knew it or not he was no relation to her, whoever his own father might have been.

Although they now had a debt at the bank for the first time in their lives, Beth and Logan felt surprisingly lighthearted and happy. The Muircumwell land was theirs to farm as they pleased and improve where and when they could in the years ahead.

'How would ye like to visit the Empire Exhibition in Glasgow?' Logan suggested at the beginning of May. 'I was speaking to James MacFarlane at the weekend and he says there will be special trains frae Dumfries.'

It was the first time Beth had been so far from home and she was thrilled by the whole experience, but the moment she knew she would remember all her life was when she saw King

George VI and Queen Elizabeth.

Logan bought her a brand-new, four-piece, walnut bedroom suite with the most elegant dressing table she could ever have imagined. It was to be specially delivered right to their own doorstep when the exhibition was over. Beth had never bought anything that was not absolutely essential in her life. Usually Logan was equally cautious. She was delighted and a little overwhelmed.

'Now I shall be wanting to show it off!' she chuckled softly. 'If Mr Sellers frae the bank hears how extravagant we've been though, he'll think we're very feckless.'

'He'll not think we're that if we make some good sales o' Fairlyden cattle after the Highland Show. Remember it's to be held in Dumfries this year, Beth. It'll never be nearer or more convenient for us. There'll be breeders there frae every part o' Scotland, aye and a good lot frae England when it's so near the Border. I intend to show as many o' our best animals as we can get ready. If other breeders like what we show in the ring, maybe they'll want to see what we have left in the fields. Will ye manage to give some o' them a night's lodging if they need it?'

'Oh aye, I'd do my best, Logan.'

'Some o' them might bring their wives. I'd like ye to be proud o' your home, Beth. I've never bought ye much i' the way o' pretty baubles and ye make finer gowns than any ye could buy in the shop. Maybe this will make up a wee bit,' he added a little anxiously. 'Are ye ever ashamed o' our home, Beth?'

'Oh, Logie! I've never been ashamed o' anything about Fairlyden. In fact every night when I lie beside ye I thank God for my blessings – and most of all for sending ye back to me when I thought ye'd died in France. Nothing – nothing at all matters beside that. I'd live in a cave if that's all we could afford, so long as we were together.'

'I'm a lucky man to have ye, Beth,' Logan murmured gruffly.

Kirsty was happy and enthusiastic when Logan outlined his plans and discussed the animals with her and Paddy in preparation for the Highland Show. It meant a good deal of extra work but she enjoyed it all. She tried not to think of James MacFarlane and the carefree days when he had helped eagerly with the Fairlyden cows. She knew he would also be planning and working to show the Nithanvale cattle at

179

Scotland's most prestigious show.

Only Luke did not look forward to the summer shows.

'It isna as if Father sells the animals after ye've spent all that time making them look better,' he complained to Kirsty. 'And they never get a lot o' money even when they win.' He could never understand his family's intense interest in cattle, which to his untutored eyes looked like peas in a pod. He simply did not believe that each one had a character all of its own, and little idiosyncrasies just like human beings.

'I keep telling ye, laddie, it's the honour o' winning, not the prize,' Logan explained when he overheard his remarks. 'Besides a show is the farmers' shop window. How will folk ken we have good cows at Fairlyden if we dinna let them see them in the show ring!'

Luke was not convinced. He dreaded the show season. All hands were needed to halter the animals and train them to walk correctly. Weeks before the shows began, as the summer evenings lengthened Paddy and Lucy, Kirsty and his father would parade round and round the farm yard leading various animals by their halters. As the cattle grew quieter and more obedient, Anna Whiteley and his mother would join the procession, and even old Thomas would be roped in to help when there were a large number of heifers to be schooled. There would be friendly arguments about the merits of the various animals and bursts of laughter, but Luke never joined in. Once or twice he had crouched in the hayloft and sketched the scene below, but more often he took himself off to one of his favourite spots beside the burn, or up to the high land at Westhill with only the sheep and the curlews for company. He had never lost his love of capturing the changing scenes and he found the peace and the creativity very soothing whenever he was troubled or uneasy.

When the date of an important show drew nearer the cows were groomed and clipped. Some revolted and tried to kick or break away; his father would shout for extra help but Luke invariably made himself scarce on these occasions. Afterwards he always felt guilty and guilt made him unhappy.

Kirsty enjoyed washing the cows from the tips of their lofty horns down to their neat cloven feet; udders were carefully examined for the slightest imbalance, and patted and powdered until they were as near to perfection as Logan and Paddy Kildougan could make them. Then at the eleventh hour came the final selection or rejection. Everyone seemed to share the excitement – everyone except Luke.

On that particular June day in nineteen thirty-eight Kirsty felt a pang of regret that she had been born a girl. She had handled all the animals since they were born; she had helped to feed them and nursed some of them through sickness. When the lorry arrived to take them to the show field some of them were too nervous to step on to the steeply sloping door and it was she who was called upon to coax and encourage them until they found themselves inside. Yet once at the show field respectable women and girls were relegated to the sidelines. Kirsty, dressed in her fine tweed suit with its pleated skirt and her best cream silk blouse, found herself standing beside her mother clasping her neatly gloved hands tensely as the animals were paraded round and round the improvised ring for the judge's inspection. Her heart jumped when she caught sight of James MacFarlane leading round a Nithanvale animal just behind her father. She knew he had seen her too but he seemed to stare straight through her.

'There's James!' her mother exclaimed with pleasure a moment later and gave him a small quick wave. James nodded and smiled back, but Kirsty was convinced he had deliberately avoided her own gaze. She pondered the reason; she had seen him several times in various places, but they had never spoken together since the foggy night in December when he had asked her to dance the polka, talked so eagerly and even kept her on the floor for the next dance. He had seemed more than friendly then. Was he regretting the relaxation of his guard, afraid she had read too much into his conversation? Into the song he had sung softly for her ears alone? Perhaps she had! Certainly she had believed they were friends again. Her face burned. It had been all too easy to forget his half-cousin, Mary MacFarlane. Kirsty glanced around the ring at the gathering crowd of spectators but she saw no sign of Miss MacFarlane.

Almost as though her mother had read her thoughts Beth murmured, 'It's a pity James seems to have no one frae Nithanvale to support him today. This will be his first really important show since he took over. I expect Miss MacFarlane is too busy nursing her grandfather. I believe he's very frail these days. Anna said they dinna expect him to see the summer out and he can scarcely see at all now, puir man! It would be nice if one o' the Nithanvale animals could win the championship for his sake and James's.'

'Oh, Mother,' Kirsty summoned a smile. 'You're supposed to

want Fairlyden cattle to win, not our main rival!'

Beth frowned. 'Surely ye dinna still think o' Nithanvale as being our rival, not now that James has taken over?'

'Why not? James is a MacFarlane! He chose to return to the clan and he's very much part o' Nithanvale now. His loyalties dinna lie with Fairlyden anymore.' She had not noticed that her father and James had already come round the ring again until they halted right in front of them. Her father was frowning and there was no doubt that both he and James must have overheard her comment, but she knew it was the bitterness in her tone which had displeased her father. She stole a glance at James but his face was set and he turned his gaze away and stared at the judge in the centre of the ring.

Nithanvale was placed first in that particular class which meant James would have at least one animal in the championship line-up later in the day. The Fairlyden heifer was only third but her father always accepted the judge's decision pleasantly and he did so now, unlike the man who was placed sixth and glared sullenly at the leading animal from Nithanvale.

'Well, well, if it isna the young MacFarlane i' the ring noo the auld man is din fer! I'll warrant yon beast willna be what it's supposed tae be if it's frae Nithanvale!' he hissed loudly. 'Cheats like yon should be banned frae the show ring.' His neighbour looked embarrassed. The cattle steward had overheard, as of course he had been meant to do. He issued a warning to the offensive exhibitor but the damage was done. Looking at James's pale, set face made Kirsty's contrary heart want to defend and comfort him. Even from where she stood she could see unhappy shadows darkening his greeny-grey eyes, and she knew the pleasure of his minor triumph was spoiled.

There were a great many classes and large numbers of Ayrshire cattle in each one so the judging was a lengthy procedure. The Nithanvale animals did not win any more of the classes and Kirsty wondered if the judge had also overheard the other breeder's remarks and whether he believed the rumours which had tarnished the Nithanvale herd's fine reputation. Kirsty was delighted when the Fairlyden animals succeeded in winning three classes and gaining places in the first four in several others but at the end of the day the supreme championship went to an animal from the famous Bargower herd belonging to a Mr Drummond.

'Och, I'm not displeased with Fairlyden's performance,' Logan assured Kirsty and Beth later. 'Paddy has done well enough with the two young bulls in the other ring as weel. Two men frae Cumberland have been asking if they can visit Fairlyden already. They want to see the dam o' the yearling.'

'Uncle Alex has done well with his horses too,' Kirsty informed him eagerly. 'Cousin Paul will be disappointed if they dinna take the Cawdor Cup back to the Mains tonight!'

It had been a long day since three-thirty that morning and Kirsty yawned hugely as she drove her mother back to Fairlyden in time for the milking. Although it had been a successful day, she was conscious of vague disappointment and she secretly acknowledged it was because James MacFarlane had deliberately avoided her. It was silly to mind, but she did.

Twenty-One

Despite the wet, unsettled weather, which seemed determined to spoil the benefits of the dry spring they had enjoyed, Logan's spirits remained high.

'I'm glad we dinna have too much corn to harvest when it's a season like this though,' he reflected to Kirsty and Paddy Kildougan as they made a dash from the cartshed to the byre, sloshing their way through several puddles and sending the ducks quacking loudly as they waddled to safety. Three geese stuck their heads in the air and watched disdainfully and the hens sought shelter under carts and barrows, looking bedraggled and miserable.

'But this is almost the second week in October and there's still five acres o' oats to be gathered in, Father,' Kirsty reminded him anxiously.

'Aye, but that's better than the thirty-five your Uncle Alex has still to harvest, lassie. I'll bet he's wishing he'd stuck to his own policies instead o' listening to young Cameron. Ach, the laddie does remind me o' your Uncle Billy. He's wanting Alex to buy a tractor now, but no amount o' machines can control the weather. We get a wet harvest in these parts more often than we get a dry one. Aye remember, lassie, Fairlyden grows grass better than anything else, especially in a wet season.'

'Aah, Master Fairly, I'm sure Miss Kirsty knows 'tis true enough, but even the grass suffers in such weather!' Paddy exclaimed, taking off his cap to shake away the rain drops. 'Sure it breaks my heart to see the cows a-tramping it into mud. The ground is like an Irish bog in that Mill Meadow down at Muircumwell. Isn't that so, Miss Kirsty? You were counting the beasts down there yesterday?'

'Yes, I was, Paddy. The bottom half o' Mill field is standing water, Father, especially since the last heavy showers. Some o' the stirks are coughing terribly.'

'Ach, it will be the flukes that are eating at their innards! Wet weather is aye bad for the young animals,' Paddy mourned dolefully. The animals were like a family to him.

'I ken the pastures are all getting sorely tramped, Paddy, but it would have been worse if we hadna managed to buy the sixty-five acres o'er the burn. There would never have been room to keep any o' the stirks. Now we own the Muircumwell land maybe we shall be able to drain half of the Mill Meadow and sweeten it up with some extra lime next year.'

'Aye, there is many an improvement a man can be making when he knows the land will be a-passing unto his own son.' Paddy sighed wistfully.

'Well, in this case I dinna think my son would thank me for it!' Logan commented sadly. 'Luke has no more interest in farming than he had the day he was born.'

'Ach, but Miss Kirsty here is as good as any laddie. My Lucy says she was always a one for the animals. She says ye were in the fields from the day you were born almost, Miss Kirsty.'

Kirsty smiled at the twinkling-eyed little Irishman. 'So they tell me. There was a war on then though. Lucy often tells me how hard Mother worked cultivating the fields with Thomas so they could get the oats sown; there were no men to spare apparently.'

'Mmm, well let us be a-hoping Mr Chamberlain has got it right this time when he says there will be peace for our time.'

'Indeed I hope he has!' Logan added fervently – too fervently, Kirsty thought with a frown. The Prime Minister had been greeted by crowds of relieved and happy people when he appeared on the Palace balcony after his return from Munich, but Luke had been discussing the situation only last night. He knew a surprising amount about the outside world these days, especially considering he was still at school, Kirsty thought. She suspected he talked to his German teacher a great deal more than he talked to his fellow students and he studies the newspapers from cover to cover. He had expressed youthful cynicism about the Prime Minister's achievements, and indeed not all Mr Chamberlain's own colleagues were happy about his appeasement of Herr Hitler either. 'I'm glad I'm a Scot and no' a Czech right now,' Logan muttered, echoing her thoughts.

'Ach well now, we ordinary mortals can not be a-doing anything to change the world out there, I'm thinking, but that nasty-tempered beast of a bull will be a-turning ours upside down if we give him half a chance!'

Logan smiled wryly, welcoming the change of subject. He hated the thought of another war, but deep in his heart he was convinced there would be one the way things were going in Europe. 'Grayson Masterful has been living up to his name, has he, Paddy?' Nothing in the cheerful tone indicated his dread.

'Indeed he has, and Paddy Kildougan is not easily frightened by a dumb-headed bull, and to be sure you know that, Mr Fairly.'

'I do, Paddy. There's none o' our own Fairlyden cattle ye havena coaxed into being as docile as a newborn lamb.'

'But that beast isna frae Fairlyden stock. If you would be asking me, he's spawned by the devil. Yes, sir!'

'Well, I think it would be safer if we took him away frae the cows so that he doesna need to come into the byre with them every night and morning. It's a pity he has such a nasty nature; he's sired some fine calves. We'll put him in a field by himself, well away frae the herd, and away frae the best pastures too. He'll need to work for his food a bit more.'

'Aye, that will get the daftness out of the beast! 'Tis the verra thing for him! Exactly the thing!' Paddy approved with a beam. 'Might I be suggesting we take him up to the small paddock at the foot of the hill, then? He'd be having a stretch o' the burn all to himself for the watering up there. Sure and it's a pretty spot with all those wild flowers. He's a lucky fellow.'

Logan nodded. 'Luke's the one to appreciate the beauty o' the place. I dinna think Grayson Masterful will think much o' flowers, Paddy, but we'll move him tomorrow – or maybe even later today if the rain goes off. Kirsty, ye'll take care not to canter across that wee field on Marocco when ye ride up to the hill to check up on the sheep, will ye, lassie?'

'Have no fear, Father. I'm as wary o' that bad-tempered old bull as Paddy. At least Lucy and I will be able to get the cows in by ourselves again if you're taking him from the herd.'

So Grayson Masterful found himself conned into taking a stroll with two of his many wives later that Friday afternoon. Keeping a close watch were two of the wisest and least fearful old collies which were no longer used for herding the sheep. After the first sharp command from Logan they were quick to nip Masterful's heels if he so much as lowered his long curving horns an inch. Logan and Paddy were each armed with a sharp pronged hayfork but they still kept a careful eye on the bull and hugged the hedge in case they had to make a quick escape. The only problem came when they had to separate him from the two milk cows which had accompanied him. Fortunately the bull was eager to explore his new domain and he failed to notice the two collies depriving him of his companions.

'I expect the poor beasts will be wondering why they had to be walking through two fields, only to turn around and walk straight back again,' Paddy grinned, 'but his lordship would not have come away without at least one of his beautiful ladies to keep him company.'

'Indeed he wouldna!' Logan agreed. 'And I dinna think he'll be too happy when he discovers he only has a few sheep for company either, but I expect he'll calm down in a week or two.'

'Sure and he will, and if he doesna then ol' Paddy will be making a blindfold for him.'

'If he doesna learn to behave himself we'll get rid o' him, Paddy,' Logan declared firmly. 'He may be a well-bred bull, but I wouldna risk anybody's life for him. This is his last chance.'

Logan announced that he and Paddy had moved the bull to the Hillanfoot Field while he was washing his hands at the kitchen sink that evening.

'Well, I'm glad about that!' Beth declared. 'At least we women willna need to wait for you or Paddy to help us bring in the cows now.'

Luke was leaning against the steel towel bar in front of the Aga cooker studying the newspaper, a small frown creasing his smooth forehead. How young and earnest he looks, Logan thought, glancing at his son with affection.

'Have ye had a good week at school, laddie? Ye look tired . . .' If he was disappointed that his only son showed no interest in Fairlyden's affairs he never gave any sign, although Luke often seemed to be in a world of his own, just as he was now; he made no reply, did not even lift his eyes from the printed sheet. Logan sighed. He was thankful Kirsty was so interested in the herd he had spent half a lifetime building up. It was not that he loved his daughter more than his son, but in Kirsty's company Logan felt his own youthful aspirations revitalised by her enthusiasm. She understood his dreams for the future of Fairlyden, just as her mother understood his most private dreams and desires – without the need for words, but with an instinct which forged an unbreakable bond. Sometimes he wondered what sort of man Kirsty would marry. Would he share her interest and knowledge, or would he be jealous – as William Fairly had apparently been of his mother's devotion to Fairlyden? He sighed again.

'What's troubling ye, Logie?' Beth asked softly.

'Och, I'm not troubled – not really. I was just thinking that Kirsty is so like my mother. I hope Fairlyden doesna come between her and her happiness.' Beth frowned slightly; she did not brush away his fears as fanciful.

'You always loved Fairlyden yourself, Logie,' she reminded him gently instead.

'Aye, but I loved ye more, Beth, and I kenned ye cared as much for Fairlyden's future as I did. I'd never have let it come between us, especially if Sadie had stayed.'

Beth nodded. Logan had only confirmed what they both knew already. Their love for each other had always transcended everything else. Privately she wondered if Fairlyden had already come between her daughter and true happiness. She sighed unconsciously, as her husband had done earlier. She would have welcomed James MacFarlane into her little family with genuine fondness. Now it was too late. Old George MacFarlane had died three weeks ago and as far as she knew Nithanvale now belonged entirely to James and his half-cousin. They would probably marry as soon as the period of mourning had passed. James had freely admitted to feeling deep affection for Mary MacFarlane and it made sense that they should marry and carry on together at Nithanvale. James would have the famous Nithanvale herd all to himself; even as a small boy he had dreamed of breeding cattle as he followed her and Logan around the byre, or helped her feed the calves. If Kirsty had been the secret love of his youthful dreams, as Beth had once fondly believed, then he must have put it behind him; certainly he had not been to visit Fairlyden for many months.

The following morning, as soon as Luke climbed out of bed he felt the sharper air which heralds a crisp autumn morning. He padded across to the window with a feeling of relief, thankful that the incessant rain and wind had been interrupted at last. There was a heavy dew but it would soon evaporate and meanwhile he gazed enraptured at the spiders' webs draped like miniature gossamer curtains over the bushes beneath his window; the berries on the rowan tree gleamed like rubies in the morning sun.

It will be a grand day for sketching, he thought, unaware that his troubled young mind craved for just such relaxation.

Luke was too sensitive and susceptible, he cared deeply about the uncertainties in the world. Many of his friends at the Academy talked eagerly of the possibilities of another war; they wanted a war! One that would last long enough for them to join in the fray. Few of them considered the consequences. Luke thought of the strange friendship which had sprung up between himself and his German teacher. The man was lonely of course, and still grieving for the loss of his only son and for the friends and family he had left behind. Luke believed him when he spoke in hushed and fearful tones of the humiliations and tribulations his people were suffering at the hands of the Nazis; and they were Germans, even if they were also Jews. What terrible fate could other nations expect to suffer if this man Hitler was not content with his easy conquest of Czechoslovakia?

Luke frowned, but he made a conscious effort to put aside the world's problems, at least for today. He reached for his canvas satchel, checked his pencils and his sketch pad. What he needed was peace and beauty to refresh his mind and soul. Today was Saturday, no cycling to the station, no train to catch, no exhausting concentration on his studies. Instead it was his job to clean out the wooden hen huts – not a pastime he enjoyed but his father had explained gravely that life was full of irksome tasks which had to be done if a man wanted to survive. His advice had been to tackle the worst things first, do them well and know they were behind him; only then would he enjoy the pleasures without guilt or irritation. Luke knew his father's advice was sound. He would not procrastinate on such a beautiful morning. As soon as he had finished he would take his satchel and follow the burn on its meandering path until he found a scene which captured his imagination – somewhere away from the farmsteading, away from the lower fields with their muddy gateways which resembled miniature deltas where the cows had tramped the grass to mud as they crowded through before fanning out into the open field.

In the big warm kitchen he found his grandmother already dishing up his porridge. Granny never lay in bed in the mornings unless she was ill. 'It's the habit of a lifetime after rising for the milking,' she always declared.

'Good morning, laddie,' she greeted him with pleasure, setting out his own small bowl of cream. 'Surely you're up early for a Saturday?'

'Aye. It's a braw morning for a change, Granny,' Luke gave

190

her his dreamy smile, but she thought his blue eyes held too many shadows and his young face seemed strained.

'A day in the fresh air is what you're needing.' She frowned, catching sight of the satchel he always carried when he went off alone to draw or paint.

'I'm going to clean the hen houses first,' he said, reading her mind. He knew she had worked hard all her life and had no time for those who shirked. 'I'll take an apple and some bread and cheese with me. I thought I'd wander up the burn when I'm finished. Maybe I'll make ye a picture o' the autumn leaves, Granny? To match the one I did for ye last spring.'

'Aye, it's a bonnie picture o' the bluebells. I can just visualise them on the bank in the wee wood at the foot o' the hill – just as they were when I was young.' Sarah smiled reminiscently. 'Your painting is the last thing I see before I blow out the lamp, Luke, and it aye brings back happy memories. It would be nice to have one o' the autumn too. You've great talent, laddie.'

Logan, Beth and Kirsty were always later returning for breakfast on Saturday mornings. The dairy, the milking buckets and churns, the cooler and pan, and even the milking stools were scrubbed and scalded even more thoroughly than usual. In fact anything which would save work on the Sabbath was done on Saturday mornings.

'The corn should dry a bit today when the sun gets up,' Logan remarked with satisfaction as he supped his porridge. 'I told Paddy we'd move the stooks to dryer ground later on this afternoon, Kirsty.'

'Very well, Father. I'll be ready to help. It will be a relief to see the last field harvested.'

'Aye, weel, it depends whether we get a single day o' sunshine or the several we're needing, lassie, but it's all in God's hands. We can only do our best with what he gives us.'

'Mmm, I'll take Marocco for a good gallop up to Westhill this morning. We'll count the sheep and make sure they're all in good health.'

'Aye. Look out for any lame ones. The footrot will be bad after this wet weather, no doubt. I think I'll study the milk records for an hour. I havena had time since the lassie was here to weigh the milk at the beginning o' the week. It's time some o' the cows were getting more cake if we're to keep up the milk yields through the winter.'

It was more than an hour later when Logan returned to the

kitchen, frowning slightly. Beth was baking at the big scrubbed table and his mother was peeling vegetables for the broth. They looked happy and content, chatting as they worked.

'What's wrong, Logan?' Beth raised her eyebrows. 'Are the milk records so bad? I expect the wet summer has pulled the yields down.'

'Och, the records are fine. Where's Luke? Is he not out o' bed yet? I've told him before he canna leave the hens for you and Lucy to clean on Saturdays . . .'

'Dinna worry about Luke,' Sarah smiled. 'He was up almost before I had the porridge ready this morning. He'll have the hens all cleaned out by now.'

'Aah,' Logan relaxed and smiled. 'He's not a bad laddie. I ken he doesna like the work but it has to be done. I expect he'll be back soon. I was hoping he would help us shift the stooks later on. It's a messy job when they're sodden.'

'Well . . . I don't know when he'll return exactly,' Sarah frowned. 'He took his sketching pad and some bread and cheese. I think he needs to relax and get some fresh air. He said he'd a mind to wander by the burn up to the foot o' the hill . . .'

'By the burn!' Logan stared at his mother's white hair and wrinkled face as though he had never seen her before.

Beth looked up at her husband's sharp tone. His face had paled. 'D'ye think Luke will ken we moved the old bull into the wee paddock at the foot o' the hill?' He stared at her intently.

'Well, he was here in the kitchen when ye mentioned it, Logan.'

'Aye, but will he remember? Sometimes he doesna even take things in!'

'I didna ken ye'd taken the bull away frae the cows,' Sarah frowned. 'But I'm sure Luke wouldna forget such a thing. He's still as petrified o' the cows as he was when he was a wee laddie.'

'Aye, but did he listen to what I said? I think I'll take a walk up there.'

'Ye'll be careful, Logie?' Beth murmured automatically.

'Of course I will.' Logan relaxed and grinned at her. 'Ye should ken I've worked too long with cattle to take any risks myself. But maybe I'll catch up with Luke and just remind him o' Grayson Masterful's presence in the top paddock . . .'

Twenty-Two

Luke strolled happily by the side of the burn, breathing deeply in the crisp clear air. After the recent rains the burn was full and it rushed merrily along, carrying twigs and leaves, brushing the long grass along its banks so that it looked, to Luke's imaginative eyes, like the streaming green hair of a mermaid. He reached the corner of the field. The gate was firmly secured with twine as well as the usual sneck making it difficult to open. Absently he wondered who had taken so much trouble and why, then he shrugged and climbed over into a smaller paddock, the last of the enclosed fields before the ground rose rough and steeper on to Westhill where the sheep usually grazed.

The burn curved away now, no longer following the hedge, but this did not trouble Luke; he knew it curled back in a wide loop at the far end of the small paddock where a cluster of silver birches grew amidst the moss and bracken. He could see in his mind the bronze curling fronds, the silver bark and the little trembling leaves. It was one of his favourite haunts.

A thick thorn hedge surrounded the paddock and provided plenty of shelter for the young lambs brought off the hill on a cold spring day. It had been planted by his grandfather and layered by him and Thomas Whiteley, and more recently by Thomas and his father. Even so Paddy had insisted on running a single strand of barbed wire along the far side, 'Just to be making sure none o' the young beasts would be a-finding their way into the wrong pasture and leading old Paddy a fine chase.'

Luke smiled to himself as he walked, quite oblivious to the great bulk of the bull slumbering on the other side of a grassy knoll. As usual his parents' discussion of the bull's removal from the herd had washed over him unheeded.

He paused to watch three young starlings pecking greedily at the glistening brambles. Behind them the rosehips glowed jewel bright in the autumn sun and Luke thought how good it was to be alive on such a day. Absently he kicked the tops off a clump of toadstools and was more startled than the birds themselves when a small covey of partridges suddenly scurried through the grass less than a foot away.

He was about half way up the field, still quite close to the thick thorn hedge. Grayson Masterful rose from his morning nap and stretched his massive bulk. Luke saw him instantly. He stared in horror. The bull moved his powerful head from side to side scenting the air, snorting irritably. He curled back his nose, making the shiny copper ring stand vertical. Luke watched, mesmerised. The bull's upswept horns seemed to gleam malevolently. They could gore a man to death in seconds and Luke knew it. Still terror kept him rigid. His feet were leaden weights yet the muscles in his stomach quivered sickeningly.

The bull began to advance. He moved purposefully, head low. Rumbling bellows echoed from the depths of his broad belly into the clear morning air. Luke's brain was paralysed with fear. His wits scattered.

Logan was still a field away when he saw his son climbing the gate into the bull's paddock. He shouted a warning but Luke had already jumped from the gate and was hidden from view by the thorn hedge and the gently rising ground. Logan cupped his hands to his mouth and shouted thrice. He waited a moment, his heart pounding but Luke did not reappear. Logan began to run up the long narrow field which now separated him from his son.

Standing on the third bar of the gate at last, panting breathlessly, Logan was just in time to see Grayson Masterful advancing towards Luke's slim, petrified figure. It was like a nightmare in slow motion.

'Move! Run! Jump over the hedge!' He almost screamed in his breathless frustration. Still Luke stared, transfixed. Logan jumped to the ground and began to run again, knowing he could never reach his son in time. 'The hedge, Luke! Jump for it! Move, Luke! Oh God help me!'

Some part of Luke's atrophied brain recognised his father's voice. He tore his eyes briefly from the bull's lethal horns. 'Jump! The hedge!' Even as Luke obeyed he saw his father sink to his knees.

He had no hope of jumping the impenetrable, five-foot hedge, but he threw himself at it, oblivious to the piercing pain of the thorns as he groped desperately in a bid to hoist himself to safety. The bull roared in fury and charged. Luke felt a searing pain tear through his thigh as he was hurtled into the air. Barbed wire gashed his cheek. Blood spurted. But he was over.

'I'm on the other side!' he gasped. It was his last coherent thought as he landed with a sickening thud.

Deprived of his quarry, Grayson Masterful bellowed loudly and pawed the ground, sending mud flying into the air. He even got down on his knees and gored the hedge in an attempt to reach the silent figure on the other side. It was futile and at last even his bovine brain realised it. He rose up and careered in a mad gallop, circling, tossing his head, scraping the ground, finally returning to the spot where Luke had disappeared over the hedge. Still there was no sport for his frustrated energy and he slunk off down the field, stopping short at the sight of Logan's exhausted figure crouched on the grass. Grayson Masterful emitted a triumphant roar. Lowering his magnificent horns, he galloped wildly at the helpless man who had been his master for the past four years. Logan saw him coming but he was powerless to protect himself. The band around his chest held him prisoner as surely as if it bound him hand and foot and manacled him to the gates of hell. He looked up at the innocent blue of the October sky. 'Dear God, help me. Aah Beth, my love. My only love . . .'

Despite the soft ground underfoot, horse and rider had enjoyed the gallop across the Fairlyden fields to the furthest point, and beyond to the top of the Westhill ground where the sheep grazed contentedly in the unexpected warmth of the autumn day. Marocco snorted gently, happy now to wander wherever his mistress wished to go, be it slithering down the slippery incline on the north side of Westhill, stepping daintily through a patch of bog or bracken or simply circling around a distant cluster of ewes. Each day Logan, Paddy or Kirsty counted every one of the cattle and sheep between them, but today Kirsty resolved to make a closer inspection of the most distant ewes, even though that meant rousing any which were slumbering, seeing each one walk, keeping a sharp eye for any which were lame or sickly. Usually she brought one of the collies but today she was content to take her time and make a leisurely tour with only Marocco for company. Some of the ewes were inclined to limp slightly. Soon the whole flock would have to be rounded up and brought in for a more thorough examination and treatment.

Kirsty sat easily astride the big chestnut gelding as they climbed once more over the crest of the hill. As though by common consent the horse paused and Kirsty gazed over the panorama of the fields, the burn looping and curving, the little woods. Almost the whole of Fairlyden was visible from here, with the roofs of the farmsteading clustered against the lea of the slope. Kirsty allowed her gaze to wander slowly, savouring the view of the distant hills, violet smudges against the soft blue of the sky, the sparkle of the Solway Firth and the hills beyond. On a clear day it was possible to see well into England and it was hard to imagine that in winter snows a man could be dead before he ever found the burn at the bottom of the hill only a few hundred yards below them. Kirsty's eyes adjusted to the nearer fields. Suddenly she stiffened, eyes narrowed. Marocco pricked his ears as the ominous roar of an angry bull reached them. Kirsty's eyes focused on the small paddock and she gasped in horror. She saw Grayson Masterful charge, saw him toss a slight figure into the air as lightly as a feather.

'Luke!' she breathed. 'Oh, Luke!' Even as she heeled Marocco into a canter and then a gallop her eyes were scanning the paddock. Surely there was someone else in the bull's field? A man? Paddy? Her father? No, it could not be! And yet?

'Come on boy! Aah come on!' All her concentration was on her mount now. Only Marocco could get her to the lower field with speed; he must not slip.

There were two gates at the bottom – one into the small paddock with the bull, and the one into the adjacent field where Luke now lay. Marocco slowed slightly, alert for her command. Kirsty's eyes scanned the bull field swiftly.

'It canna be Father!' But she knew it was. 'Oh dear God, save him! Save him!' Without further thought she urged the gelding forward, straight at the gate, her heart in her mouth. Marocco hesitated only for a split second then leapt into the air. His hind feet clipped the top bar of the gate, but Kirsty did not let him slacken his pace.

The bull had been performing some sort of mad circus but now he was heading straight towards the hunched figure.

'Move. Why don't you move!' Kirsty pleaded silently, but her breath caught in her throat when she saw her father struggling to kneel upright, saw him raise his face to the sky. Then he slumped forward and lay still, face down as though embracing the damp earth.

Before Kirsty's astonished gaze the bull slithered to a halt only inches away from the prone figure. He pawed the ground and bellowed. Seconds later he lowered his head. Kirsty screamed as one lethal horn tossed her father on to his back as though he was a rag doll. Her scream startled Marocco. The gelding reared and almost unseated her but the brief diversion had gained the attention of the bull, twice thwarted of his sport.

Kirsty knew what she had to do then. She wheeled Marocco round, kicking him into a gallop towards the far gate. If only she could reach it, dismount, open it and mount again? She was almost certain the enraged bull would follow. She had to get him away from her father, away from the field.

Marocco would have jumped the gate as he had the last one but Kirsty had to open it and the bull was almost upon them. There was no time to lose. The strings which Paddy had used to ensure Grayson Masterful remained a prisoner almost defeated her. She fumbled for her penknife and slashed the twine with sobbing breaths. She barely had time to remount. Marocco sensed her urgency and he was off again before her foot found the stirrup. The bull was much too close behind them to circle and leave him behind. There was only one thing left to do now. She must open the gate half way down this field too and lead the bull into the barley field. He would cause havoc amongst the bedraggled stooks, but surely he would be diverted long enough for her to gallop back to fasten the gate and keep him away from her father?

Grayson Masterful was tiring now but he followed the horse and rider at a steady run, his dewlap flapping from side to side. Inside the gate of the cornfield he stood still, twitching his nostrils, unable to comprehend the change of scene. For a sickening moment Kirsty wondered whether he would turn around and return to his familiar field, or whether she and Marocco would be trapped. Her faithful old gelding was tired now and sweating and he was no match for the brute strength of a bull the size of Masterful, nor had he any weapon to combat those razor-sharp horns.

Suddenly the bull made a mad dart at the nearest stook, sending sheaves flying into the air. Then he attacked the next and the next, moving further and further from the gate. The stupidity of the big bull might have made Kirsty laugh when he got a sheaf of corn stuck on his horn, half blindfolding him, but she felt too sick with fear and anxiety. She was afraid to move too soon in case the bull followed her out of the field as readily as he had followed her in, but she was in a ferment of anxiety to get back to her father – and Luke too!

'I'd almost forgotten poor Luke!' she muttered under her breath. She leaned forward and crooned in the gelding's ear. 'Come on, boy, just one last burst of speed until I shut this mad beast in with the corn stooks.'

Kirsty was dismayed to find her father still lying as she had last seen him. Surely the bull had not injured him badly, or had he attacked him earlier before she caught sight of them, even before he attacked Luke perhaps? She slid to the ground before Marocco could stop.

'Father! Father, it's me, Kirsty. You're safe now. I've shut him out o' this field. Father . . .?' She was on her knees, her heart pounding now with a nameless dread. Gently she lifted Logan's shoulders and tried to ease him completely on to his back. 'Father! Oh Dada! Dada!' The old childish name which Lucy had taught her long ago came out in an anguished sob. She could not believe that her beloved father was dead. There was no sign of injury. No blood. She got slowly to her feet like a sleepwalker. She felt bewildered; scarcely able to think; not knowing what to do next. She needed help . . . She began to shiver and her teeth chattered uncontrollably. Luke! Where was Luke? Why hadn't he come to help?

She began to walk slowly towards the hedge. Marocco followed, puzzled. He tried to nuzzle her shoulder. Kirsty did not even notice him. She had no difficulty finding the spot where Luke lay on the other side of the hedge because of the scattering of brambles and twigs made by the bull's horns.

'Luke! Luke? Are you still there?' She squatted down close to the hedge and peered through the twigs. Luke lay where he had fallen, his face and hair and his trouser leg covered in blood. 'Luke! Oh Luke! Not you too! No! No . . .' She began to sob. The sobs turned to hysterical laughter. She had to get a grip on herself. There was no one here but her. She needed help. She must get to Luke. She must bring help. Suddenly she fell to her knees and was violently sick.

Afterwards Kirsty could scarcely remember riding Marocco back to the steading. Falling into Paddy's arms, telling him and Lucy in hiccoughing sobs, taking Anna to the house to comfort her mother and summon the doctor. Everyone said how brave she had been but Kirsty did not feel courageous; she felt numb and sick. She could hardly believe her eyes when Paddy returned and helped Luke, half-carrying him, into the house. His young face, beneath the streaks of blood, was a peculiar shade of green and he looked lopsided as though he had suddenly become a hunchback. But Luke was dead! Her brother was dead, but he was still walking; his eyes, blue eyes full of pain and torment, looking at her, pleading silently – for what? She began to laugh again. Lucy slapped her face. She whimpered like a frightened child and Lucy crooned softly as she had when Kirsty was a baby.

'Tis all right, ma lamb. Doctor Broombank says Master Luke isna as bad as he looks. His shoulder is dislocated, but he'll put it right. It's the blood. All that blood . . .' Kirsty felt Lucy shudder against her and strangely she felt her own strength and composure returning. Her grandmother was sitting erect in her chair as usual but her eyes were closed as though by shutting them she could shut out the reality of this dreadful day. Her mother, deathly white, unnaturally calm, was busy, afraid to be still. Refusing to believe that Logan was dead.

'Thomas Whiteley is bringing the body down with the horse and cart,' Doctor Broombank said quietly. 'Your mother is deeply shocked, Kirsty. She will need you, when she has seen . . .'

Kirsty nodded, but she felt her own face crumple again and strove for control.

'You're shocked yourself, m'dear, and there's no wonder!' The doctor's voice was kind and compassionate. 'Could you boil me a pan o' water and bring it upstairs? I'll put some stitches in the laddie's thigh, and maybe one or two in his cheek. He'll have a scar, but it would have been worse if the barb had caught his eye. It will be some weeks before he walks easy though.'

Kirsty was astonished at the number of people who came to pay their last respects to her father.

'There's many a one I dinna ken,' she overheard her Uncle Alex remark gruffly to her mother. 'James MacFarlane seems acquainted with some o' them though – Ayrshire breeders, he says. Some have travelled a long distance to be here for the funeral.'

'It's good o' them to come,' Beth murmured brokenly. 'Maybe

ye'll see they get back to the house for a bite after ye've been to the kirk yard, Alex?'

Emma and Alex proved towers of strength. It was Emma who insisted that Luke should be brought from his room to be present during the service at the house although he was unfit to go to the churchyard to take his place at the head of his father's coffin.

'He's blaming himself for your father's death, I think, Kirsty.' Her kindly face was deeply troubled.

'But Doctor Broombank told him it was Father's heart.'

'I ken, but Luke is too sensitive, and right now he reminds me o' your mother, lassie. She didna want to face the world at all when she thought your father wasna coming back frae France. Mind you, she'd been near to death herself at the time . . . Even so, Luke is too emotional for his ain good. Ye'll have to get Paddy to help him downstairs every day until he can walk himself. Dinna let him brood. And let me know if ye need me.' Emma shook her greying head compassionately. 'Ye'll have a lot o' responsibility now for a lassie your age.'

Kirsty listened to Aunt Ellen giving much the same advice about her young brother. 'My heart aches for your mother. I was more concerned about her than anyone when I received the telegram, but somehow . . .' She eyed Beth's pale face across the room and her eyes were filled with sympathy. 'Somehow I think she will find strength to carry on. She has great faith, and I'm sure God will see her through. In time.' She sighed and her soft mouth tightened. 'I'm ashamed o' Sadie, my own sister! She should have been here for the funeral.'

'Uncle Alex sent telegrams to Aunt Sadie and Uncle Billy. Mother insisted on writing herself – to inform her of the funeral arrangements.'

'Yes,' Ellen nodded. 'It was her duty to come. She should have come for your grandmother's sake too. I see Mr Forbes came from Yorkshire on the train. Sadie could have travelled with him if Robert didna feel like making the journey – though I'm sure he makes plenty o' longer journeys when it suits him,' she added with rare cynicism.

'We had a telegram frae America frae Uncle Billy.'

'Yes, I wouldna be surprised if this brings him back to visit. He was always a bit protective towards your mother, Kirsty.' Ellen looked at her niece with affectionate concern. 'You're too young to be shouldering so much responsibility on your own, but it looks as though it will be a long time before Luke will be much support.' Kirsty followed her aunt's glance across the sitting room to where her brother was propped on the chaise longue. James MacFarlane was leaning over him while Mary MacFarlane was perched on the edge, holding both Luke's hands in hers. She seemed to be talking to him very earnestly.

Kirsty had been surprised to see Miss MacFarlane at the funeral, but James had brought her and he had lead her straight to Luke's side. Her brother certainly seemed to be remarkably well acquainted with her and more at ease in her presence than he was with anyone else. Indeed Miss MacFarlane had scarcely left Luke's side.

Shortly afterwards Ellen went to speak to someone else but Kirsty was no sooner alone than James came towards her. It was months since Kirsty had spoken to him but her heart was too heavy with grief now to have room for joy. She looked at him dully. His face was grave but his eyes held sincerity as he took her hand and held it firmly between both of his.

'Don't hesitate to send for me, Kirsty, if there is anything you need.' Kirsty made no response. She felt numb, like a carved wooden puppet. 'If there's anything at all, ever,' James insisted quietly. 'There is another matter I have been asked to mention. Finlay MacPhail was at the funeral. He had to leave to catch his train back to Glasgow and you were occupied so he did not manage to speak to you himself. He had a great respect for your father. He asked me to pass on his condolences.' Kirsty nodded. There had been so many fellow breeders. 'Mr MacPhail also asked . . . and I know this is not the time or the place to mention it, but I supposes you will have to reach some sort o' decision—'

'Decision! What about?' Kirsty asked more sharply than she had intended.

'About the bull, Grayson Masterful. MacPhail thought you might send him for slaughter. He would like the chance to buy him. He has a specially constructed pen. He assures me there would be no fear of anyone else being injured. However I told MacPhail you wouldna want to think about that today. He's left his address on a card in the hall.'

'Thank you.' Kirsty's face felt stiff with the effort of keeping her emotions under control. Despite his months of silence, she longed to throw herself into James's arms, to feel their strength as she had done so often in the past; to weep and hear his comforting words . . . feel his gentle touch. Her mouth trembled.

Suddenly she felt alone and frightened of the future – so terribly alone.

'Remember, Kirsty, if I can help at all? Your father . . . he was a fine man and a good friend to me, the very best. For – for his sake I'd like to help if I can. Kirsty . . .?' She felt her whole body stiffen with those words – 'for his sake'. Hastily she withdrew her hand from his firm clasp. Her head came up, her square jaw tilted proudly.

'Thank you,' she said stiffly. Moments later she heard James say much the same words to her mother; then he was gone, back to Nithanvale with Mary MacFarlane at his side. Kirsty knew his offer was sincere enough but she made a silent vow – she would never ask James MacFarlane for help. Never.

Twenty-Three

In the ensuing weeks Beth's grief and shock were almost tangible but gradually, with the help of the Reverend Morrison and her own devout faith, she accepted Logan's heart attack as God's will. The joyous spark was missing from her eyes and from her smile but she had a stoic calm, at least on the face she showed to the world. She was determined to carry out her daily tasks; indeed it was evident to Kirsty that her mother did more work than ever; she sensed her need to tire herself during the day and she could only guess at the loneliness of the long winter nights.

Luke, on the other hand, seemed unable to concentrate on anything, least of all the studies he had once enjoyed. He blamed himself for his father's death and several times Kirsty was wakened in the night by her brother's nightmares.

'He reminds me o' your mother, Kirsty,' her grandmother commented anxiously.

'I know. Aunt Ellen and Aunt Emma were worried too, but Mother seems to have accepted Father's death better than any of us.'

'Accepted, aye. She's grateful, in a way, I suppose. I believe she treasured each and every day o' the past twenty years as a gift frae the Almighty. She'll be true to your father's memory for the rest o' her life, but she'll never rail against his death, or question God's will – not this time. It's Luke I'm worried about. He canna seem to get it into his head that his father had a heart attack.'

'I know, Granny, and I've tried to convince Luke o' that but he gets quite angry. He says I don't understand. At other times he – he bursts into sobs like a bairn and then he's ashamed afterwards.'

'Aye,' Sarah sighed. 'He's all mixed up and I dinna know how to help the laddie either. He'd be better if he worked out in the fresh air, I'm sure. I canna understand him being afraid o' animals when he's been brought up with them all his life. The things he reads in the newspapers and the stories he

203

hears from that German teacher dinna help him either. He keeps talking about innocent women and children being persecuted. Luke is far too sensitive about the world and its problems, and I'm just a useless old woman, for I dinna know what to say to the laddie to ease his mind.'

Kirsty felt far older than her twenty-two years; she worried about Luke, but she also had other problems. Fairlyden was no longer a place of refuge, a secure haven; it was an awesome responsibility – hers. People depended on her for their home and their living, as they had depended on her father.

Thomas Whiteley was now sixty-five and he had suffered several attacks of bronchitis, but between them, he and Logan had managed all the ploughing and cultivations for the oats and turnips, as well as the reaping and other field work. When, on the second of January nineteen hundred and thirty-nine, Anna came to tell her that Thomas was again confined to bed with his bad chest Kirsty felt the new year had made a bad beginning. She hoped fervently that it was not going to be as bad as the one which had just ended.

One thing was clear to her, they would need another man to help Thomas before the spring sowing began. Paddy was an excellent stockman but he admitted frankly that he was a hopeless ploughman. Behind his cheery façade she detected his anxiety and unspoken questions.

'You are needed to look after the cows, Paddy – more than ever now . . . I am depending on you.'

'Ach, Miss Kirsty, there's no man can replace Master Fairly,' he muttered gruffly, 'but you'll be knowing ol' Paddy will do his best – his very best.'

'I know that, Paddy. I dinna like the idea o' going to the hiring fair myself, and we shall need help before the May term anyway.' She chewed her lower lip anxiously. 'Maybe I should ask Uncle Alex if he knows of any ploughmen who want to move.'

'That will be another wage to be finding then, Miss Kirsty? They were saying at the Crown and Thistle that the prices for mutton and wool are so low they're scarcely worth the keeping?' Paddy looked at her uncertainly. Kirsty knew he was wondering whether she would be able to make all the right decisions, and he knew nothing of her other problem – the debt to the bank for the purchase of the Muircumwell land.

'It's true the sheep are a poor trade but most o' the land on Westhill isna much use for anything else yet and Father felt

204

they improved the fertility. They wouldna be worth much in the markets even if we wanted to sell them and we still couldna manage without a ploughman. So, Paddy, whatever happens, we need you here at Fairlyden. Father also said you had an uncanny instinct for the wellbeing o' all the animals, so I know you'll not let me down?'

'Did Master Fairly really say that, Miss Kirsty? And him one o' the finest stockmen in Scotland! Ach, to be sure he taught me many a thing about cows, he did. You're his own daughter and I'll not be a-letting you down.'

A week later Anna approached her diffidently and Kirsty realised she should have reassured her and Thomas too.

'Paddy was saying ye'll be hiring a new ploughman, Miss Kirsty. I ken Thomas isna as fit for his work as he used to be. Maybe we . . . Well, maybe we should be moving out o' the house? Ye'll be needing it for a new man, I suppose.'

'Ah Anna!' Kirsty was dismayed. She had not considered the question of housing a new man if he had a wife or lived some distance away. She shuddered. 'I couldna stand any more changes! Is Thomas wanting to leave Fairlyden?'

'Wanting to leave! Och, Miss Kirsty, Thomas would never leave Fairlyden unless ye tell him there's no place for him here anymore.'

'I'd never do that, Anna! He's been here all his life. He's as much a part o' Fairlyden as I am.' Even as she uttered the words she knew Mr Sellers, the bank manager, would tell her that sentiment had no place in running a business.

'If ye really mean that, Miss Kirsty, about wanting us tae stay, well I'd be willing to give bed and board to a ploughman laddie, especially now we've a spare bedroom.' Anna sounded eager. 'James kens o' a young fellow who might interest ye?'

'Aah! Was this James's idea?' Kirsty's colour rose indignantly.

'Weel, he kens I'm worried about Thomas, and I dinna want to leave Fairlyden either, ye see. Your grandmother and your mother have been good to me. We've kenned each other through many a trouble.'

'Of course you have, Anna, and I've never thought o' asking you to leave. You know as well as anybody how important the hens are for paying the wages and keeping the house going, and Mother couldna manage them on her own. Then there's the milking. It seems we never have enough pairs o' hands for that.'

'I ken. I was telling James it's just the ploughing and such

205

like.' She sighed heavily. 'If only he'd been here now! I told him he should never have left Fairlyden after all your father had done for him! And I'm sure he's worried about his ain affairs for all he doesna tell me much. A mother aye kens when there's something troubling her ain son. He should never have gone near Nithanvale!'

'But he did, Anna, and there's no going back. He could never return to Fairlyden now.' Kirsty knew she couldn't bear to have James at Fairlyden again, seeing and working with him every day and knowing he had Mary MacFarlane as his bride. Fleetingly, she wondered why they had not married already, but Anna went on.

'I suppose ye're right, Miss Kirsty. Anyway he was at Lizzie's on Sunday and he said he kenned o' a single fellow he'd like to recommend as a young ploughman. If ye'd consider him I'd be pleased to have him bide in the house wi' Thomas and me.'

'Did James give you his name and address? I could arrange to see him perhaps.'

'He wrote his name on a bit paper. Joey Little. He . . . er, he works at Nithanvale. He's worked there for five years, ever since he left school. He's nineteen. His father and grandfather have been there all their lives. James says they're all grand horsemen and Joey is good at the ploughing . . .'

'Then why is he leaving Nithanvale – if his roots are there, and if he is so good at his work?'

Anna flushed. 'I dinna ken exactly, Miss Kirsty. I – I just ken in my ain heart that James is worried about something . . . He said he'd like to see Joey Little fixed up at a good place.' She frowned. 'James looks pale and worried and he's thinner. I thought he and Mary MacFarlane would be planning to wed by now, but there's no word o' it. He willna talk about her when I ask questions.'

'Maybe they've had a lovers' quarrel.'

'No, I think it's more than that. I ken Nithanvale cost more than James and Miss MacFarlane could afford. Lizzie reckons they only bought it for the sake o' the old man, so he wouldna have to leave afore he died. She loaned them her ain wee bit savings. Now I'm wondering if they'll have to get out o' farming like so many others have had to do. I expect that's why he wants to see this young ploughman fixed up with a job.'

'I'm sure James will do what he considers best. I'll make enquiries about Joey Little, Anna, and let you know.' Privately she wondered whether James was looking for a way to keep his mother and uncle at Fairlyden because he and Mary MacFarlane could not provide a home for them at Nithanvale. Were things really as bad as Anna feared?

Kirsty had no wish to visit Nithanvale so she asked her uncle to make discreet enquiries about Joe Little.

'Good family. Hard workers,' Alex reported. 'Can't think why James is letting him go. The other men at Nithanvale are getting old, at least so I'm told. In fact . . .' He frowned. 'There's a lot o' speculation going on about the MacFarlanes. Nothing wrong with the laddie though, Kirsty. I think ye should hire him, lassie.'

Kirsty trusted her uncle's judgement and she knew he was not a gossip. He was a respected member of several committees too, including the Farmers' Union and Chamber of Agriculture for Scotland.

'What sort of speculation, Uncle Alex? I mean about Nithanvale?'

'Och, ye'll likely know more than me, lassie. I havena seen James MacFarlane since your father's funeral, and I didna have a proper conversation with him then. As ye ken his Aunt Maggie and his cousin Ben are still working at the Mains, but they dinna ken any more than I do. I expect James is too proud to burden his family with his problems. Pity times are so bad because he's a grand farmer and your father always said he was one o' the best young stockmen he'd come across.'

'We havena seen him either. Or at least I think Luke sees him, but I'm sure they dinna discuss farming! Luke goes to Nithanvale sometimes after school and comes home on the later train.'

'Does he now? Weel, it's just as well the laddie talks to somebody.' Alex frowned. He considered his nephew a strange laddie. 'We all have problems. I have enough of my own with Cameron. He says he'll join the air force if there's a war! Join the air force indeed! Better keep his feet on the ground, I told him. Just like my brother, your Uncle Billy, he is. I had a letter frae him again this week. He seems concerned about your mother. He wonders how she is managing without Logan.'

'Mother seems to find great comfort from her bible these days.'

'Aye.' Alex said no more. Luke had certainly inherited his mother's sensitive nature and perhaps he got the idea of being a minister from Beth too. If only he was a more normal young fellow – more like Paul. After all they were the same age but they weren't at all like cousins. Paul had left school the moment he got the chance. Alex smiled. Emma had not approved but at least Paul had stuck in at his work at the Mains and he was making a fine job with the pigs and cattle.

Joey Little started work at Fairlyden at the end of February. His cheerful whistle and jaunty smile lifted everyone's spirits.

Apart from her anxiety over Luke, Kirsty's main problem now was keeping up the payments to the bank. She had had an uncomfortable interview with Mr Sellers but he was wise enough to realise there was little hope of recouping his money by selling Fairlyden's fertile pastures. No one wanted an investment as immovable as a farm in such unpredictable times. There had not been a single offer for Avary Hall and its extensive grounds. The place was rapidly going to ruin.

Kirsty missed her father terribly, both for his company and his wisdom. She was grateful to Aunt Emma and Uncle Alex. They came regularly each week to see her mother and grandmother and it was comforting to know she could discuss many of her problems with people who understood them; but at the end of the day the responsibility was hers now and even small decisions took on a new importance. Paddy and Thomas looked to her for guidance as they had looked to her father: when to move the cattle to a different field, when to sell a cow from the herd, when to change them from field to field or alter their feeding rations. Even more onerous were the decisions affecting the field work, spreading the farm yard manure, buying and carting lime, when to plough and sow and reap . . . She agonized over all these everyday matters which her father had taken as part of the daily round.

Anna MacFarlane was pleased to have the company of Joey Little in her home. Thomas's hearing had deteriorated to the stage when normal conversation was impossible. Joey also visited his family at Nithanvale most Sundays and brought more news of James.

So the year progressed slowly and to Kirsty at least the rumblings of war barely touched her daily life. Even the weather was favourable. It was Uncle Alex who first made her realise the changes a war might bring.

'A tractor!' she gasped. 'You're going to buy a tractor, Uncle Alex, and you're the breeder of the best Clydesdales in the whole county and beyond!'

'I can scarcely believe it either, Alex,' Beth said quietly as she served the soup for Sunday lunch. Her glance strayed to Emma and she noticed how pale her sister-in-law looked and there were dark shadows beneath Emma's eyes too. Usually her face was so pleasant and placid but today she looked strained and pinched.

'I'm hoping a tractor will be enough to keep Cameron frae joining the services.' Alex's tone was flat.

'It willna keep the laddie if he's determined to try his wings,' Sarah commented almost to herself. She rarely joined in serious discussions these days. Since Logan's death she had withdrawn more and more into herself. Alex looked at his mother and their dark eyes met and held.

'Ye're thinking o' Billy?' He sighed. 'In my heart I ken Cameron will go if there is a war and it seems more and more likely with every day that passes.'

'Aah Alex, dinna say that,' Emma pleaded. 'Anyway the government has already said that farmers and agricultural workers will be in reserved occupations this time. They ken frae the experiences o' the last war how essential it is to produce as much food at home as we possibly can.'

'Aye, but if Cameron *chooses* to go, they'll take him, I'm afraid.' Alex looked at his wife. 'He's intelligent and capable – and he wants adventure.'

'But you still bought the tractor, Alex . . .' Beth mused softly.

'Aye, partly for Emma's sake.' He looked lovingly at his wife. 'I shall do all I can to keep him at home, but apart frae Cameron, we shall have to be ready to move with the times. The government is wakening up to the serious state o' British agriculture, and the plight we shall be in if we canna get the ships through with the usual quantities o' imported foods. The politicians reckon we need another one and a half million acres under the plough. That will take a lot o' extra men and horses over the whole country. I canna see how it can be done. Ye canna wave a magic wand and find a pair o' fully grown horses all ready to pull a plough! There'll be a scarcity o' men too, even if some are exempt frae joining up. Ye'll be planning to plough extra land at Fairlyden, Kirsty?'

'N–no. It will be a struggle getting this year's harvest in as it is. Paddy and Joe Little are the only strong men.'

'That's true,' Beth agreed. 'Thomas isna fit for hard work and long days now.'

'Besides Father always said Fairlyden grows better grass than corn, especially when we get so much rain. I dinna understand much about growing grain either, and neither does Paddy. At least we know a bit about cows and producing milk . . .' She didn't like to disagree with Uncle Alex when he had been so generous with his time and help. She looked anxiously at her mother.

'Ye're doing fine, lassie.' Beth smiled gently. 'We couldna have kept going without ye.'

'Aah, but that's not the point!' Alex frowned. 'There are plans already to compel farmers to plough extra land if they dinna cooperate voluntarily. The government are offering a subsidy of two pounds per acre for ploughing up permanent pasture, aye and cheaper lime to improve it. They say they will need more home grown cereals and potatoes if Hitler goes on.'

'But surely people will need milk too, Uncle Alex?'

'Aye, aye, they will that, lassie,' Alex sighed. 'But ye canna produce as much food for the nation frae an acre o' grass as ye can frae an acre o' corn. A lot o' the corn is imported, and feed we use for the cows to produce the winter milk. I tell ye, lassie, we shall all need to be more self sufficient if Britain joins in a war against Germany.'

'I expect ye hardly get time to read the newspapers these days, Kirsty,' Emma broke in kindly. 'And it's gloomy news anyway, but there's already provision to give young children and nursing mothers priority if milk becomes scarce, and the price is to be controlled to two pence a pint.'

'Two pence a pint! But that's sixteen pence a gallon. That's a fortune!' Kirsty exclaimed. 'And somebody has to produce it. Surely it's better for us to do what we can do well at Fairlyden and leave the corn to the farmers in the south and east who know about grain and potatoes?'

'Aah, but the milk producers willna get sixteen pence a gallon,' Alex reminded her. 'That's the price limit for folks buying it frae shops.' He sighed heavily. He had already been asked to join a committee which would make decisions about the cropping on the local farms if war was declared. He could see just how unpopular the task was going to be. There was a proposal for setting land aside near villages and towns for allotments too, so that householders could grow their own potatoes and vegetables if the situation became as desperate as it had in the last war. Kirsty was intelligent and he could understand why she would not want to make changes when she was still struggling to find her way without her father. There were a lot of farmers, even in Muircumwell, who made a worse job of their farms than his niece ever would, but he could see it would be difficult to make changes, even with the government's incentives to encourage ploughing.

'Maybe ye should buy a tractor for Fairlyden, Kirsty. Ye can drive a car so ye'd be able to drive a tractor with a bit o' practice and it would be a lot easier than walking behind the horses.' Kirsty frowned. She could hardly believe Uncle Alex was serious.

'How can the lassie afford a tractor, Alex!' It was her grandmother who sprang to her defence. Sarah spoke sharply, though it was an effort to rouse herself these days. She listened, but she had no heart to join in the plans o' the young generation. 'Have you forgotten Logan borrowed money frae the bank to buy the land at Muircumwell Mill?' She sighed wearily. 'I blame myself. My father always counselled against borrowing money.'

'Oh no,' Beth protested softly. 'It wasna you who—'

'I encouraged him. I wanted the Guillymans' contemptuous old lawyer to . . . I wanted him to know the Fairlys had survived, aye and flourished, in spite o' his arrogance and disdain all those years ago. I was a foolish old woman. The man is probably retired, or even dead by now. Kirsty's paying for my pride, my ambition.'

'Oh Granny, that's not true. We all wanted to keep the Muircumwell land. You canna blame yourself.'

'No indeed,' Beth declared firmly. 'None o' us would be at Fairlyden today if ye hadna struggled to keep it. Besides . . .' Her eyes were shadowed as she mentioned her husband's name and her voice shook a little. 'I know how much satisfaction it gave Logan to buy that land himself, aye, and to let Simon Guillyman see that he could buy it.'

'Maybe ye're right, Beth,' Sarah murmured wearily, her flash of spirit fading, but her brown eyes were steady as they looked across at Kirsty. 'You'll win through, lassie,' she said softly. 'I know you will. You'll never let them take Fairlyden away from you either, will you?'

'Of course not, Granny.'

Twenty-Four

It was impossible to look up at the clear blue of the late summer skies and think that war had actually been declared, that men and women were already fighting, the long-talked-of air raids a real possibility, the gas masks an essential part of daily life. It was Lucy who made them all realise how far-reaching the awful effects of war could be. Some months ago there had been an appeal for householders to register if they had room for evacuees. The childless Lucy, with a wealth of love and compassion to offer, had registered eagerly. Now she was filled with a mixture of trepidation and excitement.

'The evacuees are really coming! They're expected at the station some time this afternoon. Any that arena placed are to be brought to the village hall until places can be found for the puir wee mites. Oh Mistress Fairly, I asked for a wee bairn, even a babe if there were any, but d'ye think I'll be able to look after one?'

'Of course ye'll manage fine, Lucy,' Beth smiled. 'You helped to look after Kirsty when ye were little more than a bairn yourself.'

'Oh I do hope the wee soul will like the bedroom. Paddy helped me paint it weeks ago in case it came to this. We dinna ken whether we'll get a boy or a lassie so we painted it pale green and Paddy stuck a border o' flowers round the walls and I've made new curtains out o' the ones I had in the old cottage, and I've lined them well for the blackout regulations.'

'I'll drive you to the station, Lucy,' Kirsty volunteered. 'I don't suppose children from the town will be used to walking very far. They'll miss the buses and trams.'

'Ach, that would be good o' ye, Miss Kirsty. We shall be back in good time for the milking. What about the petrol rationing though?'

Kirsty grimaced. 'Six gallons a month. We shall just have to get used to walking again. I have plenty of petrol for now though.'

'Aye, and the children will be tired and excited,' Beth sighed.

'And I think some o' the mothers are supposed to accompany the young ones. They'll be glad to reach their destination. Maybe we should have prepared a room too, but I couldna face the prospect o' welcoming strangers at the time o' the registrations.'

'Of course ye didna,' Lucy agreed sympathetically, 'and ye've plenty to do with the auld Mistress and Master Luke, as well as the milking and hens to attend to, and that big hoose to keep. Is the Mistress any better today?'

'No, but she isna any worse. She says she is just very tired. Doctor Broombank says it's her heart. She is still in bed.'

'Well, that's a sure sign she isna in good fettle! I remember weel how she was aye the first to rise in the auld days when Miss Kirsty was a bairnie.'

'Yes. She still likes to get up early and make sure Luke eats his porridge before he cycles to the station.'

'How much longer will Master Luke stay at school?' There was no criticism in Lucy's tone or in her expression, yet Beth felt guilty that she had encouraged her only son to continue his studies when everyone else at Fairlyden had to work so hard.

'This is his last year at the Academy. He would like to go to the university so that he can become a minister after . . .'

'A minister!' Lucy's brow puckered, then cleared. 'Weel, weel . . .' she murmured. 'Master Luke would make a good minister, him being so soft hearted and kindly wi' folks. But what about all the languages he kens. Would it no' be a terrible waste for him to be an ordinary minister?'

'I dinna ken, Lucy, I just dinna ken what will happen now that war has been declared. Rabbie Burns was right enough when he said, "The best laid plans o' mice and men gang aft a-gley." None o' us ken what we might have to do.' Beth frowned. Luke had had his seventeenth birthday in May and already men from eighteen to forty-one were being called up for the armed services. Luke and his contemporaries had been registered. Beth shuddered. It was like history repeating itself; this time it was her son instead of her husband. For a moment or two her mind darkened and her steadfast faith in an 'Almighty and Everlasting God' wavered. Yet there was a difference. This time the government was prepared. Perhaps not as prepared as it should have been according to Alex; the politicians had considered the storage of imported cereals and fertilisers too expensive and now the war was really upon them and there was little food in reserve. Consequently every farm was to retain essential workers, at least within reason. Beth was not sure what that meant, but she was becoming convinced that the best way to safeguard her only son was to persuade him to work at Fairlyden. Such selfishness was alien to Beth's gentle nature but there was no talk of this war being over within a few months; indeed it promised to be bitter and prolonged, and even more destructive than the last war; there were no boundaries in the sky, and no distinction between civilians and soldiers.

When the train drew into the little station at Muircumwell it was already more than an hour later than expected. Some of the host families had already gone back to the village hall with demands for better organisation or refreshments; others waited irritably, impatient at the delay. Kirsty stood beside the car when the train whistle blew at last, while Lucy scurried on to the platform, eager to be presented to the young stranger who was to be placed in her care by the billeting officer, a harassed-looking woman by the name of Clare Lawson.

Kirsty watched several small groups appear; tired, grubby children, gas masks slung around their necks, clutching each other's hands or the hands of equally tired-looking mothers. She was astonished to see a stunned-looking Lucy approaching, leading a boy of about nine or ten by the hand and accompanied by a thin, sharp-featured woman with lank, greasy hair and a pasty face, her coat held together by a large safety pin and with a large hole in her stocking. The woman held a screaming baby on one hip and a brown paper parcel under her arm, while another boy tagged along behind, clinging to her skirt, looking more belligerent than shy.

'Miss Lawson says I'm the only one who volunteered to take a wee bairn when I filled in the registration form,' Lucy gasped in bewilderment even before she reached Kirsty and the motorcar. 'She says I've to take the whole family!'

'Did you tell her you have only one spare room?'

'Aye, she says it isna – isna policy to split them up . . .' She glanced down at the boy beside her and lowered her voice to a hushed whisper. 'She says some o' the families only have one room! For cooking and sleeping – and everything. She says some o' them share a closet with about ten or more families! I canna believe that, can ye, Miss Kirsty?'

'It's true, Missus! We'll be all right if ye hae a drawer for oor

215

Irene. Ye told that auld . . . that woman ye'd a big bed. It'll dae. Oor Arf an' me can sleep at the bottom an' me Ma will sleep up top.' He looked back. Kirsty and Lucy followed his gaze to see the woman standing open mouthed, staring around her and looking anything but pleased to be nearing the end of her journey.

'Come on, Ma! What ye're gaping at?'

'Shut up, Lenny! Eeh, you!' she glared suspiciously at Lucy. 'Where's t'other hooses then? An' t'pub?'

'There's houses in the village,' Kirsty answered when Lucy seemed to have been struck dumb. Then to Lucy she said softly, 'Dinna worry. Maybe the boys could sleep at our house. I'm sure Mother . . .'

'No, no. Miss . . . er . . . the woman wi' the lists said none o' the families are tae be separated.' Kirsty was about to argue but as she glanced down at the younger boy she saw him wipe a stream of yellowish green mucus from his nose on to the sleeve of his jacket, and from there on to the leg of filthy grey shorts – at least she assumed they had once been grey, and might even resume something of their original colour if Lucy had her way with them in her peggy tub. She swallowed a sudden feeling of nausea as Arf poked his finger as far into his slimy little nose as he could get it. She averted her eyes swiftly.

The Glasgow family piled into the back of Kirsty's car with varying comments and exclamations while Lucy seated herself stiffly in the front beside Kirsty. She gave a sideways glance and wrinkled her nose expressively as their eyes met briefly and slid away. Kirsty too had detected the smell, a malodorous mixture of stale sweat, tobacco, urine and worse.

'I expect the bairn needs changing,' Lucy muttered under her breath, but they both knew it was not just the youngest member of the family, or even the two scruffy little boys, who were the culprits.

'Is someone bringing your luggage later?' Kirsty asked. 'We shall have to get on. We shall be late for the milking as it is.'

'Luggage? I've got me claes here.' The woman indicated the brown paper parcel. 'And they've got their ain . . .' She glanced at the pitifully small bundles attached with string to the straps of the boys' gas mask cases. Kirsty's eyebrows rose involuntarily.

'That's all you have?'

'The man at the depot i' Glasgae said we'd be sharing

everything wi' oor new families.'

Beside her Kirsty felt Lucy give a slight shudder and she let in the clutch with less than her usual expertise so that the car bumped and jerked for a moment before proceeding along the road to the village. They had driven through Muircumwell, past the high wall which surrounded the Manse and the glebe and over the bridge before anyone spoke again.

'Where's the hooses ye talked aboot? And what about t'Picture hoose and t'pubs?'

'We've just passed through the village, Mrs McGuire,' Kirsty answered with a faint note of consternation in her voice. 'Surely you saw it – the post office and the tearoom, with Miss Lizzie's grocery shop attached, and the smiddy down the lane at the side.'

'Ye mean that wee bunch o' hooses was a village! Bloody hell! Where was the Picture Hoose then?'

'We dinna have a cinema in Muircumwell. We have to go to town for that. To Annan or Dumfries.'

'Guid God! They've sent us intae the bloody wilderness, richt enuch! Ye'll no' get Gladys McGuire biding here! I want tae gang hame richt noo . . .' The sleeping baby wakened at the sound of her mother's screeching voice and began to howl.

'Aw Ma, we'll hae tae bide forty days and forty nichts if we've come tae the wilderness!' Lenny reminded.

'Bide forty bloody nights! Here? What are ye haverin' aboot?'

'The school maister read it oot o' the bible.'

'I'm no' interested i' the school maister an' his bible thumping! I want tae gang hame, I tell ye.'

'There's no train back to Glasgow tonight, I'm afraid,' Kirsty said and the regret in her voice was quite genuine, though for very different reasons than sympathy towards the plight and desires of Gladys McGuire and her brood.

'I thought the wilderness was all rocks and ravens and big stanes . . .' Lenny ventured. 'But I reckon this is a'richt. I never seen sae much green afore! Look! Look, oor Arf, there's a bull! Three o' them – and mair,' he yelled in excitement and Irene stopped howling to stare at him.

'They're not bulls, they're cows, laddie,' Lucy corrected with a wan smile, but a smile for all that. Kirsty felt a slight relief. Maybe once the McGuires reached Fairlyden and were bathed and fed things would not seem quite so bad. 'Is your brother's name really Arf?'

'He's Arthur, after his Grandfaither McGuire.'

217

'He lived in t'country once, didn't he, Ma? Grandfaither, I mean? Said there were hosses as big as elephants. I seen an elephant in a book at school once. It didn't half look big beside the wee Injun man!'

'Ye canna tell whether it's big or no' if it's just a picture!' his mother scorned. 'Ye're as bad as your Grandfaither McGuire wi' your tales and 'maginings. He tellt me t'countryside was a braw place tae bide, not like this wi' nowt tae look at but fields!'

'There's trees tae,' Lenny argued defensively and Lucy's heart warmed towards him a little. 'An' look, there's a bird sitting on a bush! Aw, he's flown awa' . . .'

'Dinna look sae disappointed, laddie. Ye'll see lots o' birds, and if ye're here in springtime ye'll see them building their nests and maybe ye'll even see the wee eggs if ye're lucky. Lovely colours some o' them – as blue as the sky and . . .'

'I'll thank ye no tae fill the lad's head wi' sic rot, Mrs Kildougan,' Gladys McGuire snapped. 'Eggs as blue as skies indeed!' Lucy opened her mouth to insist before she caught Kirsty's eyes, shrugged her shoulders and closed it again.

'If you're not too tired, Lenny, maybe you'll be able to help my mother and Mrs MacFarlane gather in the hens' eggs,' Kirsty suggested tactfully. 'We need a pair of sharp eyes like yours to search for hidden nests.'

'Ye mean ye've got real hens! D'they make real eggs then? Aw, missus, I'd like tae see 'em! Is't like the zoo? Where ye live?' Kirsty grinned widely. 'Sometimes it's just like a zoo!' Even if the animals are not quite the same, she thought.

'Aah, Miss Kirsty, that's the first time I've seen ye wi' your old smile since the Master died,' Lucy said warmly. Maybe some good might just come out o' this lot . . . Maybe.

It was later than usual before the milking was finished and the cows returned to the field, the pigs and hens fed and the horses groomed and watered. Beth was just as dismayed as Lucy had been by the number and state of the evacuees allocated to the Kildougans. She immediately offered to accommodate the two boys, knowing that Lucy would prefer to keep the baby, even though that meant putting up with the mother.

'I'd best do as they say and keep them all together, at least for now, thank ye, Mistress,' Lucy muttered despondently.

218

'But the first thing I'm going to do is bathe them all – even her.' She shuddered. 'Did ye notice how she keeps scratting her head? And the laddies too ... They're loozie if ye ask me. She hasna even got a clean nappy for the babe either. Her puir wee buttocks are red raw! No wonder she keeps greeting. I had to cut up a good towel to make two dry nappies. I dinna ken what we're going to do ... I mean Paddy and me canna clothe the lot o' them! We didna expect to be landed like this. I'll need to make the laddies a pair o' breeks frae Paddy's second-best pair afore I can wash the ones they've got on!'

'Och, Lucy, surely they have at least one change o' clothes!'

'No, honest, they havena a stitch, Mrs Fairly.' Lucy's face crumpled. 'They'll be a disgrace to Fairlyden, and to me, when they gang to school tomorrow ...' Beth saw she was near to tears.

'No one can blame you for the state o' the bairns, Lucy. Anyway I'm sure I have some old trousers that Luke used to wear, and I'll send up some old towels for the baby's nappies. We shall all have to unravel our old woollens and start knitting for the poor waifs. Make do and mend, that's what the government is urging us to do frae now on, so we'll start with the laddies.'

'Aye ...' Lucy murmured, biting her lip to stop it trembling.

'Is something else worrying ye, Lucy? Kirsty said the mother was a rough, unkempt woman?'

'Aye, she is that. She's a slovenly, handless critur if ye ask me. I just popped back into the house to change into my working clothes ready for the milking after I'd been to bring in the cows with Anna. I found Mrs McGuire in ma bedroom trying on ma best goon, the one I keep for the kirk.'

'Surely not! She has only just arrived!'

'I ken. And – and she smells. I told her she couldna take my clothes and she shouldna be in my room either. It's Paddy's room as weel.'

'Quite right! The woman canna have any manners at all!'

'She – she gave an awfy cackle. Nasty it was! Said she didna mind seeing Paddy in there, either wi' his claes or without! She says it's share and share alike frae now on. That's what they told her when they packed her and her bairns off frae Glasgow.'

'That's ridiculous, Lucy! Has she no clothes of her own at all?'

219

'Just a wee parcel and I think that's mostly cigarettes and a pair o' shoes that're needing to be taken to old Mr Turner for mending afore she can wear them.'

Twenty-Five

The sun was setting over the Galloway Hills, gilding Criffel, the highest and most distinctive mountain, with a golden crown instead of the ghostly cloak of mist which usually heralded rain. The birds were already settling down for the evening with a last joyful trill when Kirsty walked back up the short track and crossed the farm steading to the Fairlyden cottages after supper. It had been a long day and she was tired, but she knew how worried Lucy was by the unexpected invasion of her home. She guessed she might need a little moral support over the question of bathing too. Neither the boys nor their mother looked as though they had ever bathed before.

Beth was concerned and angered by the burden which had been thrust upon Lucy, and Paddy too. She had gathered up some nightshirts which Luke had outgrown, and a nightgown of her own, as well as some underwear and a cotton dress. Kirsty was only too glad to return to the cottage with the garments and she hoped Lucy would realise she was not without support in coping with the evacuees.

She had been lost in her own thoughts as she walked and she was almost at the door when she looked up. She was startled to see James MacFarlane sitting on the old stone slab which had been outside the original farmhouse at Fairlyden since the steading was first built. She realised he must have been watching her approach from beneath those hooded eyes of his. She began to tremble inwardly. She had not spoken to him since the brief exchange at her father's funeral and before that she was convinced he had deliberately avoided her. His long legs were stretched out in front of him and he looked surprisingly contented, especially after Anna's assertion that he had serious problems concerning Nithanvale. Of course he had spent the major part of his twenty-nine years at Fairlyden so perhaps its familiarity was comforting to him now. Kirsty wished the colour would not ebb and flow in her cheeks the way it always did at the sight of him. She bit her lip and frowned in annoyance at her own volatile emotions.

'I'm sorry if I'm disturbing the peace of the evening for you, Kirsty,' he remarked dryly, misinterpreting the reason for her frown.

'Disturbing? But you're not. It is rather a surprise to see you here in the evening though . . .?'

'I wanted to make sure Mother and Uncle Thomas were not too anxious. It's not every day that war is declared after all.'

'No,' Kirsty reflected gravely. 'It hardly seems possible.' Her eyes moved over the well-loved landscape. Everything seemed so tranquil. 'But we know it is a fact, unfortunately. I came to bring Lucy some clothes for her – for the evacuees. I thought she might need a little support to get them into a bath.'

'A-ah, she needed that all right!' James gave a chuckle which reminded Kirsty of the Jamie MacFarlane of her teenage years – before she had become so aware of him as a man and herself as a member of the opposite sex, with all the complications such awareness can bring to what had once been a delightful, if volatile, friendship.

'What happened?'

'The laddies flatly refused to go anywhere near the bath, or to get undressed. I think poor Lucy was half drowned herself. I was sitting out here chatting to Paddy when we heard the hullabaloo. I've never seen him move so fast. He thinks the world o' Lucy so he will not stand any nonsense from them.'

'I'm glad he was handy. They both have hearts o' gold, but the McGuire family might try their patience. I do hope Lucy doesna end up being too miserable. She was really looking forward to having a lovable youngster to mother. She was only doing her best to cooperate, as the government requested. I think the authorities have taken advantage of her good nature.'

'For once, my dear Kirsty, we are in agreement.' She could see a gleam of humour in his eyes now. 'Come and take a seat and tell me how Joe Little is doing?'

'He's fine. I – Thank you for recommending him.'

James nodded, but his eyes seemed suddenly shadowed. 'He's a good lad. What do you think of this business of being at war? Nobody seems to know what to expect. I notice you have not built an air raid shelter.'

'No-o. Do you really think they might bomb the farms, James?'

'Well, they canna bomb them all, and I suppose they'll aim at the factories and the towns first. We'll just have to pray for deliverance. Aunt Lizzie says they've made a shelter in the village but she vows she willna use it.'

Suddenly there was a loud scream followed by a stream of invective from Gladys McGuire.

'I think I'd better go in there,' Kirsty frowned. 'Paddy canna threaten a woman! Neither can he forcibly strip the clothes from her back.'

'We-ell . . . he could.' A smile twitched at the corners of his mouth. 'And from the little I've seen of her, I dinna think Mrs McGuire would object to that.' Kirsty blushed. James's dark brows rose slightly and he eyed her pink cheeks speculatively, and with faint surprise. Surely Kirsty could not still be the innocent girl he had known if she had really spent the night at Avary Hall with Simon Guillyman?

'I-I've brought her some clean clothes so she might be persuaded rather than forced.'

Kirsty was right. Gladys agreed to bathe if she could keep the cotton dress which Beth had sent. As for the nightgown, she declared she never wore one, but she would keep it for a dress and tie it in the middle with a string.

'Thanks for coming, Miss Kirsty. I dinna ken how I'm going to manage that one. The bairns are no' so bad and wee Irene looks real bonnie since she's been washed and changed. She's sleeping now.'

Kirsty nodded. 'Well, see that Gladys does her share o' the work, Lucy. After all they are her children and she would have had to look after them if they'd stayed in Glasgow.'

'I dinna ken what she feeds them on for she says she's never peeled a tattie or made a plate o' soup in her life, or porridge either! Can ye believe it! They buy chips frae a shop, and peas when they have enough money. The rest o' the time they eat bread and jam. Yon wee Arthur wouldn't drink the milk because he'd seen it coming frae the cow. "It ain't proper milk" he says!'

'I expect he'll soon learn what's good for him,' Kirsty smiled. 'I'll see you at the milking in the morning, Lucy.'

Kirsty was surprised to see James still sitting on the stone slab outside.

'I'll drop you off at the house.' He jumped to his feet and opened the door of his car which was standing nearby.

'But it's only a couple of hundred yards!'

'Well then, you've nothing to be afraid o' in such a short distance, have you?'

'I'm not afraid!' Kirsty climbed into the car with a defiant toss of her head.

Jamie swung the handle and the engine burst into life but he did not drive off. He half turned and looked her straight in the eye. 'I'm glad you realise I dinna trick girls into spending the night with me,' he remarked cryptically and let out the clutch. Kirsty stared at his profile. A muscle was pulsing in his cheek and she remembered it had always been a sign of tension with him.

'What do you mean by that remark, James?'

'We-ell, since you didna go back to America with Simon Guillyman, I've come to the conclusion he must have tricked you into spending the night with him at Avary Hall after the Dumfries Farmers' dance.'

'Simon never tricked me . . .'

'So, you did go with him willingly.'

'I don't know what you're talking about.'

'Don't you? Have you forgotten the night of the dance? It was foggy. Guillyman's car was seen at the fork in the road – abandoned. Yet there was nothing wrong with it the next morning.'

'Maybe the engine was flooded then, or damp, or something. It certainly wouldna fire the night before or I wouldna have had to walk all the way home!'

'You *walked home*? All the way to Fairlyden? In that fog? Did you walk alone?'

'Of course I did!'

'But Aunt Lizzie thought . . . She said . . .' James's mouth tightened. 'She certainly had the impression you had spent the night with Simon Guillyman at Avary Hall.'

'Then Miss Lizzie shouldna jump to conclusions!' Kirsty exploded indignantly.

'She saw Guillyman the next day. He must have misled her deliberately!'

'Well, if you were so interested you should have known I was at the milking the morning after the dance.'

'I was interested. I did ask. Mother said you looked terrible, as though you'd never been to bed. I thought Guillyman must have collected his car and driven you back in time for the milking.'

Kirsty opened her mouth in a furious protest, but then she slowly closed it again; several things were falling into place. She recalled Simon's pique because she had resisted his charm, refused to respond to his desires, his demands; she remembered Miss Lizzie's coolness in the weeks which had followed. She was certain James himself had been avoiding her since that night when they had danced together, laughed together. He had scarcely spoken to her until tonight . . . Now Britain was at war; no one knew from one hour to the next what lay ahead. She stared at him.

'So? You really believed that I had spent the night with Simon Guillyman!' she muttered accusingly. Yet even as she said the words she remembered how anxious her own mother had been, how her beloved father had felt it necessary to take her to task. At the thought of her father's earnest, loving face her eyes filled with unexpected tears. She turned her face swiftly away.

'I'm sorry, Kirsty! Dinna cry, lassie. I didna mean . . .' James looked away, frowning fiercely at the track as he drew up at the garden gate. Kirsty blew her nose, struggling to regain her usual composure. At least she knew why James had been so cold and contemptuous towards her. How long ago it all seemed now, and how unimportant in comparison to the events of the past year. She felt a deep thankfulness that she had not disgraced her family or given her father real cause for distress over Simon Guillyman.

'I should have guessed how it was, Kirsty. I'm sorry.'

Kirsty nodded, accepting his apology more readily tonight than she would have done even a few months ago. Besides, she knew how easily rumours could start in the small community of Muircumwell and at least James must have cared enough to be concerned, if only as an old friend. 'Will you come in to see Mother and Luke? Granny will be in bed. She retires early now.'

'Not tonight, thanks. I must get back.' Suddenly his lean face took on a haunted look and his eyes were troubled.

'Jamie?' She barely noticed the old affectionate name had slipped out in her concern. 'Is – is something wrong?' He grimaced, but then his eyes seemed to search her face. She thought he would confide in her, but to her astonishment he reached out and cupped her chin gently between his hands; he gazed down into her eyes with an intensity which bewildered her.

'Everything's wrong! Everything! I'm right back to where I started, and this time there aren't even dreams left! I know it's useless to cry for the moon!'

'I dinna understand?'

In answer he bent his head and pressed his lips to hers. It

was not the kiss of a friend, but it was not the kiss of a lover either. There seemed to Kirsty to be an unspeakable yearning, a desperate need behind James's kiss. Then he was turning away, releasing the brake, ready to leave. Feeling confused she got out of the car, but she could not shut the door and leave him with that awful bleakness in his eyes.

'Mary – your . . . your . . . Is Miss MacFarlane well?'

'Oh yes, Mary is in good health. She has been patient and she deserves to be happy. I have achieved that at least.' He lifted a hand in a brief salute, dismissing further questions. 'Good night, Kirsty. Take care,' he added softly, so softly that his words were almost drowned by the noise of the engine.

Kirsty stood and watched until the car was lost to sight, and long after that. At least we are friends again, she thought gratefully. The war has done that. But friendship isna enough, her heart cried silently. I love him and he's going to marry Mary MacFarlane. So why did he seem so unhappy, so frustrated? Was he marrying his half-cousin to keep a promise to old Mr MacFarlane perhaps? Was that the real price he had paid for Nithanvale? Or maybe he needed her share of the money to keep the farm? Kirsty's jaw tilted. Why should she worry if that was the cause. Yet why do I feel I've failed him tonight? Why should he need comfort from me, or anything else? 'Och, Kirsty Fairly, you're imagining things!' she muttered impatiently. 'James MacFarlane needs nothing from you now he has a farm and a herd of cows to call his own – and his gentle Mary!' She turned and strode up the garden path and round to the back door.

The following morning Beth and Anna were washing up the buckets and milk cooler in the dairy while Kirsty measured the milk in the churns and carefully sealed the lids with the lead tags which would remain unbroken until they reached the creamery. She felt Anna's brooding gaze on her as she rolled the last of the churns out to the raised area in front of the dairy where Thomas was waiting to load them into the cart to take them to the collecting point at the end of the Fairlyden track.

'Jamie came over frae Nithanvale last night,' Anna remarked. 'He wanted tae make sure Thomas and me arena too worried about this war business.'

'He's a good laddie. Always was,' Beth responded, but she sensed Anna had something else on her mind.

226

'Aye, but he'll no' get over to see us so easily now the petrol's rationed.' She turned as Kirsty reentered the dairy. 'He gave ye a lift down to the hoose didn't he, Miss Kirsty? He aye talked to ye a lot when ye were bairns together. I – I wonder . . . did he give ye an inkling o' what's troubling him?'

'He mentioned the war, and yourself and Thomas, Anna.'

'Na, na, it's more than that!' Anna was almost impatient, as though she felt Kirsty was being unusually dense.

'He's bound to be worried about the war, Anna,' Beth intervened peaceably. 'Everyone is. Farmers will be under pressure, even though they arena going away to fight this time. There's a scarcity o' men already, according to Alex. Everybody will be expecting us to work miracles to produce enough food.'

'Oh aye, I ken there's that, Mrs Beth, but James was never feart o' hard work and he'll do his best. But there's more than that troubling him, I ken there is!'

'James looked contented when I saw him sitting on the stone outside your house last night.' Kirsty tried to reassure Anna. There was nothing to be gained by repeating her son's parting words, or dwelling on the bleak desolation she had glimpsed in his eyes.

'I suppose he's worried about money, Anna,' Beth suggested gently. 'Remember he and Miss MacFarlane had to buy Nithanvale and everyone is being urged to buy machinery to replace the men who have already gone to fight.' There was sadness, even a trace of bitterness, in Beth's soft voice. She had found it hard to accept there could be another war after the carnage and waste of the last one. Kirsty knew she blamed the effects of the last war, far more than the bull or Luke, for her father's death.

'It isna money that's causing James to look so miserable when he thinks nobody is watching him. I'm not saying he's wealthy, mind ye, and I ken he hasna bought a tractor yet, or one o' these newfangled milking machines, but lack o' money would never make my laddie look like that – so desolate! Anyway . . .' Anna lowered her voice and moved closer to Kirsty and her mother. 'He gave me fifty pounds last night. Fifty pounds! That's nearly a whole year's wages! I didna want to take it frae him. I told him Thomas and me are more than comfortable wi' our wee house and the pig, the milk and tatties and a wee bit o' butter when we want it. We dinna lack for anything at Fairlyden – except our youth,' she added with a brief flash of her old humour. 'But he insisted on putting the money intae the wee teapot where I keep a bit for emergencies. He said, "No one knows what's going to happen, Mother. Nithanvale could be destroyed for ever for all we know, so I want you to have this for now. I've had a good year with the milk and the heifer sales." Then he muttered something like, "Not that it'll do me any good now." He sounded fair depressed, and James was never one to lose heart.'

'Then it must be the war that's worrying him,' Beth frowned. 'Though James shouldna need to fight. Farmers with his knowledge and experience are needed at home. Is there any word o' him getting married to Miss MacFarlane, Anna? Maybe he wouldna feel so depressed if he knew their future together was settled.'

'Miss MacFarlane?' Anna sniffed disapprovingly. 'She's awa' to some sort o' training. She's hired a housekeeper to look after James at Nithanvale.'

'Aah, then that's why James will be so depressed,' Beth declared. 'Is it first aid she's learning? I expect she'll soon be home again, then everything will be all right. I'm thinking o' going to the first aid classes in Muircumwell when they get started. Kirsty's coming too, aren't ye, lassie?'

Kirsty was lost in her own thoughts, recalling the bleakness that had appeared in James's eyes the previous evening. He had looked as though his whole world had fallen apart. Yet earlier he had appeared contented, and almost happy, sitting on the stone slab outside his mother's house. 'Kirsty?'

'Miss MacFarlane isna awa' to first aid training,' Anna stated categorically. 'Anyway, she is like young Luke – too meek and milk for this wicked world if ye ask me. James needs a wife wi' a bit o' spirit, a lassie to work at his side when things go wrong. Just like you and Master Logan did. Like I'd hae done wi' my ain man. No,' Anna shook her head emphatically, 'I've never thought Miss MacFarlane was right for James, even if she'd owned Nithanvale, the whole o' the Carnland Estate! I thought he might hae confided in you, Miss Kirsty, I really did.' She glared almost accusingly at Kirsty.

'Well, I'm sorry, Anna,' Kirsty said stiffly, 'I think I would be the last person James would confide in. Maybe you should ask Luke if he knows what is wrong – though as Mother says, it's probably the war that is worrying him and I suppose it will affect all of us now that it has finally been declared.'

Twenty-Six

The baby, Irene McGuire, was the only one of the evacuees who seemed to have settled happily at Fairlyden. Neither of the boys liked the local school although they knew some of the other evacuees also attending it. They were clearly dismayed at having to walk four miles each morning until Paddy and Thomas good-naturedly renovated a couple of old bicycles for them. Gladys McGuire was even worse than her sons. She grumbled continuously at the isolation, the lack of shops and entertainment, the absence of neighbours, the scarcity of Woodbine cigarettes – and her deprivation of male company.

'If the idle besom would be doing some work now, she would not be having the energy to complain all day!' Paddy exclaimed in exasperation one morning after Lucy had been reduced to tears with exhaustion and frustration.

'Well, she should certainly look after her own children and help Lucy with the cooking. Mother has brought down our old perambulator from the attic for Irene but from what you say, Paddy, I wonder if it will just make Gladys think she can leave her in Lucy's care more than ever?'

Paddy's face softened. 'Ach, but she is a pretty babe now that Lucy has her cleaned up and a-wearing the wee white jacket the Mistress knitted, Miss Kirsty. We could manage the bairns if it wasna for their mother! Mind you, young Arf is a deil of a boy – like his mother if you'd be asking me! Arf! What a name for a laddie!'

'Isn't it short for Arthur?'

'Ach, maybe so, but it sounds as though the laddie is only half there!'

'There's no doubt he's all there! At least Lenny seems to be settling better now that we've finally convinced him he has to go to school whether he likes it or not.'

'Ach yes, we could be making a farmer of that one! He follows Anna and the Mistress like a shadow, a-feeding the hens and collecting eggs. To be sure he was that excited when he found a nest under the old cart in the shed! And he eats his egg like a man now!' Paddy chuckled. 'He'd never seen a boiled egg before. Would you believe it, Miss Kirsty, he was going to be eating the shell and all, if Lucy had not caught him in time! For certain the rationing canna be any worse than these lads have been used to!'

'Maybe you're right, Paddy, though they say things are scarce already in the towns.'

The McGuires had been at Fairlyden for almost two weeks when Gladys received a postcard from her husband to say he had been given a forty-eight hour leave and was coming to visit her before being posted south. Gladys seemed delighted at the prospect, despite the number of times she had cursed the boys and told them they were just like their father and no use to anyone.

The day after Josh McGuire's arrival was a Saturday and Lenny could hardly wait to show his father round the farm.

'Uncle Paddy says we shall see some ducklings if we're still here i' the spring and—'

'Who the h . . . Who is Uncle Paddy when he's at hame?'

'Ye ken fine it's Mr Kildougan, Faither! He tellt me tae call him that.'

'Oh aye? And the woman then, what d'ye call her?'

'Aunt Lucy. She makes smashing cakes and—'

'What's t'other one called. The young'n?'

'Ye mean Miss Kirsty?' There was a note of awe and pride in Lenny's voice as he walked with his father across the Fairlyden farmyard that autumn morning. 'Paddy says all this belongs tae her – all the hooses and sheds and even the fields. The cows and horses and a' the hens and things belong tae her and her mother and her brother. She has a pony tae – a big yin! It's called Marocco. She's promised tae gie me an' oor Arf a ride on him and . . .'

'Marocco? That's a stupid name for a horse.'

'It isna!' Lenny was irritated. He'd forgotten how argumentative his father always was. 'Anyway he's a nice horse and she's nice tae. They're all nice here – all except Miss Fussybum anyroad. She's—'

'Fussybum!' Josh McGuire gave a loud guffaw. 'Who the . . . Whaes she then?'

'She's the new teacher o' course! Her real name's Miss Fosserby but she's a fussy auld co . . . Oh, there's Miss Kirsty! Miss! Miss! This is me faither. He's come frae Glasgae tae see

230

us. Are ye mucking oot the byres again? Can I help this time then?'

'Good morning, Lenny.' Kirsty set down the wheelbarrow carefully and straightened her aching back. She grinned down at the youngster's eager face then turned to his father. 'Pleased to meet you, Mr McGuire.' She frowned. Josh McGuire's eyes were roving over her appreciatively, but she had no desire for his sort of admiration. Indeed, remembering her first impressions of his wife and children, Josh McGuire was a bit of a surprise. It was clear that he fancied himself from the way he stroked his trim moustache, and his hair was brilliantined into symmetrical waves. She wondered whether he had always been vain about his appearance or whether his brief acquaintance with the army had smartened him up as Lucy had smartened up his sons. 'Lenny has adapted very well to country life. He wants to have a go at everything.' Kirsty deliberately recalled his wandering eye and pointedly ignored the message in it. Josh shrugged.

'Not like his mother then, is he! Everything's dead around these pairts, she says. Nae life at a'. Maybe she's right after all.' His eyes challenged Kirsty. 'Nothing tae dae, it seems.'

'There's plenty of work for anyone willing to have a go, Mr McGuire.' Kirsty's tone was cool. Lenny was quick to notice it.

'Are ye going tae empty that barrow i' the midden, Miss Kirsty? Uncle Paddy says I'll mak a gran' worker some day. Can I wheel the barrow for ye?'

Kirsty looked ruefully at the heavy barrow. The contents resembled runny brown porridge. 'I only wish you could, Lenny, but it's heavier than it looks. It will not be quite so bad when the cows begin to sleep in the byre instead of in the fields. We give them straw to sleep on then. It absorbs the liquid you see and that helps to make the manure.'

'And the manure helps the crops tae grow when ye spread it on the fields. Uncle Paddy tell't me that tae!' Lenny announced with pride. 'He said I could help spread the wee heaps if I'm still here when they dae it.'

'Eh, I remember ma ain father telling me about that when I was a wean!' Josh McGuire interrupted. 'Scalin' dung, that's what he called it. Loved the country, he did. Moved tae Glasgae tae earn mair money though, when he was young. Maybe the laddie has inherited some o' his ancestors' love o' the land, eh Miss Kirsty?'

'Maybe you're right, Mr McGuire. You'll have to excuse me

now. I've another barrowload to bring yet and several more jobs to do before midday.'

'Och, that's no job for a woman. See here. I'll soon tak this tae the midden for ye.' He shouldered Kirsty out of the way before she could protest. 'That's the midden, is't? T'other side o' the stane dyke?'

'Aye, Father, that's it! But ye've got tae push the barrow tae the top o' the plank so it goes intae a neat heap and disna spread all o'er! That's the hard bit.'

'Och, there's naething hard aboot that, laddie, not for a man as strong as your faither! Just ye watch this!'

Josh almost ran towards the midden, mounting the plank without hesitation. Everything might have gone all right if the plank had not wobbled slightly, or if the contents of the barrow had been less sloppy, or even if Josh McGuire had not been so intent on showing off to Kirsty and his son. As it was he was not ready to hoist the handles of the barrow and tip out the contents. Before Kirsty could shout a warning the barrow wheel had run off the end of the plank. The barrow slipped, turned upside down and Josh McGuire followed in an undignified heap of arms and legs.

Kirsty tried hard to suppress her laughter at the inelegant spectacle. Her eye caught Lenny's, she saw his thin shoulders shake; he clutched his hands to his face and tried in vain to stifle his mirth but he could not contain an explosive splutter. Kirsty felt the tears running down her cheeks as Josh floundered and stuttered in the stinking midden. At that moment Paddy returned from the small paddock behind the steading where he had been helping a heifer to calve. He stopped short at the sight of Josh McGuire with his neat ginger moustache and carefully arranged hair now plastered in dung. Paddy's involuntary guffaw could have been heard a mile away. Certainly it brought Lucy and Anna and Gladys McGuire to their respective doors. Still laughing as though he might burst Paddy disappeared into the stable where Thomas was unharnessing the mare which he had used to cart away the milk cans. Paddy pulled the bewildered old man out into the yard, quite unable to explain the reason for his uncontrollable mirth. Thomas's eyes widened. A deep chuckle began in the region of his boots; it grew and grew as it reached his wrinkled face and Thomas Whiteley enjoyed the best laugh he had had since the influenza left him deaf many years ago.

Josh McGuire floundered on to clean dry ground at last and stood there like a stranded, but exceedingly angry, fish. He glared at the two men, at Kirsty, and at his son, then gave vent to a stream of invective which made even his wife wince, though it did nothing to curb her own hilarity. Josh charged towards her and Lucy like an enraged bull, leaving a slimy brown trail in his wake.

Just in time Lucy realised his intention; before he could dash into the house, and possibly even up to the bathroom, she slammed the door shut with a little scream of laughter and indignation.

Paddy controlled his hilarity with an effort, strode towards the angry Josh and grasped him gingerly by the cleanest part of his shirt.

'Now, now!' He held up his other hand in warning, but laughter threatened to convulse him once more as he looked into the filthy and enraged face of McGuire. 'Don't you be a-shaking your filth on to me! 'Twas not Paddy Kildougan who was a-making you take a dive into the midden, now was it?' Again laughter threatened to overcome Paddy and his leathery face worked in an effort to control himself. 'No doubt you would be a-showing Miss Kirsty and that laddie o' yours what a verra fine man you are, eh? Now come along to the horse trough . . .'

'Horse trough! Not on your sweet, bloody life! I'm—'

'You're a-coming with me!' Paddy's voice grew stern, despite his quivering lips. 'Get the bucket from the byre, young Lenny, and we'll soon be having this father o' yours washed down, eh? Thomas!' He raised his voice and gesticulated for another bucket and the yard brush. Thomas gave an unholy grin and disappeared.

'I'm not getting in there!' Josh screamed, interspersing every word with an oath.

'Of course you're not,' Paddy agreed pacifically, but his eyes sparkled devilishly and he turned his face towards the house and winked hugely. Kirsty followed his glance and saw Lucy, Anna and Gladys still watching from the window, while a sleepy-eyed Arf peered from the window above.

'Where are ye taking me then?' Josh demanded suspiciously.

'You'd only contaminate the water for the horses if we put you in the trough, and to be sure Lucy would flay me alive, and yourself too, if I was a-letting you into her house looking and stinking . . .' Again Paddy had difficulty controlling his laughter and Kirsty had to turn away as she caught his eye. 'Stinking like the midden to be sure . . .' Paddy choked. 'We'll dowse you with the buckets before we strip off your clothes.'

'The water will be cold! Wait! Wait!' But Paddy chuckled and jumped away to seize a bucket for himself as Thomas poured the clean cold water over the unfortunate Josh.

Kirsty left them to it.

When Kirsty went to bring in the cows for the milking later that afternoon, Lenny ran across the field to join her. She saw at once that he had been crying but was too tactful to comment.

'Ma faither's gone.'

'Gone? Left you mean, Lenny?' The boy gulped and nodded. 'But I thought he wasna due back at camp until tomorrow?'

'He isna. Ma mother's gone tae. She isna coming back.'

'B-but I dinna understand! Where's Arf?'

'Gone tae. I didna want tae gang back tae Glasgae, Miss Kirsty! Ma faither flayed me wi' his belt, but Uncle Paddy and Aunt Lucy ran up the stair and stopped him.'

'I-I see. Well, I expect your mother will come back tomorrow when your father returns to camp.' Kirsty comforted.

'She isna coming back, not ever and – and she said she doesna care about me an' oor Irene an' if we want tae bide here and wait for Hitler tae get us we can. Will Hitler get us here, Miss Kirsty?'

Kirsty swallowed hard as she stared down into the boy's grubby white face and wide fearful eyes.

'No. Our soldiers and sailors and the men who fly aeroplanes will not let Hitler come to Britain.'

'Ma faither says he will!'

'I'm sure your father is wrong, but even if Hitler did come he would not know where to find us at Fairlyden. Didn't you know, Lenny, that's what "den" means – a safe place to hide? And Fairlyden is a safe place for the Fairlys – and all the people who live and work here, like Lucy and Paddy, Anna, Thomas and Joey Little.'

'An' oor Irene an' me?' Lenny asked uncertainly.

'Of course. You belong to Fairlyden too, for as long as you want to stay.'

'That's what Aunt Lucy and Uncle Paddy said and they said you and Mistress Fairly would say it tae!' Lenny's face brightened, but his brown eyes still looked troubled. 'Ma faither was mad because I laughed . . .'

'We all laughed.'

'I ken. That's why he's gone. But I dinna care sae long as I can bide here!' Kirsty detected the uncertainty beneath the defiant words. Josh and Gladys McGuire were not very good parents, she thought sadly.

'Paddy and Lucy will be pleased you have chosen to stay with them. They love children. You'll be all right, Lenny.'

'I ken . . .' Lenny bit his lip and turned away abruptly to hide the sparkle of tears which had sprung to his eyes again. 'I just wish oor Arf hadna gone tae – even if we dae fight sometimes.'

Twenty-Seven

As autumn progressed the people of Muircumwell still waited for the dreaded effects of bombs dropping from the sky but, apart from wisps of white cloud, it remained clear and innocent; the beauty of the Scottish countryside was unblemished; the killing gases and invading armies had not materialised. In fact the declaration of war had had little affect on the daily routine at Fairlyden. Even the weather had been favourable and the harvest had yielded well; the scent of woodsmoke mingling with the evening mists lent a warm sense of continuity and security. In an effort to comply with the blackout regulations Beth had made heavy curtains for every room, including the tiny attic window. Since there had never been cinemas or street lighting in the village, or anywhere near it, the regulations caused little hardship to the locals.

Even so people were more wary when they met together in small groups – in Lizzie's store or at the smiddy, the inn, the village hall or even the kirk. Two men from the outskirts of Muircumwell had been taken away; rumour claimed they were suspected aliens; an enemy plane had been sighted over the Firth of Forth and that brought renewed fears and emphasised the fact that there were no boundaries to this war; the sea no longer rendered Britain invincible. Indeed the sinking of the Royal Oak in its home base of Scapa Flow sent shivers of fear down many a spine and Beth's was no exception.

Her resolve to protect her only son increased as the weeks passed. If only Luke could be persuaded to work at Fairlyden for the duration of the war. At least he had a choice – to farm, or to fight – a choice which had been denied his father. Moreover, since Logan's death and the departure of his teacher and counsellor, the little German Jew, Luke's interest in his studies had waned considerably. Although she did not fully understand them, Beth was aware of her son's inner conflicts and confusion, his need for guidance and direction, but she was too wise to dictate to him.

'Your Uncle Alex was telling me the government plans to

reclaim one and a half million acres o' derelict land so that we can grow enough food,' she remarked conversationally one evening when there was only herself and Luke in the small sitting room off the kitchen. Luke was not deceived by his mother's light tone. He tensed inwardly and remained silent as she went on knitting without raising her eyes, her needles clicking rapidly as they fashioned a brightly coloured jersey out of a bag of wool ends for Lenny McGuire. 'Every farmer is supposed to plough more land for corn and potatoes. I canna imagine how we'll manage the extra work next harvest time. There's no idle hands to call on now that so many young men have gone to the army.' Beth's sigh was genuine. 'Your father always said Fairlyden was fine grazing land, but it's not good for corn. Ploughed land needs more horses and men to work it.'

'Kirsty will find a way, Mother. James MacFarlane thinks she's managed splendidly since – since Father was killed.'

'Aah, Luke! How often must I tell ye, laddie? Your father wasna killed. He died o' a heart attack.' Beth's voice choked a little, her thoughts momentarily diverted by memories of Logan.

'Well, he wouldna have had a heart attack if it hadna been for me. I-er . . . I've been thinking . . . I ought to try to make up for Father's absence, especially now.' Beth looked up, her blue eyes questioning. 'I know nothing can ever make up to you, Mother. But I suppose Kirsty misses him too. Maybe I could help her with the work. I would try – for Father's sake, as well as for the people who will need food if our ships go on being sunk by the German U-boats. I used to dream about being a spy if we ever did have a war but—'

'A spy!' Beth almost dropped her stitches as she stared at her son across the hearth. Luke grimaced.

'I'm good at learning languages,' he muttered defensively.

'B-but, I thought ye wanted to go to the university and be a minister?'

'I do want to be a minister, but there's no chance o' that now, not until the war is over, Mother.' Luke spoke patiently, as though Beth did not understand such things. She lowered her eyes. 'But I know I'd never make a spy either. It takes more than languages learned at school. It needs knowledge – great knowledge. Most of all it needs courage . . .'

'I'm sure ye'd have courage, Luke. B-but . . .' Beth floundered.

'We both know I didna have courage when I needed to run

238

frae the bull,' Luke muttered with rare bitterness. 'Father knew too, that's why he came after me, and that's why I've got to try to help now.' Beth's heart soared. It had been so much easier than she had expected.

'I heard Kirsty telling Uncle Alex she would have to study the records and sell the worst cows to make room for the extra corn and potatoes she has to grow. Maybe I could help her with the accounts and the milk records and pedigrees and things like that . . .' Beth's spirits plummeted again. How ignorant Luke was of all the tasks Kirsty had to do! Of course she spent time poring over books. It was probably the only thing Luke noticed because she did such things in the evenings. Sometimes she even fell asleep over them, but that was because she had already done a hard day's work. She sighed.

'I'm sure Kirsty will be glad o' any extra help,' she agreed quietly. She resumed her knitting with a sigh. 'I know she's planning to grow fifteen acres o' corn on the Muircumwell land for next harvest, as well as four acres o' potatoes. She doesna want to do it, any more than ye want to work here, but she says we've all to contribute as much as we can, even if it isna what we like.'

'War! It's such a waste!' Luke muttered with unexpected vehemence.

'Aye.' Beth sighed. 'It is. But the Scottish Agricultural Executive Committees want two hundred and sixty thousand acres o' Scottish grassland under the plough before next harvest, so there'll be plenty o' other folks disgruntled too, laddie!'

> 'Wee, modest, crimson-tipped flow'r,
> Thou's met me in an evil hour;
> For I maun crush amang the stoure
> Thy slender stem . . .'

Luke quoted the lines softly, his thin sensitive face shadowed.

'What did ye say, Luke?' Beth looked up from her knitting. 'Was that Rabbie Burns?'

'Yes. I expect he didna want to walk behind a plough all day either. It must have hurt him to uproot the daisies when he wrote that.'

'I suppose it did, but it's worse to see wee bairns starving for want o' food.' Beth's tone had a faint note of reproof.

'I suppose Uncle Alex and Aunt Emma are still upset because

Cousin Cameron has joined the air force?'

'Aye, I'm afraid they are.' Beth stopped knitting again and stared into the fire. 'I pray he'll come back safely,' she whispered fervently. 'I hate war!'

'Cameron could easily have ploughed the extra land here, as well as at the Mains, with his new tractor. D'you think Joey Little will manage to do it all?' Beth sensed Luke's apprehension even before he added, 'I dinna think I could handle the horses.'

Beth bit her lip. She often wondered how she and Logan had produced a son with so much academic intelligence, so much artistry, and yet with so little practical ability when it came to farming. Fairlyden had meant so much to her and Logan for as long as she could remember. Even now that Logan was dead she knew it would break her heart if ever she had to leave the place which held so many happy memories of their life together.

'Luke, I hope ye'll try to do whatever's needed, for all our sakes, as well as for the British nation. Thomas is getting old and there's only Joey Little for the field work. Paddy helps as much as he can, but he has plenty to do. There's jobs ye could do I'm sure. I remember harrowing the corn maself when your father was in France during the last war. Aye, we've always managed somehow. There were bigger families then, though, and more folk in the countryside.'

'James MacFarlane says more people will buy tractors to take the place o' horses and men.'

'We canna afford to do that yet! Kirsty has done well to keep up the payments to the bank for the Muircumwell land as it is. There are controls on the prices o' the food we produce already, even though the government hasna started the rationing yet, so there's no' much hope o' increasing the profits enough to buy a tractor. Mind ye, we're to be paid two pounds an acre for ploughing up the old pastures, I think, and there's help with lime, if folks can afford to buy any in the first place.'

'Yes.' Luke frowned thoughtfully. 'I wonder why James should give up now after all the problems he must have had when he first went to Nithanvale.'

'James MacFarlane? He's giving up? Whatever d'ye mean, Luke . . .?'

'He's selling the Nithanvale herd. I thought you and Kirsty would know?'

'Selling some o' the cows ye mean? He canna be selling the whole herd! Ye must be mistaken, Luke.'

'It's true. One o' the lads on the train told me it's advertised in the *Scottish Farmer*. I looked tonight. It's there all right. There's not much notice either.'

'No! I canna believe that! Anna says he's not short o' money and he thinks the world o' his cows. He's devoted himself to building up the Nithanvale herd again after that rogue o' a factor almost ruined it – and the MacFarlane name! I'm sure ye've made a mistake.'

'Here's Kirsty coming. Maybe she'll know.'

'She'll be tired, poor lassie. She was helping Paddy calve a heifer. A lot o' them have had difficult calvings recently.' Beth looked up and saw Luke's thin face flush with embarrassment. 'Aah, laddie, it's all part o' nature: births and deaths. Ye'll have to get used to such things.'

'Used to what things?' Kirsty asked, coming into the cosy room and flinging herself wearily into a chair in front of the fire. She stifled a yawn.

'Luke is going to leave the Academy. He's going to help you here until the war is over,' Beth said carefully. 'Ye'll be glad o' extra hands, won't ye, lassie?' Beth's blue eyes met her daughter's startled gaze. Kirsty saw the pleading in them. They both knew Luke would never be much use at farming, however hard he tried.

'Er . . . y-yes, yes of course we need all the help we can get.' Kirsty sighed. They missed her father's help dreadfully, especially when Thomas's arthritis was bad, or his chest rendered him breathless at the least exertion. Anna was not getting any younger either. They did not have enough money to buy one of the new milking machines yet, but she knew they would have to try to save enough money for one if the war continued, as people seemed to think it might, unless the fanatical Hitler could be defeated soon. 'We havena even started the ploughing yet,' she said aloud. 'Most o' the turnips are still to lift and there's all the manure to be carted and spread before Joey can begin. There's certainly plenty of work for you, Luke.'

'Ye look worn out, lassie. Did the heifer calve all right?'

'Bessie is all right, but the calf was dead.'

'Oh dear.' Beth sighed softly. She knew how much both Paddy and Kirsty hated to lose a calf. It meant more than money to them. It was a life, and they cared deeply.

'It was coming with its hind feet first. And the new bull hasna helped! All his calves are big, too big for heifers!'

Kirsty muttered in frustration.

'Luke says James MacFarlane is selling off the Nithanvale herd.' Beth successfully diverted her daughter's thoughts. 'Had ye heard that, Kirsty? Has Anna mentioned it?'

'No! I dinna believe that!' Kirsty stared at her brother. 'You see James more than any of us, Luke. Did he tell you that?'

'I havena seen him recently. He was – sort o' dejected. He must have been worried for ages, I think. But he never said anything. Besides things aren't the same since Mary went away to the convent. James has a grumpy old housekeeper now and she doesna welcome young folks like me.' Kirsty had jerked upright in her seat. Beth laid aside her knitting completely this time. 'Wh-what are ye staring at me like that for?' Luke asked defensively.

'Did you say a convent? Miss MacFarlane has gone to a convent?' Kirsty repeated incredulously.

'Yes. I thought you'd know. Her grandfather didna like Catholics or she'd have gone before; she didna want to upset him. Anyway he needed her to look after him. She's always wanted to be a nun. All her life. That's – that's why I liked to talk to her. She understands . . . things . . .' Luke's voice was low and he gazed wistfully into the fire.

Kirsty stared at her mother but Beth could only shake her head wonderingly. 'I'd no idea. Anna didna say anything . . .'

'She couldna have known either. No wonder James seemed so – so depressed,' Kirsty mused softly. 'Mary MacFarlane owned half of Nithanvale. I suppose that's why he has to sell the herd. It is the only way he'll be able to pay her share o' the money, I suppose.'

'That's not true!' Luke protested indignantly. 'Mary didna want any money. She told me so. She told James too – once when I was there and she was telling me what she planned to do. She said she wouldna leave Nithanvale until her grandfather's affairs were all settled and she had found James a housekeeper. She said he deserved everything because money couldna repay him for what he'd done to restore her grandfather's good name, and for the way he'd worked to keep Nithanvale and let the old man end his life there, in peace.'

'I canna think of any other reason why James would sell his beloved cows,' Kirsty declared.

'Mary is – is a real Christian, honestly.'

Kirsty did not sleep well that night despite being utterly

exhausted. She was up even earlier than usual, impatient to see Anna, but Anna was as surprised and shocked and incredulous as Kirsty had been.

'Surely he'd have told me, his ain mother? And whatever will he do if he has no cows, Miss Kirsty?' Kirsty had no answer.

It was evening before James drove up to Fairlyden to explain to his mother. Kirsty saw the car going by and paced round the garden several times before she went indoors.

'I want to check on the heifers in case any more are calving, Mother. I'll shut in the hens while I'm there.' Beth nodded, understanding the cause of her daughter's restlessness even better than Kirsty herself.

It took longer than Kirsty had expected to shut in all the hens. Although the evening shadows had long since disappeared and it was almost dark, the pullets were still reluctant to roost in their own quarters; it needed more than a little time and patience to coax them all inside their wooden huts. She shut the door at last and hurried up the slope towards the yard, afraid she might have missed James if his visit had been a brief one.

James had been watching her slim shadowy figure for the last five minutes, leaning against the rough stone wall which separated the steading from the burnside field where the hen houses were situated. Then she saw him, his long easy stride covering the distance between them as he came to meet her instead of hurrying back to his car and Nithanvale. Her heart leapt in spite of her determination to keep calm, in control. After all she had no right to demand or expect any explanation for James MacFarlane's decisions.

'Hello, Kirsty. I meant to call to see you at the house but I saw you shutting in the hens.'

'You would have called?' James had hardly been to the house since her father's death.

'Yes. I – I want to ask a favour of you, a big favour.'

'Oh? We . . . er, we saw the sale of the Nithanvale herd advertised in the *Scottish Farmer*. We were surprised. Your mother is very worried.'

'I detect a note of reproof in your voice. Believe me I would have told Mother, if I could. But you know she would have told Aunt Lizzie, who would have whispered in confidence to one or two of her favourite customers, or to Willy and Adam Taylor and their wives. They're fine people and they're good company

for Aunt Lizzie but you know how innocently posties pass on
information.'

'Yes. It sounds as though Luke was right though. You must
have known for some time that you were going to sell your
cows. He says you havena been your usual self.'

'I didn't know for certain that I would have to sell the
Nithanvale herd. I've hung on to the bitter end, just hoping it
wouldna come to that.' His voice had sunk suddenly and even
in the dim light Kirsty glimpsed that haunted look again, saw
the rapid pulse beat in his lean cheek. 'I was still hoping they
wouldna choose Nithanvale even when war was actually
declared.'

'I dinna understand. I thought you were selling to pay your
half-cousin her share of her grandfather's estate?'

'Oh no, nothing like that, Kirsty. I've insisted Mary must
have her share, even if she gives it all to the convent eventually,
but I could have paid her in small amounts, when I could
afford it.'

'I see . . .' Kirsty frowned, not seeing at all.

'I still don't know whether the government wants Nithanvale
for an air force base, or for an army camp, or whatever else
governments require in times of war. I only know it's a threat
that has been hanging over my head ever since war became a
possibility.'

'Y-you mean the government is taking over Nithanvale –
the land? The steading? Everything?' Kirsty stared up at
James incredulously.

'I havena any option. There were other farms being
considered, of course, but meetings with the officials were
confidential so I don't know which the others were. I just wish
they hadna chosen my land.'

'How awful. I'm so sorry, James.' Kirsty thought how dreadful
she would have felt, and her mother, and grandmother too, if
anyone had commandeered Fairlyden. 'What did your mother
say . . .?'

'She was a little hurt.' He grimaced ruefully. 'I should have
come yesterday to explain, before the sale of the Nithanvale
herd appeared in the paper. It was all finalised at the very last
minute. This damned petrol rationing is beginning to bite too
– at least it has recently. I've had so many extra journeys to
make, trying to sort out this business, make some sort o'
plans. Not so long ago there were farmers who couldna get out
quick enough, now most o' them are sitting tight, especially if

they have sons who would be forced to go to war . . .'

War . . . Suddenly Kirsty experienced an icy shiver. What would James do if he was not farming? Did he want to return to Fairlyden? Her heartbeats quickened. 'What was the favour you wanted to ask me, James?'

James bit his lip and frowned, then he took a deep breath. 'I want you to come to my sale. I . . .'

'Of course I shall be there! Paddy too. Everyone with an interest in pedigree Ayrshires will be at Nithanvale. Will you be ready in time? It's short notice for the sale of a whole herd surely?'

'Aah, but I've been half preparing for months, sorting out pedigrees and records and things like that. But Kirsty . . . the favour I wanted to ask is this, will you buy four Nithanvale cows at the sale? If you could come to Nithanvale beforehand I will show you the ones I think are the very best in the herd.' There was no doubting his enthusiasm and eagerness. 'I want you to buy them publicly, no matter how much . . .'

'James, I canna do that! I . . .'

'I see.' James stiffened immediately. She could not see him clearly but she knew the light had left those expressive greeny-grey eyes and her heart sank when he muttered coldly, 'I'm sorry I mentioned it. Forget it.'

Kirsty chewed her own lip now. It was common practice amongst farming friends and neighbours to attend each other's sales, to put in a bid here and there, even to buy if possible, to help make the sale a success. In the case of the Nithanvale herd there would be any number of people there willing and eager to buy. The stock was excellent and even in these uncertain times there were always fellow breeders keen to seize the last chance of acquiring a famous bloodline for their own herd. If her father had been alive he would certainly have wanted to purchase at least one animal, both for James's sake and because he would be proud to own almost any of the Nithanvale cattle.

'You dinna understand.'

'Oh yes I do, Kirsty. I know you have always held it against me for leaving Fairlyden. I expect you still believe some of the filthy rumours about the MacFarlanes cheating and faking pedigrees, but remember—'

'Will you listen to me a minute, James MacFarlane!' Kirsty almost stamped her foot in frustration and disappointment. For a moment she had actually believed James wanted to return to Fairlyden, that that was the favour he had in mind. 'I know my father would have bought at least one of the Nithanvale cows if he had been alive, but there are several reasons why I can't buy any.'

'I said forget it!' James turned away.

'Wait!' Kirsty grabbed his arm angrily. 'You always were the most proud, stubborn creature I ever knew!'

'And you always had the most furious temper of any girl I ever came across!'

'Only with you! No one else ever provokes me like you do!' She sighed and strove for calm. 'Please, don't let us quarrel. I canna buy your cows because we havena any money to spare! You must realise that Father bought the Muircumwell land soon after he had spent most of his money on the improvements to the cottages and extending the byre? The bank only loaned him the money in exchange for a bond on the whole of Fairlyden. We are managing fine, so far,' she added proudly, 'but you must see I really have to keep up the bank payments before I spend money on buying extra cattle – or anything else, and I really think we should try to buy a milking machine soon – what with your uncle and your mother getting older and if there's to be no spare labour available.'

'But Mother said you were thinking of selling some o' the Fairlyden cows.'

'I am. We have more than we can keep at Fairlyden, if we plough up grassland for corn and for potatoes as the government is urging us to do. I've been sorting out the records so that I can sell the least productive.'

'Aah, well lack of space is another obstacle altogether,' James agreed more calmly. 'You see, Kirsty, I was not asking you to use *your* money to buy the Nithanvale cows – at least only until the sale is over and my affairs are sorted out. Then I will repay you. I just want you to bid for and buy my four best cows and bring them back to Fairlyden. I need someone I can trust – and whom I think trusts me?'

'Of course I trust you, but . . .'

'You must see I canna bid for my own cows at my own sale. I could keep them back for myself, but people would be suspicious, especially after Metcalfe ruined the reputation o' the MacFarlanes and the Nithanvale herd. Anyway people would soon realise I have no other land to keep them on and they would wonder. I'm not wanting to cheat anyone, Kirsty, believe me! I just canna bear to see all my cows going to

246

strangers. I had just begun to think I was getting them as near perfection as a man can get with livestock.'

'I know . . . I-I understand now, Jamie. Father would have felt just the same.'

'If you could do this for me I promise you the four I choose for Fairlyden will produce at least as much milk as your own top producers. You would have their milk in return for their keep, and you could sell more of your own least productive animals. You would have the money you get for them and you would still have as much milk to sell. I'm not wanting you to be out of pocket,' he added proudly.

'B-but what if anything happened to the Nithanvale cows while they were at Fairlyden?'

'I've every faith you would do your best to take care of them, and Paddy too. I'm sure they'll still be here, or their calves will, if ever I get the chance to start breeding my own herd again.' He sounded so desolate and dejected that Kirsty's heart ached for him. She knew how much cattle had always meant to him, and these were his very own, bred and reared by him.

'I'll buy the cows, James, and I'll do my best to take care of them until you can get another farm.'

'I doubt if that will be possible until the war is over,' he grimaced bitterly. 'I've no idea how much the government will pay me for Nithanvale yet.'

'But what are you going to do? Would you consider com . . .'

'I'm going to join the army.'

'The army! Oh James, no!' Kirsty's hand clenched on his arm, but there was no anger in her now, only a dreadful fear.

'Dinna tell me you'd miss me after all the quarrels we've had since I left Fairlyden,' James peered down into the pale blur of Kirsty's face. He wished it was not quite so dark. He wished he could see her expression, her eyes . . .

'Of course I shall miss you,' she muttered huskily. 'Dinna go, James, please? It – it's such a waste. You love farming. You know so much about it.'

'I'm afraid there's not much alternative.'

'Yes there is. You could come back to Fairlyden. Luke is going to leave the Academy and work at home and he hates farming. I think he's doing it to please Mother. He still blames himself for Father's death.'

'Yes, I know he does, and it would upset your mother if he had to join the forces now. Mother told me tonight how relieved she is that he was going to leave school and start work. It is one more reason why I canna return to Fairlyden, Kirsty.'

'Because of Luke? But you've always got on together. He respects you more than anybody. You would be good for him . . .'

'Kirsty, the government has exempted farmers and their workers from the forces for the time being because they recognise how important it is that we grow enough food, but they will not allow any farmer to keep more than his fair share of labour. If I came to Fairlyden now it would almost certainly mean that Joey Little or Luke would be called up to serve in the forces. I knew when I sent Joe to Fairlyden to work that there was a chance Nithanvale would be taken over by the government. It was the reason I encouraged him to look for another job. I canna come along and displace him now. Anyway . . . it wouldna work, even if there was no war,' he ended implacably.

'Why not?'

'I have my pride, Kirsty. I'm used to being my own boss now, making the decisions, not taking orders, especially frae a lassie I've known since she was in nappies.' Kirsty blushed in the darkness.

'I wouldna give you orders . . .'

'You couldna help it. The answer is no.'

'Do you detest Fairlyden so much then?'

'I've never disliked anything about Fairlyden.'

'It's me then; me you resent. Isn't it?'

'Resent!' He gave a mirthless laugh. 'No, damn it! Don't you know the reason why we canna work together!' Before Kirsty realised his intention he had pulled her roughly into his arms, crushing her against his chest. His mouth searched for hers. He kissed her with a hunger that made Kirsty feel weak all over. Then she was responding to his kisses, abandoning her pride, clinging to him as though she would never let him go. She heard his gasp of surprise and exultation, she felt his lips exploring her face, her neck, returning again and again to her mouth like a moth to the candle. She had not the strength, nor the desire, to draw away. To Kirsty's mortification it was James who regained control, who drew himself stiffly away, disentangled himself firmly from her clinging arms.

'Now you know why I canna work with you at Fairlyden!' James's voice was harsher than Kirsty had ever heard it, even when he had been angry with her. He almost pushed her from him. Then he was striding away through the darkness. Kirsty pressed her fingers against her bruised lips and strove to control the hot tears which sprang to her eyes as she heard the engine of the Vauxhall being revved impatiently, as though its owner could not escape quickly enough. Hot shame washed over her and yet she shivered violently.

Twenty-Eight

Two days later Willy Taylor, the postman, delivered a letter to Kirsty, along with the news that he had been called into the army and would be leaving the following day. His wife would be delivering the letters until he returned. 'Ma brother, Adam, will be going into the navy any day now so Miss Lizzie is looking for a young girl to help her in the store.'

The man was clearly excited and anxious and Kirsty tried hard to make all the appropriate comments. She liked the young postman and she was genuinely sorry he had to go away to fight, but she had recognised James MacFarlane's handwriting on the envelope of the letter.

The tone was stiff and stilted. James offered his apologies for his behaviour. If she could still bring herself to purchase four of his best cows, and keep them until he was in a position to reclaim them, he would ensure neither she nor her family would lose by the transaction. He enclosed the records and sale numbers and further details of the pedigrees for her to study. It was clear that he had changed his mind about her visiting Nithanvale before the day of the sale.

'I shall leave the decisions regarding the mating of the cows to you and Paddy Kildougan, though if the opportunity arises to use the young bull out of Grayson Masterful, which I believe is presently in your uncle's possession at the Mains, then I trust you will endeavour to arrange it. I expect to be away indefinitely once my affairs at Nithanvale have been completed. If it is necessary for us to meet, you have my word that such meetings will be strictly for business. Perhaps I am expecting too much of you in the circumstances, but I truly hope you will secure the cows for me, for the sake of past friendship.' There was a little more but Kirsty screwed the paper into a tight ball and threw it across the room in frustration, only to retrieve it seconds later and smooth it out carefully.

She and Paddy went to the Nithanvale sale a fortnight later and bought the four cows which James had requested her to keep for him, as well as two more for the Fairlyden herd.

'They're fine beasts to be sure, Miss Kirsty, and they have excellent milk records, but I was thinking we had too many cows at Fairlyden already if we're to grow corn in the hay field and potatoes on the calf pasture?' Paddy looked anxious.

'Yes, we do have too many but I shall sell more of our own than we have bought and if the Nithanvale cows live up to their reputation we shall have as much milk from these six animals as we could get from eight of our poorest yielders. Don't forget, Paddy, we shall have some of the famous Nithanvale blood too.' Her smile had a faintly bitter twist which puzzled Paddy. 'I'll bring the milk record book up to the cottage and we'll decide which of our own cows to sell at the next pedigree sale at Castle Douglas. Uncle Alex says even our worst cows are a lot better than average, thanks to my father's skill as a breeder,' she added softly, her voice suddenly gruff.

'Ach, Miss Kirsty, your father was a fine man, sure he was, but he would have been proud of the way you have carried on.'

'Mmm,' Kirsty muttered doubtfully. 'I've been thinking, Paddy . . . if we get a good price for the cows we have to sell, we may be able to afford the milking machine a bit sooner than I had thought . . .'

'A machine! To be sure, Miss Kirsty, and what would we be needing such a thing for?' Paddy's disapproval was evident.

Kirsty bit her lip. 'Because it would save labour. There's never a winter passes now without Thomas being troubled with his chest, and his rheumatism is getting worse. Anna has to look after him. My grandmother is getting very frail too. Mother worries about leaving her in the house alone while we are all at the milking. And I'm sure Lucy would be pleased to miss the milking sometimes too, especially now that she has Irene and Lenny to look after.'

'Ach, she gets a bit tired sometimes, but there's Master Luke to help now. When is he going to learn to milk? There's no machine can soothe a cow like the touch of a hand.'

'I dinna think Luke will ever learn to milk,' Kirsty sighed. Luke still had a terrible fear of the cows and they sensed it immediately he went near them. The horses were almost as bad. Only the other day she had found him cowering against the trough in the stable because Ron, the big gelding, had moved across his stall and Luke had been too afraid to push him aside.

'Thomas asked me to harness him to take the cart up to the turnip field,' Luke had complained. 'He said Ron was as gentle as a lamb, but the stupid horse threw up his head and moved about the stall when I tried to put his collar on.' Kirsty had scarcely known whether to laugh or to cry with frustration when he held up the leather collar and tried once more to shove it over Ron's powerful head.

'No wonder the poor horse is objecting! He's shaking his head because you're putting the collar on the wrong way!'

'No, I'm not!' Luke had held up the big oval collar with the metal aimes attached.

'Luke, you must have seen Thomas or Paddy harness the horses dozens of times! You have to hold the collar upside down to get it over their head, and then turn it.' She had demonstrated with the ease of long practice and Luke had looked so ashamed and dejected that she had felt guilty for being so sharp with him. To make matters worse Thomas had grown tired of waiting for him to take the cart to the field and had hobbled to the yard himself to find the cause of the delay. His aches and pains had not improved his temper and Luke had been thoroughly downcast for the rest of the day and several days after that.

Kirsty had a brief note from James a week after the sale and with it he had enclosed a cheque for the four cows she had purchased on his behalf as well as a legally worded statement setting out the fact that she would retain the value of the milk produced while the cows were in her care. Any calves produced by the cows would be his property but she would be fully recompensed for the labour and food costs they incurred. It was as formal as any business arrangement between two absolute strangers and Kirsty felt cold and empty inside – until she came to the last paragraph of the document. She drew in her breath sharply. In the event of his death, James Thomas MacFarlane had stated, any animals he owned would be hers to do with as she wished.

'Dear God, please send him back safely,' she prayed silently. Why, oh why do I act so foolishly in Jamie's company? she asked herself. Because you love him and you're too proud to tell him so, she admitted honestly.

It was nearly Christmas when Kirsty learned from Anna that James had not been assigned to the army after all, although he had passed his medical. Instead he had been recommended for a government department dealing with the improvement and handling of food supplies. He had been dispatched to Edinburgh for further instruction; afterwards he was to move to East Lothian to inspect and advise farmers in that area with a view to getting the maximum production from each and every acre in that fertile corner of Scotland.

'I'm pleased to hear he is in safe employment, Anna,' Kirsty remarked fervently.

'Aye lassie, so am I. I was worried when he told me he was joining the army, and he wouldna have been happy away frae the land. At least he'll still be connected to it, even if he canna look after his own cows and horses.'

If the summer and autumn had been good during the first months of war, the bitter winter weather certainly made up for it and the misery and discomfort were not improved by the additional rationing of butter, sugar and ham.

'At least we're not as badly affected as the townsfolk yet,' Beth murmured one snowy morning as she cut generous slices from the big ham hanging from the kitchen ceiling. 'Lucy says Gladys McGuire's weekly letter to Lenny is nothing but grumbles these days, but the cost o' a packet of Woodbines seems to trouble her more than the shortage o' butter and sugar.'

'Lenny is better off with Lucy!' Kirsty commented with feeling. 'He seems quite settled too. I think he will be a useful young worker when he is a bit bigger. By the way, Uncle Alex says the government is bringing in controls for all the livestock in the country so we may not always be able to kill a pig when we need one.'

'Aye, and Lizzie Whiteley was saying she canna get enough eggs or enough butter, but there's no wonder the hens aren't laying with this dreadful weather,' Beth sighed.

Although the winter weather of nineteen hundred and forty finally gave way to spring the world was not a happy place. The government was in turmoil.

'They seemed to have lost confidence in Mr Chamberlain as their leader,' Emma reflected anxiously, on one of her Sunday visits.

'Aye, well let's hope it's not too late to save the day now that they've elected Winston Churchill as head o' this Coalition government. I was talking to two farmers at the smiddy yesterday and they're full o' doubts – what with Hitler already taking over Holland and Belgium.'

'Well, at least the new Prime Minister is honest,' Emma grimaced. 'Blood, toil, tears and sweat – that's all he can promise.'

'He is strong in spirit. He will lead the way,' Beth declared with conviction. She had listened with undivided attention to Mr Churchill speaking on the wireless.

'What do you think about the new Act that's just been passed,' Kirsty asked gravely, 'giving the government unlimited powers over all persons, all property, all wealth and work?'

'It has to be done, I suppose, for there's no telling what we're going to need,' Alex frowned. 'I just hope some folks dinna let a wee bit o' authority go to their heads and become wee Hitlers themselves.'

'What d'ye mean, Alex?' Beth asked anxiously. She had been shocked to see how much her brother-in-law had aged in recent weeks. She knew he and Emma were desperately worried now that Cameron was flying regularly with his squadron and her heart went out to them.

'Och, there's always one or two who throw their weight around unnecessarily, and even an odd one who'll take advantage to feather his own nest.' It was unlike Alex to be cynical or bitter and he stared unseeingly at Kirsty. 'I've seen it already,' he added quietly.

'But surely most o' the men concerned with the War Ag are farmers, aren't they, Uncle Alex, like you?'

'Aye, they are at a local level, lassie. They're mainly volunteers and they give a lot o' time and do a good job. But there's the County Executive Committee as weel – men frae the Department of Agriculture, some frae the universities and colleges, land agents – all sorts o' folks with different kinds of experience. The Minister of Agriculture canna see to everything. He delegated a lot o' power last September for regulating the cultivation and management o' the land. They can even take it over if they consider the farm isna as productive as it could be – maybe if a farmer isna in good health, or hasna the knowledge or the money, or whatever is needed to do as well as he should in these desperate times.'

'I see . . .'

'Dinna look so worried, Kirsty. Ye're doing fine, better than many a man. Maggie told me her nephew has left four o' his best Nithanvale cows in your care until the war is over and he gets a farm of his own again. I believe he's doing some sort o' work for the Ministry in another area, isn't he?'

'Aye, so Anna says.' It was Beth who answered. 'He writes every week but she doesna see him much, what with his work and the petrol rationing. She says he's supposed to encourage the farmers up there to grow more sugar beets, as well as wheat and potatoes. She thinks James would have been a lot happier advising stock farmers, rather than arable. There's to be some sort o' survey though, isn't there, Alex?'

'The National Farm Survey, ye mean. It will be a record o' every farm in the country when it is finished. The acreage, soil type, crops grown – even the state o' the buildings, fences, whether it has electricity – all that sort o' thing. They might test some o' the fields. We're sadly lacking in lime in this part o' the country – always have been, especially where there's peaty soil and with the heavy rainfall we get. Your father aye believed in liming when he could afford it, Kirsty, so Fairlyden shouldna be too bad.'

'No-o . . . I hope not. Father concentrated on the better land. He couldna afford to lime all the fields and we havena spread any this year.' She looked uncertainly at her uncle. She knew a lot about cattle and caring for them and even selecting the right bull for breeding, but her knowledge of the soil and growing crops was sadly lacking, and she was as inexperienced as Luke when it came to ploughing, although she did know how to harness the horses and roll or harrow. She also knew how exhausting it was, walking up and down the field behind the horses all day long.

Any problems Kirsty or anyone else in the country might have, seemed small in comparison to the plight of the thousands of soldiers stranded on the French beaches as first Holland, and then Belgium, were beaten into submission.

Despite her own frailty Sarah still insisted on listening to the news at least twice a day. She also confessed to enjoying the music of Sandy MacPherson on the theatre organ.

'Granny still has more spirit than any of us,' Kirsty smiled when she came in from the milking one evening to find her grandmother grasping the bar of the Aga cooker with one hand while stirring a pan of stovies for the supper with the other.

'Aye, that's true,' Beth agreed with a grateful glance at the old woman who had been her friend and guide for as long as she could remember, as well as the most loving mother-in-law any woman could wish for. 'We're late tonight,' she added apologetically, 'but the very smell o' the stovies makes me ravenous.'

'Och, stovies were one o' the first things I learned to make when I was a bairn,' Sarah reflected. 'We didna have money to buy meat then, and now there's not much to buy, even for folks that can afford it, or so Emma was telling me when she visited last week.'

'That's true,' Beth agreed ruefully, 'and Lizzie Whiteley says things are getting worse. Still we'll not miss the meat tonight. I hope ye havena tired yourself out,' she added with an anxious look at Sarah's lined face.

'No, no. I can still do a wee thing like that. Anyway I remember what it feels like to come in frae the milking and have to set about making the supper, Beth. Though you and Ellen were always ready to lend a hand, even as young lassies . . . Sadie never liked cooking . . .'

Sarah often talked of the past these days and Beth made no comment. She had no desire to remember her sister-in-law's dislikes. Sadie had had so many, and she had been so spiteful that Beth had no happy memories of her at all.

Twenty-Nine

As the months wore on German air raids over southern England became almost a daily occurrence. It was painfully clear Hitler was determined to conquer Britain, as he had conquered the rest of Europe, but it became equally clear that Winston Churchill was just as firm in his resolve that Britain would never surrender. The successful rescue of thousands of the soldiers stranded on the French beaches at Dunkirk had proved a powerful boost to British morale. There was renewed pride in being British, a resolve to give the last ounce of effort in any and every way.

Local defence groups were renamed the Home Guard. Even in the relative peace of the Scottish countryside men from seventeen to sixty-five met to practise drills and manoeuvres with enthusiasm, no longer the butt of local jokes. Luke Fairly accompanied Paddy Kildougan and Joe Little to the Muircumwell practices, except when the hay or harvest demanded their prior attention.

Unfortunately the exercises only made Luke more introspective than before.

'It is wrong, Mother, wrong and wicked to shower bombs so – so indiscriminately! Burning and killing – all that suffering and destruction . . .'

'Aye,' Beth agreed heavily, with a troubled glance at her son's pale strained face. 'War is cruel, terribly cruel.' She spoke with feeling. 'But we canna let Hitler take Great Britain without a fight. The man must be insane; we have to defend our country.' She studied Luke's set young face and her heart sank. He was far too sensitive for the wicked place the world had become; he listened tensely to the news whenever he could, and he read every report in the newspaper. 'Ye mustna take it all to your ain heart so much, laddie,' Beth urged. 'We all have our work to do and yours is helping to feed the nation. They're even appealing for schoolboys, and men and women who have never seen a cow or a field o' corn to help on the farms. We all have to do our best with the talents God has given us, and do the tasks He has set us to do. We canna do more than that.'

'I'm beginning to wonder if there really is a God after all.'

'Luke!'

'I'm sorry, Mother. I didna mean to shock you. I dinna want to upset you either because I know how much your faith has helped you, especially since Father was killed.'

'It has, aye it had indeed, and God will help ye laddie, if ye'll let Him . . .'

'But what God of mercy could allow such – such destruction of human lives?' Beth could not give her son the satisfactory answer he needed so badly.

Luke knew his outburst had distressed his mother and he was genuinely sorry. He did not mention his wavering faith or his confused feelings to her again, but Beth often saw his brooding eyes and she sensed the doubts and fears which filled him – sensed and understood, for she too had been lost in the wilderness. It was Sarah, her mother-in-law, who had helped her find her way again, and Logan who had brought her the happiness of supreme love. The memory of that happiness lived on and no one could take it away. She could only pray that the war would end soon and the suffering cease, so that Luke and the millions of young men and women like him would be able to resume their lives and live in peace.

Beth did pray fervently, and as the sun shone for the hay and again for the harvest, and the blue skies above Fairlyden looked so innocent and clear, she was convinced that God must be in his Heaven, even though all was far from right with His world below.

Lenny McGuire certainly considered Fairlyden the most perfect place in the whole world. He spent every minute of his spare time running to the fields after Paddy or Joey, or accompanying Kirsty to feed the young calves and pigs. Any young animal fascinated him. Earlier in the spring he had been delighted when he saw a chicken pecking its way from the shell to join its ten brothers and sisters beneath the anxiously clucking brown hen, and he was absolutely thrilled when one of the ducks proudly presented eight fluffy yellow ducklings which she had hatched in secret. But his greatest excitement had been the birth of Star, a long-legged Clydesdale filly foal whose mother had been born when Kirsty herself was ten years old.

'I told James in my last letter that the roan mare had had

another foal at last,' Anna smiled, watching Lenny's eager face with pleasure. 'I remember when she was born, you would scarcely leave her, Miss Kirsty. The mare was a wee bit flighty and your father told ye not to go near her on your own. James would be sixteen then; he couldna resist ye when ye pleaded with him to go with ye to see her.' Anna sighed. 'They were happy days, even if we were all short o' money. James was just as bad as young Lenny for wanting to see the calves and foals and your father was so patient wi' him.'

'My father always liked James, Anna.'

'Aye, they had the same love o' animals.' Anna sighed again.

'Is something troubling you, Anna?'

'James doesna like the work he's doing now, inspecting fields o' potatoes and sugar beet and telling other farmers what they ought to be doing to improve them. He says he'd rather be doing the work himself – even if it does mean working as a labourer for somebody else. But he's applied for a transfer back to this area. At least he would be dealing more with stock farmers and things he understands best.'

'I didn't know. James never writes, not even to ask about his cows.' Kirsty knew she had been sharper than she intended when she saw Anna's keen gaze. Had she revealed her secret hurt? 'I'm sure James willna be as bad as the man, Steel, who came to inspect Fairlyden, however miserable he feels.'

'I hope not indeed! I heard Paddy saying he was a nasty piece o' goods. Picking faults where there were none to find. It's just as weel Thomas canna hear so weel or he'd have been telling him what to do with himself.' Kirsty smiled wanly at Anna's indignation, but Mr Steel's visit had troubled her. She felt he had been searching for faults because she was a woman. 'A flighty bit lass', he had called her sarcastically. He had been back again and taken samples of soil. She would not have known about that, if she had not seen him when she happened to be down at the little Muircumwell meadow checking up on the young calves which they had put out to graze the day before.

'I told Uncle Alex about him. He didna say much but he doesna know him very well. Apparently he lives at the other side o' Lockerbie.'

'Aye, it's a pity your uncle decided to give up his own work on the War Ag committee. He's a fine man and a good farmer. Ma sister, Maggie, says it's aged him and your Aunt Emma terribly since Master Cameron started flying, especially since these last raids started.'

'Yes, Hitler doesna seem content to confine his bombs to London and the south anymore either,' Kirsty agreed worriedly. 'The German planes seem to be everywhere recently, or at least wherever there's a city or a big town, or a special target.'

'Aye, Master Cameron and his friends are doing a fine thing for their country. "Never in the field of human conflict was so much owed by so many to so few",' she quoted, puffing out her chest and putting on the deepest voice she could muster in an imitation of Mr Churchill. Her mimicry brought a faint smile to Kirsty's face as Anna had intended. She was fond of Kirsty and she felt Fairlyden was too big a responsibility for a young woman alone, especially in this time of stress and shortages. Even the cattle cake was rationed now and still they were expected to produce as much milk as ever.

'Miss Kirsty! Miss Kirsty, can I ride on the empty cart wi' Uncle Paddy. He's going to load it wi' the stooks o' corn frae Woodside field. The ones I helped ye set up like Indian tepees. He says I can help, if ye'll gie's permission! Please, Miss Kirsty?'

'All right, Lenny, but do be careful not to fall off the cart. If you fell under one of those iron-rimmed wheels there'd be no Lenny McGuire left, and then what would your mother say!'

'She wadna care aboot me. She's on'y bothered aboot oor Arf.' For a moment the eager light vanished from Lenny's grubby young face and Kirsty's face softened.

'Of course she cares about you, Lenny. It's just living at Fairlyden your mother doesna like. Off you go then, or Paddy will be away to the field without you.'

'Gee, thanks, Miss Kirsty! I dinna want to gang back to Glasgae, ever . . .' he called as he ran off on bare brown feet to where Paddy was waiting to hoist him up on to the cart.

'Gladys is expecting another bairn soon, did ye ken?'

'No! Josh McGuire must have been home on leave sometime then . . .?'

'Maybe he has – and then again maybe he hasna . . .' Anna held Kirsty's gaze steadily, almost defiantly. Kirsty's eyes widened. 'Oh, Anna surely you dinna mean . . .' Kirsty's fair skin flushed beneath its tan.

Anna shrugged. 'They're not all as innocent and good as yoursel', Miss Kirsty. Lizzie was right sorry she believed ye'd spent the night up at Avary Hall with Mr Guillyman that time. Anyway Gladys wrote to tell Lucy about the bairn because she wants young Lenny to gang home to keep an eye on that brother o' his when the babe is born. Lucy is fair upset. She's grown fond o' Lenny.'

'I think we all have.'

'Aye, we'd miss him now, puir laddie. Lucy hasna had the heart to tell him yet.'

'Mother was afraid Lucy and Paddy might grow too fond of the McGuire children,' Kirsty reflected with a troubled frown.

'Weel, if ye ask me they'll get wee Irene for keeps – or at least until she's old enough to earn her ain keep,' Anna retorted cynically. 'All Gladys McGuire thinks about is the next packet o' cigarettes – and men.'

Everyone at Fairlyden worked hard to gather in the harvest, even loading and carting corn from the fields late into the night when there was a full moon and a clear sky.

'We have to make the most o' the fine weather,' Kirsty urged when Luke grumbled about his aching back and hands stinging from the thistles in the sheaves. 'It canna go on for ever, but neither will the harvest.'

'Kirsty's right, laddie,' Beth assured her white-faced son. Luke simply did not seem to have the stamina for hard work and it troubled her. 'If only ye would eat more meat and drink some milk . . .' she coaxed for the umpteenth time. 'Good food would give ye more energy.'

'Meat and milk are supposed to be rationed.'

'They are, but I dinna need all my rations o' meat and we've plenty milk and butter, thank God. We're luckier than most folk, even if we havena much sugar. Paddy is talking o' keeping some bees next summer, did he ask ye about it, Kirsty?'

'No, but there's no reason why he should if he mentioned it to you, Mother. Fairlyden is yours too, remember.'

'No, no, lassie. It was meant for you and you were meant for it. We all depend on ye, and that's a fact.' Beth sighed heavily. 'Mind you I think it's too big a burden for ye on your own, but I dinna ken what any o' us would have done without ye – including Paddy and Lucy, Anna and Thomas. They ken their living depends on you, lassie. You're just like your grandmother. She kept Fairlyden going and she must have had a hard time often.'

'Speaking of Granny, how is she this morning? I see there's a letter for her with a Yorkshire postmark . . .?' Kirsty looked curiously at her mother and was surprised to see a wary, almost frightened expression on her gentle face. 'Do you know who it is from, Mother? Could it be bad news?'

'I'm almost sure it's your Aunt Sadie's writing, lassie.'

'Aunt Sadie's! B-but she's never once written to Granny since – since Grandfather's funeral . . .' Her voice tailed away hoarsely. They all knew how hurt her grandmother had been by Aunt Sadie's silence, but she had accepted it with resignation eventually.

'She was jealous because you got Fairlyden, but there's nought for ye to fear,' Beth declared firmly, compressing her lips. 'Fairlyden is yours and nobody can take it away frae ye.'

'Then why were you looking so – so troubled yourself a minute ago, Mother?'

'Och . . . well, to tell the truth, lassie, your Aunt Sadie has always seemed to signify trouble in one way or another. She made me feel guilty when we didna hear frae her . . .'

'But it was her own fault. You've always sent her a Christmas card and she has never sent one back since Grandfather died, not even to Aunt Emma and Uncle Alex. Even if she hates me for inheriting Fairlyden she should have considered Granny.'

'Aye. Maybe she's repented now there's a war on and nobody kens what each day might bring . . .'

'There's only one way to find out.'

'Ye're right, lassie. I think I'll take the letter up before your granny gets out o' bed. I'll take up a cup of tea as well.'

'You're expecting it to be bad news, aren't you, Mother?' Kirsty suggested gently.

'I've no reason to think it must be bad. It's just that I find it hard to remember anything good coming o' any contact I ever had wi' your Aunt Sadie.'

'You take the letter to Granny then. I'll bring the tea and say good morning before I go back up to the steading. The mornings are nippy now. I'm glad the harvest is almost finished. I wondered how we should ever get the extra corn gathered in and built into the stacks.'

'God is merciful – even to this sinful world o' ours. He has always sent a time for sowing, and He'll aye send a time for reaping.'

'Mmm, I shall feel happier when the last sheaf o' corn is gathered in and the stacks are all thatched though,' Kirsty smiled. She had noticed how often her mother quoted the bible these days and she envied her unshakeable faith in God.

* * *

Sarah's wrinkled hand shook as she held up the single sheet of paper which was the first communication she had had from Sadie since Crispin died. Dear, dear Crispin. She thought longingly of her late husband, her friend and companion through the troubled waters of her life. Her mouth trembled and then firmed resolutely. She sat up straighter in the big bed and looked up into Beth's concerned face.

'She's afraid o' the bombing.' Her voice was flat. 'She says industrial areas are prime targets for the Germans to bomb.'

'I see . . .'

'No, Beth, you dinna see. How could you? You with your gentle, kindly nature! You could never understand a mind like Sadie's.' There was anger in Sarah's dark eyes. She always had such lovely brown eyes, Beth thought irrelevantly. 'If it was just the bombing she wanted to escape, she has at least two other houses to choose from. She wants to come to *live* at Fairlyden until the war is over, and she intends to bring Robert. Help me out o' this bed, Beth. As soon as I'm dressed I'll write her a letter. She canna come here.'

'B-but she is your ain daughter. Her place is here with you if she—'

'She's waited too long to remember that!' Sarah's hand shook but her eyes sparked with anger; despite her age and her nightclothes she looked as dignified as a queen, sitting up so straight in bed. 'It is not me she wants to see even now, Beth, so dinna distress yourself. The trouble with Sadie is she has never been able to get on with her maids and now there are no maids to be had. She's tired of looking after Robert; she does not like the rationing.'

'Surely Aunt Sadie hasna written you a list o' complaints, Granny?' Kirsty asked with a smile, carrying the tray of tea into the bedroom.

'That's exactly what she has done!'

'Oh, surely not!' Kirsty sobered in the face of her grandmother's anger. She had not seen her with those twin flags of colour in her cheeks and her eyes blazing indignantly since she was a child – and her grandmother was older now and she had a troublesome heart . . .

'Please, dinna distress yourself so,' Beth pleaded, thinking exactly the same as her daughter.

'Dinna distress myself! Not once in this epistle of complaints and demands,' she tapped the thick paper sharply, 'not once

265

does Sadie ask after my health! Here, Kirsty, read it for yourself then you'll understand. I'm not being a selfish hard old woman when I refuse to have Sadie here. She almost ruined your mother's life once before. I shall not give her the chance to try again. She thinks we have no rationing up here; she wants to live off our food, she wants you and your mother to do her work and her washing and her cooking and cleaning while she acts like a lady. She even wants you, Beth, to nurse her husband now he's no use to her any more!' Sarah began to shake uncontrollably. 'She still thinks she has a right to live at Fairlyden.'

'Oh Granny! Please, please dinna upset yourself so . . .' Kirsty thrust the tea tray at her mother and pulled Sarah into her strong young arms as though she would imbue her with her own strength.

'You needna worry about your Aunt Sadie, Kirsty,' Beth assured her later. 'She always survives. My own fear is for your grandmother and the effect of all this upset and excitement. She has always forgiven Sadie in the past and it isna her nature to harbour a grudge, but I fear Sadie has hurt her too deeply this time.'

Beth had good reason to be worried. Doctor Broombank had warned her that too much excitement was as bad as exertion for someone with a heart condition like her mother-in-law.

During the night Kirsty was wakened by the sound of the little bell which her grandmother always kept beside her bed. She jumped up instantly, pulling on her robe as she went, oblivious of her bare feet on the cold linoleum.

'The – pain . . .' Sarah's words were slow and slurred as Kirsty reached her side. There was a movement in the doorway and she looked up to see her mother's white face, her hair falling down her back in a long golden pleat.

'I'll telephone Doctor Broombank.' Beth's voice was hoarse. Sarah waved a feeble hand but Beth had already run downstairs to telephone. '. . . too late . . ., lassie.'

'Ssh, Granny. Dinna talk. It'll pass. Please . . .' Kirsty smoothed the soft white brow with a gentle finger. Sarah's eyes, dark as ever, looked up into her granddaughter's face. 'Dinna fret, bairn . . . I'm ready . . . I've had a good life . . .' Her eyelids drooped wearily, then opened again, her eyes suddenly alert. Her fingers plucked restlessly at the air until Kirsty cupped them tenderly in her hands. 'Dinna let them take Fairlyden, lassie!'

'I'll take care of Fairlyden, Granny. I promise,' she whispered soothingly.

'You're a good . . . lassie . . . but dinna . . . be proud . . . take his help . . .' Her eyes closed again. Kirsty frowned. Was her grandmother's mind wandering? But when she looked upon the lined face again the brown eyes were fixed on her own face; gentle, loving eyes . . . Sarah smiled. '. . . need love as well . . . can do anything . . . anything if you . . . have love . . .' The papery eyelids drooped and closed for the last time.

Thirty

Sarah had lived all her eighty-one years in the parish of Muircumwell and during her eventful lifespan she had befriended many; if she had occasionally found criticism, she had also earned love and respect. Her funeral was well attended; more than the usual proportion of women were present, many representing their soldier husbands, and the absence of two members of the Fairly family – Billy, and his sister, Sadie – was duly noted. Billy could be excused; it was a long and dangerous journey across the Atlantic Ocean and he could not have arrived in time. Sadie's absence was a different matter; it was discussed freely in Lizzie Whiteley's store while customers waited patiently for their rations.

'I dinna ken anything about Mistress Bradshaw's family,' Lizzie snapped irritably when pressed. 'I only ken she was guid to all o' us Whiteleys and that brother o' mine is grieving as badly as he did for oor ain mother. Mind you, the auld Mistress was as guid as a mother to him, God rest her soul. He's worked at Fairlyden for fifty-three years, ever since he was a lad o' thirteen. Miss Kirsty is the third generation o' Fairlys he's worked for, though I dinna ken how much longer he'll keep going wi' that chest o' his and being out in all weathers.' Her listeners had not come to hear about Thomas and soon dispersed as Lizzie had intended. If she was curious about the Fairly family, she was also intensely loyal.

It was true that Thomas Whiteley had taken the news of Sarah's death very badly and Anna was worried about him. It was a welcome relief when she received a letter from James.

'He hopes to pay us a visit at the end o' November,' she told Beth as they worked together in the dairy. 'He says all the potatoes are gathered in now and most o' them safely stored for the winter. He's still hoping to get a transfer back to the southwest o' Scotland, though he admits he has learned a lot about growing crops while he's been in the Lothians.'

'It will be nice to see James again,' Beth nodded as she scrubbed the ridges of the milk cooler with less than her usual vigour. 'I wish he could be transferred to the Dumfries area. He might have some authority over the likes o' that man Steel who keeps interfering. He criticises every plan Kirsty makes. He's undermining her self-confidence over the ploughing o' the extra land. He's even insisting some o' Westhill should be ploughed this time – the steepest part o' it too!'

'Mercy me! None o' the horses could plough up yonder! Joey Little would be exhausted in half an hour as weel, trying to turn a furrow on that ground. The man must be crazy! It would take a machine to plough any o' Westhill.'

'That's exactly what Kirsty told him. "Then it's high time you bought a tractor, Miss!" he snapped nastily and he eyed her slyly as though he'd won some sort o' contest. They were talking outside the kitchen window and the door was standing open. I could see Kirsty looking pale and upset.'

'Miss Kirsty aye had plenty o' spirit and she kens what needs to be done. I hope she told him where to gang!' Anna exclaimed in disgust.

'Aah, but Mr Steel is supposed to be representing the government so she darena tell him what she really thinks o' his ideas. She did tell him we couldna afford a tractor yet. She said we had other fields which were more suitable for the horses and she was willing to plough one o' them if he really insisted on the extra acres. He didna want to hear that. "I've told my colleagues a farm like this should not be left in the hands of an ignorant young woman in a time of war," he crowed. Aa-gh!' Beth clenched her fists, remembering. 'He looked so pompous I wanted to go out there and slap the smile from his great, sneering face! "Don't you understand girl, the nation is desperate for food. I shall put in a report and I shall not hide the results of samples of soil taken from your land either! It's wasting for want of lime." He wouldna even listen to what Kirsty had to say and we ken he only took samples frae the wettest fields and the peat meadow down at Muircumwell,' Beth finished anxiously.

'No wonder the puir lassie has been looking sae pale and worrit!' Anna exploded.

'Och, I shouldna be burdening you with Fairlyden's troubles, Anna,' Beth summoned a smile.

'Aah, but Fairlyden's troubles are oor troubles as weel, Mistress Beth. Anyway we've kenned each other a long time and it does a body good to talk whiles. I'm glad I ken what's wrong with Miss Kirsty though. I thought she was grieving too much o'er her grandmother.'

'Aye.' Beth sighed. 'There's that too. I must admit I miss her presence in the house more than I ever expected.'

'I ken. She was a wise woman anyway, but I always thought ye were closer to her than her own daughters, especially after Miss Ellen went away to nurse.'

'She was as close to me as my own mother.'

'I suppose there's no word o' Miss Sadie, I mean Mistress Smith, coming to pay her last respects – even belatedly?' Anna probed.

'No.' Sadie had not replied to the funeral letter; she had refused to speak to Alex on the telephone even, but Beth would not tell Anna that. 'It was lovely to have Ellen's company for a whole week after the funeral.'

Anna accepted the change of subject. She knew better than most people how nasty Sadie had been to Beth when they were young, but Beth had always been too loyal for her own good, long before she'd become Mistress Fairly herself. 'Miss Ellen was aye kind and compassionate. It's a pity her and Doctor Leishman never had any bairns.'

'Ellen would have been a wonderful mother,' Beth agreed warmly. 'As it is she's spent her life caring for others.'

'Aye, but she looked older than her years, I thought. She's fifty-four, the same as maself.'

'Aah, I had forgotten that.' Beth looked keenly at Anna. 'You certainly carry your own age well, despite being widowed so young, and having had your share o' troubles.'

'Aye, weel, if ye've finished with me for the dairy work,' Anna grinned wryly, 'I'd better get back to the sink and peel the tatties or I shall be in real trouble with Joey and Thomas. It's no' easy feeding working men when there's so little meat to be had.'

'At least we've plenty o' vegetables. Growing the beetroot and carrots in the tattie fields was a grand idea o' Thomas's. They help the potatoes down and at least they're no' rationed.'

'Not yet anyway!' Anna reflected darkly. 'Oor Lizzie reckons we're fortunate compared wi' other folk. She was saying auld McFie at Burnend has killed more than his two pigs already. He thought he could get awa' wi' it because they were his own and he'd killed them on his ain premises but the police found out and he's in trouble o'er it. Oh, and I nearly forgot to tell ye, Lizzie is collecting clothes for the Women's Voluntary Service, if there's anything that belonged to the Mistress that ye want to give. I'm sure she'd be pleased to think she was helping folks still.'

'I'm sure she would. Ellen helped me to sort out her things before she left and I suppose some o' the women who have lost all their possessions in the bombing might be glad o' some good warm clothes. Thanks for telling me, Anna.'

She watched Anna hurry off to her cottage and her thoughts returned to those few days she had spent in Ellen's company and the brooch they had found in a scuffed leather box amongst Sarah's cherished mementos. Ellen had ignored her protests and insisted she should keep it, adding, 'I think the stones are diamonds and I've no cause to wear jewellery now, and no daughter to pass it on to.' She had smiled that sweet, serene smile. 'You looked after Mother well, Beth, and I'm grateful. I know she never wanted to leave Fairlyden and sometimes I felt guilty that my work came before my family . . .'

'Your mother understood, and she was proud that you could help so many who were wounded, men whose lives were turned upside down fighting for our freedom.'

'Yes,' Ellen had sighed softly. 'They are so dependent on us, and so grateful for everything we do. Who would have believed that the world could be filled with so much strife again after the supreme sacrifice made by so many!' Her voice had held a faint note of bitterness then but a moment later she had smiled and changed the subject. 'What about Mother's old blue bowl? It's been at Fairlyden as long as I can remember. Sadie would have smashed it long ago. She thought it was ugly, but I always liked it myself.' Ellen had smiled reminiscently then, her fingers tracing the blue figures absently. 'My grandmother brought it from Galloway with her, but I think it had been a wedding gift to her grandmother before that. It is a bit old I suppose.' She had smiled apologetically. 'You'll just have to throw it away if you dinna want it, Beth, but wait until I've gone, will you? I'd take it with me for sentiment's sake but it would probably get broken on the train. The railways are so crowded with soldiers.'

'I always liked the blue figures. So did Logan. I shall keep it.' Beth smiled as she remembered her promise. She had always been a bit fanciful about the blue bowl; it seemed like a sort of talisman to her.

So they had disposed of the auld Mistress's possessions but Beth felt her spirit would always linger around Fairlyden – unless the likes of the man Steel had his way, she thought grimly. She was sure he must have an ulterior motive for hounding Kirsty so continuously. Or perhaps he really believed a young woman on her own could not manage a place like Fairlyden.

James MacFarlane arrived at Fairlyden late on Friday night, the sixth of December, nineteen hundred and forty. Even Anna was not sure when he would arrive as his intended visit had already been postponed once with only the vaguest explanation. So Kirsty was astonished when he strolled into the warmth of the byre early the following morning just as she and Paddy were collecting their stools and pails to begin the milking.

'James!' Her eyes glowed involuntarily. Her smile was a welcome straight from the heart – before her brain had time to register its usual frantic messages of caution. James MacFarlane drew in his breath sharply but there was nothing in his deep pleasant voice to reveal how much Kirsty's smile had affected him.

'It's good to be back in the Fairlyden byre again,' he grinned almost boyishly. 'I see I'm just in time to help with the milking.' Instantly he saw wary shadows darken Kirsty's expressive eyes. She thought he must have come to check up on his own cows, to see whether she was caring for them properly; were they in calf? well fed? were they producing sufficient milk to continue their excellent records? Well, his cows were in fine fettle despite the rationing of cake. She lifted her chin proudly but before she could speak James remarked quietly, 'I offered to milk in place o' Mother. She didna get much sleep last night. Uncle Thomas couldna get his breath. I believe she must have been boiling kettles half the night to try to give him ease.'

'I see . . .'

'I wish she had called me but I arrived very late and I must have slept like the proverbial log. Anyway she seemed relieved when I offered to take her place this morning.'

'Yes, I'm sure she would be.' Kirsty relaxed and smiled; although her eyes did not have their earlier radiant light, James was satisfied, at least for the present. He had vowed that he would tread so carefully and guard his tongue so well that not a single misunderstanding would occur between them during this brief visit. After all he had had plenty of time for reflection since their last encounter.

'Maybe you would like to start with your own cows? I usually milk them myself but I'll start on the opposite side this morning. They have all milked well. I hope you'll be satisfied with them . . .' Kirsty could not prevent a faint note of uncertainty creeping in, even though she had done her best. That man Steel sometimes made her wonder whether she knew anything at all, and James was a perfectionist where his cows were concerned.

'I know I shall be more than satisfied, Kirsty. I'm just happy to know that I still have some cows to call my own . . .' Kirsty glanced at him sharply but he was not humouring her; there were shadows in his eyes, and a wistful look on his lean face as he patted the rump of the nearest cow.

'You have more than the original four now, James.' Suddenly she was eager to banish his melancholy. 'Nithanvale Queenie had a fine bull calf and she is milking well so he will be in great demand when you want to sell him for a stockbull. Jessie and Ringa have had heifer calves and Lupin is due to calve in about three weeks.'

'Aah, Kirsty, I dinna know how to thank you!'

'You dinna need to thank me.' Her tone grew brisk again. The defensive shutters were back in place. 'We've had the milk frae them, remember. I sold six o' our own and we got quite a good price, even though they were our lowest yielders.'

'I should think so too. I can think of many a breeder who would be glad just to get the chance o' some Fairlyden breeding.'

'Yes, Father had built up a good name and it helps a lot. I've nearly enough money to install a milking machine and we mean to do that in the spring.' Her expression grew grave. 'There's some people wouldna agree,' she muttered darkly, thinking of Steel telling her to get her priorities right. 'But milking is our biggest job, twice a day, seven days a week and it isna right to depend on your Uncle Thomas turning out every morning and evening, or your mother. I suppose you know this is not the first time he has had a really bad attack o' bronchitis this year and there's still most o' the winter ahead yet.'

'Mother admitted as much this morning,' James nodded as he settled himself on his stool and eased his head comfortably against the warm flank of a cow. 'I wish this damned war was over so that we could all resume our lives again.' He sighed heavily and this time there was no doubting the yearning in his voice.

'I dinna think anything will ever be the same again even when it is over.' Kirsty spoke softly, taking her own place between two cows straight across the centre walk from James's pair. 'I see you havena last your touch,' she added as the milk streamed rhythmically into his pail.

He smiled back companionably and Kirsty felt a rush of warmth course through her.

'Why hello, James!' Beth had just come into the byre followed by Lucy. 'I didna know you were home . . .'

'Good morning, Mrs Fairly,' James smiled warmly. One of his earliest memories was of a very young Beth Fairly dancing him around his mother's kitchen table singing *Alexander's Ragtime Band*. He had always had a deep affection for her. 'I arrived last night on the late train. By the time I'd walked the four miles frae the station everybody was in bed.'

'How's Thomas this morning?'

'Not good, I'm afraid. Mother tells me he has been just as bad many a time. I'm worried about her as much as Uncle Thomas . . .'

'Yes, it will be better for everyone when we get the milking machine. Lenny looks after Irene while Lucy is at the morning milkings but he's only a laddie and he has to go back to Glasgow for a while soon to help his mother with young Arf.'

'We should have the milking machine in by then,' Kirsty assured them, moving on to the next stall and another pair of cows while her mother and Lucy went off to the far end of the byre. James glanced up and down as he also changed stalls. 'I only see Paddy down the other end . . . Does Luke not come to the milking?' He raised his eyebrows.

'No.' Kirsty bit her lip. 'He has never got over his fear o' cattle.'

'I see . . .' James frowned but said no more. He had gathered from his mother's letters that Luke was not particularly good at anything to do with the farm work, but even so he had assumed he would have a go at everything, if only to assist Kirsty.

'Joey usually lends a hand if we're still milking when he has attended to his horses – unless he needs to make an early start on the ploughing or some other field work. There's such a lot for him to do now that your Uncle Thomas isna so fit.'

'Yes, the labour situation is difficult and likely to get worse, I think. The government is encouraging women to become land girls.'

'Yes, there's three in Muircumwell parish already. I've met one of them. She seems to be enjoying the work although she had never been on a farm in her life before.'

It seemed to Kirsty that they had scarcely started the milking before it was finished.

'Come down to the house and have your breakfast with us, James,' Beth smiled. 'I'm looking forward to hearing your news and it will save Anna's rations.'

Kirsty was surprised to see James looking at her questioningly before he accepted her mother's invitation. She was annoyed to find her cheeks flushing as she nodded. 'Yes, we may as well all eat together and Luke will be pleased to see you. He misses Granny's company and he likes more varied conversation than mine,' she added ruefully.

'I don't remember you ever being short of conversation, Kirsty, or a variety of topics,' James laughed, raising a quizzical brow.

'Mmm, these days my conversation seems to consist solely of farming budgets, farming crops, breeding cattle and how to satisfy the government – or at least one nasty representative . . .'

'Yes . . .' James frowned. 'Mother said you were having problems with a man named Steel. Maybe I can help? If you want to talk about it before I leave?'

'We'll see,' Kirsty said shortly. She hated to admit to James that she couldn't manage, but there were times when she felt so alone, so weighed down by responsibility without her father's help and guidance. Sometimes she wept in the darkness until her pillow was soaked, then she would turn it over and punch it viciously – but it did not help. Nothing had ever changed in the morning; the decisions were still hers; the responsibility for her mother and Luke, for Lucy and Paddy, for Anna and Thomas and Joey Little, with his earnest young face and eagerness to please. Even Lenny looked to her for permission to do this or help with that.

Thirty-One

James's stay at Fairlyden lasted four days and during that time he took his mother's place at every milking. He helped with other work too, but more important to Kirsty were their stimulating discussions, their shared interests – the return of their old camaraderie. Yet it was not quite the same as of old, for they were no longer children. She knew the tensions were only just beneath the surface, that the spark could flare into an uncontrollable blaze if either of them provoked the temper or aroused the passions of the other, but it seemed to Kirsty that there was a new understanding in James, a silent resolve to preserve their friendship.

James's last day was bitterly cold but they were well wrapped against the biting wind as they walked over the fields up to Westhill ground.

'This afternoon we'll walk down to the Muircumwell land too,' James suggested. 'I really canna understand why Steel is insisting you plough the only steep land there is when you've offered to plough an extra ten acres of lower ground.'

'Because there's fifty acres o' permanent pasture on Westhill and he wants to write up in his reports that he's persuaded us to plough and improve twenty-five acres this year and twenty-five next. He says if it is limed and cropped it will grow better grass.'

'Well, he's probably right about that,' James conceded. 'But it would take years to gain any improvement and it's extra cereals that are most needed and they are needed now. Even oats wouldna make a decent crop up there.'

'Even if we did have a tractor to plough Westhill, which we havena, as Steel already knows,' Kirsty muttered flatly, kicking ruthlessly at a tuft of frost-encrusted grass. 'And even if we did manage to plough and drill twenty-five more acres, however would we manage to harvest it?'

'You must tell Mr Steel that you refuse to plough Westhill, or at least the steepest area. If he still insists, ask him to supply you with a tractor and plough and a man to drive it.'

'Could he do that?' Kirsty asked eagerly.

'Most o' the War Agricultural Executive Committees are trying to gather a supply of implements for use by farmers in their area. I believe the government has arranged some sort o' lend and lease agreement with the United States.'

'You mean the same as for weapons? Britain gets implements frae America now and pays when the war is over?'

'Something like that.'

'Do you arrange such things in your well-paid job, James?' Kirsty teased gently, but James's face was grave and he frowned.

'As a matter of fact I did when the local inspectors felt the farmers in their area couldna manage to do all that was needed or reasonably possible. I-er . . . I've given up my job with the Department of Agriculture though. When I return tomorrow I shall be going to work on a farm myself.'

'Oh James!' Kirsty could not hide her disappointment. 'Your mother said you had applied for a transfer back to Southwest Scotland . . .'

'So I did, but there's not much chance o' getting one.'

'But your mother was so proud of your official employment. She kept telling us all how lucky you've been to get such a well-paid job. Now you're giving it up to work for forty-eight shillings a week as a labourer?'

'The wages are going up to three pounds a week next month,' he grinned. 'I shall earn a bit more than that, but I've learned that money is not everything, Kirsty. I'd rather be doing than telling. Besides, the man I'm going to work for is in desperate need of someone he can rely on. He has a young wife and three children and he needs a serious operation. Labour is just as scarce in the east and good dairymen are almost non-existent in that area at the best o' times.'

'I see . . .'

'No, you dinna see, Kirsty, and neither does my mother. I told her last night. She thinks I'm crazy! I've been lodging in a cottage belonging to Billy Henderson's family. He and his family have had one stroke o' bad luck after another. His father died four months ago. Billy's wife had her third baby son six weeks ago. Billy has neglected his own health because he didna want to worry them. He canna put off the operation any longer. The Hendersons have one of the few dairy farms in that area so I have been helping with the milking occasionally in the mornings and at weekends. I've agreed to take over the

278

dairy and oversee the cropping until Billy has recovered. The doctor thinks that could be as long as six months.'

'But what will you do then, when this Mr Henderson is well again?'

'There will be a job for me as long as I want it. He uses a lot of casual labour for growing vegetables as well as the usual crops. There is a constant shortage of labour these days, but once he is fit I shall consider myself a free agent. Who knows, maybe the war will be over by the summer!' James spoke cheerfully but without conviction.

'If only you're right!' Kirsty breathed fervently. 'No more of that awful Steel!'

'Hey, come on, Kirsty! It's not like you to let things get you down! Anyway men in his position are supposed to help with their advice, not frighten folk to death.'

'He wouldna frighten me at all in normal circumstances because I know – I just know! – I can manage to make the Fairlyden herd a success! But I don't know much about growing potatoes and corn and that man Steel seems to delight in reminding me that the Emergency Powers Act gives the government absolute authority over everything.'

'Well, in time of war I suppose everything does have to be under State control, but it doesna mean Steel can do just as he likes, you know. Maybe he's overstepping his authority? Some people do if they like power. You must stand up to him, Kirsty. There's more than him on the district committee surely?'

'Yes. He brought two other men with him on one of his visits, but he kept interrupting whenever I tried to tell them anything – even when I was answering their questions. Of course he had already shown them the results o' the soil samples frae the fields that need lime. That had them half convinced that I couldna manage Fairlyden as well as it ought to be managed. they gave me paternal smiles and told me Mr Steel would keep an eye on things and not to worry. But I do worry, James! Fairlyden is my home and Mother's! It's our living! And more than just ours . . .'

'I know, I know, Kirsty . . .' James soothed. 'I just canna see what Steel is making such a fuss about. Fairlyden is as productive as any similar farm in this area, and more productive than some, I'll bet! Maybe he has an ulterior motive. Does he have a farm of his own?'

'Yes, I believe so. According to the information Paddy gleaned in the Crown and Thistle, he has a small farm of his own. He

279

certainly has plenty o' labour to do all that has to be done,' she added bitterly.

'What do you mean by plenty o' labour?'

'Apparently he has two sons and a daughter working at home already and another son due to leave school soon.'

'Three sons *and* a daughter! All working at home . . . I wonder what Paddy's informant meant by a *small* farm?'

'It's easy to tell others what to do when you've plenty o' resources yourself!' Kirsty muttered. She did not notice James's frown or the sudden concern in his grey eyes.

James was beginning to suspect that Steel really did have a motive for suggesting Fairlyden needed other supervision; he had good reason for insisting it could not be farmed to its full potential by a woman, if he wanted to have it taken over for the duration of the war by one of his own sons! It was true that farmers and farmworkers were in a reserved occupation, and indeed were forbidden to move to higher-paid employment in industry, but no farm was allowed an excess of labour; workers who were not essential were liable to be called into the armed forces and the longer the war went on the more desperate the situation was likely to become. James felt Kirsty had enough worries without adding to them with his suspicions, which might easily prove groundless, so he said nothing.

Nevertheless he almost wished he had not committed himself to helping Billy Henderson, although in his heart he knew he had had little alternative. He liked the Hendersons and Billy's condition was a matter of life and death; he could not renege when he had given his word. Anyway Kirsty might resent his interference as much as Steel's. If only Luke had been more use, more support, more capable of providing the practical help Kirsty needed, he thought, instead of being just another burden, however unwittingly.

Kirsty drove James to the local station the following morning.

'Are you sure you can spare the petrol?'

'Yes, I have some small tools to collect at the smiddy on my way back and I can call for the groceries as well. We never use the car if we can help it these days.'

James nodded but as they drew into the station yard he turned to her and she was surprised by the urgency in his voice.

'I shall be staying in one of the cottages on the Hendersons' farm for the next six months, Kirsty. I don't know when I shall get home again. It depends on Billy's health.' He took a small card from his waistcoat pocket and handed it to her almost diffidently. Kirsty took it and turned it over in her hand, puzzled. 'It is Billy Henderson's telephone number. Mother has my address, of course, but there are no telephones to the cottages and – and if ever you need help, Kirsty . . . If you're in trouble, I want you to promise to get in touch with me. I know Billy's wife, Elsie, will be more than willing to pass on a message. Will you promise to contact me?'

'Well, yes . . . of course. You mean if your Uncle Thomas is very ill? I don't think you should worry too much, James . . .'

'It's not Uncle Thomas I'm worried about, Kirsty! It's you.' He groaned softly. 'Here comes the train! Promise you'll telephone me if you're in any kind o' trouble?'

'Y-yes. Yes, all right – Jamie . . .' Kirsty's voice was suddenly soft, her smile luminous.

'I've got to go!' James reached out and cupped her face in his hands. Very gently he touched his lips to hers. 'Take care, Kirsty,' he whispered gruffly, then he was out of the car and sprinting across the cobbles. He reached the train and leapt into the carriage just as the porter was slamming the door.

In the spring of nineteen forty-one it took far longer than Kirsty had expected for the dairy engineers to fix the vacuum pipes around the byre for the installation of the new milking machine. Although Thomas Whiteley wheezed incessantly his health had improved with the approach of spring and he had followed Joey Little up and down the fields harrowing in the corn. Unfortunately his temper had not improved. He was becoming a cantankerous old man. Certainly he severely tried the patience of the elderly man and the young boy who were doing their best to install the milking machine.

'The old man doesna want any changes,' the engineer told Kirsty. 'But ye'll only need two milkers instead o' the six or seven hand milkers ye have just now. Of course ye'll need somebody to carry the milk to the dairy all the time but even that young brother o' yours should be able to manage that, and it's quicker if ye've somebody to wash the cows and feed them their cake – if ye can still get any cake to feed them, that is!'

'I hope the machine is as great an invention as you say, Mr Paton. Thomas is sixty-seven, we can't expect him to go on milking forever, but he has never liked changes.'

'Aye, weel I'm sixty-five masel but there's no hope o' me giving up either, not while this war goes on,' the man reflected. 'There's no others to take ma place. I expect young Ned there will be getting his papers afore long, just when I'm getting him intae the way o' things. Ye're lucky to get this machine as a matter o' fact, Miss. Guid job ye had it ordered afore the winter. They say there's a shortage o' metal.'

Kirsty nodded. 'I just hope the cows dinna take too long to get used to the noise,' she frowned. Part of her sympathised with Thomas. She did not look forward to the peace of the byre being disturbed either.

'Och, it'll no' be easy to begin wi'. The kie will skitter all ower the place.' The man grinned almost gleefully. 'But ye'll wonder how ye ever managed without it in a few months. Least that's what other farmers tell me. Ye'll ken a difference when ye get the electric light in here as weel. It'll save ye a lot o' time trimming all the oil lamps every day, and ye'll see what ye're doing.'

'I hope so.' Kirsty bit her lip. 'It's a big expense.'

'Aye. I dinna ken why your faither didna bring the electric up to the farmsteading when he had it put intae the big hoose. Are ye sure ye dinna want it connected intae the stable and the other buildings, or the cottages?'

'No, we don't want it any further than the byre yet.' Kirsty's tone was firm.

The man grinned again. 'Na, yon cantankerous old devil told me I hadna to bring sic a thing as 'lectrics near his hoose. He thinks it's an invention o' the devil.' Kirsty smiled. Thomas did not like changes, it was true, but neither Anna nor Lucy had been eager to have electricity; Kirsty had not pressed the matter. Although Fairlyden's profits had improved since the war had brought such an increase in demand, there was always a shortage of capital to buy such things as a tractor and the plough which would go with it; moreover the animal feed had increased in price and it was impossible to get enough. It was proving as great a curb on increasing production as the lack of money.

Kirsty was crossing the yard, thinking of all the eggs they could have sold now, if only they could get enough meal for the hens. As it was they all saved every scrap and every vegetable peeling to boil up to mix with the meal and make the rations stretch as far as possible. Suddenly Lenny ran out of the stable to greet her, distracting her thoughts.

282

'Hello, Lenny! I'd forgotten this was Saturday and no school today.'

'Aye. Miss Kirsty, ye said ye'd teach me tae ride your horse before I went back tae Glasgow,' Lenny burst out breathlessly. 'Aunt Lucy had another letter frae ma mother yesterday. I've got tae gang this time . . .' He gulped and his lip trembled but he controlled it manfully. '. . . next Tuesday.'

'Ach, Lenny.' Kirsty rumpled the boy's hair affectionately. He had found a place in all their hearts with his enthusiasm for every aspect of life at Fairlyden, and his eagerness to help and to learn. 'You'll be back here in no time, don't you fret. I'll give you a ride on Marocco this afternoon though, I promise.' Kirsty smiled. 'I've scarcely had time to ride him recently so he'll be pleased to see us.' Kirsty tried to cheer him.

'If only I could wait a bit longer . . . Ma is arranging for some woman she kens tae meet the train on Tuesday though. Mr Paton says he'll no' hae the machine finished for milking the cows. I canna understand how a machine can milk them, can you?'

'I expect we shall all have to get used to it.'

Lenny took to riding Marocco as though he had been born in a saddle.

'It's incredible,' Kirsty told her mother and Luke at suppertime. 'He's a natural rider. He's desperate to have another ride before he leaves. I think he's afraid his mother will not allow him to return.'

'Lucy says she'll soon send him back when she sees how much he can eat!' Beth smiled reassuringly.

By the time Lenny came home from school on Monday, Kirsty was busy with the milking but to Lenny's relief she had not forgotten her promise. 'I've saddled Marocco. Luke will help you up on to his back and lead him round the small paddock, Lenny.'

'Aw, thanks, Miss Kirsty!'

'I don't want to lead that great beast anywhere!' Luke hissed softly. 'You shouldna have promised him a ride today.'

'But he has to leave tomorrow, Luke, and he's so keen. Besides Marocco is getting old now and he's as quiet as a lamb. Surely you canna be afraid of him?'

'Of course not.'

'And I don't suppose you'd start milking for me while I give Lenny a proper riding lesson, would you?'

'No! I would not!' Luke sighed. 'You know how I hate the cows, Kirsty. All right, I'll take Lenny round the paddock.'

It was about half an hour later when Luke ran into the byre, his face as white as the milk in the pails.

'I didn't mean to let him go!' he stammered. 'He only wanted to try a bit faster. He . . . I . . . honestly. You'll have to come, Kirsty . . . come quickly. Please!'

Thirty-Two

Kirsty rarely allowed anything to interrupt her in the middle of milking a cow, knowing how it disturbed the animal and spoiled the day's yield, but one glance at her brother's face brought her into the middle of the centre walk of the byre almost before she was aware of moving.

'Lenny?' she breathed, feeling as though her heart was in her mouth. 'Calm yourself and tell me, Luke!' Her voice was sharp with fear as she grabbed Luke's arm, already turning him towards the wide door at the end of the byre. Everyone else had stopped milking, though they still sat rigid on their stools. The cows moved restlessly, already sensing the tension in the air. 'Has Lenny fallen? Is he hurt, Luke?'

'I think he's bruised. He fell. I didna mean to let go of the reins, Kirsty . . .'

'Where is Lenny?'

'I told him to lie still. Not to move. The first aid! Mother told us—'

'I'll get her.' Kirsty hurried to the end of the byre, but Beth was already on her feet, sensing she was needed. As they passed Paddy and Lucy, Kirsty saw their white faces and the anxiety in their eyes. 'You'd better come, Paddy. I'll come and tell you what's happened soon, Lucy. Irene will howl if you leave her.' She glanced briefly at the rosy-faced toddler strapped in the old pram in the centre of the byre.

Kirsty ran after the others, surprised to find her mother so fleet of foot at forty-two.

'I'm all right, I tell ye, Mistress!' Lenny protested, trying hard to stem the tears which had gathered in his eyes. 'Miss Kirsty!' he cried in relief as Kirsty knelt beside her mother. 'I didna mean tae make him jump. 'm sorry!' He gulped back a sob.

'Hush, laddie,' Beth soothed. 'Ye'll have some awful bruises by tomorrow, but I dinna think there's anything broken. Did ye hurt your head at all?'

'Naw, naw. Miss Kirsty . . .' He struggled to sit up.

'Take it easy now, son,' Paddy muttered huskily, clearly relieved to find the boy seemed to have suffered no more than shock and bruises from his fall. But Lenny's lips trembled and the tears streamed down his grubby face. 'Marocco!' he wailed. 'He fell. Ye've got tae find him, Miss Kirsty!'

'He'll be all right,' Kirsty reassured him. She glanced round, expecting to see the quiet old gelding nibbling grass nearby. There was no sign of him. Her gaze returned to Lenny and she found his wide frightened eyes fixed on her imploringly.

'He jumped o'er the wall, over yonder,' he whispered tearfully. 'Master Luke let go the rein because I was managing fine. I made him go faster but I didna mean for him tae jump.'

'I'll look for him, Lenny. Will you take him back to the cottage, Mother?' Beth nodded, noting her daughter's face was even paler than before and her eyes were puzzled. She strode across the small paddock and Beth watched her scramble over the stone dyke and disappear swiftly on the other side. Paddy nodded at Lenny. 'Mistress Fairly will look after ye. All right, laddie?' Then he turned and followed Kirsty.

Marocco lay on the other side of the wall and just to see him lying stretched out like that made Kirsty's heart plummet sickeningly. He was grunting quietly, his chestnut coat dark with sweat. She was beside him instantly, murmuring his name over and over. He recognised her voice at once, nickered softly in response. He tried to raise his head.

'Oh dear God. No!' Kirsty stared at the unnatural angle of his hind leg, the ivory gleam of exposed bone. She felt sick, yet her hand stroked the velvety nose as it had always done, her eyes gazed back helplessly into the large liquid eyes of the horse as they pleaded silently for help.

Behind her Kirsty heard Paddy land softly on the grass as he jumped over the wall.

'Holy Mary, Mother of God!' He was standing over her, staring in disbelief. He muttered a string of expletives and they seemed to hang in the clear air of the late April afternoon. Paddy was not a foul-mouthed man. Kirsty knew it was his reaction to the heart-rending sight of an animal in pain and his own helplessness to cure that pain.

'Lenny . . .'

'I dinna blame Lenny.' Kirsty's voice was choked. 'I blame myself.' Her fingers caressed the soft muzzle.

'You know . . . what has . . . to be done, lass?' Paddy's voice was thick, hesitant, full of compassion. Kirsty nodded, unable

to speak, the tears streamed silently down her cheeks
unheeded.

'I'll get Joey, and bring the gun. 'Tis better . . . Sooner . . .'

'I'll wait with him. Please . . . hurry, Paddy . . . I canna bear
to see him suffer . . .'

Later that evening Luke miserably hung Marocco's saddle
and bridle on the high wooden pegs at one end of the stable.
No one had asked him to bring them from the paddock but he
wanted to save Kirsty from further pain; he wanted to keep
out of the house too. Somewhere in the yard he heard the
rumble of deep voices and recognised them as Paddy's and
Joey Little's. He had no intention of eavesdropping, but by the
time he realised he was the topic of their conversation it was
too late to escape.

'I dinna suppose he thought Lenny would try to canter . . .'

'If you're asking me, young Luke is not for thinking at all!
Leastways not about the farming! Sure he's just another
liability to Miss Kirsty . . .'

'Och Paddy, ye're angry because young Lenny is upset and
ye feel responsible for the laddie. Ye got a shock as weel.'

'Ach, the laddie is blaming himself right enough. It is a
terrible memory for him to be a-taking back to Glasgow with
him.'

'Thank your Irish stars that he didna fall under the horse or
break his neck. He wouldna hae gone back at all then.'

'He is not wanting to be going at all!' Paddy muttered
unhappily.

'It's not Master Luke that's making ye irritable at all, it's
because the laddie has to leave against his will, isn't it?'

'Ach, for sure I'm not for trusting that woman McGuire.
Even so you'll be admitting that Master Luke canna be trusted
to do anything without blundering like an idiot. I cannot
understand him! All the brains he is supposed to be having in
his head!'

'Och, come on, Paddy, it's not like you to be bitter or so
critical o' a man!'

'Man! Luke is not a man, he is a—'

'Whisht! What was that?'

'I heard not a thing.'

'I thought I heard a cough, or a sob, or something . . .'

'And I think pigs might fly! All right, Joey. I will not be
criticising of Master Luke again this night since it is disturbing

the ghosts for you!' Paddy did his best to summon his usual grin and failed miserably.

'Did I tell you about that man Steel? The big fellow with the red face and beaky nose?'

'What about him?'

'He came to speak to me in the field on Friday. I had just finished harrowing. He didna come up to the big hoose to speak to Miss Kirsty as he usually does.'

'She would not be sorry to miss him!' Paddy declared with feeling. Then he frowned. 'But I wonder why he did not come to speak with her? The last time he went to the fields alone he stole away with soil. Took it to have tests of some kind.'

Joey shrugged. 'Maybe he was in a hurry. It brought him to mind, you speaking about Master Luke like that. Steel asked a lot o' questions about him.'

'About Master Luke? What sort of questions?'

'How old he is. What he does here. He said he hadna kenned Miss Fairly had a brother until a neighbouring farmer mentioned him being so wonderful at the schooling. He asked about you as weel, Paddy.'

'And what would he be a-wanting to know about Paddy Kildougan now? I've met him and he did not so much as speak a word to me.' Paddy tapped his pipe out on the wall beside him and proceeded to fill it with a pinch or two of his precious Ogden's Flake.

'Och, he just wanted to ken how old ye are and what ye do at Fairlyden, and whether ye're married. Tae tell ye the truth, now I come tae think o't he asked an awfy lot o' questions about everybody at Fairlyden. He wanted to ken who helped with the milking. I told him Mistress MacFarlane and Mistress Fairly were aye busy, what with the milking twice a day and all the poultry. Then he asked how old Mistress Fairly might be. I told him that was nane o' my business and nane o' his either. I've been wondering though, Paddy, d'ye suppose he's interested in Mistress Fairly? Looking to find himself a wife I mean . . .?'

'I cannot tell you that, Joey, my laddie, but I can guess what Mistress Fairly would say if Steel had the impudence to be asking her such questions. It is as well you told him to mind his business! Now I'm going inside to see if Lenny is settling down. It is his last night . . .'

Kirsty drove a subdued Lenny to the station the following

morning, accompanied by Lucy, struggling hard to restrain her tears. As Beth had feared, the children from Glasgow had made their own niche at Fairlyden and particularly in Paddy's and Lucy's hearts. Irene, at eighteen months, was the only cheerful person in the car that particular spring morning. Lenny gazed out at the fields and trees and the lane as though he might never see them again and when Kirsty drew up at the station she heard him give a loud and determined sniff. Out of the corner of her eye she saw him wipe his fist surreptitiously over one eye and then the other.

'Ye've got a clean handkerchief, haven't ye, Lenny, and your gas mask, and your sandwiches?' Lucy asked for the umpteenth time. 'And ye'll not forget the wee parcel o' eggs and butter and ham Mistress Fairly sent for your mother . . .?' Her face was pale and Kirsty guessed she had not slept any better last night than she had herself. Lenny nodded silently, his dark eyes round and strangely fearful.

'I'll see you safely on to the train, Lenny,' she assured him now. 'I'll ask the guard to watch out for you when you get to Glasgow. You'll be all right.' Again he nodded silently and gave another loud sniff. 'You look very smart in your new trousers and the jersey Lucy has knitted for you.' Lenny bit his lip and blinked rapidly.

'I'll no' come right to the train with ye, laddie,' Lucy croaked huskily, coming round to their side of the car. 'Kiss Irene goodbye.' Irene gabbled merrily, not understanding her brother's solemn face, or the sparkle of tears on Mama Lucy's eyelashes.

'You'll be back before you know it, Lenny,' Kirsty assured him, doing her best to raise a cheerful smile despite the unexpected lump which seemed to be blocking her own throat now that the moment of parting had actually arrived. Lenny stopped and turned to her then. He looked up at her.

'Ye really mean it, Miss Kirsty?'

'Of course, Lenny! We are all expecting you back just as soon as your mother can manage without you. Who is going to help my mother and Mistress MacFarlane look after all the chickens if you don't hurry back?'

'Oh I will come, I will! I'll gie the new wean all my rations tae mak it grow big real quick!' Lenny's eyes gleamed with more than unshed tears now. There was renewed hope, and determination.

'We shall all come to the station again to collect you,' Kirsty promised huskily. 'Look, there's a seat in that carriage and I'll speak to the woman in the corner. She'll keep an eye on you until your mother's friend meets you in Glasgow. You'll remember and write to Lucy soon, Lenny?'

She bent and gave Lenny's bony young body a warm hug before two soldiers helped him and his small bundle into the carriage and grinned kindly at his anxious expression.

'Ye'll be all right with us, pal!' One of them assured him.

'We'll look after yer laddie, missus,' the other nodded to Kirsty.

'I didna mean tae let your horse die, Miss Kirsty,' Lenny called urgently as the doors slammed all down the platform and the train began to chug slowly. 'Honest I didna!'

'I know that, Lenny. Don't worry. He's flying over the clouds with the angels now . . .' She pointed up at the fluffy white clouds in the April sky. Lenny squinted upwards, nodded and gave one last wave.

As Kirsty had suspected Lucy had dissolved in tears the moment Lenny had turned his back; the journey home would have been a melancholy one, except for Irene's childish prattle.

Lenny's departure, coming on top of Marocco's death and a sleepless night, would have been enough for one day, but when she drew up outside Lucy's cottage, Kirsty found Mr Steel's car already parked in the yard and her heart sank.

Thirty-Three

Mr Steel had been peering into the stable but he turned as soon as Kirsty stopped the car. She went to open the passenger door before greeting him. Irene had fallen asleep on the way up the track.

'I hope the bairn sleeps until I've made Paddy his dinner,' Lucy had whispered. 'And got masel' in control a bit more,' she added, sniffing fiercely at the thought of Lenny's forlorn little figure waving from the train.

'I see you've plenty of petrol for joy riding, Miss Fairly,' Steel boomed behind them. 'Plenty of time too it seems,' he added, raising his sleek grey eyebrows as Lucy scrambled out of the car.

'Miss Kirsty wasna out for pleasure!' Lucy began indignantly. 'She—'

'It doesn't matter, Lucy. It is none of Mr Steel's business,' Kirsty interrupted firmly. Lucy wanted to protest, but when she glanced up she saw the twin patches of colour which stained Kirsty's cheeks, the coldness in her level stare; she knew that her young mistress was as angered by the man's inference as she was herself. Everyone at Fairlyden dreaded Steel's visits. He always set everyone on edge with his criticism and they all knew how much that upset Miss Kirsty when she was doing her very best for the war effort, Fairlyden and everyone who depended on her for their living. Lucy nodded at Kirsty and lifted her own chin determinedly. Kirsty knew that small defiant gesture was offering all the silent support Lucy could give her and her mouth softened faintly before Lucy turned away with the sleeping child and hurried into her cottage.

Surprisingly Steel seemed less critical than usual, almost smug in fact, although he questioned her about the fields which had been sown with oats and barley, how much land had been ploughed for potatoes and turnips. He already knew the answers to his questions, having questioned Joey Little, but Kirsty was unaware of his earlier surreptitious visit.

'So, Miss Fairly, you have not ploughed any of the old pasture as I suggested?'

'Oh yes. We have ploughed more than ten acres of permanent pasture, but not on Westhill.'

'You are ignoring my advice?'

'It is impossible to plough the Westhill land with horses. It is steep and in places it is boggy. We have compromised. We have sold the sheep and we are doing our best to rear the heifer stirks on Westhill, even though they need more supplementary feeding. We have taken them from the Muircumwell land and ploughed it instead.'

'The area I recommended would have provided twenty-five acres of corn, instead of the ten you have ploughed on the outskirts of the village.'

'We shall have a better crop from ten acres down there than frae twice as much up on Westhill – and more chance o' harvesting it.' Kirsty explained patiently for the umpteenth time. 'Besides which, I understand fresh milk is one of the best foods the people could have, according to the pamphlets just issued by the government, and it is in short supply too. Surely it doesna make sense to cut back too drastically on something we can do well at Fairlyden—'

'Miss Fairly!' Steel interrupted sharply. 'Government instructions are to increase the acreage of wheat and potatoes. They are the staple diet of the British people!' Kirsty knew this was true; it was one of the things which troubled her in her dealings with Steel. Yet surely if every farmer ploughed most of his land there would be no milk, no beef, no mutton. Already the number of pigs and hens had been drastically reduced.

'I do understand the need for home-grown cereals, Mr Steel,' Kirsty sighed, 'and we're doing our best to increase them, but wheat does not grow well here. Our little corner of Southwest Scotland is more famous for its cattle because grass grows so readily with the heavy rainfall.'

'Then you must increase the acreage of oats and barley. We want more and more and more! Are you aware that our ships are being attacked daily by the German U-boats, girl? Thousands of tons of good food are being lost every . . .'

'Yes, Mr Steel, I understand that.' Kirsty sighed wearily. 'But surely it is important to maintain a balance if the farm is to go on producing milk as well? I assure you we are doing our best to produce as much food as possible all round.'

'You are not!' Steel looked almost triumphant. 'You have not ploughed the land I instructed you to plough.'

'If you insist on Westhill being ploughed then you must arrange for a tractor and plough from the local War Ag.'

Steel glared suspiciously. 'Has someone been inciting you to make such demands on our limited resources?' His displeasure was plain. 'I have heard that Fairly from Mains of Muir is a relative of yours?'

'Uncle Alex? I have not discussed your ideas about ploughing Westhill with him, Mr Steel.' He would probably ridicule the idea as James had done, she thought. 'He has enough worries of his own. One of his sons is a pilot.'

'Umph...' For some reason Kirsty could not fathom Steel's face reddened and he looked at her sharply. 'Fairly has resigned from his local committee, and from the NFU, I understand. I suppose he used his son as an excuse when he couldn't stand the responsibility,' he sneered.

'Uncle Alex would never need to use anyone as an excuse,' Kirsty stated proudly. 'You would know that if you had lived in this area for any length of time, Mr Steel. He has been lame all his life but it has not prevented him building a fine reputation as a farmer. He is known throughout Scotland as a breeder of some of the best Clydesdale horses too. He has enough demands on his time and his health if he is to make the best he possibly can of the Mains, especially without Cameron and one of his other young workers. His neighbours still go to him for advice, but he admits frankly that he does not enjoy criticising other men's methods.'

'There's no room for sentiment! I am doing this job for the good of the nation,' Steel announced pompously. 'Now are you going to plough that land up there or not?' He inclined his head sharply towards the steeply rising ground three or four fields away behind the farmsteading. Kirsty stared at him.

'It is too late for this season, even if we had a tractor...'

'You are refusing to obey my instructions?'

'Yes I am!' Kirsty's control finally snapped but before she could say another word Steel had turned on his heel and was heading for his car. She did not see the sly gleam in his eye as she watched his retreating figure with a mixture of relief and exasperation.

Two days later Kirsty felt slightly comforted when she received a letter from James commiserating over Marocco's death.

Apparently Anna had written to tell him of Lenny's return to Glasgow. She had also mentioned the riding lessons and the subsequent accident. James understood better than anyone how much the old horse had meant to her. Marocco had been a part of the happy years of her youth, part of James's own youth too. She was warmed by the thought that he understood how she would feel and had taken time to write. A day or so later she wrote a short letter in return, acknowledging his thoughtfulness, making a determined effort to sound cheerful. She even described her confrontation with Steel with a touch of humour, as well as recounting the trivia which made up the daily life at Fairlyden.

When she received another letter from James within a week, Kirsty felt happier and more lighthearted than she had done since her father's death. He had made no secret of his desire to correspond regularly with her. So why not? Kirsty thought. Mary MacFarlane is no longer an obstacle to our friendship. Moreover James had once understood the running of Fairlyden almost as well as her father. He understands the problems the war has brought too, she thought, and the decisions I must make. It would be a relief to share my thoughts, my worries, with someone who really understands. Who better than James? He knew her weaknesses and her strengths; he had watched her growing up, dried her tears and shared her laughter; he had taught her to ride Marocco; he had quarrelled with her too, but until he went to Nithanvale and she had believed he was going to marry his half-cousin, they had always returned to their youthful camaraderie. Yes, she would enjoy corresponding with him.

Only the last paragraph of James's letter had troubled her slightly. He seemed to think Steel might take advantage of his authority and position and he urged her to be wary. He also commented on the new extension to the age limits for the registration of men and girls. At forty-one, Paddy fell within the age group concerned, but he had already registered and been assured that he was classed as an essential worker. Kirsty smiled faintly, tenderly, knowing James was concerned that she should not transgress the regulations and give Steel grounds for criticism.

Yet she had a niggling feeling that James was more anxious for everyone at Fairlyden than he had actually stated in his letter.

* * *

The milking machine was finally installed at Fairlyden in the last days of April. Kirsty did not like the constant chug chug of the Lister engine which drove the pump, creating the necessary vacuum. Mr Paton assured her it was the most reliable on the market, but she could not blame the cows for jumping about like a flock of nervous old hens. The first few milkings were dreadful. It was not only the cows which needed to get accustomed to the unwieldy buckets with their heavy lids and tubes and rubber-lined cups. Whenever she turned on the tap the vacuum hissed and sucked; straws, dirt and debris disappeared like magic; to Kirsty's horror they reappeared in the milk. The cotton pad in the sieve below the ridged cooler, which had been reasonably clean when they were milking by hand, was now a dirty greenish brown after every milking, quite contrary to what Mr Paton had led them to expect. Even the quietest cows tried to kick away the offensive contraptions and more than once Kirsty almost ended up in the gutter herself.

Lucy and Anna absolutely refused to stay in the byre while the machine was in use, and Paddy had found the operation just as difficult as Kirsty until Mr Paton arrived late one afternoon to see how they were progressing.

'Ye see these four cups for the teats are called a cluster,' he explained patiently. 'Now ye must stop the vacuum escaping until the instant when ye're ready tae slip it on the cow's teat. Like this see . . .' There was more than a gleam of amusement in his eye as he carried the bucket and tubes between two quiet-looking older cows and Kirsty guessed he had seen it all before and was enjoying a private joke at their expense. Not for long though. He had no sooner crouched on his haunches and extended one hissing cup towards the first of old Bertha's teats when he suddenly found himself sprawling in the centre walk of the byre at Kirsty's feet, glaring up into her astonished face, while the tubes hissed and fissed, writhing like snakes, and the startled cows almost broke their neck chains as they tried to jump over the wooden partitions.

'That silly auld b—' Mr Paton bit off the expletive with an embarrassed glance at Kirsty, and wiped a hand across his face where Bertha's wet tail had swiped him. Behind him Paddy exploded with laughter. A slow smile eased the tension on Kirsty's face too. It was a relief to find even the experts did not find this new machine as easy to use as a child's toy.

'Of course some o' the older cows never take tae the machine,'

Mr Paton announced defensively.

'What!' Kirsty stared at him in dismay. 'You should have told us that before you sold us the machine then!'

'Och, only one or two will be awkward, Miss. Ye'll see! The rest will soon get used tae it and the heifers will be nae bother at all after the first one or two milkings; they've never kenned any difference see.'

'I hope you're right,' Kirsty breathed fervently, thinking of the money she could have used towards paying off the bank loan, or purchasing a hundred and one other necessary items. Then she thought of all the times during the winter when Thomas had been too ill to come to the milking, and Anna too afraid to leave him alone. On these occasions it had been a terrible rush to get the milking finished and the churns down the track to the milkstand in time for the collecting lorry. Lucy would be relieved too. Since Lenny had gone she did not like to leave Irene in the house alone in case she wakened and climbed out of her cot. Instead she roused the little girl from sleep at five o'clock each morning, bundling her into the old pram and trundling her to the byre. Irene was getting too big to sleep in the pram now and she hated being confined. Even the novelty of the new electric lights did not distract her for long. Consequently she was often fractious long before the milking was over so that Lucy grew tense and impatient to be finished, a condition which the cows always seemed to sense.

Gradually all except four of the cows became accustomed to the new machine and Kirsty and Paddy washed, fed and milked one side of the byre each, working with precision. Beth placidly undertook the milking of the four cows which had continued to resist. Luke, with help from one or other of the women, carried the pails of milk to the dairy to be cooled, leaving Thomas and Joey to attend to the horses and make an early start on the field work. At last it seemed things were all under control.

Mr Steel called later than usual one afternoon and Kirsty was proud that everything was running with smooth efficiency. He had never offered anything but criticism, however, so she was not surprised when he muttered little more than a greeting and took himself off again. Beth almost collided with him at the door.

'Mr Steel is looking awfy smug today,' she remarked dryly. 'I suppose our problems with him are small though, compared to the misery o' the people who have lost everything with the bombs.' Certainly there appeared to be no end to the air raids – indeed the Germans seemed to have intensified their activities. Every morning there was news of more destruction and suffering. Early in May the bombing over London was particularly vicious and the tragic results of war touched many families throughout the land. The families at Fairlyden and the Mains of Muir were no exception.

Beth had returned to the house to make the evening meal in readiness for Luke and Kirsty. The telephone was ringing when she opened the door.

'Paul?' she murmured uncertainly, wondering why Alex's youngest son should be telephoning at all, and particularly at this time of day when most people, including those at the Mains, were either feeding and milking their animals, or preparing for their own evening meal.

'I didna know who else to phone, Aunt Beth.' He sounded young and vulnerable, more like Luke than the confident, capable young man Beth knew he had become. 'It's Mother. She – she's shattered by the news . . .'

'What news? Paul . . . What—?'

'Cameron. His plane was shot down over the Channel. One of the other pilots saw it.'

'Cameron! Oh, dear God, please not Cameron . . .'

'Can ye come over? Please, Aunt Beth? I-I canna get Mother to speak to me . . . and – and Father's so lost when Mother goes to pieces like this . . .'

'I'll come. Yes, of course I will, Paul. Just as soon as Kirsty comes in frae the byre. She'll not be much longer.'

'Th-thank you, Aunt Beth.' She heard the relief in his voice.

'Paul? What did—? I mean is there any hope?' she asked softly. Paul shook his head, unable to speak over the painful lump in his throat, but forgetting she could not see him. 'Paul?'

'N-none,' he whispered hoarsely. 'Very brave . . . they said . . . last out . . . Ye'll be here soon?'

'Aye, laddie, soon as I can.' Slowly Beth hung up the receiver. Her heart ached for Emma and Alex. This was the thing they had feared since the day their laughing, dark-haired, devil-may-care son had declared he was going to fly over the top of the world. So young, so full of life, of joy . . . she thought sadly.

Kirsty opened the back door and removed her clogs from leaden feet a quarter of an hour later. Her face was pale and shocked but for once Beth did not notice as she met her at the kitchen door. 'There's bad news, lassie,' she said carefully.

'I know. I've just heard . . . I canna believe he could do this.'

'But . . .' Beth faltered, frowning. 'Paul has only just telephoned. Did ye overhear then? He wants me to go to the Mains. Now. Tonight. I ken ye must be weary, lassie, after the busy day ye've had . . .' Beth went on anxiously, setting out a plate of steaming vegetable pie in which an odd piece of meat might or might not be found. 'But Emma and Alex were always kind to me and your father. Paul says there's no hope. Cameron's plane came down in the sea and he was last out . . .'

Kirsty stared at her mother, stunned by this second shattering blow within half an hour. Beth looked at her then and came round the table, pressing her into her seat. Kirsty had an almost overwhelming desire to turn into her mother's arms and bury her head against her soft, sweet-smelling bosom as she had done when she was a child. 'You must eat, lassie,' Beth murmured gruffly. 'We all depend on you. You must keep up your strength whatever happens. Och, if only Luke would learn to drive!' For the first time her exasperation with her son's total lack of practical ability showed. Kirsty sighed and made an effort to pull herself together. 'Indeed I think I must learn to drive myself!'

'I-I'll take you to the Mains, Mother.' Her voice was dull, flat. 'Whenever you're ready.'

'Ye're a good lassie, Kirsty.' Beth looked at her daughter's strained white face and frowned. 'There's nothing else troubling ye, is there? No other bad news?'

'We'll manage, if you've to stay the night. Don't worry.' Kirsty avoided answering directly. She knew her mother's thoughts were with Aunt Emma and she would not add to her anxiety tonight.

Thirty-Four

It was very late when Kirsty returned from Mains of Muir, leaving her mother behind with the difficult task of comforting Aunt Emma and Uncle Alex. Her cousins, Paul and Alexander, had also been understandably upset. Their youthful optimism had been shattered by harsh reality and Kirsty had found it hard to leave them despite her own weariness and depression. It had been a slow journey home too with the hooded lights of the car scarcely penetrating the darkness of the moonless night.

Kirsty had intended writing to James, telling him of her latest anxiety. There was nothing he could do about it. He could not even visit; Mr Henderson was still in hospital and James was in charge of the livelihood of his young family – but she wanted to write, she wanted advice, if he had any; she needed his reassurance. She arrived home to find Luke still up, sitting at the kitchen table, his head in his hands and with the remains of the evening meal still strewn around him.

'Oh, Luke!' Kirsty could not hide her reproach. She felt utterly weary. 'Surely you could have cleared the table and washed the few dirty dishes?'

'Sorry.' Luke mumbled miserably. He did not even look up at her.

'Mother is staying at the Mains, for a day or two at least! You'll have to help more.' Kirsty knew her voice had risen; she felt like bursting into tears but she strove for control. 'Joey has left . . .' Her voice came in a shaky croak. Luke looked up then and she saw the haunting shadows in his blue eyes, the stark pallor of his thin face. He looked far younger than his twenty years, but he showed no surprise at her announcement. 'You knew?' She stared at him.

'Not until tonight.'

'Is that all you can say! I-I don't know how we'll manage, Luke! Don't you understand? We need Joey so badly! Why, oh why did he have to go?' Kirsty slumped down on to a hard wooden chair, her eyes vacant, despairing.

'He didna have a choice,' Luke whispered hoarsely. 'It's my fault. I heard Paddy and Joey talking in the barn just before supper. They were saying goodbye. It was him or me. If I hadna come home Joey wouldna have gone, Kirsty . . .'

'That's nonsense.'

'It's true. Joey said the authorities had been informed that Fairlyden has three men registered for call up, as well as a man over fifty and several females resident on the farm. They reckoned that's more than we need for the production we . . .'

'Man over fifty . . .' Kirsty muttered, frowning. 'Surely they couldna mean Thomas? He's well over sixty . . . nearer seventy.'

Luke shrugged miserably. 'Joey's known for days. That's where he went last Saturday, to some office or other. They had a report on Fairlyden. He told Paddy he's been bracing himself to tell you. He didna want to go, Kirsty! I heard his voice, thick and croaky. Then he rushed from the barn, away from Paddy and down the track. It's all my fault. I should never have come home to work, not even to please Mother. I'm no use to you here anyway . . .'

'Don't say that, Luke,' Kirsty protested weakly. 'It would have broken Mother's heart if you had joined the army so soon after losing Father . . . Anyway at least I know that Joey didna go voluntarily. Tomorrow I shall write a letter appealing for his release.' Kirsty spoke with more confidence than she felt. If only James had been here, or if she could have sought Uncle Alex's advice . . . but she could not trouble him in the midst of his grief.

'Did you tell Paddy I had to drive Mother to Mains of Muir tonight?' she asked suddenly.

'No. Should I have done?' Luke looked genuinely puzzled.

Kirsty sighed heavily. 'The cows are still sleeping in the byre at nights until the weather improves . . .' Luke still looked back at her askance.

'Aah, Luke, surely you know one of us always checks the cows before bedtime, especially in the byre – in case any of them have slipped out of their chains, or are sick. Paddy would have looked them over if he'd known I had to go away this evening.'

'I'd forgotten. Surely they'll be all right for once?' He yawned.

'Probably.' Kirsty was deadly tired and she was tempted to skip the routine check as Luke suggested – then she remembered how diligent their father had always been. 'You go to bed, Luke. I willna be long.'

The byre was the newest building in the Fairlyden steading and since it had been extended it had a large sliding door at either end. Kirsty slipped inside and switched on the electric lights. What a blessing they are when it is really dark, she marvelled silently. She made a careful inspection down one side of the byre, her tiredness and depression temporarily forgotten. The warmth, the soft rustling and gentle rhythmic breathing – even the familiar pungent odour – were oddly comforting. The cows were fine specimens and in excellent condition; she knew in her heart that she had reason to be proud of them, whatever men like Steel might say.

At the far end of the byre she opened the other door and crossed the yard with the lantern she had brought, checking the horses in the stable, then the pigs, the calves, and last of all the small loose box where two of the cows had been housed. They were due to calve soon and it was less risky if they slept in the loose box than being tied by the neck in the byre. There were not enough loose boxes to house all the in-calf cows and it was one of several reasons why it was important to check them all thoroughly before going to bed. One of the farm collies crept silently across the yard and nuzzled gently at Kirsty's hand.

'It's all right, Tig,' she murmured softly, 'they're all behaving splendidly so far.' She returned to the byre, closed the big wooden door securely behind her and proceeded to inspect the cows down the second side. They were all chewing their cud, apparently happy and content. Kirsty yawned as she reached the far end; she switched off the lights and closed that door too. A few minutes later she was back at the house, too weary to write a letter to James. She would do it in the morning.

'Ach, Miss Kirsty, all these changes, it gets folks down. First Lenny leaving, and now Joey,' Paddy grumbled the following morning as he followed Kirsty into the dairy with the milking machine buckets and tubes ready for washing. 'Young Lenny has not written a single line for more than a fortnight now. Lucy thinks he's forgotten Fairlyden, changed his mind about coming back maybe.' He grimaced. 'Ach, I keep telling her he will not be forgetting us. Don't you agree, Miss Kirsty?'

Kirsty pushed aside her own worries over Joe Little's departure and gave him her attention, aware of the anxiety behind his brusque tone. She saw the doubts in his eyes too.

'I'm certain Lenny will never forget you and Lucy, Paddy. He thought the world of you both. I expect his mother is keeping him busy with Arf and the new baby to look after, or maybe he couldna buy a stamp this week.'

'Lucy sent him stamps and postcards.'

'Maybe Gladys sold them.'

'Ach! 'Tis a sin that such women as Gladys McGuire should be blessed with babes, when Lucy . . .' Paddy shrugged and turned away.

'Paddy?' Kirsty bit her lip uncertainly as Paddy turned back to face her, his rubbery face now under control. 'Joey . . . he didna really want to leave Fairlyden either, did he?'

'Bless you, Miss Kirsty, indeed he did not!' He frowned thoughtfully. 'To be sure and I was wondering if Joey has been called up because of that devil of a man, Steel. Him and his questions . . .'

'What do you mean, Paddy? What questions?'

'He talked to Joe one day when he was working down at the Muircumwell fields – by himself he was – but the man was for asking him questions. Joey told me so himself.'

'Wh-what sort of questions?'

'Just questions . . .' Paddy shrugged. 'About his work, about me and my work . . . I cannot be telling what else he asked, Miss Kirsty, but Joe said he did not come up to the farm to see you that day.'

'I see . . . I don't think Steel has anything to do with men being called up for the armed services . . . unless – unless he put in some sort of report or complaint about Fairlyden. I'm going to write a letter appealing for Joey's return.'

Paddy grinned and looked more relaxed than he had been since he appeared in the byre two hours earlier. 'Sure and that would be fine indeed! It's needing him we are. All the turnips still to be drilled and this here Paddy Kildougan scarce able to walk in a straight line himself with his legs bowed like a beer barrel, so how can I be making a fine straight drill with the horse? As for old Thomas . . .' He shook his head. 'You be sure and get young Joey back here quick, Miss Kirsty.'

Kirsty wrote the letter immediately after breakfast and she had just sealed it when Madge Taylor delivered the mail.

'Aah, you're early this morning, Madge,' Kirsty smiled, handing her the sealed letter to take to the post office. 'I meant to write another letter but I have not had time yet this morning.'

'I've a letter to take up to Mrs Kildougan this morning. I'll call on ma way back, if ye like? It would save ye a journey to the village.'

'Thanks. I'll see if I can get it written in time. Mother is away at the Mains so the work is all behind this morning.'

'Aah . . . Of course. I heard about Master Cameron. I am sorry, Miss Kirsty.' Madge's cheery smile died. 'War is awfy cruel!' Her eyes had filled with apprehension.

'Yes. Let's hope it will all end soon!' Kirsty remembered Madge was doing her husband's job because Willy was in the army. She changed the subject tactfully. 'I'm glad you've brought a card for Lucy. She was beginning to think Lenny had forgotten her.'

'Oh, but it isna the usual postcard frae the wee laddie who was an evacuee. This one's an official-looking letter frae Glasgow.' She frowned suddenly. 'I hope it's not bad news. One o' the women biding i' the village comes frae Glasgow. She said the Germans had bombed Clydebank something terrible.'

Kirsty felt a shiver run down her spine. She stared at the young postmistress. 'Please, please, dear god, let Lenny be safe,' she prayed silently.

'I'll get up to Mrs Kildougan's then and call in for your letter on ma way back.'

Kirsty watched Madge leave the kitchen, hurry down the path and jump on her red bike, but she could not move to write the letter to James; she could not think; she had the most dreadful premonition of more trouble hanging over Fairlyden and its families.

Take a hold on yourself, she admonished sternly. Just because Lenny has not written, just because Paddy was secretly as worried as Lucy, just because there's an official letter . . . none o' these things mean anything! But bad things always go in threes, she thought superstitiously, and Kirsty had never been superstitious in her life. Joey gone, Cameron dead . . . Her thoughts would not be calmed . . .

It did not take long for Madge Taylor to come peddling across the farm yard and down the short length of track back to the house. Kirsty had been standing at the kitchen window, subconsciously waiting. She dashed outside and ran down the path. Madge's face was pale, her eyes wide. Kirsty's heart thudded.

'Mrs Kildougan . . . she needs ye,' Madge gasped. 'The laddie, all o' them . . .'

'Lenny?'

'All killed. Mrs Kildougan's in a terrible state.'

'I'll go to her now,' Kirsty whispered hoarsely. She pictured Lenny's earnest young face peering from the train window . . . Tears blinded her eyes as she ran towards Lucy's cottage. She blinked them back determinedly. She would need to be strong and calm for Lucy's sake. Poor Lucy.

'The letter says the McGuires were all killed,' Lucy repeated over and over punctuated with hiccoughing sobs while Kirsty spooned some of the precious tea ration into the warmed pot and found cups in the cupboard.

'Drink this, Lucy, and I'll find Paddy.'

'Oh God!' Lucy groaned. 'He loved the laddie as though he were his ain for all we had him so short a time. He'll be upset, I ken he will.'

'Yes.' Kirsty agreed desolately.

'The letter is frae a woman, a Miss Mackintosh, frae some sort o' office. Read it, Miss Kirsty. Read it in case I've misunderstood,' Lucy pleaded.

Kirsty scanned the typed formally worded lines obediently.

'There's no mistake,' she whispered hoarsely. 'It says four families in that block were killed that night . . .' Kirsty frowned as she read the last two lines. 'Josh McGuire was not with them though. He – he's been back to Glasgow! He's returned to his regiment . . .'

'Aye,' Lucy said flatly. 'I ken.'

'Surely he could have written himself. He should have come to see you, and Irene . . . to tell you!'

'I hope he never comes!' Lucy sobbed vehemently. 'He'll never love Irene like we love her. Lenny knew he didna love him either!' Lucy began to sob hysterically.

'Dear Lucy . . . Please drink some tea,' Kirsty urged gently. She felt so helpless, but gradually Lucy calmed down and sipped gratefully at the hot, sweet tea.

'They shouldna put this on ration.' She gave Kirsty a brave, wobbly smile. 'It's the on'y medicine worth having.'

'Just you sit and drink the pot dry then.' Kirsty did her best to respond to Lucy's heroic effort. 'I'll run next door and ask Anna to bring Paddy. He and Thomas are mending the fence in the Long Meadow. I'll not be long.'

* * *

It was evening and the end of a long and stressful day before Kirsty had time to think of James and the letter she had meant to write. Suddenly she had a terrible urge to talk to him. 'You could telephone,' he had said. Why not? she thought. James had been fond of Lenny too; he had known her cousin Cameron well; it was he who had sent Joe Little to Fairlyden. Yes, she thought eagerly, I will telephone.

She fetched the card and dialled the operator. It was not either of the local operators but she seemed quite efficient as Kirsty heard her asking for the other exchange and then the telephone ringing in some strange house. Suddenly Kirsty felt nervous and foolish and her mouth went dry. She didn't know what to say. A woman's voice answered. She sounded young and tired and a bit impatient. Kirsty heard a baby crying in the background and a child calling stridently, 'Mama, Mama!' She began to stammer but she managed to ask Mrs Henderson if James could telephone Fairlyden.

'Is it urgent?'

'Y-yes, I-I mean no ... well ...'

'Would it do tomorrow?' the voice asked wearily.

'Y-yes, of course.'

Kirsty hung up the telephone and stared at it glumly. She felt more depressed than ever. There was no word of her mother returning from Mains of Muir tonight either and Kirsty missed her quiet strength, her comforting presence. She was glad that Anna was so kind and motherly to Lucy and Paddy. It seemed such a tragic waste that a young eager life like Lenny's should be snuffed out like a candle in the wind.

Beth returned home the following day. Kirsty had just finished bedding the young calves when she saw the Mains' car coming up the track and she breathed a sigh of relief. Anna had been doing the morning round of the hen houses. The eggs were too precious now to allow any to get broken in the nests if it could be avoided. 'There's your mother home by the looks o' it,' she said as she drew level with Kirsty in the yard. 'I'll give ye this basket o' eggs to take to the house if ye're going to see her now.'

'Thanks.' Kirsty relieved Anna of the big wicker basket. 'It will not be much of a welcome when I tell her about Lenny.'

'No. Paddy has taken it badly too, even worse than Lucy, I think. Irene claims her attention ...' Anna frowned and sighed. 'I wonder what'll happen to the bairn after the war?

It's taking the heart out o' good folks, all these partings . . .'

'Only time will tell. I can't imagine Josh McGuire caring much about a baby daughter he has hardly seen. He didn't seem to care all that much about his sons and he had lived with them. I'll go and break the news to Mother. I'll have to tell her about Joe leaving too.' She glanced up at the sky. 'The weather seems to have settled for the present. We really must get the turnips sown.'

'Aye, Thomas was saying the same thing when he came in frae feeding the horses first thing. He's willing to make a start, Miss Kirsty, but he kens he's no' fit . . .'

'I know, Anna, I know. I wouldn't care whether the drills were straight or not. I shall have to persuade Paddy to have a go, or try myself.'

'Well, it would take Paddy's mind off Lenny maybe,' Anna reflected doubtfully. 'But there are so many other things to be done with the cattle. I suppose there's nae chance o' Master Luke . . .'

Kirsty shook her head. 'He canna manage the horses.'

Luke had seen the Mains' car too and he had already broken the news of Lenny's death and Joe Little's departure to his mother by the time Kirsty reached the house. She put the eggs safely into the outer pantry for her mother to clean and sort later in readiness for the van which now collected them to take to the local packing station. At least that will be one job less to do tonight, she thought wearily.

'Kirsty! Lassie, ye look exhausted!' Beth exclaimed as soon as she entered the kitchen. 'And so much trouble and I've only been away two nights.'

'Yes.' She summoned a wan smile. 'How's Aunt Emma, and Uncle Alex?' She looked from her mother to her Cousin Alexander.

'My mother is beginning to accept the inevitable,' he said quietly, 'thanks to Aunt Beth's help and understanding.' He gave Beth a brief, sad smile. 'Father seems to be suffering from delayed shock though.'

'They both have courage,' Beth said staunchly. 'It's harder when there's nothing . . . no body . . .' she added under her breath. 'It doesna seem real.'

'We are not alone though. But what about you, Kirsty? You seem to have enough problems here at Fairlyden without adding ours?'

Kirsty grimaced. 'I have appealed against Joe Little's call up, but I'm afraid it may be too late. He didna tell us until the night before he had to report. He may already have been sent to a training camp.'

'Very likely he has,' Alexander agreed frowning. 'There seems to be such a demand for more soldiers and airmen – indeed there just aren't enough men for all that needs to be done and it's amazing the jobs women are tackling.'

'If we'd just had the turnips drilled before Joey had to leave it wouldna have been quite so bad,' Kirsty told him, trying to sound optimistic, and feeling weighed down with problems. 'We can all hoe them once they've grown. Some o' the women frae the village came to help us last year, and they came again to gather potatoes. It's the jobs that need a good ploughman that I find hardest to manage.'

'I just wish we could help you with the turnip drilling but we only started our own this morning. That's the trouble with turnips: if you plant too soon they get frosted and bolt away to seed, and if you're too late and the season happens to be dry they just lie there in their corky clusters and dinna even germinate. I suppose it might help if you had a tractor?' he suggested tentatively.

'Maybe it would if we could afford one,' Kirsty said wryly. 'But even if I could drive it myself it doesna mean I could manage all the cultivations, does it?'

'I've never heard o' you giving up without a darned good try, Cousin Kirsty!' Alexander smiled encouragingly. 'If Father was more like himself I'd ask him to telephone some o' the officials he's acquainted with and see if he could help you get Joe Little back, or at least send you some temporary help from the War Ag.'

'I—I tried to telephone James MacFarlane last night, in case he knew anyone who might help.' She glanced at her mother. 'But he hasna contacted me yet. I expect he'll telephone tonight.'

James did not telephone that night, or the next. Neither was there any reply from the War Ag office to give her any hope of Joe Little being returned to Fairlyden. Thomas and Paddy had made a start on the turnip drilling. She had even made a reasonable effort herself and discovered just how exhausting it was trying to make the drills let alone plodding behind the horses, up and down the field all day long. Thomas was too

307

lame and too short of breath to get from one end to the other without several rests. Paddy was disgusted with his own efforts and he tended to take out his frustration on Luke who had made no attempt to try any cultivations. He simply could not handle the horses, even less the machines. In desperation Kirsty telephoned the local War Ag office and demanded to know why they had not acknowledged her appeal or sent her some temporary help. She was informed that help had already been arranged and would be with her that very afternoon; she hung up the receiver with a heart-felt sigh of gratitude.

'Help' arrived in the form of Mr Steel and a younger man whom he introduced as his eldest son, Peregrine.

'He has come to take charge. You have the option of cooperating fully, Miss Fairly, or moving out of the farm with your family. Fairlyden must make a worthwhile contribution to the nation's larder. You will do well to remember that I have full authority as an agent of His Majesty's government.'

Thirty-Five

Kirsty gasped. The colour drained from her face as she stared at Steel's implacable expression. She fancied there was a smirk of satisfaction on his thin lips; certainly there was a glitter in his eyes.

'Fairlyden already contributes well to the nation's larder!' she declared indignantly. 'And nothing – absolutely nothing – will make me, or my family, leave our home.' She saw Steel catch his son's eye, saw him nod and watched Peregrine Steel's flaccid lips curl derisively. Fury boiled in her. 'This farm is my heritage! My parents and grandparents have given sweat, toil and tears for its survival.'

'There is no such luxury as heritage in our present climate. We are at war,' Steel declared coldly. 'The State controls your land and it controls you – through me. Me, Miss Fairly. Now good day to you. Peregrine,' he beckoned his son with a jerk of his head. 'Come to the car and collect your portmanteau. Telephone me if you have any trouble.' He glared quellingly at Kirsty but she tilted her square jaw and glared back at him defiantly. Inwardly she felt sick with apprehension, but she followed them outside, unwilling to allow them any opportunity of discussing her. Could this really be happening? Had she really made such a terrible job of managing Fairlyden? In her heart she knew she had not, even if she had not obeyed Steel's instructions to the letter. If only they hadna taken Joe away, she fumed silently.

'I'll get a tractor and driver sent over from the local depot,' Steel informed his son, 'probably by tomorrow.'

'You'll what? If you can send a tractor and a driver for him, you could have done the same for me! We dinna need your son! And we certainly dinna want him here!'

'He is here to stay and he has absolute control from now on. You'd better get used to that, *Miss* Fairly.' Why had he emphasised her single status and looked back at his son like that? Kirsty was bewildered and uneasy, but she was also frustrated by her own impotence as she watched Steel shrug his shoulders and get back into his car, leaving his son and his luggage standing on the steps of her home.

Kirsty did not know whether to be glad or sorry that her mother was still gathering the eggs in the small field behind the byre. It was hatching time again and the hens took a lot of Anna's time as well as her mother's.

'Well, Miss Fairly, you had better show me to my room,' Peregrine Steel ordered smoothly.

'Since you have come here uninvited, unannounced and certainly unwanted, then you will just have to wait until it is convenient for someone to find you a room.' Kirsty turned away, her head high, but Steel caught her arm roughly and twisted her back towards him.

'Now look here, you—'

'Take your hands off me!' Kirsty's eyes blazed. 'Or I shall report you to the authorities.' Steel's hazel eyes wavered but he did not release his hold. 'Don't doubt my word,' Kirsty advised through gritted teeth. 'My uncle is well acquainted with most of the officials, even though he is no longer one of them.' She remembered Uncle Alex's grey, drawn face and knew she would never pester him with her own problems at such a time. 'They will have a good deal to say about your father's abuse of his position.'

Peregrine did release her then. 'I regret that it is necessary for me to take over like this, Miss Fairly, but you have brought it on yourself. You will soon get used to having me around.' Kirsty found his excessively smooth tone even more repulsive than his father's pomposity. 'I'm only doing the job I have been asked to do, you know.'

'Asked to do! Commanded to do, by your own father, you mean! I don't believe Fairlyden needs anyone like you. All we need is Joe Little's return. Your father's interference is excessive. It is so unjust!'

'War is a desperate state calling for desperate measures . . .'

'Even if Fairlyden does require a manager, or a supervisor, or whatever you choose to call yourself, I canna help wondering how your father managed to wangle the job for you, his own son. What are your qualifications, Mr Steel?'

'My qualifications do not come into the matter, Miss Fairly.'

'No? What are your father's real motives in bringing you here, to Fairlyden? You certainly don't look like a farmer to me. Perhaps he is abusing his influence and position to keep his "wee laddie" frae having to join the forces?' Kirsty watched a red stain colour Peregrine Steel's sallow skin and realised her bitter taunt had accidentally struck part of the truth at least – not that it made her own position any better. Steel was here, and presumably someone in authority had sanctioned his employment. Again she felt her heart give a sickening jolt. She couldn't bear to have anyone else take over Fairlyden. What would her father have thought of this situation? Her grandmother too – working so hard and struggling for years to keep her family at Fairlyden.

'Whatever I have to do to prevent it, I shall never let you take Fairlyden from me and my family!' she said aloud, her jaw clenched, her blue-grey eyes sparkling with anger.

'I'm sure we shall find an amicable arrangement for working together, Miss Fairly – very amicable indeed . . .' His voice was silken now and Kirsty realised why she found it so abhorrent. His eyes were skimming over her figure, limb by limb; she saw the speculative appreciation in them but she was not flattered by it; that glitter was unmistakable in a man's eyes. 'I think we should start by being a little more friendly. Your name is Kirsty, I believe?' Kirsty did not answer. Her mind was grappling with this new problem. He was expecting to live under the same roof as her, share the same table; she would have to deal with the man as well as his authority. 'You may call me Peregrine.'

'Mr Steel,' Kirsty said deliberately. Icily. 'You may stand here all day and wait for my mother to return and show you to your room, if you wish. I have work to do.'

The hazel eyes narrowed angrily. Peregrine Steel was not a handsome man, but he was not used to being rebuffed by women, let alone by a haughty chit of a peasant girl. Still, he reflected, he had plenty of time to tame this one and teach her a lesson – all the time in the world; living in the same house he would have ample opportunity too; it might prove to be rather good sport. He hadn't reckoned on such pleasant diversions.

His father had told him only that the farm was occupied by a stubborn, ignorant girl who should not be difficult to oust. He had not told him how easy on the eye she was, nor that she was proud, haughty and damned spirited. Of course she had probably attended the village school and she would know little more than how to write her name and add one and one together, but he could put up with that for the duration of the war if he had to. Yes . . . now that he had seen her he might well consider her as a wife until the war was over. That would serve his purpose very well.

Gaining possession of a farm had been his father's idea – how he did it was immaterial. He had not been particularly enthralled by the prospect himself, except insofar as it kept him out of the hands of all those sergeant majors and similar boring disciplinarians. His thick lips curled. He had had enough regimentation at boarding school. He was his own man now and he intended to stay that way. He eyed Kirsty's retreating figure speculatively. She was tall, slim, erect – extraordinarily graceful in fact, but she certainly wouldn't be allowed to stand in his way. After all it was not only his own freedom which was at stake. There was always the possibility that one of his brothers would be called to serve their country too, unless the family had more land under its control. His father had bought a large house but the land belonging to it was no more than seventy acres; he had lost no time in inveigling himself on to several committees and cultivating the most influential men he could find, but that would not be sufficient to keep his sons at home the way that devil Hitler was shaping up.

He was still watching Kirsty when a small middle-aged man in uniform came puffing up the track on a bicycle. He rang the bell to attract Kirsty's attention when he saw her hurrying towards the farm buildings. He continued peddling as fast as he could, giving no more than a cursory glance at the well-dressed stranger standing beside his initialled leather luggage.

Kirsty heard the insistent ringing of a bicycle bell and turned, puzzled. She began to retrace her steps reluctantly and they were less than a dozen yards apart before she recognised Dick Anderson, the village joiner.

'Why hello, Mr Anderson.' She gave him a strained smile. 'I hardly recognised you in that uniform.'

''Afternoon, Miss Kirsty.' He jumped off his bike and stood holding it awkwardly. There was no place to prop it unless he walked to one of the walls of the surrounding buildings but this he seemed disinclined to do; neither did he seem to know what to say. He looked ill at ease and Kirsty frowned slightly.

'Did you want to see my mother?' she asked helpfully. Mrs Anderson and her mother attended the same first aid class and they were both members of the local Women's Voluntary Service and in the Women's Rural Institute. Sometimes Mrs Anderson helped Beth with the Sunday School too. Still Dick

Anderson hesitated. Over his shoulder Kirsty could see Peregrine Steel approaching.

'I'll find Mother,' she suggested.

'Er . . . no, Miss Kirsty. That is . . . well it's not your mother I've come to see . . .'

'Oh. There's nothing wrong, is there, Mr Anderson? N-no bad news for anyone? Miss Lizzie? Is she all right?'

'Och, she was in fine fettle when I came by the shop!' His face lightened a little. 'Grumbling about folks grumbling about the rationing . . .' He chuckled, then sobered. 'Truth is, Miss Kirsty, I'm here officially as the local ARP warden. We've had a complaint about Fairlyden contravening the blackout regulations.'

'A complaint? Mother has all our windows covered if we have even a peep of light inside, especially since those poor men were killed at Gretna last month. We could scarcely believe the Germans would drop bombs almost on our own doorstep.'

'Aye, 'twas a sorry business,' Dick Anderson agreed gravely. 'It was a Monday night ye see; some folks reckon a bomber must have been flying o'er just as they opened the door to come out o' their meeting. Must have showed a chink o' light. Other folks reckon 'twas the gleam o' water Jerry saw . . . We'll never ken. Made us all realise we canna be too careful though. Never know where the enemy is.'

'We try to be careful,' Kirsty murmured thoughtfully. 'The cottages still use lamps or candles and I'm sure Anna and Lucy have blackout curtains. So . . .'

'It wasna the houses, lassie. The man who complained didna leave his name. Likely he'd be poaching up here. But he did say he'd seen a light when he was up the hill above the steading. It looked like a long line o' light, he said, and t'was a danger to the district . . .' Dick Anderson looked more uncomfortable than ever and Kirsty was aware of their uninvited guest almost within hearing. 'I've got to investigate all complaints, ye understand, Miss Kirsty?' he muttered, dropping his voice.

'Yes, of course.' Kirsty frowned. 'But a long line of light? I canna understand it . . .'

'Weel, I did wonder if it could be the byre? I heard Les Paton had been installing electric lights for ye?'

'Yes, we have the electric in the byre now, but it doesna have any windows.'

'Not in the walls, lassie, but there's windows in the roof and along the ridge o' the roof, if I remember rightly, that is? I was at the building o' it with ma father.' He rubbed his hand nervously over the saddle of his bicycle and avoided Kirsty's eye. He did not enjoy showing his authority to people who had given his family work.

'You're right! I never thought o' that,' Kirsty agreed, her eyes widening in horror. 'But even so, we dinna need the lights just now. It's daylight when we are milking.'

'Aye. But this was very late one night – just before the weather improved. The complainant should have reported it earlier, whoever he is. Maybe Paddy Kildougan was helping one o' the cows to calve, eh?'

Kirsty's brows creased in thought, then she remembered. 'The night we got word o' Cousin Cameron . . .' she muttered in dismay. 'I was late doing the rounds. I turned the lights on. I remember thinking what an improvement the electric light made for checking up on them . . . Oh, dear!' She clapped a hand to her brow.

'Weel, there's no harm done yet, thank God. We'll no' be giving 'em another chance though, eh? Maybe I could just take a look at the byre and give ye a bit o' advice?'

'If there's any advising to be done here I shall be doing it from now on, Mr . . .?'

Dick Anderson turned and found himself looking into Steel's plump pasty face. He looked back at Kirsty.

'Who's he then?'

Kirsty bit her lip. 'Mr Steel. From the War Ag.' Her words were clipped, cold. Dick Anderson registered her disapproval. He turned his back on the intruder, cocked an eyebrow and half winked. 'You an' me . . . we'll just tak a walk through the byre then, lass, shall we?'

'I shall be in charge here from now on,' Steel informed him sharply. 'If you're here to make some sort of inspection I will accompany you. If you have any reports to make you will show them to me first, my man.'

Dick Anderson scowled at the dictatorial tone and looked at Kirsty questioningly.

'Anything I have to say, I'll say to Miss Fairly, if ye dinna mind,' he declared when she remained silent, her lips pursed, her face tense with dislike. They walked together to the long byre and Dick propped his cycle against the wall. He patted the wooden door.

'Fine bit o' wood, Miss Kirsty. Ma father and me, we made a good job o' the joinery when it was built, eh?' He beamed proudly. 'They're using every scrap o' wood they can lay hands on now. There'll no' be a bit o' well-seasoned timber when this here war is o'er.' He went inside and Kirsty followed miserably, watching as he frowned consideringly up at the roof ridge which was always open for ventilation except in the coldest wintry weather. Apart from that there were three rectangular windows set into both sides of the sloping roof. She realised now that these would all need to be blacked out before the winter. Another unexpected task; another expense; her heart sank.

'Mmm . . . weel, we canna be having any more complaints, or risking Jerry coming o'er again and emptying his bombs onto oor wee neck o' the woods . . . . Ma father's too old to do much nowadays but I reckon he could make ye some frames for the roof lights, Miss Kirsty? Maybe that brother o' yours could nail some pieces o' felt on and think o' a way to fix 'em up. He has plenty o' brains they tell me, so likely he'll find a way. As for that ridge . . .' He squinted up at the high peaked roof. 'The windows all along the top will have to be painted. There's dark paint available for that sort o' problem. When I get back I'll telephone through to Annan and explain what's needed, if ye like. They'd put it on the bus to Miss Whiteley's Store for ye to collect.'

Kirsty smiled gratefully and with relief. Surely it would not be such a terrible problem after all, even though the byre ridge was very high and difficult to reach. 'That would be fine. Thank you very—'

'I shall decide what to do about any problems,' Steel interrupted sharply. 'I've told you, I'm in charge here now.'

'Fairlyden belongs to Miss Fairly and I ken fine she'll put things right.' Dick Anderson declared firmly.

'I shall see to it. I tell you I'm in charge here.'

'Mmm . . . so ye keep saying. Ye'll be telling me ye've bought the place next,' Dick Anderson muttered.

'You havena got a car to go into Annan,' Kirsty protested.

'I shall use the farm car of course.' Steel gave Kirsty a pitying glance as though she had no brains at all.

'Use my car! Indeed you will not. Please order the paint, Mr Anderson and I will collect it at Miss Lizzie's.'

'Miss Fairly! You would do well to remember—'

'As the local air raid warden I'll decide what's to be done and

315

I said I would order the paint, Mr what's-your-name . . .' Dick Anderson intervened with uncharacteristic rudeness. 'No use wasting petrol. You'll see that it's put on before ye use the lights again, Miss Kirsty?' He had pulled his own rank with Steel, but he winked at Kirsty as he jumped on his bicycle. She knew the complaint was a serious matter but he trusted her to rectify it. She also sensed that he did not like Peregrine Steel any better than she did herself and that thought brought her a little comfort, though not a lot. The whole situation was intolerable.

Thirty-Six

Beth was just as dismayed and indignant as Kirsty when she heard how Peregrine Steel had been thrust upon them; not only on the farm, but also as an uninvited visitor in their home. She felt an instant dislike towards the pasty-faced young man, with his sulky mouth and close-set eyes. She mistrusted him instinctively, without reason, and she chided herself for such hasty judgement. Beth was usually very tolerant of other people's failings. She had been sorely tempted to telephone Alex to ask whether Mr Steel had overstepped his authority, or whether there was anything they could or should do to change the arrangements which had been made without their consent; but like Kirsty, she was reluctant to involve Alex and Emma in Fairlyden's problems when their grief for Cameron was still so raw.

Beth was sitting in the kitchen, already warmed by the big Aga cooker, but she had kindled a fire in the front parlour for Peregrine Steel, despite the coal shortage. It was more to keep him out of her way than to make him welcome. The weather was getting warmer now and Luke had retired to his bedroom with his books as usual in the evenings.

She looked up from her seat at the kitchen table, her fountain pen in her hand with its cap still in place. Kirsty paced restlessly from the cupboard to the sink, moved aimlessly to the cooker, lifted first one hot plate cover then the other, then put them down again; she went into the small adjoining room which had been Logan's study and where she still did the accounts. Minutes later she was back again.

'Maybe you should telephone James again.' Beth suggested, guessing the reason for her daughter's restlessness.

'If he had wanted to telephone he would have done so by now. Anyway I don't like to bother Mrs Henderson when we don't know her.' It was her turn to write to James but she had kept putting it off, waiting for the telephone call which had never come.

'Perhaps he couldna get to a telephone if he's busy.'

317

'It's three days since I left a message for him. He's had time to write if he couldna phone. Oh Mother, I am sorry! I didna mean to snap.'

'I understand, Kirsty dear,' Beth sighed.

'Who are you writing to tonight.'

'Your Uncle Billy. I owe him a letter.'

'Yes, he's written to you regularly since Father died, hasn't he?' Kirsty eyed her mother curiously. 'Was he like Father?'

'Oh no, not at all,' Beth smiled. 'And he used to be a terrible correspondent. But he was always a good friend to me when I was a bairn, living in the cottage – especially when my father died . . .' Beth's eyes took on a reminiscent look.

'Who was he like – Uncle Billy, I mean?' Kirsty welcomed any subject which took her mind off Peregrine Steel's presence in the house, or James's failure to contact her.

'Cameron was the image of him,' Beth reflected softly. 'It's a pity Billy never managed to get home to see his nephews, and you, his only niece.'

'Maybe he will come, when this awful war is over. It will be too late for him to meet Cameron, though.'

'Aye, but I dinna think Billy is well enough for such a journey now. He has seemed a bit homesick recently. I think that's why he looks forward to my letters so much.'

'Do you enjoy writing to him mother? Or is it another of the duties you undertake with such grace?'

'It isna a duty, lassie. Billy kens Fairlyden well, but he sees our problems differently, and it helps me to get things in perspective, writing to him. He wrote such lovely things when Logan died . . .' She sighed softly but a gentle smile curved her lips and Kirsty thought how young and pretty her mother looked despite her troubles and hard work. 'He thought we should have borrowed more money frae the bank and bought a tractor.'

'You didn't tell me that.'

'No.' Beth frowned. 'I hate the thought of owing money to anybody and ye've had such a lot o' responsibility since your father died, Kirsty. I'm afraid I havena been much support to ye, and I was selfish encouraging Luke to come home to work. I realise now that he's more of a burden than a help, for all ye've been so patient with him.'

'Oh, Mother, you have been a wonderful support! Just being here, looking after Luke and me, being so brave when your world had fallen to pieces . . .'

'Aah, ye're a good lassie, Kirsty. Ye dinna deserve this man Steel.'

The following morning a middle-aged man arrived driving a green tractor with wide metal-spiked wheels. There was no machinery with the tractor however and the man had to set about converting the horse drill. Kirsty was despatched to the village to have a specially shaped iron made at the smiddy, while Thomas and Paddy found and shaped a suitable pole. Luke kept out of the way and Peregrine Steel succeeded only in annoying everyone with his supercilious comments.

Fortunately the War Ag man seemed to know what he was about; he tackled the conversion with quick efficiency and by midday had started sowing the turnips. It seemed to Thomas and Kirsty that he worked with remarkable speed but by the end of the day there was a definite atmosphere at Fairlyden and it was not a pleasant one. Thomas, always hard of hearing, simply made no effort to listen to Steel's numerous instructions and went about his usual work muttering derogatory remarks – not quite under his breath – about idle men who came to work dressed like gentlemen and did nothing but give orders. After his third confrontation with the new manager of Fairlyden, Paddy also had a sullen look on his leathery face instead of his usual wry smile.

Kirsty had silently resolved that she would not allow Steel to provoke her, but she followed Luke's example and avoided him as far as possible. This was relatively easy since it soon became apparent that he knew little about the care of cattle and pigs and absolutely nothing about poultry. It was almost the end of the following day when Peregrine Steel succeeded in arousing Kirsty's temper. She and Paddy had finished the milking and the early summer evening seemed wonderfully peaceful when the milking machine engine was switched off and silence reigned once more. Paddy was ushering the cows back to their pasture for the night and Kirsty was alone in the dairy, draining the heavy milking units and checking all the tubes in readiness for the morning milking. She had thought Steel had gone back to the house an hour ago so she was surprised when she turned and found him close behind her – too close. She was trapped in a corner. She frowned and glanced up at him irritably when he made no effort to move out of her way.

'Excuse me.' Her voice and her expression were cold and

impatient. She was tired and hungry and she could not imagine what stupid triviality he had come to complain about this time.

'It is time you and I had a little talk, *Miss* Fairly.' His voice was suave but Kirsty was not impressed. She prodded him with her elbow and would have pushed past him to finish her few remaining tasks, but he gripped her arm and pulled her up sharply so that she was held close against his chest. When she looked up she could feel his breath, hot and none too sweet, on her forehead.

'For goodness sake! If you've so much strength and energy to spare you might try doing some real work for a change. Now let go of me!' She heaved hard and succeeded in jabbing him in the chest with her elbow, temporarily winding him. It was sufficient to allow her to move away from the corner, if not out of the dairy, and she seized the last small pail of water which she had saved to scrub the milk cooler.

'Don't come near me or I'll throw this right at you,' she warned through gritted teeth. 'If there's anything we need to discuss about the farm there will be time when we have had our meal. Mother will have it ready and I've no intention of keeping her waiting.' Peregrine Steel hesitated and it seemed he would agree but then Kirsty saw the look in his eyes – anger, determination, but worst of all, lust. He moved towards her, his intentions plain. She threw the water straight into his face, then she dropped the bucket with a clatter and ran. Steel almost fell over the rolling bucket as he wiped the water from his streaming hair and face but he was not so easily thwarted and the insult of such a rejection fuelled his angry determination. Despite his square overweight body he moved with surprising speed and Kirsty had only just reached the far side of the yard when he caught her. An open-fronted cart shed was the nearest building and he pushed her roughly against the stone pillar which supported the roof. Kirsty could not move backwards for the stone nor forwards on account of Steel's heavy panting body. She glared at him and her lips curled in contempt.

'You may think you can say what you like to the men and get away with it but if you touch me just once more, I'll see you regret it!'

'Quite the spiteful little cat, aren't you, Miss . . . sss,' he hissed into her face. 'Then let me tell you! No woman drenches me with a bucket of water and gets away with it!' He pushed his face against her and fastened his lips on her mouth so suddenly and so ruthlessly that Kirsty had not even time to draw breath. His marauding tongue filled Kirsty with revulsion and still she could not twist her head away. She felt her body sagging for want of air and an awful blackness seemed to be descending; but her spirit was not so easily conquered. She summoned her last ounce of strength, lifted her knee sharply and caught Steel in the groin. It was a valiant attempt but it was not enough to do more than make him lift his head to utter a curse. His hold barely slackened except to grasp her wrist and twist it viciously behind her back. It took all her willpower to suppress a cry of pain. When Steel's lips claimed hers again she forced her mind to become a blank, and her limbs sagged.

'That's better, you little hellcat!' Steel muttered against her bruised and bleeding mouth. 'I knew you'd see sense in the end. Arrogance like yours is not a quality I appreciate in my women, but you'll . . .'

'I'm not your woman!' Kirsty hissed through swollen lips, but the words were silenced at once by a sharp nip from Steel's big yellow teeth and another of his brutal kisses. She had forgotten about Paddy until he rounded the corner of the cart shed. She heard his bellow of rage and felt Steel almost lifted away from her.

Paddy was small for a man, barely half an inch taller than her own five and a half feet and he had bowed legs, but he was wiry, and he was furious. His clenched fist connected with Steel's flabby cheek twice before the man had pulled himself together sufficiently to deflect a third blow. When he did he gave such a howl Kirsty almost jumped out of her skin, but at least it brought her to her own senses and made her realise that Paddy might very easily be seriously hurt; instinct told her that Peregrine Steel was not a man who would fight fairly. He was like a sulky spoiled boy but he had strength and weight. Swiftly she scanned the cart shed and her eye fell on a bundle of the thin wooden laths which were used to hold the binder canvasses flat. She tugged one from the strings and ran to the fighting pair.

'Stop it! Stop fighting at once!' Paddy glanced at her and hesitated but Steel seized the opportunity to land a vicious blow at Paddy's right eye. Kirsty wielded the thin stick across his broad shoulders which all the strength she could muster and she did not stop until she knew Paddy was safely on his feet and Steel had agreed to abandon the fight.

'Thanks, Paddy,' she gasped, 'but you'll have a terrible black eye in the morning . . .'

'Ach, it'll not be as bad as his, and it was worth it I'm thinking,' he grinned lopsidedly and nodded towards Peregrine Steel's broad figure already slinking down the short track to the house.

'No doubt he's hoping to get to the bathroom and clean himself up before Mother sees him,' Kirsty muttered darkly.

'Indeed you'll need to be watching that one, Miss Kirsty,' Paddy wagged his head anxiously, all traces of the grin now gone. 'Maybe ol' Paddy Kildougan will not be around the next time he tries his nasty tricks.'

'I shall be wary of him now,' Kirsty agreed, but inside she felt sick and depressed. It was impossible to avoid Steel all the time. 'I shall report his conduct, but it seems impossible to lodge any sort of request or complaint when his father has so much influence.'

'Aye. That yellow-bellied rat is a-hiding behind his father if you ask me. That one should be sent to fight the Germans, instead of them taking young Joe and us needing him so badly. Ach, Miss Kirsty you're a-trembling! It's the shock, eh! Or did that – that scoundrel hurt you?' Paddy looked at her anxiously. 'Will you come to the cottage with me, eh? Lucy will make you a cup of tea now and she . . .'

'N-no th-thanks, Paddy. I'd better get home or Mother will wonder when I am.'

Kirsty managed to wash her hands and face and tidy her hair before she encountered Beth in the kitchen but she could do little to hide her pale face or the bruise which was rapidly discolouring her cheek.

'I've taken Mr Steel's supper into the sitting room on a tray, same as last night,' Beth declared tightly. 'He's better out o' the way. His presence in my kitchen spoils everything. Even the stovies aren't as good as usual tonight . . .' She set down a plate of the hot savoury potatoes which was usually one of Kirsty's favourite meals, even without the wartime rations which had made the dish a substantial part of their weekly diet. 'He's never produced his ration card yet either,' Beth grumbled as she brought her own plate and took her seat at the end of the table. It was only then that she noticed Kirsty's unusual pallor and saw the way she chased the food around her plate instead of eating with her usual relish, but Beth was sensitive and there was something about her daughter's shuttered expression which forbade questions. Beth's brains raced. Steel had rushed up to the bathroom in a great hurry when he came in but she had seen the half-closed eye which would certainly be black and blue by morning. She had assumed he had had a minor accident. Now she wondered and her heartbeats quickened.

They had barely finished their meal when the telephone shrilled. It was just the excuse Kirsty needed.

'I'll answer it. I'm afraid I've lost my appetite for stovies tonight.' Beth watched her rub her arm and flex her shoulder as she moved stiffly into the little room off the kitchen. The telephone had been installed there for Logan's convenience since there was also access via another door opening off the front hallway.

'James!' There was joy and relief in Kirsty's eyes as she recognised James MacFarlane's deep voice, but as she listened the spurt of happiness drained away. Her face grew even paler than before, and she sank on to a nearby chair.

'B-but you canna blame me for that!' she whispered hoarsely.

Thirty-Seven

'James, I tried to appeal! I did not know Joe had received his call up papers – not until the night he left! They said it would be looked into, then they said they were s-sending . . .' her voice sank to a choked whisper, 's-sending other help.'

'I really believed Joe would be secure at Fairlyden, whatever happened. That's why I persuaded him to come to you as soon as I knew there was a possibility of Nithanvale being taken over. I trusted you, Kirsty. Joe's heart is in the land . . .' There was a catch in James's voice and Kirsty realised he was really upset. Yet how could he hold her responsible? Fairlyden needed Joe desperately, but James was blaming her because he had gone. 'Haven't you heard of the Essential Workers' Act, Kirsty? Why, oh why, do you have to be so proud? So damned independent!'

'But I tried to ph—'

'Maybe I could have intervened if I'd known earlier. I was shattered when Mother's letter arrived today. Even that was later than usual. And you've not written at all,' he accused.

'James, will you listen to me? Please?' Tears were running silently down Kirsty's cheeks now. James's condemnation was the last straw. Life was so unjust. She stifled a sob and tried to swallow a knot of tears. 'I t-telephoned Mrs H-Hend . . .'

'Kirsty?' Consternation replaced James's anger.

She sniffed hard but the tears would not be denied; they choked any words she had to utter; they caught at her breath and gathered in an aching lump in her chest. She hung up the receiver.

What was there to say anyway? James had already judged her and found her guilty. She buried her head in her arms on the back of the chair and sobbed. Nothing mattered any more. Everybody believed she had made a mess of things. She hadn't sown enough corn; she hadn't sown it according to Steel's instructions, or put it in the right field; Joe had gone to the army; Paddy had fought and might even have been injured because of her; she had even been careless over the blackout regulations and she could only thank God that the Germans had not been making one of their frequent reconnoitres of the Solway Firth on that particular night. She shuddered; she might have been responsible for killing most of the people in the village.

Maybe she should leave? Move away and find some useful work like the thousands of women who were swelling the ranks in defence of the nation . . . Maybe Fairlyden would be better in the hands of the Steels. The black cloud of depression made Kirsty's tears flow faster than ever. But whatever her befogged brain might consider, her heart belonged at Fairlyden. She found her handkerchief and blew her nose. The tears still squeezed out from under her swollen eyelids and she hiccoughed on a sob, but at least the storm was abating.

The telephone rang. Its shrill bell, so close, startled her. She did not lift the receiver immediately. She stared at it and blew her nose, her throat working frantically, knowing she must control her voice before she could answer coherently.

'Hello, Muircumwell 213,' she said thickly.

'Kirsty? Is that you?'

'Y-yes.'

'Thank God I've got through! I'm phoning from the farm. The operator thought I'd been cut off . . . Kirsty, you werena . . .? Were you crying?' James voice was gentle now, full of concern. It only served to start Kirsty's tears off again. 'I'm sorry. I shouldna blame you for Joe leaving. Mother seemed to think Luke might have been called up if he hadna gone, though I'm sure that canna be the case with a herd the size o' Fairlyden's.'

'It isna Luke's fault. He-he never wanted to come home to farm. He . . .' Someone opened the door from the hall and she turned her head. It was Peregrine Steel. He saw she was speaking on the telephone but he made no effort to leave. He knew this room was private. Still he came forward. There was a bruise on his temple and his eye was almost closed, but he had a mean set to his mouth and Kirsty trembled inwardly. 'This room is private,' she muttered in an undertone. 'Mother has told you that already.'

Steel's thick lips curled. 'I think I can regard this as my study.' He closed the door and sauntered towards the small desk which had belonged to her great grandmother.

'Kirsty? Did I hear a man's voice? It's not Luke, is it?'

'No, it's an unwelcome intruder. Please, can you wait a

moment.' She turned back in time to see Peregrine Steel flipping through some accounts which lay on the desk. Anger boiled in her at his deliberate impudence. 'Those papers are private.'

'I shall decide what is private now.'

'We'll see about that! Right now I am in the middle of a telephone conversation! Have you no manners at all, Mr Steel?' Her voice was icy despite the quivering inside her.

'Telephone calls are my business too,' he drawled, eyeing her tear-stained face and reddened eyelids speculatively.

'This is private!' Kirsty's indignation banished any lingering depression. All her fighting spirit returned. 'Now will you get out of this room?'

'It sounded more like business to me. You were discussing your brother's dislike of farming. Perhaps I should arrange something more useful for him to do for his country.'

'I was discussing my family with the man I'm going to marry!'

'Kirsty! Hey, Kirsty . . .'James's voice came clearly over the crackling wires and Kirsty stared at the instrument in her hand. Had she really spoken those words aloud? Could James have heard? She glanced at Peregrine Steel and saw his good eye had narrowed; he looked startled and far from pleased. He probably thought her cheeks were flushed with anger instead of burning with embarrassment. 'Kirsty, are you still there?' James sounded eager, or was it impatient?'

'I-I'm s-sorry we canna talk just n-now, James.'

'But what?' For the second time that evening Kirsty hung up the telephone on the man whose voice she had longed to hear for days.

She turned back to the room and faced Steel, now standing insolently with his legs apart on the hearth rug in front of the empty fireplace.

'My mother has gone to a lot of trouble and wasted precious coal lighting a fire in the other room for you. Now I suggest you return to your own quarters and if—'

'You suggest! Let me tell you *Miss* Fairly, you are not in a position to suggest anything. And how is it my father has never heard that you are planning to get married?'

Kirsty's eyes widened incredulously. She stared speechlessly at Steel's angry face and petulant mouth. Then her own eyes narrowed.

'Your father has been prying into my private life?' She

327

remembered the emphasis both he and his father had used when addressing her directly, scornfully – *Miss* Fairly they had said as though the word and status had some special meaning. 'If he has . . .'

'Oh come now. My father has tried his best to help you because he believes you are a single girl with too much responsibility. I shall do my best for you too, if you will only cooperate a little.' Kirsty scarcely knew which was more sickening – Steel's ingratiating tone or his unspeakable arrogance. He gave a thick-lipped smile and moved towards her. She remembered the sharp nip she had received from those horrible big yellow teeth.

'Don't dare come near me!' She put up her hand instinctively and glared at him with chilling dislike. His fatuous smile faded. His expression was menacing now.

'And what are you going to do about it?' He allowed his glance to move slowly over her body, then round the room. 'Kildougan will not come to your rescue this time and that milksop of a brother would not be much help to you.'

'You have not seen Luke in a temper!' Neither had she, and these days Luke was more like a wraith living in a world of his own than a man. 'Artistic people like Luke can become quite insane with anger if they think anyone is molesting one of their own family,' she fabricated and wondered how she was dreaming up so many fantasies in a single evening – first a marriage, now a wildly possessive brother. She risked a glance at Peregrine Steel's pasty face and saw him gingerly fingering the bruise around his eye. She guessed he was a coward as well as a bully. 'What is more, Mr Steel, I intend to see my father's solicitor,' she bluffed.

'Solicitor?'

Kirsty frowned. Was that alarm, or even fear, she had glimpsed in the one eye which remained open? 'That's what I said. Your boorish behaviour is intolerable and I can not believe your father has the authority to send you here, to live in our home, to pry into our private affairs – even though the country is at war.' She had been watching his face closely and she was almost convinced his face had gone a shade paler. Was it possible that she had stumbled on some particle of truth? Oh, she thought, if only we could get him out of the house, away from the daily running of the farm.

'Then you can tell your solicitor I intend to have Kildougan charged with assault,' he announced sullenly, but he strode out of the little room, slamming the door behind him. Kirsty gasped. Had she only succeeded in putting the idea of solicitors into his head? Had she stored up more trouble for Paddy? Oh, James, if only you had telephoned days ago, she thought, I need you so badly. Then she remembered her words: 'the man I'm going to marry.' Her face flamed anew as she wondered if James could possibly have heard them over the telephone.

The following day was full of tensions. Peregrine Steel strutted around in his tweed suit and leather boots as though he was a country gentleman, though his image was somewhat marred by his half-closed, multi-coloured eye. Thomas sniggered openly when he saw it and Paddy caught Kirsty's eye and gave a broad wink, despite the fact that his own weatherbeaten face was not unblemished either. Steel found fault with everything and some of his criticisms and alternative ideas were so ludicrous when applied to farmlife that even Luke gazed at him askance.

'I know now how Mr Steel received his bruises,' Beth announced the first time she managed to speak to Kirsty alone after the midday meal. 'Lucy told me this morning.' She looked at her daughter anxiously. 'I-I hope he willna—'

'Please dinna worry, Mother,' Kirsty said with more confidence than she felt. 'As a matter of fact I tried to telephone Mr Carsewell this morning but I canna get an appointment until tomorrow afternoon.'

'The solicitor?' Beth's eyes widened with alarm. 'Steel didna . . .?'

'He didn't harm me at all, thanks to Paddy. But I've been wondering whether any man in Steel's position can have so much authority all on his own, even though the country is at war. I don't know who else to ask to look into things except Uncle Alex and we canna trouble him just now.'

'No-o, I thought that myself.' Beth brightened. 'Well, I'm glad ye've thought o' some other solution, lassie, because I'm convinced ye ken more about farming than that young man will ever ken. D'ye believe, he's instructed Paddy to cut out all the meal frae all the stock, even the young calves?'

'He canna do that! They would starve.'

'Paddy told him he was crazy. I think they might have come to blows again if I hadna been there. Mr Steel was telephoning somebody too. He must have come in while I was cleaning the bedrooms. I heard him speaking when I came down to make the dinner. He must have thought I was outside because he looked quite guilty.'

'Maybe he was telephoning his solicitor?'

'No.' Beth frowned. 'It must have been somebody he kens weel. I thought perhaps his father . . .?' Though he seemed angry and he was talking about somebody getting married.'

'Oh.' Kirsty blushed. 'Maybe you didna hear correctly,' she mumbled. Beth watched her thoughtfully as she left the kitchen.

Long before the evening milking Kirsty was strained almost to breaking point by Steel's petty niggles and she was half afraid he might deliberately provoke Paddy into losing his temper so that he could have him charged. As she was assembling the milking units Beth came into the dairy.

'Lizzie Whiteley has just telephoned to say the Friday bus has dropped off a big can o' paint for us frae the store in Annan. It'll be the stuff to black out the byre windows I suppose.'

'Yes. I'll collect it tomorrow when I collect this week's rations.' A shadow darkened the doorway and she looked up to see Peregrine Steel.

'You must collect the paint now.'

Kirsty frowned. 'It willna make any difference. No one will be painting the windows tonight.'

'I said fetch it now.'

Kirsty took a deep breath. Beth watched anxiously. 'Mr Steel, it is time to start milking now. The cows are already coming into the byre and they do not like their routine upset. Moreover we do not waste petrol on two journeys when one would do. Lizzie will have our groceries ready for Saturday.'

'Someone else might take the paint. You must collect it now.'

'Och, no one else would dream o' such a thing!' Beth intervened, 'Not in Muircumwell anyway. Besides Lizzie Whiteley wouldna give it to anyone else.'

'That is not the point, Mrs Fairly. I am ordering your daughter to collect it now and you will kindly mind your own business!' Steel's mouth set stubbornly. Kirsty turned to him, her eyes blazing.

'And I am refusing to go now because there are sixty cows in that byre and Paddy is already tying them in their stalls and I am going to help him.'

'You are refusing to carry out my orders?' Steel's eyes popped incredulously.

'I am refusing to bow to your tyranny.'

'Then your brother must go! Now!'

'Luke doesna drive. Anyway he is needed to help Mother carry the milk to the dairy.'

'Mistress Whiteley can do that.'

'Anna has plenty to do with hens and chickens and Lucy is feeding the calves and the pigs and looking after young Irene into the bargain. Thomas is helping the man frae the War Ag to finish the turnips. He has promised to stay until it's dark if need be to finish drilling today. *You* are the only one with nothing to do.' Kirsty turned and marched to the byre, her clogs clacking furiously. Beth glanced at Steel's furious face and followed her.

Kirsty had not slept well the night before and such altercations increased her tension so that by the end of the milking she felt utterly drained and exhausted. She and Paddy were usually the last to leave by the time the cows were returned to the field, the byres cleaned for morning and the dairy utensils washed and set up for an early start.

'I will walk down to the house with you, Miss Kirsty, if you would not be minding my company?' Paddy suggested tentatively as he followed her from the dairy.

'What? O-oh, I'm sure Mr Steel willna risk an encounter with your Irish wrath again, Paddy.' She tried to make light of the previous evening's trouble.

'Maybe he will not but . . .' His gaze suddenly became alert, 'But then again, he might, or why is he hanging around under the tree down there, instead of getting himself into the house for his supper?'

'Oh no!' Kirsty groaned, following his glance. 'I canna face any more disputes tonight!' Paddy fell into step beside her.

'To be sure it would be a pleasure to make his other eye match the beauty I gave to himself last night, if you'll just be saying the word . . .'

'I'm sorely tempted to. No! Look, Paddy! That's not Steel! It's – it's James . . .' she breathed. Paddy glanced up and saw the light in her eyes and cocked an eyebrow quizzically, but Kirsty was not even looking at him as her steps quickened involuntarily.

'Ach well, Miss Kirsty, you and James have had many a quarrel, the pair of you, but I think you will not be a-needing ol' Paddy tonight. Indeed and I would not like to be fighting young James – not even for your bonny self.'

'Och, Paddy!' Kirsty chuckled a little breathlessly. 'I'll see you in the morning.'

'To be sure and you will. I wonder if I should be putting my head round Anna's door to tell her to lay an extra place at the table and to be putting another tattie in the pot, eh?'

'I'm sure Mother will make our meal stretch for James. Good night, Paddy, and thank you . . .'

''Tis a pleasure.' He winked and his leathery face split into a wicked, knowing grin which brought a delightful blush to Kirsty's cheeks and made him laugh aloud. He performed a step or two of an Irish jig as he made for his cottage; then he thought of young Lenny McGuire and his kindly Irish heart ached for the young laddie whose life had ended almost before it had begun.

Thirty-Eight

'I didna expect to see you here, James,' Kirsty felt suddenly breathless and unable to meet his eyes. She wondered for the umpteenth time whether he could have overheard the lie she had told to Peregrine Steel, and felt hot with embarrassment again; yet she was pleased, oh so pleased, to see him.

'It is a very short visit, but I had to come, Kirsty. You mentioned an unwelcome intruder. You sounded upset . . . more than upset, on the telephone. You did not even finish our conversation. Surely Steel is not staying at Fairlyden?' He took her hands in both of his and Kirsty felt their warmth and strength. She heard the genuine concern in his voice too.

'Oh, James . . .' Her voice was unsteady. 'Mr Steel has put his son in charge of everything! He is even living with us at Fairlyden! He-he's a horrible man.' She shuddered.

'Horrible?'

'Yes. He criticises everything and offends everybody, especially Paddy. I thought of asking Mr Carsewell to check on the Steels, but I don't really believe a lawyer will interfere with government officials. What am I going to do, James? They want to take Fairlyden away from me, I know they do!'

James did not answer for a moment. He was still clasping her hands and his thumbs moved over the backs of them, soothing, almost hypnotic; she looked up into his face. She saw that slow, almost lazy smile which had been so familiar when she was a young teenager. She watched in fascination as it spread over his lean strong face until it reached his eyes – and there was warmth and tenderness in their greeny-grey depths. Her heart jolted.

'You're not angry now? I wouldna have let Joe leave if I could have prevented him, you know.'

'I'm sorry I blamed you, Kirsty. I'd just opened Mother's letter when I returned to my cottage. I rushed back up to the Henderson's house to telephone straightaway. I owe you another apology too. I didn't know you had tried to telephone me. Elsie only remembered when she realised something was wrong and I was trying to telephone you a second time. The night you left a message with her she was desperately worried about Billy, her husband. The first operation had been a failure and that day they had operated again. She was terrified every time the telephone rang.'

'But he's all right?'

'Well, he pulled through. Now they think the second operation has been a greater success than they had dared to hope but he will have a long convalescence. He's to go home next week, and at least he will be able to give some instructions and advise generally, even though he has not to work for a year. I confess I'm almost as relieved as Elsie. It was her idea that I should visit you – a sort of compensation because she feels so guilty. She's made all sorts o' complicated arrangements so that her cousin could take over the milking and keep an eye on things until I get back there tomorrow night.'

'Oh.' Kirsty's face fell. 'So soon?' She did not know what she had been expecting, but she knew James would never go back on his promise to the Hendersons.

'Kirsty, we have to talk . . .'

'Y-yes. You must be starving though. You'll share our meal?'

'You said Steel's son was staying with you?'

'Yes, but Mother gives him his meals on a small table in the sitting room so that we dinna see any more of him that we can help.' She grimaced. 'Truly, he is awful, James.'

'I believe you.' He grinned and squeezed her hands and she realised he had never released them. 'I'd rather not meet him yet. Don't tell him I'm here or mention my name. I telephoned a man named Morley in the Department of Agriculture; he was extremely helpful to me when the government was taking over Nithanvale. I asked him if he could tell me anything about Steel. Mr Morley says he is on a lot of committees and he has cultivated several influential men in the county. He likes to organise. He made his money from warehouses he owned in Liverpool but he got out just before the war. He bought a big house and some land up here and moved in with his wife and three sons and a daughter. Morley thinks it may have been a ploy to keep his sons out of the services if war was declared. Mr Morley is going to get in touch if he can give me any more information, especially if Steel is overstepping his authority. So you see why it's better if young Steel believes I'm just another peasant visiting my poor widowed mother in her cottage.'

'Oh, James . . .' Kirsty sighed. 'You've always had such an inferiority complex about your background, and without any justification.'

'Maybe I had once,' he agreed ruefully, 'but not any more. I've always been proud to be a MacFarlane, just as you are proud to be a Fairly of Fairlyden, but I've got life into perspective now, I think. Nothing stays the same for ever – good or bad.'

'Well, I shall certainly not stay as a Fairly of Fairlyden much longer if the Steels have their way,' Kirsty commented darkly.

'Mmm, we'll have to see about that. Can you meet me up at the little wood beside the burn, as soon as you've had your meal? We have a lot to discuss if we're to keep these Steels in their place. We should not be interrupted there.'

'All right,' Kirsty smiled up at him. 'And James, thank you for coming all this way,' she said softly.

He squeezed her hands again and released her. 'You might not thank me when you hear some of the ideas that have been buzzing around in my head all day! We shall probably have an almighty quarrel again. You might decide I'm worse than young Steel—'

'Never! Few men could be worse. I'll see you in three quarters of an hour then.'

The early summer evening was calm and peaceful as Kirsty made her way towards the farm steading. She had changed into a pale blue sweater and her pleated skirt swirled around her knees and emphasised her long shapely legs. The shadows were lengthening, making purple silhouettes over the distant hills as she crossed the farmyard, heading for the small field and the burn. Here and there birds still darted to their nests with fragments of straw or dried grass; a pair of swallows perched on the new electric wires, swaying gently in the breeze. She smiled at the sight of them. Her father had not relished the idea of wires and poles marring the well-loved views at Fairlyden, but the birds seemed to welcome them.

It was hard to believe that men and women in other parts of the world were fighting for their freedom, and suffering and dying in hundreds, even thousands. Most evenings, as she lay in bed she heard the drone of aeroplanes in the night sky and cuddled further into the comfort of her warm blankets, wondering whether they were friend or foe. Thoughts of Lenny and his family always saddened her whenever she heard the ominous sounds of the distant aeroplanes. However bad her own day had been she always thanked God for her blessings. She did so now, silently but with sincerity, and the balmy evening air soothed her troubled spirit. Soon she would be able to share her problems with James and she realised with humility that she longed for his advice and support.

She rounded a bend where the burn had carved a wide loop over the years; she saw James was already at the little wood, sitting on a fallen log, waiting patiently for her. She slowed her steps; she had the strangest feeling that she was moving towards her own destiny.

James rose and came towards her. 'Hello, tortoise,' he teased, giving her that slow warm smile which seemed to turn her heart upside down. 'Anyone would think you were putting off an evil encounter the way your steps are dragging.'

'You make it sound as though I've come to meet the devil himself,' she quipped, but she could not quite hide the strain of the past months and it showed in her wide blue-grey eyes and in the faint droop at the corners of her mouth.

'We'll sort something out, Kirsty, never fear.' James's voice was gentle, understanding. He sighed softly. 'I'd forgotten how peaceful Fairlyden always is; how beautiful. You know I could sit for hours – just gazing at the green fields and the hedges, the long line of the hills on the horizon.'

'I know . . . Oh James, I'd hate to leave it all.' There was a catch in Kirsty's voice and she had to blink hard to control a sudden rush of tears. James looked at her keenly. Kirsty had never been one to cry easily – even as a little girl she had been far tougher than Luke. He watched her swallow hard.

'Is – isn't the countryside lovely where you live now then?'

'Yes, it is . . . but it's different. Maybe you'll see it for yourself one day. The fields are much bigger . . . rich red soil; it's flatter with not so many hedges. In fact some of the Hendersons' neighbours are pulling out hedges to make the fields even bigger.'

'Pulling out hedges? But why? I mean don't the hedges keep their cattle from straying and provide shelter?'

'Big fields are easier to cultivate and a lot of the farms are selling their cattle now. There are very few dairy herds in that area. As a matter of fact Billy Henderson is thinking of selling his herd too if I insist on leaving when he has recovered. It's almost impossible to get herdsmen up there just now. He has had plenty o' time to think while he has been in hospital. It would be easier for him without the cows to milk seven days a week and it's what the government wants . . .'

'You mean . . .' Kirsty turned to stare at him aghast. 'You mean you agree with the likes o' Steel?'

'I didna say that. Come and sit down on this log and I'll explain.' He took her hand and led her to the log where he had been sitting earlier but he did not release her fingers even when they were seated. 'First I want you to promise to listen to all – and I mean all – I have to say before you blow up at me in a rage.' He half smiled, but his eyes were grave, his gaze steady and Kirsty knew he meant exactly what he said. She nodded.

'Where the Hendersons live, in the Lothians, they could grow almost anything. They have already tried some sugar beet. It has done exceptionally well and the government are desperate for more. So it makes sense to grow that instead of turnips; they can use the pulp to feed the cattle after the sugar has been taken out. They have a better climate for wheat than we have and better soil. They already grow fine crops of potatoes. So you see it makes sense for them to stop growing grass for cows and concentrate on what the country needs.'

'But the country needs milk too! The government have had to give priority to babies and nursing mothers because there's such a shortage of milk. Imagine being rationed to two pints a week when milk is one of the most nutritious foods there is.'

'I know, I know,' James sighed patiently. 'And I do agree, Kirsty. But I dinna think our friend Steel realises there canna be one rigid rule applied to the whole country. It's either that, or he's intent on causing trouble at Fairlyden. That's what I need to find out. He is right in one way though: every farm has to produce some cereals if it's at all possible. We imported so much to feed our animals as well as people, before the war started. No wonder the numbers of pigs and poultry in the country have halved. Elsie Henderson was using dried eggs! I could never have imagined such a thing possible.'

'I know, your Aunt Lizzie depends on them to keep her customers half satisfied. But James we've grown extra cereals at Fairlyden. When I went to the smiddy, old Mr Kerr said we had ploughed more acres than most o' the farms round Muircumwell, even the larger rented ones. The Mains is an exception of course. Uncle Alex was on the committees and he tries to set an example of what is needed, and he has a tractor to do his ploughing.'

'Yes . . . I can't help wondering whether Steel has the impression that his area must have a higher percentage of extra acres of corn than any other in this region to make it appear that he's doing a successful job, or whether he is using the present guidelines to his own advantage and keeping his son in safe employment. He must realise you have made an effort to comply with the regulations; he knows you have no tractor for ploughing or harvesting. I wonder whether he knew anything about Joe Little being called up or whether he even had a hand in it? Removing a good ploughman from his employer is against present government policy unless there's been a serious complaint from one or the other.'

'But it wouldna make sense for Steel to have Joe taken into the forces, and then expect us to get even more land ploughed.'

'It would if Steel pulled a few strings which made it possible for him to justify putting someone in charge at Fairlyden – someone like his own son.'

'Yes. I almost accused Peregrine Steel of that last night when I got so angry. He didna deny it, but I still feel so helpless to fight back when his father seems to have so much authority. I'm sure there must be some one who has power to question his decision.'

'I'm sure there is – and I intend to find out who. In the meantime I think we have to prove young Steel's presence at Fairlyden is unnecessary, and soon. Once decisions are taken by people in authority it can be a long time before they are reversed, even though they were unjust in the first place. Sometimes it's impossible to reverse them – as with Joe Little,' he added bitterly. 'I pray he'll come back safely.'

'So do I,' Kirsty agreed fervently. 'I think Luke feels guilty because he believes Joe has taken his place out there. You know how sensitive he is; he'll blame himself if Joe doesna come back.'

'Mmm, well we must think positively and make sure there is still a Fairlyden and a job for Joe when he does return. That is what I wanted to discuss with you, Kirsty. Whether we agree with them or not, everyone has to go along with the regulations to some extent and if Steel does want an increase in cereal acreage we'll give it to him. We'll play the game his way, but not at the expense of the milk.'

'We? And how can we do things his way any more than we've done already?'

'I've given it a lot of thought so dinna interrupt.' James squeezed her hand and gave a wry smile to take the sting out of his words. Kirsty nodded meekly. 'Fairlyden must have a tractor for a start, and a plough to go with it. Most of the other machinery can be converted from shafts to a single pole when it is necessary. Aah-ah . . .' He grinned and laid a finger gently over her lips. Lingeringly he traced their shape before he withdrew, sending a tingle through Kirsty so that she barely heard the next sentence and had to gather her wandering thoughts. 'I know you havena got money for a tractor, but I have . . .' Again he laid a finger over her lips. 'Silence,' he growled. 'I'm coming to the bit when that temper of yours will flare. The one thing I don't have at the present time is my freedom to return to Fairlyden to give you the physical help you need – unless I break my word to Billy Henderson, and you know I canna do that.'

'I understand that, but—'

'I expect to be free before harvest time comes round. I think you could manage until then – with help from the village folk for the turnip hoeing and the hay?'

Kirsty nodded.

'So, Kirsty, as soon as Billy Henderson is well enough to look after his own affairs again, I'm willing to return to Fairlyden, but are you willing to share Fairlyden with me? Your land, my money for machinery, our joint labour; in other words – can we be partners? He held her gaze then, his eyes steady yet inscrutable.

Kirsty's heart had soared when he mentioned his return to Fairlyden; now it seemed to plummet like a rock and disappointment washed over her. James had always dreamed of owning a farm like Fairlyden, even when he was a little boy. Now he was offering her a business deal.

'Well, Kirsty?'

'Your mother told us you had a good job when you were working for the Department. We still have a bank overdraft for the purchase of the Muircumwell land so Fairlyden couldna afford to pay you more than three pounds a week, and you would be using your savings to buy a tractor.

'The Nithanvale herd sold well, remember. Then there were the horses and pigs, as well as the implements. Even they made more than I expected on account o' the sudden scarcity due to the war increasing demand.'

'Yes, but surely your half-cousin owned some of the stock?'

'I have put money in trust for Mary. She has agreed to leave it there until she is absolutely certain about her commitment to the church. So you needna worry about that.'

Kirsty nodded, but she chewed anxiously at her lip.

'What else is worrying you,' James asked. We have to be frank with each other.'

'I remember my father saying you had a loan from the bank when you had to buy Nithanvale. Surely three pounds a week . . .'

'I had repaid some of the loan before the war began. I repaid Aunt Lizzie and the rest of the loan when the government took over Nithanvale . . .' Despite his own advice to be frank he did not add that he had received a far bigger sum for the compulsory purchase of his land than he had ever anticipated. Even so, at the time it had seemed a poor exchange for having to dispose of his cherished herd and relinquishing all his plans for the future. He had made sure his mother was provided for but he still had money in the bank, and he had invested more in war bonds than he had ever hoped to possess. Once lack of money had been the greatest obstacle between himself and Kirsty – at least in his own mind. Now he feared that having enough to buy Fairlyden lock, stock and barrel might prove an even greater obstacle – this time from Kirsty's point of view. Steel's constant harassment had severely dented her confidence but he knew her pride was just as great as his own.

'B-but are you sure you're being wise? You may regret coming back to Fairlyden?' Kirsty said slowly. How much worse it would be if James went away a second time, she thought with a shiver.

'Wise?' He laughed almost harshly. 'No, probably not. Maybe I'm a fool to dream after all that has happened. Let me tell you exactly what I expect from an alliance with you, Miss Kirsty Fairly . . .' Her hand trembled and his clasp on her fingers tightened almost painfully. 'I know you felt I deserted Fairlyden once, but I've always loved this place.' He raised his eyes and his mouth softened as he gazed down the glen at the patchwork of fields, the neat hedges, the roof tops of the buildings and cottages, all spread out before them in the fading light. 'I would not make this proposition if I believed either of us would regret it. I'm not trying to take Fairlyden away from you, Kirsty, as I suspect Steel may try to do. But I can never return as an ordinary worker like Uncle Thomas. I have my pride too, remember.'

'I know that, James MacFarlane.'

'Can you blame me?'

'No, I suppose not, especially when you proved yourself so successful at Nithanvale.'

'I want us to be partners. Equals. Sharing everything – problems and triumphs, joys and sorrows . . . When this war is over, when things return to normal, I'm sure we can do great things together.'

'So long as the Germans dinna take us over first . . .' Kirsty whispered, voicing one of the secret fears that haunted her sleepless nights.

'Britain will win! We must not doubt it. If we lose hope we lose everything.'

'I know,' she nodded meekly once more.

'So you see I'm not just talking about tomorrow or next year. I'm talking about sharing the future – our whole lives.'

'Our lives . . .' Kirsty breathed. 'But what if . . .?'

'If we quarrel?' He gave a wry smile. 'Then we make up again as we have always done. After all we do have one bond in common,' he added rather dryly. 'The future of Fairlyden. We are the next generation, Kirsty. The future depends on us.' He looked away from her then and stared into the middle distance. 'Marriage,' he said softly. 'It is the most legal, the most binding agreement for life partnership I can think of. There would be no going back for either of us if we were married.'

'Married. . .' Kirsty echoed. She stared at him but she could not tell what he was thinking from his profile. 'J-James, are you serious? Or d-did you overhear wh-what I said to Peregrine Steel?' She sat up suddenly. 'Are — are you mocking me?'

'I did hear,' he admitted frankly, 'but I'm certainly not mocking.'

He is so controlled, Kirsty thought in frustration. He might have been making a deal to buy a cow. She felt a kind of panic rising in her. 'I-I only thought Steel wouldna be so – so arrogant if he thought . . . if . . .'

'If he thought there was a man in your life who would probably give him two black eyes instead of the one Paddy gave him?' James's jaw clenched grimly.

'You heard about that?'

'It was the first thing Mother told me. You were right, Kirsty, having a husband would make Steel think twice before making unwelcome advances. I presume they were unwelcome?'

'Of course they were! I told you! He's a horrible creature,' she declared hotly and James laughed, easing the tension between them.

'That's better! I wondered what had happened to the spirited Miss Fairly I've always known. Anyway, there could be other advantages to taking me as your husband. Once the authorities know you are married and that I shall be joining you at Fairlyden, I think we shall be able to get rid of young Steel, especially if we make a few compromises, like buying a tractor and agreeing to plough some of the Westhill ground next year – or at least attempting it. Yes, my dear, I think we may get rid of your unwelcome intruder very quickly indeed.'

'That would be wonderful!'

'Even if that means being tied to me for the rest of your life?' James quirked one dark eyebrow, but his eyes were watchful and they looked more green than grey in the evening light.

'You make it sound as though I shall be your prisoner,' Kirsty responded flippantly rather than tell him the truth: that she wanted to be his wife – a real wife – more than anything in the world. But he was marrying her for all the wrong reasons: he had always envied her because she belonged to Fairlyden; he had made no mention of love. Was that because Mary MacFarlane was the girl he had really loved? But she was married to the church now, and Nithanvale was lost to him too. Perhaps Fairlyden and herself were both second best? She tossed her head with a small defiant gesture which reminded James of the old spirited Kirsty of their youth, the girl who would have died rather than let him see the merest glint of tears in her lovely eyes.

'Anything would be better than letting the Steels have Fairlyden,' she said, striving to keep her voice light, although her next sentence reflected anxiety. 'Do you think Mr Steel would still be able to dictate to us?'

'He might try, but he'll probably look for some other farmer to bully, especially if he considers the farm would make a safe haven for his dear boy.'

'It doesna suit you to be cynical, James MacFarlane.'

'No, and it doesna suit you to be the meek little lady, either. You have not given me a proper answer yet. Is it a pact?' His voice softened. 'Perhaps you need time to think about it?' He had never known Kirsty to be so vulnerable before; perhaps he was taking advantage. 'I could return for a couple of days in about three weeks I think, if Elsie's cousin will take my place again.'

It all sounded so official, Kirsty thought, a real business deal, but in her heart she knew she would rather have James on his terms than risk losing him again. She needed him; everyone at Fairlyden needed him.

'I've known you all my life, James MacFarlane, so I dinna need time to think about it! The answer is y-yes.' For a moment James showed no reaction, then he let out a long breath as though he had been holding it deliberately. When she dared to look at him his eyes seemed to have a different glow but whether from joy, or triumph, or just the changing light of evening, she was uncertain. He took her other hand and his eyes searched her face as he leaned closer. She thought he was going to kiss her again; she wanted him to kiss her, to hold her close and kindle the flame of passion between them, but James held back and in the end his lips did no more than brush her bruised temple.

'You will not regret it, I promise,' he murmured gruffly.

Thirty-Nine

Kirsty was astonished that neither her own mother nor Anna MacFarlane seemed at all surprised that she and James were to marry. Beth's pleasure and even relief were evident. Her only qualms were how she could prepare for a wedding, however small, in only three weeks, for James had suggested they should be married without delay, preferably on his next visit.

'I know I shall not be free for some weeks to take up my responsibilities as a husband, or to do my share of the work,' he apologised to Beth. 'But it is essential to get young Steel away from Fairlyden as soon as possible, for Kirsty's safety and her peace of mind.'

'For everyone's peace of mind,' Beth agreed wholeheartedly.

'I must keep my agreement and return to the Hendersons unfortunately. I almost wish I had never promised . . .'

'We all understand, James,' Beth assured him, smiling. 'And I ken it is not in your nature to break your word, especially to a sick man – and I'm glad. If ye care so much for others, I ken ye'll care twice as much for your own wife.'

'Indeed I do already,' James agreed and his look brought the colour rushing to Kirsty's cheeks. 'But we must not allow young Steel to become entrenched here or he may be immovable for the duration of the war – and who can tell how long that might be! It is vital that we notify the authorities; aye, and prove to them that changes are already taking place.'

Kirsty was bemused by the plans everyone seemed to be making on her behalf, but she was too busy organising all the tasks to keep the Fairlyden cattle in good health to have time to consider. At first Peregrine Steel had refused to believe she was to be married so soon. Although he had made no move to molest her again Kirsty found him as domineering and aggravating as before, and the annoying thing was that he made absolutely no attempt to help with any of the tasks he insisted were essential. He had a long and apparently heated discussion with his father on the telephone, followed by a short, sharp exchange the following day. Early the next morning

Mr Steel arrived in person. Beth and Kirsty were surprised when Peregrine appeared in the front hall with his luggage already packed and, with no more than a muttered goodbye, departed from their lives as swiftly as he had come.

Mr Steel was less pleasant. His gimlet eyes surveyed Kirsty suspiciously and he looked down his beaked nose.

'I have read the proposals submitted to the authorities by MacFarlane. They appear to have made an impression on those officials with less practical knowledge of this country's situation than myself.' Kirsty gasped incredulously. Practical experience of farming was the one thing neither he nor his son seemed to possess in the slightest degree. 'Make no mistake, Miss Fairly,' he continued grimly. 'I shall return to Fairlyden within the month. Unless there is evidence of the proposed changes taking place I shall take steps to have you and yours removed from here. The farm will be taken over on behalf of His Majesty's government for the duration of the war, and probably longer.'

Kirsty was worried by his threats; the more so because she sensed malice behind them rather than a feeling that Steel was genuinely working for the good of the nation.

Arrangements for the wedding ceremony had been made with the Reverend Morrison, but James himself had admitted that little would alter until he was free to take up his life at Fairlyden, which would not be for some months yet. That evening she wrote to tell him of Steel's threats. He replied by return. Although he made little reference to their personal relationship she felt warmed and reassured.

'James has already ordered a new tractor,' she informed her mother and Luke during the midday meal. 'He hopes it will be delivered within a fortnight and he seems to think I shall learn to drive it without much difficulty since I can drive the car. He does admit that learning to plough may prove rather more awkward though, but he should be here himself by the time that is needed. He intends to convert the mowing machine so that I can cut the hay with the tractor. Just think how much easier that will be!' Her eyes were shining. 'I really wondered how we should ever manage it without Joe.'

'I hope it willna be dangerous,' Beth frowned.

'I'm sure it won't,' Kirsty assured her jubilantly, 'and even Mr Steel canna say things are not changing then.'

'That's true,' Beth conceded. 'Now, Kirsty, as soon as we've washed the dishes I'd like ye to try on your dress. I think the cream brocade material is going to look splendid, especially as ye're so slim. It was a marvellous suggestion o' Miss Harrison's to look at the curtain materials. Due to everybody having to buy blackout curtains nobody wanted the light brocades.

'It seems such a lot of extra work for you, Mother,' Kirsty murmured. She felt a little guilty that her mother and everyone else seemed to be so excited and taking so much trouble to make her wedding day special, despite the wartime restrictions. Did they realise that nothing would really change? The ceremony would be little more than a formality; afterwards they would all have the milking to do; the following day James would be away again. Life would just go on as it had before.

'Ye're sure ye want to be married so soon, lassie?' Beth asked anxiously as she slipped the half-made dress over Kirsty's head a little later.

'Yes, of course. It's just that James will not be staying and . . . well, his mother and Aunt Lizzie are going to such a lot of bother too. They're so excited.' Beth proceeded to pin and tuck, kneeling to check the hem, her mouth full of steel pins.

'Mmm, 's a pity James must return, 's like the soldiers, coming home for forty-eight hours . . . getting married, going 'way again . . . There!' She removed the pins from her mouth. 'I think that will be fine once I've stitched the seams and pressed them flat.' She stood back and beamed with pleasure and Kirsty had no heart to tell her that she and James were only entering into a business partnership and not a real marriage. 'I am pleased Alex agreed to give ye away . . .'

'Yes.' Kirsty pulled her thoughts away from James. 'I know he and Aunt Emma are still grieving for Cameron but they never spoil things for other people.'

'Your Aunt Emma's a fine woman. She promised to bring a big tin o' salmon that Billy sent frae America so that I could make a salmon mousse. I am glad I didna use all the dried fruit he sent in his parcel at Easter or I'd never have had enough, even for a small wedding cake. Lizzie Whiteley's been very good at saving me a bit of extra sugar. She says some o' the women dinna want the extra rations for preserving so she set a bit aside for us. The icing sugar is terribly lumpy though. We shall have to hammer it with the rolling pin before I can make the icing,' Beth chattered on, apparently unaware of Kirsty's silence.

'Aunt Ellen sent a lovely set of embroidered pillow cases and sheets for a wedding present,' Kirsty made an effort to respond. 'I'm sorry she canna come to the wedding.'

'Mmm. So am I. There, ye can get dressed again, lassie. I shall have the dress finished in good time.' She looked round Kirsty's bedroom critically. 'At least ye have a double bed and plenty o' room in here. We could move in the walnut wardrobe and the tallboy . . .'

'Mother!'

'Aye? What is—?' She saw her daughter's flushed face. 'Och, Kirsty, lassie. There's no need to be . . .' Beth did not finish. Instead she turned and hugged Kirsty. 'Ye're a good lassie. I'm sure – as sure as a mother can be – that Jamie will be good to ye. I've always liked him, ever since he was a wee fellow.'

'I-I know that. It -it's just that we . . . we have not discussed things like . . . like living arrangements.'

'No, well ye've scarcely had time, I suppose. But it's only right ye should both live here after ye're married. We'll leave things as they are though, for now. You and Jamie can decide yourselves what ye want in the way o' furniture. There's some nice pieces in your grandmother's old room . . .'

Later, alone in her room, Kirsty looked round in a dazed state. She had thought no further than the wedding ceremony and then the time, still months ahead, when James would come back. She had not even considered where he would stay . . . until now . . . She put her hands to burning cheeks. Had he considered such aspects of married life?

When she wrote to James Kirsty still avoided the question of their accommodation once they were man and wife, but it filled her thoughts throughout the letter. When she received his last letter before their wedding day it seemed to Kirsty that James had sensed her confusion.

'I have managed to book two nights in a small hotel in Galloway, right on the edge of the Solway Firth. I thought it would give us a breathing space away from all our friends and family. However tactful and wellmeaning they may be, we need a little time to ourselves before our lives resume their separate ways again.' Kirsty stared at the letter, and amidst her relief at James's thoughtfulness there was the strangest feeling of disappointment, as she had experienced the night he went away. He had taken her in his arms and she had thought he was going to kiss her with all the eagerness of a lover; instead he had kissed her as gently and tenderly as a loving father or brother might have done. She read the rest of the letter, her eyes widening. He had even made plans for Lucy to help with the milking while she was away.

So that's why Lucy keeps appearing in the byre asking so many questions, she thought, Lucy who had vowed she would never attempt to use 'those things like giant shiny spiders.'

'I shall travel down by the early train in time for the wedding,' he had written, and even reading the words made Kirsty tremble with nerves. There were a few more lines, all equally light and pleasant, but not a single word of love such as a man might write to his bride almost on the eve of their wedding. Kirsty chided herself for her conflicting emotions. She barely knew what she wanted, or expected. She supposed she ought to feel pleased that James was being so considerate and not making too many personal demands on her.

The day of the wedding dawned bright and clear and in spite of her nerves and doubts Kirsty's heart rose when she looked out of her bedroom window before going to the morning milking. The hollows were filled with a fluffy white mist like a gently billowing sea with miniature trees and hills rising out of it like a fairytale land. It's going to be a lovely day, she thought, drawing in a deep breath of the clear, fresh air.

Kirsty did not see James until she walked down the aisle on her uncle's arm. He looked tall and broad in his best dark suit and the muscles in her stomach tightened. His smile was one of tender affection as she approached, but when she reached his side and looked up at him, his eyes darkened. For a moment they seemed to drink in the sight of her in her cream brocade dress and the filmy veil which had belonged to his own mother.

'Kirsty . . .' he breathed softly, 'you are truly beautiful.'

Despite the wartime shortages Beth had provided an excellent meal and the small gathering of Whiteleys and Fairlys was a happy one. An invitation had been sent to Mary, James's only remaining MacFarlane relative. She had sent her blessing to the happy couple but had begged to be excused on account of her religious duties. She had also sent a wedding gift. It was a fine lawn tablecloth with twelve matching serviettes, all exquisitely embroidered with white fleur-de-lis and drawn threadwork.

'I remember Mary stitching that in the evenings when she sat with her grandfather,' James smiled. 'She says she left a space and now she has added our joint initials in one corner.'

The meal was almost over when Luke got to his feet and

cleared his throat nervously. He was always shy in public but he proposed a simple and sincere toast to the bride and groom. Kirsty blushed and James looked pleased and proud. Then Luke further startled everyone – everyone except his mother – when he continued.

'You all know that I have not made much of a contribution to Fairlyden's survival. Indeed I have realised for a long time now that I am achieving nothing here except my own survival. That does not make me feel proud of myself, nor can I claim with justification that I am proud to be British because I have done nothing for my country either. In a few months James will be returning to Fairlyden permanently. He will bring with him knowledge and support, as well as practical help, which I could never give, and which I know Kirsty has missed so badly since . . .' Luke's voice shook and he glanced briefly at Beth, then went on more firmly, 'since Father died . . . I think, and I hope, I do have something to contribute to the world out there, but it has taken me a long time to find enough courage. I thank God that I have found it now. I have been accepted by the army and I shall be leaving Fairlyden the day after Kirsty and James return.'

There was a stunned silence, then all eyes seemed to turn questioningly to Beth. She looked pale but serene.

'I know Luke stayed at home for my sake. He goes now, to do his duty for his country and his fellow men, with my blessing.' She smiled tremulously.

'Bravo, Master Luke.' It was Paddy who broke the silence, his voice husky, his kindly eyes too bright. He had expressed his frustration with Luke several times in recent weeks but he was genuinely sorry to hear he was to go.

'Hear, hear!'

'May God go with ye, laddie.'

'God bless you, Luke.'

Luke smiled, accepting their good wishes, but Kirsty saw her Aunt Emma surreptitiously wiping away a few tears and knew her thoughts were on Cameron, the son she had sacrificed in the name of freedom. She felt James's hand on hers. He squeezed her fingers in silent support.

'Whatever the future holds for him, Luke is his own man now,' he whispered. 'I'd like to speak to him while you change . . .'

She nodded and stood up. The sober atmosphere dispersed and Luke smiled gratefully across at them. He had never enjoyed being the centre of attention.

Kirsty changed into her best summer dress of blue crepe-de-chine sprigged with pink and white summer flowers, and a wide-brimmed straw hat. Then she was descending the stairs amidst teasing laughter, feeling slightly unreal. James clasped her hand and laughingly hurried her to the car in a vain attempt to avoid the rose petal confetti.

'Alone at last,' he grinned cheerfully as they drove through the village and turned on to the main highway towards Dumfries. 'I never expected to feel so nervous on my wedding day!'

'You were nervous?' Kirsty echoed incredulously. 'You didna look it – not once, James MacFarlane!' He turned his head briefly and his smile was warm, almost boyish.

'Well I was, especially when I glimpsed the beautiful vision at my side. I wondered whether I was worthy of such a bride . . .'

'You're teasing me,' Kirsty retorted with mock severity.

'Truly I am not, Mistress MacFarlane. Mmm . . . Kirsty MacFarlane – that sounds all right to me. How about you?'

'I'd quite forgotten I've changed my name!'

'You'll soon get used to it. How does it feel to be married?'

'It doesna feel any different,' Kirsty shrugged with a nonchalance she did not feel, especially when James glanced at her again and she saw the expression in his eyes.

'Then I must remember to beat you every night to remind you that you belong to me now.' He chuckled softly and Kirsty wondered if she had imagined the darkening of his greeny-grey eyes, or mistaken simple admiration for something more.

It was a small hotel built almost on the edge of the shore and the landlady welcomed them warmly and enquired when they would like their evening meal. Then she led the way up a wide staircase where polished brass rods held a pretty, if faded, carpet firmly in place. She opened the door into a large bedroom with a wide bay window facing on to the Solway Firth and the hills beyond.

'This is the best room we have, as ye asked for in your letter, and the bathroom is straight opposite. I hope you'll be comfortable, Mrs MacFarlane, but please tell me if there's anything ye need . . .' Kirsty stared at her speechlessly for a moment, then she pulled herself together.

'Th-thank you. It's a-a lovely room.' The woman nodded and her eyes twinkled merrily.

'We'll see you in the dining room around seven o'clock then. Oh, and ye'll not forget to draw the curtains if ye switch the light on, will ye?' she reminded gravely before she closed the door, leaving them alone together. Kirsty stared at the big double bed with the blue satin eiderdown and the matching bedspread. She felt mesmerised by it. Her eyes moved to the carpet, fawn with blue flowers, and a fawn lino surround; the large heavy wardrobe; washstand and dressing table; blue basket chair; the window on the far wall ... Slowly, reluctantly, she raised her eyes and found James watching her intently. Her heart began to hammer. Did he know what she was thinking? He had so often read her thoughts in the past ... He had known her so long, so well and yet ... and yet in some ways we're almost strangers, she thought, feeling a surge of panic. James was such a complex character – proud and prickly and aloof one moment, teasing and boyish, considerate and kind the next – not at all like Simon Guillyman. She had known exactly what he wanted!

'D-did you know? D-did you intend us t-to ... sh-share the same r-room?' she stammered. He came to her then and took her hands.

'Not only a room,' he said softly, but his deep voice was firm. 'A bed too, my dear ...' Her head jerked up then and her eyes were wide and dark. He gazed down at her but he had his back to the window and she could not read the expression in his eyes.

'Surely you understood?' he asked gently. 'We agreed to share everything, did we not? We promised to share a whole lifetime?'

'B-but you didna ... We n-never talked of ... of ...' She broke off, unable to meet his eyes.

'Kirsty, I'm a normal man with a man's desires and you're a beautiful girl.' His mouth curved in a faint smile, but his eyes remained grave and unfathomable. 'Unless I've made the greatest mistake of my life, you have the passionate nature to match your beauty – and your temper ... Surely you understood why I could not return to Fairlyden as an ordinary worker? I could not spend each day at your side – except as your husband. You and I, Kirsty, we could never live like monks!' There was a tinge of laughter in his deep voice now and Kirsty frowned.

'You never mentioned ...'

'Mentioned what?'

She wanted to say 'love', but maybe men didn't need love to desire a woman. Simon Guillyman had not loved her, had not even wanted to marry her, but he had desired her. She trembled.

'Aah, Kirsty!' James's arms closed round her then, warm and protective. He cradled her head against his broad chest as though she were a child in need of comfort. 'I don't know what it is I failed to mention, but whatever it was, I hope you're not afraid of me?' She did not answer and he put a finger under her chin, tilting her face gently to his. 'Are you afraid of me, Kirsty?'

'N-no, I don't th-think so. I-I . . .'

'I do believe you're shy,' James murmured incredulously, 'Even after your friendship with Simon Guillyman . . . I scarcely dared to hope . . .'

'What has Simon Guillyman to do with anything?' Kirsty demanded with a spark of her usual spirit. She leaned back to see his face more clearly and felt the muscular hardness of his arms holding her.

'Nothing, my dear Kirsty MacFarlane, nothing at all . . .' he said happily and lowered his mouth to hers. Kirsty's knees went weak, and as James's kiss deepened the weakness spread deliciously until she was barely aware that she was clinging to him, murmuring soft responses which fired James with a passion he had fully intended to control – at least for several hours more.

He had waited a long time to make Kirsty Fairly his bride; there had been times when he had despaired of achieving his heart's desire, and when the goal had seemed almost within reach he had practised the most painful self-restraint, afraid that he might overwhelm her if he could not keep a tight rein on his desire. Now her body was soft and pliant in his arms, her lips yielded willingly to his probing kisses. He raised his head with a groan and looked down at her flushed cheeks, her eyes slumberous with a desire to match his own.

'Oh Kirsty, my love . . .' he groaned and buried his head against the soft curve of her neck. 'I never want to hurt you, or to frighten you . . .' he whispered softly and his warm breath tickled her ear and she moved her head until her mouth found his and they clung together. 'I've loved you so long . . . so long . . .' he murmured against her lips.

'Loved?' Kirsty breathed. 'Loved, James . . .?' She leaned

back again, eager now to see his expression, her eyes searching his, her face soft and vulnerable and too lovely for James's fragile hold on his control. His mouth descended almost ruthlessly, demanding a response to match his own desire. When he lifted his head again Kirsty saw his eyes were dark with passion, the same darkness she had glimpsed before. 'Yes,' he growled softly, 'I love you. What other reason could there be for making you my wife?' Kirsty searched his face, gazed into his eyes. She saw the truth in them.

'I can hardly believe it,' she breathed joyfully. 'I-I thought Fairlyden and I were – were only second choice in your life.'

'Dear heaven! Second choice to who or what?' James studied the face so close to his own.

'To Mary MacFarlane and Nithanvale . . .' Kirsty faltered, seeing that he was waiting for an answer. His eyes widened, then he shook his head in disbelief. 'I only went to Nithanvale because I needed to make something of my life before I dared to think of the fiery young girl I wanted for a wife. When I heard that your grandfather had actually left Fairlyden to you, instead of your father – or Luke . . .!' he grimaced, 'that you were not just the daughter of Fairlyden, but the owner of it, I really believed you were beyond my reach.'

'Oh Jamie,' Kirsty murmured softly. 'You were always so proud and independent, and yet . . .' She frowned. 'Do you know, before she died, Granny's last words to me were "dinna be too proud", so perhaps we're a bit alike.'

'Maybe.' James smiled faintly. 'I was certainly jealous of your friendship with Simon Guillyman but I can't understand how you could believe a girl like Mary could ever mean more to me than you, Kirsty?'

'It was all too easy. I once heard you tell Father you considered her a very special person . . .' Kirsty admitted.

'So she is. Not many pretty young women wish to devote their lives to the church, serving the sick and the poor. I often felt Mary's spirit was too mild and gentle for the ordinary world and yet I think she had a different sort of strength to the rest of us – not at all the kind of spirit I want for my wife though . . .' His eyes strayed back to her lips. Kirsty trembled at the latent passion in them. 'I suppose you think we should go for a walk along the shore . . .? Or unpack? Or something?' he suggested, but he made no move to release her and Kirsty's heart danced with happiness.

'"Or something . . ."' she murmured.

'What?' James blinked.

'The "or something", sounds the most er . . . interesting . . .' she dimpled up at him, then blushed rosily at the light that blazed in his eyes.

Sometime later Kirsty opened her eyes and yawned sleepily. For a moment she could not think where she was when she saw the wide window and the glitter of the water beyond; then memory came flooding back. She blushed and turned her head. Beside her James's body was long and lean and warm; he smiled as her eyes met his.

'Hello, Kirsty MacFarlane,' he said softly. She turned into the circle of his arms and felt them close around her.

'Oh Jamie, I'm so happy . . . so very happy.'

'Mmm, you always used to call me Jamie, except when I disagreed with you or made you angry, then you stamped your little feet and called me James . . .'

'Did I, Jami-e-e-?' Kirsty stretched languidly against him and felt the desire rise in him. His arms tightened. 'I think it will always be Jamie from now on,' she murmured softly. Over his shoulder she saw a path of molten gold spreading over the restless waters of the Solway Firth as the sun began to set behind the hills. It bathed the room with its mellow light and the whole world seemed beautiful. But Kirsty felt nothing could ever compare with the beauty of the love she shared with Jamie.

Forty

Kirsty missed James terribly when he returned to the Hendersons, but she knew he had to keep his promise. Their brief time alone had passed in a blissful dream, a dream which had ended far too soon. The ecstasy she had experienced in James's arms had exceeded her wildest fantasies and now she yearned only for his return.

'I am beginning to understand how the thousands of wives and sweethearts must feel when their men leave them,' she had murmured as he held her tenderly in his arms to say goodbye in the privacy of her bedroom at Fairlyden. 'It must be even worse when your man is going to war. The future is so uncertain.' She had shuddered and James had held her tightly.

'I certainly intend to return safely, Kirsty, but none of us know what tomorrow may bring.' His face was grave, his voice more urgent. 'You've heard the slogan "Lend to defend the right to be free"? When I intended to join the army I thought I should be helping the war effort if I put the money frae Nithanvale into government bonds, but if anything should happen to me, you . . .'

'Don't, Jamie! Please dinna think o' such things. I-I couldna bear it if anything happened to you now that we've found each other – really found each other.'

'I know what you mean, my dearest love. But I did say we should have no secrets and—'

'I understand, Jamie. Mother has a few bonds too. The war is costing millions of pounds every day, so every little bit must help.'

'Yes, but you should know the certificates are in the oak writing box, the one which my father inherited frae Grandfather MacFarlane.'

'I dinna care about certificates, Jamie. All I want is you,' Kirsty whispered insistently and hugged him tighter.

'How am I to drag myself away frae you?' he groaned softly. Everything else was forgotten in the bitter-sweetness of their parting.

* * *

As the weeks passed Kirsty looked forward eagerly to James's letters. Even separated by so many miles she still felt the glow of warmth which only mutual love can bring. She no longer felt alone and weighed down by the responsibility of Fairlyden. The burden was lightened now that she knew James would soon be sharing it with her. Steel no longer frightened her with his threats of taking over and eviction. Her confidence had returned, and increased with the knowledge that she had James's love and respect. Mr Steel's visits were still unwelcome but now she could deal with him firmly and effectively.

The Fordson tractor had arrived and she had learned to drive it, after some initial confusion between the petrol and paraffin tanks and a few problems with the controls.

After Luke's departure, Anna had offered to accommodate one of the girls recruited into the Land Army if Fairlyden was eligible for one. James had arranged it. He knew Kirsty could use all the help she could get, but he also understood his mother's desire for company in the house. His Uncle Thomas's asthma attacks could be alarming, and even when he was well the old man seemed to have little desire for conversation at the end of a day's work. So Jane Bennet, a doctor's daughter from Ayrshire, arrived at Fairlyden in time to help with the haymaking. She was slight and pretty and seemed too timid to be much help with the varied and demanding work of Fairlyden.

'Och, we must give the lassie time,' Anna declared, instantly bristling with maternal loyalty towards her new protégée when she thought Paddy and Thomas might be criticising. 'She canna be much more nervous o' the cows than Master Luke was and she seems willing enough.' Indeed Jane proved to be cheerful and eager to learn; what she lacked in physical strength, she made up for with ingenuity and a sense of humour.

Twice James managed to travel down to Fairlyden for a brief visit, arriving very late on Saturday and leaving again straight after lunch on the Sunday.

'It's such a short time to be together,' Kirsty sighed wistfully as they walked hand in hand to the station, on the Sunday of his second visit.

'I know, but Elsie's cousin has his own farm to run and he's the only man the Hendersons know who has any experience o' milking cows. His father used to have a dairy herd when he

358

was a laddie. Anyway, Kirsty, it's better than nothing. I couldna wait any longer without seeing you.' The look in his eyes brought the colour rushing to Kirsty's cheeks and he stopped when they reached the shade of the last beech tree at the end of the track. As they went eagerly into each other's arms neither of them guessed that the same tree had witnessed the tender loving of an earlier generation, and a parting which had proved far longer than the young lovers could ever have anticipated.

Eventually they walked on again, a little faster now, on account of the delay.

'Billy Henderson has definitely made up his mind to sell all the cows – with some persuasion from Elsie. She understands how impatient I am to return to you, my love, so she knows I shall not be persuaded to stay a moment longer than necessary, and she's afraid her husband will wreck all the doctors' good work if he starts lifting heavy milk churns again.'

'How long will it take to arrange a sale for his cows?' Kirsty asked eagerly.

'Well, they're not pedigree but they are mostly in good condition so I'm hoping I shall be back at Fairlyden by the middle of August.' He sighed and paused to kiss her lingeringly. 'I had hoped to be here in time to help with some of the haymaking, but that willna be possible.'

'We shall manage,' Kirsty assured him with more confidence than she felt. 'Jane is getting quite good at managing jobs which only require one horse. She will rake the hay into heaps.

'Mmm, Mother seems happy to have her company in the house. Uncle Thomas is looking much better too.'

'Yes, the fine weather helps and Jane's father sent him some medicine for his chest. Didn't he tell you? He says it eases the congestion quite quickly but it smells just like camphor. Oh Jamie, look at the time on your watch!'

'Aah, you're a temptress! You distract me so I canna hurry away. Come, I'll steel another kiss in the shade o' the Manse wall, then I'll leave you and run the rest o' the way to the station . . .' He clasped her hand and they ran, laughing like two young children, to the high sandstone wall which surrounded the glebeland. They clung together, reluctant to part.

'I must go . . .' James groaned, but still he bent his head for another kiss.

'The Reverend Morrison wants us to rent the glebe when you return, Jamie,' Kirsty breathed against his lips. 'I forgot to tell you.' She returned his kisses urgently.

'So many things to say, so little time!' James lamented. 'The Kirk Session will have a fit if they think we're taking over the glebe.'

'Mr Morrison says we shall make better use of the land.'

'Aye, no doubt. I meant to tell you, Kirsty: I intend to buy a couple of Billy Henderson's cows for Fairlyden . . .'

'But you canna do that, Jamie! They're not even Ayrshires. You told me they were black and white!'

'They give a lot o' milk though!' James grinned and silenced her protest with a long kiss. 'I must run like the wind now, my lovely lassie. I'll come again as soon as I can . . .'

It was only later Kirsty remember his mention of the black and white cows. Surely James could not be serious? The Fairlyden Ayrshires were all pedigree and attested and renowned for their purity and true breeding.

The haymaking was almost finished. It had taken longer than they expected and in two days James would be home to stay. Kirsty could scarcely believe they would soon be together again. She walked exhaustedly into the yard and stifled a yawn. Jane Bennet followed and swung the gate closed behind her. She grinned.

'I never really believed farmers worked from dawn to dusk before.' She stifled a yawn herself. 'It must be nearly ten o'clock.'

'Yes, it's been a long day,' Kirsty mused, leaning her arms on the top bar of the gate and looking back over the shadowy fields. 'But a satisfying one.'

'It's strange to see all the hay fields looking so brown and shorn; hard to believe they'll ever be green again.'

'Oh, but they will. Another week and you willna recognise them, especially if we get a gentle shower o' rain.' Kirsty glanced up at the night sky and sniffed the air instinctively. 'I dinna think it will rain tonight though. I certainly hope it willna. We should be finished carting by midday tomorrow.'

'It's so calm. So still . . .' Jane spoke softly, almost reverently, as though afraid to disturb the evening peace. 'It's hard to believe there's a war going on out there.'

'Yes. We had a letter a few weeks ago though – a warning to farms in the area that soldiers may be sent into Muircumwell and neighbouring parishes for training. That would shatter the peace – but at least they would be our own men.' She shuddered. 'It must be dreadful to be taken over by the German armies . . .' She wondered where Luke was now. He wrote long letters home but they told little about his work except that his ability to write German and French was proving very useful. He had failed one of the medicals and had been drafted to London as some sort of clerical aide. 'Do you ever hear from you brother, Jane?' Kirsty asked curiously.

'Mostly through my parents. Though he seemed quite interested to hear I've joined the Land Army.'

'He's in the RAF isn't he?'

'Yes.' Jane sighed and looked pensive. 'He'd just finished his degree when war was declared. He enlisted immediately. Father aged ten years in as many months. He had hoped Hamish would join him in his practice.'

'War is such a cruel, stupid waste!' Kirsty declared vehemently. 'My cousin Cameron was in the RAF too.'

'Was?' Jane asked quietly.

Kirsty nodded. 'Was . . .' she repeated sadly. 'He was shot down over—'

'Kirsty!' Beth's voice called out of the shadows and both girls straightened and moved away from the field gate.

'Mother?'

'Oh, there ye are, lassie.' Beth hurried towards them. 'There's a message for ye frae the station master at Muircumwell. He couldna get through on the telephone so he sent his laddie up. They've got three cows there. He says they're bound for Fairlyden!'

Kirsty gasped. 'James!' Surely he wouldna—

'I told the laddie there must be some mistake. He says the cows are black and white . . .'

'I see.' Kirsty said tightly and her lips pursed. Jane looked at her speculatively and even in the dim light the twin patches of indignant colour were plain.

'I . . . er, I'll go in for my supper and get to bed now then, Mrs MacFarlane? Unless you need me for anything?'

'What? Oh yes, you go in, Jane. It's too late to walk the cows frae the station now; it will soon be dark. Mother, did young Tommy MacAllister say what his father had done with the cows?

'Aye, he's put them in his ain wee paddock behind the station house until morning. But, Kirsty . . .?'

'I think James must have bought them at the Hendersons' sale. I'd forgotten it was today.' Kirsty's voice was brittle. 'He mentioned them, but I didna believe . . .'

'Mmm . . . well, wait to see what he has to say before ye lose your temper, lassie,' Beth counselled wisely. 'Remember marriage is a partnership.'

'A joint partnership – or so I thought!'

'Aye. But ye're tired now. Ye've had a hard day and things will be clearer in the morning.'

Kirsty did not sleep well that night. She felt angry, hurt and upset by what she considered James's high-handedness. Were they going to quarrel as soon as they started their life together? She did not want any black and white cattle mixing with Fairlyden's Ayrshires. They would lower the standard and reputation which her father had spent years building up. She knew the black and white dairy cattle were supposed to give large quantities of milk; they were originally imported from Friesland – large, ugly beasts – at least from the little she had seen of them at the shows. She disliked their long misshapen udders which bore no resemblance to the neat square udders for which the Fairlyden Ayrshires were now famous. Her thoughts went round and round and she wondered what her father would have done. Would he have forbidden James to bring them back to Fairlyden? Forbidden? She was James's wife now. She was in no position to forbid . . . At last she fell into an uneasy sleep.

She was wakened by a loud knocking on the back door. It was never locked and she heard someone enter the kitchen. She lifted a head which felt twice as heavy as usual and peered blearily at her clock. It was quarter to five – almost milking time, but she had not overslept. Outside, the early morning mist still clung to the hollows and the birds were already well into their dawn chorus.

'Mrs MacFarlane! Mrs MacFarlane!' It was Jane Bennet's voice calling softly but with a note of urgency. Kirsty was out of bed and groping into her dressing gown before she had time to think. She stared over the polished bannister at the pale blur of Jane's upturned face. 'It's Mr Whiteley. He – he's dead . . .

'Thomas!' B-but he was fine last night.' Kirsty ran down the stairs. Automatically she moved towards the kitchen. Jane followed. 'What happened? Did Anna send you?'

362

'Yes. Mr Whiteley always gets up first. He likes to feed the horses in good time. Habit, he says . . . he said. He was not up when Mrs MacFarlane went through to kindle the fire. She says . . .' Jane gulped, 'she says to tell you he – he looks very peaceful; he must have died in his sleep. Will you telephone for the doctor?'

'Yes, yes, of course I will – if the telephone is working again. Mr MacAllister said he would report it. I'll need to contact James.' Kirsty pushed the kettle on to the hot plate of the Aga. 'Make yourself a cup of tea, Jane, while I wash and dress.'

The day passed in a whirl of activity. The telephone was still out of order. The milking had to be done and finished in time to catch the milk collection lorry. Kirsty had to drive into the village to notify Doctor Broombank and tell Lizzie Whiteley. Miss Lizzie was sixty-five and she accepted death as part of life, but she was understandably shocked at the suddenness of her brother's passing. She motioned Kirsty to use her telephone to contact James at the Hendersons and her sister Maggie at the Mains of Muir.

It was Beth who remembered about the three black and white cows still waiting to be collected from the station paddock. She took charge of two-year-old Irene herself and dispatched Paddy to the station with Lucy and Jane and two of the collie dogs to help him bring them home to Fairlyden.

James arrived at Muircumwell station late that night. He stood on the dark and deserted platform surrounded by his worldly goods. The Fairlyden telephone was still out of order so he had been unable to contact Kirsty to ask her to meet him. Wearily he stowed the heaviest of his cases in the waiting room and set off to walk. It was not a good beginning to his new start in life at Fairlyden.

Kirsty took one look at his white exhausted face and her earlier anger over his purchase of the alien cattle was forgotten, at least for the present time. She sprang out of bed and into his arms.

'I didna know you were coming tonight Jamie! But I am glad – so very glad you're here.' He kissed her tenderly.

'I couldna get through on the telephone. How is Mother? Is it too late to see her tonight?' He slumped on to the edge of the bed.

Kirsty glanced at the clock. 'It's well past midnight. I think she will be asleep. She has taken it all very well. Your Aunt Maggie has been with her most o' the day and Mother and

363

your Aunt Lizzie were there this evening . . .' Kirsty pulled on her robe as she talked. 'They're waiting for you to make the funeral arrangements though. I'll make you some tea and some sandwiches. You look all in.'

'I am. It's been a busy week preparing all the cows for the sale, and today has seemed endless! I was up at four and there were so many loose ends to finish, even before I got your telephone call about Uncle Thomas. At least I dinna need to return. Aah, Kirsty, it's good to know we shall be together from now on.' He drew her close once more, but a moment or two later Kirsty ruffled his hair and gently disentangled herself.

'I'll make those sandwiches or you'll be asleep on my lap, Jamie MacFarlane.'

When she returned to the bedroom with the tea and a plate of sandwiches James was stretched out on the bed, sound asleep; except for his boots, he was still fully dressed.

Forty-One

Thomas Whiteley had been a part of Fairlyden for as long as any of its present occupants could remember, but as Anna herself declared, 'Time waits for no man'. This was certainly the case at Fairlyden. It seemed to Kirsty that Thomas had scarcely been laid to rest in the Muircumwell Kirkyard before the first fleet of army lorries advanced on Fairlyden, disgorging soldiers here, there and everywhere.

'Poor Thomas, he certainly wouldna have liked having so many strangers all around.'

'We must be thankful they're not enemy soldiers,' Beth declared philosophically. 'I suppose they have to train somewhere.' She was less calm when the tanks began to arrive, however. Their broad heavy tracks churned the Fairlyden lane into a mire, tearing up the grass verges, uprooting the primroses and bluebells, and even the clump of shy wild violets which had nestled at the foot of a hawthorn bush for as long as she could remember. When she witnessed the destruction of the beech tree, at the narrow end of the track nearest the Manse, she felt some of her most treasured memories were being destroyed. Kirsty was dismayed at the swift, almost ruthless desecration, but her mother's distress was almost tangible.

'When the war is over we'll plant more trees,' she comforted gently.

'They would never be the same. I'm glad your grandmother didna live to see such changes. The beeches were planted by your Great-Grandfather Logan and James's grandfather, Louis Whiteley. They made the road too. Your father and I kenned every inch o' it frae the day we went to school together . . .' Kirsty sensed the majestic old tree and the flowers had held more than schoolgirl memories for her mother, but she did not probe.

The soldiers came and went, often sleeping in the farm buildings and at other farms in the area. They constructed a bridge to carry the lorries across the Strathtod Burn.

'It's all part of the exercise,' one of the officers informed James. 'I'm sorry about the mess we've made of your farm track. I'll put in a memo for repairs when the war is over. The authorities might even make a tarred road right through to the Strathtod village.'

'Is there any sign of an end to the war?' James asked eagerly. The man hesitated, then shook his head.

'No end in sight at all. In fact if we can't stop these bloody U-Boats from sinking our ships the bloody Nazis will starve us into submission – but that's only my opinion,' he added hastily. 'Don't be spreading scary tales.'

'I understand.' James nodded. 'Keep up morale and a stiff upper lip – even if we are about to die. We're doing our best to provide as much food as we can on the farms, but there's a shortage o' everything we need here too. If your men have any time to spare frae their exercises we could always use some help with the harvest.

'Mmm, I'll remember that.'

The officer kept his word and from time to time during the long weeks of the harvest, groups of soldiers, including officers, came to help stook the corn, or fork the sheaves on to the carts and into the stacks. Whenever the weather permitted the work went on from dawn until dusk and even into the night when the light of the harvest moon turned the golden fields to silver.

Sometimes Anna fretted when the eggs she collected were fewer than they should have been. She was convinced some of the soldiers had been round the hen houses before her, but for the most part they were all cheerful young men a long way from home and the petty thefts were overlooked. Jane Bennet erected a barrier of reserve which kept even the most forward young servicemen in their place, and James made it very plain that Kirsty was his wife, and that he would stand no nonsense if any of the soldiers tried to become too familiar with the Fairlyden women. There had been several affairs in the village and a few broken hearts; some said there would be worse to follow. While he was willing to cooperate, James had no intention of allowing Fairlyden to be disrupted any more than he could help.

Kirsty and James worked as hard as anyone else and were frequently exhausted by the end of the day, but their love, and the simple satisfaction of just being together, made even the most serious problems seem lighter.

It was the beginning of October when Joe Little paid a fleeting visit to Fairlyden.

'I had three days' leave so I travelled north to see my parents. They told me of your brother's death, Mrs MacFarlane. They knew ye were both kind tae me when I was biding beneath your roof. I wanted to tell ye how sorry I am, but I'm not much good at the letter writing.'

'It was good o' ye to think o' me, laddie.' Anna was touched by his earnest young face. 'We all have to go when the good Lord calls,' she declared stoically. 'Though to tell the truth, young Joey, I've missed Thomas more than I would have believed, even though he was a mite cantankerous at times. He had a good heart and he was very good to me and James when I was a young widow ... Mind ye, I've a new lodger in your old room and I've been glad o' her company these past months.'

'Her company? Ye have a lassie biding here?'

'Aye, Jane Bennet is her name. She's frae the Women's Land Army. She kenned nothing about farming when she came to Fairlyden, but she's a grand help with the hens and pigs now, and she's even learning to use that new-fangled machine for milking the kie.'

'So ye've replaced me with a lassie?' Joe's eyes crinkled goodhumouredly.

'Och no! Jane came after Master Luke went intae the services. If ye'll wait for a bite o' supper ye'll meet her. They're lifting tatties i' Burnside field, down at Muircumwell. It's a long road for carting, but we have a tractor now, ye ken. Noisy thing it is tae,' Anna snorted in disgust, 'wi' iron spikes on the big wheels. Mind ye, Joey, it does save the horses some hard pulling up yon track. Have ye seen what a muddy mess that is since the tanks started coming up it?'

'I could scarcely miss it! The mud would have been over my boot tops in places if I hadna clung to the hedge. How is young Irene McGuire? Is she still with Lucy and Paddy Kildougan?'

'Aye, she is. That Josh McGuire has never come once to see his ain bairn! He's never even written to enquire for her either. Mind ye, I do believe Lucy is hoping he'll leave her with them. She loves that wee lassie like her ain flesh and blood. Paddy thinks they should try to adopt her so that Lucy kens where she stands.'

'Well, that might be the best thing all round if McGuire

doesna want to be bothered with a bairn.'

'Aye, it might be best,' Anna agreed slowly. 'But Lucy is spoiling her because she has no mother o' her ain. "Spare the rod and spoil the child", my mother used tae say. I didna think she was right when 'twas me on the end o' the rod, mind ye! But in my heart I ken she was a wise woman and I'm telling ye, Joey, young Irene rules the Kildougans already. She'll break Lucy's heart when she grows up if she doesna put her foot down now. I dinna ken how a pair like the McGuire's bred such a bonny bairn. She's a bright wee thing. She's not three years old until January but she kens how to get her ain way already, even with Paddy.'

Joey grinned. 'I'd like to see Paddy again, if ye're sure ye dinna mind me staying a while?'

'Ach, I dinna think it's Paddy ye're wanting to see at all, Joey Little.' Anna teased. 'Jane's a pretty lassie. A bit small, but she's tough enough so dinna be deceived. And she stands no nonsense frae young men in uniform – even handsome fellows like yourself!' Suddenly Anna sobered. 'To tell the truth, Joe, I'm thinking o' leaving Fairlyden, but I dinna ken where Jane would stay then.'

'Leaving Fairlyden! But ye've been here all your life.'

'No, not all of it. I was born here, but we moved to the rooms above the shop in Muircumwell when ma father died. Then I married and went to live at Highmuir farm. I came back to Fairlyden to keep house for Thomas when I was widowed. I've always got on well with all the Fairlys, especially Mrs Beth . . . I shall miss her, aye and the hens and such like work, but we're none o' us getting any younger. It's nearly four miles to the village but it seems longer than it used to do, and I like a bit o' company. Lizzie, ma sister, will be sixty-six soon and it isna easy to get help at the shop, what with all the women needed for the ammunitions and the canteens, and even taking over frae the bank clerks and other office jobs. There's plenty o' rooms above the shop and Lizzie says she'd be glad o' my help as well as the company.' She frowned. 'I dinna ken why I'm telling ye all this, Joe laddie. I havena even mentioned it to James and Kirsty yet, or Mrs Beth.'

'I do believe ye're serious,' Joe mused. 'I'd give my right arm to be back at Fairlyden!' He grinned wryly. 'Not that I'd be much use here without it! I wish this was over, I truly do. Mind you I've learned a few new tricks in the army. I can drive a jeep and a tank now, ye ken.'

'Well, I expect that'll be useful, Joe,' Anna said sympathetically. 'Maybe ye'll be able to drive the tractor when ye come back.'

'If I come back, Mrs Mac. If I come back . . .'

'Oh, Joey laddie, I'm sure ye will!'

'Mmm, maybe . . .' He frowned. 'I wonder . . . if ye'd do me a favour?'

'If I can, I will, Joey.'

'If ye do decide to leave Fairlyden, would ye ask Mr MacFarlane if he'd consider giving my father a job here, and this house? He's working over at Lower Nithside but he doesna like it. I ken they're not supposed to move frae one farm to another while the war is on but he's never liked working for that miserable auld Beckman. Ye'll ken the wages went up tae sixty shillings, but Beckman says Father is too old for a full wage so he only pays him forty-two and sixpence a week. He's forty-seven but he's strong as a horse. He works all the hours God sends to do his bit for his country, but he isna allowed to keep his ain pig, and he doesna get any milk or eggs or even a rotten tattie for nothing! Mother helps in the house and the dairy but Beckman says they get the cottage for that – and it's a damp, miserable hole, I'll tell ye! They dinna even have a cold tap in the house for running water.'

Anna frowned and bit her lip. 'What will your father say about ye arranging his life and never even asking him, Joey?'

'Ach, he'd jump at the chance to work for Master James again, I ken he would. But I'll not mention it until ye've made up your ain mind, Mrs MacFarlane. My family worked for the Nithanvale MacFarlanes for four generations. Father couldna believe it when Nithanvale was taken over by the government!'

'No, I think it was a shock to James at the time, but it's all worked out for the best. If ye ask me I reckon he and Miss Kirsty were meant for each other. He needs a woman with a bit o' spirit.' She looked Joey straight in the eye. 'I think ye've helped me make up my mind, laddie. It was bothering me a bit, ye ken – leaving just when every pair o' hands is needed. What about Jane though?'

'I expect Mother would be pleased to keep a dozen lodgers if she was moving to a house like this,' Joey assured her.

Anna moved to the rooms above the Muircumwell Store at the end of November and James arranged for a cattle lorry to move all Albert Little's worldly goods to Fairlyden the following day. The arrangement was welcomed by all concerned. Kirsty suggested that Jane Bennet should move into the farmhouse – at least until the Littles had settled into their new home, and Beth and James agreed. Jane was three years younger than Kirsty herself, she was intelligent and keen to learn all she could and they got on well together.

The night Jane moved into Fairlyden James declared, 'I have a complaint to make, Mistress MacFarlane.' In the darkness of their bedroom Kirsty could not see the twinkle in his eyes and she missed the mock seriousness in his tone.

'Oh?' she frowned, trying to think what she had done to displease him. They had had a serious, if belated, discussion after his purchase of the three black and white cows and they had agreed to consult each other fully over all major decisions in future. James had acknowledged that at least one of the cows had proved a poor bargain and he had agreed to sell her as soon as she finished her lactation. 'Are you complaining because I . . .?' James chuckled and rolled towards her in the big feather bed, enfolding her in his arms.

'My complaint is that I am now surrounded by women. I need some male support. I suggest it is time we had a son . . .' His voice thickened and deepened as his hands moved over the warm soft curves of her body. Kirsty gave a relieved and happy sigh as she responded eagerly to his caresses.

'I fully agree with your suggestion, Mr MacFarlane,' she whispered saucily. 'But I don't know how such things can be achieved – do you?'

'Indeed I do, my beautiful witch . . .'

Forty-Two

Far from drawing to an end, the war and its attendant troubles seemed to have intensified and spread throughout the world by Christmas – the first Christmas James and Kirsty had spent together as man and wife. Early in December the relative peace of the Sabbath was shattered by the news that hundreds of Japanese bombers had attacked the United States Fleet as it lay at anchor at Pearl Harbor in the Hawaiian Islands.

'I suppose it was inevitable that the United States would declare war after such an outrage,' James reflected the following day as he anxiously scanned the Glasgow Herald. 'The destruction seems to have been devastating, and to make matters worse the Japs wrecked the American base in the Philippines as well.

'Our poor soldiers seem to be fighting in all corners of the globe now,' Kirsty observed in troubled tones. 'There's no wonder the government is calling up all unmarried women – at least those between twenty and forty.'

'Aye, and extending registration of men up to the age of fifty-one,' James frowned. 'Everything is tightening up alarmingly. No wonder Peregrine Steel wanted to insinuate himself into a safe harbour for the duration.'

As the weeks passed they listened tensely to the news bulletins. Christmas passed and the New Year dawned, but there was little to bring cheer. The bitter winter weather only added to the misery.

'We must be thankful we still have our homes, Beth reminded them all gravely, 'The poor people in London and the other big cities must be suffering dreadfully. I think I should teach ye to knit socks and gloves for the war effort, Jane.'

'Well . . . I could try,' Jane agreed slowly. 'But I expect I'd be very slow compared with yourself and Mrs MacFarlane,' She glanced at Kirsty's flying fingers. 'You put me to shame. Yes, I will have a go!'

'Good lassie!' Beth approved. 'Every little bit helps. Anyway ye're much better at the first aid than we are so we'll teach each other.'

It was early in the spring when two men in dark suits and ties came to Fairlyden and asked to speak to James.

'He is ploughing a field o' stubble ready for the drilling,' Beth informed them. 'My daughter will be going down there with a can o' tea shortly. If your business is urgent I will ask her to summon James.'

'It is urgent. You are . . . Mrs Fairly?' The younger man asked politely.

Beth nodded. 'That's right.'

The two men exchanged glances. 'My name is Morley, Mrs Fairly, and this is my superior, Mr MacArthur, from the Department of Agriculture in Edinburgh. I know how important it is for Mr MacFarlane to get on with the spring cultivations, but believe me, our business with him is indeed urgent and Mr MacArthur is due in Aberdeenshire tomorrow.'

Beth nodded, but she wondered why they had not sent a letter ahead if Mr MacArthur was such an important official and his time so precious. 'Please come in and have a seat. I will send a message to the field for James.'

Half an hour later Mr MacArthur frowned with annoyance at James as they faced each other across the hearth in the small room which was still used as an office-cum-living room.

'I'm sorry, Mr MacArthur, but I will not take over another man's farm behind his back!' James was equally annoyed and his jaw was set in a stubborn line. 'The same thing almost happened here – to my wife, less than a year ago! Now you say we are making an excellent job . . .'

'Aah, yes, that was our friend Steel . . .' Mr Morley interrupted. 'That was a very different matter, James. He acted on his own authority, and mainly for his own purposes. You'll be interested to hear that his younger son has gone into the navy since the new regulations tightened things up. His eldest son, Peregrine Steel, is looking after their own place, but for how much longer I cannot say. It is a small acreage and he seems to know very little about farming.'

'I see,' James said tightly. 'But that does not help the two farmers you are asking me to displace. We are neighbours with Strathtod Estate! Surely you can imagine the bad blood it would cause!'

372

'I appreciate your point – and your principles – Mr MacFarlane,' the senior official declared more peaceably. 'I understand from Mr Morley that you worked for the Department yourself before your marriage?'

'I did.'

'Then you will understand that the last thing men in our position should do is to cause alarm to the public, or to lower the morale of our soldiers . . .' He lowered his voice and his face was grave. 'So I am speaking to you in confidence. Do you understand?'

'Yes,' James frowned now. 'I know all government ministers are sworn to secrecy, and their—'

'Good. The situation is serious, Mr MacFarlane. So serious that Britain is on the verge of being starved into submission by the German U-Boats. The navy is doing everything possible, and many things which are impossible, to protect our shipping. The rest is up to us – the British farmers, smallholders, gardeners, in fact anyone who can grow any damned thing that can be used for food. Parks, public gardens, golf courses – all the land we can turn into vegetable patches. Now the widow over at Burnside Farm and the old couple in the Strathwood Holding are quite incapable of cultivating their farms to their full potential . . .'

'Surely Mrs Brown has a son?'

'He's dying of tuberculosis. She knows he can't last the year out. She wants to stay in the house for as long as he lives, but she would not mind you taking over her land – so long as you pay the rent of course. Much the same applies to the Rogers.'

'You mean you have already spoken to them?' James demanded indignantly.

'We have not mentioned you specifically, Mr MacFarlane, but they know that some other farmer must take over – someone capable of bringing the land to full production – and soon. As a matter of fact both Mrs Brown's son and old Mr Rogers told us they consider Fairlyden to be the best-run farm in the district, and—'

'Do they indeed!' James gave a hoot of angry, mocking laughter which startled his visitors. 'You can sit here and tell me that! Do you realise the anxiety my wife experienced because she thought she was about to lose this "well-run farm" and her home? All because she would not – indeed could not – plough the Westhill land as Steel suggested?'

Both men looked uncomfortable. 'I . . . er, I'm afraid we were not responsible for some of Mr Steel's advice or his decisions, Mr MacFarlane. He has been relieved of most of his authority, you know. Anyway I understand you have ploughed half of the Westhill land this year now that you have acquired a tractor?'

'We have, but only to comply with orders, not because we agreed with them. I can tell you now it will be a waste of time and seed and a lot of damned hard work for next to nothing.'

'Er . . . umph . . . I understand the army have taken over the other half of the hill for training purposes?'

'They have. They find it hard going, even in their tanks, after a week of wet weather!'

'Perhaps this other land which we are suggesting you take over will compensate for the loss of the hill, and it is conveniently situated across the burn from your own land. I understand Fairlyden was in fact part of the Strathtod Estate at one time?'

'Yes . . . so I believe; long before my time though.'

'So things have come full circle,' Mr MacArthur suggested smoothly. 'Quite an achievement for you, young man, to be spreading your wings so widely.'

James frowned. 'I will ask my wife to bring in a tray of tea. We must discuss your suggestion.' He ignored MacArthur's raised eyebrows.

Kirsty and Beth had already anticipated the request for tea and Kirsty carried in a laden tray without delay.

'I see you are not affected by the rationing in the country, Mrs MacFarlane!' MacArthur quipped and Kirsty suspected there was veiled criticism behind his jocular tone.

'Indeed we are as affected as anyone else. We have plenty of potatoes and a good supply of oatmeal though, as you can see from the potato scones and the oatcakes. They are freshly baked and the raspberry jam is homemade. Where there is a will there is a way!'

'I see. Yes, I suppose you are right. My wife says it is impossible to bake anything these days. You're a fortunate man to have such a thrifty wife, MacFarlane.'

As she poured the tea Kirsty listened to the mens' conversation. Her first reaction was one of angry indignation towards them, and sympathy towards the two small farmers whom they planned to remove from their farms.

'Believe me, Mrs. MacFarlane, they are struggling to pay the rent as it is and they are making a desperately poor living. If they can stay in their homes, and perhaps keep a few hens and a pig, in return for carrying out seasonal work . . . I believe they would come to consider that you and your husband were doing them a favour eventually.'

'Eventually!' Kirsty repeated darkly. 'I think we should speak to them ourselves first and gauge their reactions personally.'

'As you wish, Mrs MacFarlane,' the senior official said stiffly. 'But I must warn you there is little time to waste.'

'I think that is a splendid idea, Mrs MacFarlane,' Morley agreed warmly. 'The personal touch. After all, we do want to retain friendly relations all round as far as possible, don't we, sir?'

'That is not always possible in the present critical situation, Morley. One way or another half of that land must be ploughed this spring, and sown with corn. The rest of the pasture land on both holdings is badly in need of lime and some stock to graze it. Some of the fields need draining too, though I realise that would be a longterm plan and it would require some form of government incentive.'

'Is the owner of the Strathtod Estate aware of your plans?' James asked shrewdly.

'The owner is a Major Christie-Hall, who lives in Bedfordshire now. He is an old man; had a stroke two years ago, apparently, when his son insisted on joining the RAF instead of the army. He has never spoken since – according to his factor and his lawyer, that is. I gather the son is not interested in the estate and plans to sell it when he inherits – if he survives that long. He does have a wife and a young child but they also live in Bedfordshire at the present time.'

'I see . . .' James nodded thoughtfully and looked at Kirsty, a silent question in his eyes. She gave an imperceptible nod. 'My wife and I will go over to Burnside and Strathwood this evening and I will telephone Mr Morley at his office tomorrow.'

'Very well,' MacArthur agreed reluctantly and rose from his chair. 'There will be about ninety-five acres between the two holdings, which should all be ploughable eventually. If you take it on, Mr Morley will see that you are allocated another recruit from the Womens' Land Army. It's surprising what some of these young women have managed to do,' he mused wonderingly and Kirsty hid a smile.

'I didna like that Mr MacArthur much,' Kirsty said two evenings later. 'But I have to admit he was right. The Browns especially seemed desperately poor – far worse off than Paddy and Lucy have ever been, and the son looks dreadfully ill.'

'Aye,' James agreed, 'And so long as they can keep their homes, both families seemed almost relieved to be rid o' the pressures o' responsibility. Of course it will all have to be done officially with the laird's agreement but Mr Morley promised to see to all that. He's a good man, Morley. He's sending us another girl. I mentioned it to the Littles and Mrs Little says she's willing to provide lodgings now that she's settled in at Fairlyden herself.'

'Mmm, I'm glad. Mother has plenty to do really, though she never complains.'

'No, she's one in a million!' James grinned. 'And her daughter is, er . . . almost as good.'

'Only almost, James MacFarlane!' Kirsty aimed a playful punch at his broad chest. He caught her hand and drew her close, stealing a kiss and releasing her hastily when they heard Jane's footsteps approaching.

'I do believe Uncle Billy would agree with you about Mother being one in a million. Do you know he's offered to pay her fare if she wants to join him in America. I think he is quite eager to see her again.'

'Perhaps he shares Simon Guillyman's sentiments and believes there's little hope of Britain winning the war this time,' James mused glumly.

'Well things certainly dinna sound very good and I'll bet we dinna know the half of it,' Kirsty agreed anxiously.

'What did your mother say – about your uncle's invitation to join him, I mean?'

'She said she would never dream of such a thing – whether there was a war on or not.' Kirsty smiled and turned as Jane entered the room. 'I don't suppose she'll tell Uncle Billy as bluntly as that though. She thinks he must be very lonely.'

Forty-Three

Rhoda Gledd, the new girl from the Land Army, was the complete opposite to Jane in every conceivable way, or so it seemed to Kirsty. She was tall and broad, with flaming red hair which she wore loose most of the time, either floating behind her like a wild pennant or obscuring her freckled face completely – depending on the direction of the wind. Several times Kirsty asked her to confine it beneath a cap or secure it with a ribbon, especially when she was working in the byre or dairy. Although Rhoda nodded, and she was neither sullen nor defiant, nothing changed. She was like a large placid cow herself – though not always as particular about her grooming, Kirsty suspected. Her home was on the edge of a small town in Lanarkshire and she considered herself a country girl although she had never before had anything to do with animals or any other form of country life, except for a pet rabbit which her brother had kept for three weeks and then turned loose to forage for itself in their pocket-handkerchief garden.

'Oi kens aboot animals, Mrs. Ye divna need tae tell me what tae dae . . .' she announced in her slow gruff voice whenever Kirsty gave her instructions. James fared little better when he told her to bed the calves with clean straw; not only did she use precious hay reserved for the winter feed, she simply shoved large forkfuls down from the hay rick and spread it on the ground; then she turned the calves from their sheds into the yard. James found them frisking and dancing like devils at Halloween, while Rhoda clutched her hands around her ample girth and rocked with mirth.

James, striving to keep a hold on his temper, demanded to know why she had let the calves out of their sheds. She looked at him askance.

'Ye told me to make them a bed o' straw! I couldna carry the stack tae them, so I brocht them oot tae mak their ain bed. I use ma heed, ye see.' She thumped her temples with both hands.

Beth, the most forbearing of women, lost patience altogether

377

after the first two weeks of trying to instruct Rhoda in the simple science of setting eggs to hatch chickens.

'She muddles the fresh eggs with the eggs frae the broody hens every time she comes near!' Beth exclaimed in exasperation. 'And they aren't even in the same shed! I canna imagine how anyone could be so stupid! I darena let her touch any more eggs or she'll waste them all. I set her on to clean the dropping boards and she put all the droppings on to the floor o' the hut instead o' in the barrow, then she asked what she should do with the empty barrow!' The final straw came when they were sitting down to breakfast round the kitchen table at Fairlyden one morning in the middle of May. A boiled egg had become a Sunday morning luxury in an effort to comply with the stringent rationing which had been enforced. When Kirsty sliced the top from her egg with eager anticipation she was confronted, not by a bright yellow yolk, but by a chicken which had been almost ready for hatching. No one enjoyed their breakfast that morning and Kirsty felt she could never face a boiled egg again.

For days following this episode Kirsty felt nauseous whenever she thought of breakfast. Gradually it occurred to her that the sickly feeling had little to do with boiled eggs – good or bad. It began to dawn on her that it was her own condition which was responsible for the morning squeamishness. Despite the privations and problems of war her spirits soared at the prospect of presenting James with the child they both longed for. As the weeks passed so did the nausea.

'If it is possible, you're even more radiantly lovely than before,' James whispered as he held her tenderly, almost reverently, in his arms in the privacy of their bedroom. 'But you will be careful, my love? I know how hard you work but I couldna bear it if anything happened to you.'

'Och, Jamie, you know I've always been disgustingly healthy, and everyone works hard . . .'

'I know, I know.' He hugged her closer. 'But you are so special, Kirsty. Nothing would be worthwhile without you. You don't know how much I need you.'

'Och, Jamie, I need you too and I do intend to take care – if only for our son's sake.'

'I dinna care whether it's a boy or a lassie – just so long as you are all right, Kirsty.'

She chuckled in the darkness. 'You could fill the byre with black and white cows to your heart's content if you got rid of me!' she teased. 'There'd be no one to argue with you.'

'Aah, but I need you to argue with me, state your opinions, understand the problems and share our successes.'

'I was only teasing, Jamie,' Kirsty said gently.

'I know, but you were right about the cows I bought frae the Hendersons' sale. They havena come up to Fairlyden standards at all. The last one will have to go as soon as she finishes her present lactation.' He sounded so like a bewildered little boy who had displeased someone he loved that Kirsty turned into his arms and kissed him lingeringly.

'I love you, Jamie . . . and who knows – some day the black and white Friesians may be just as good as the Fairlyden Ayrshires.' She sighed. 'If only there was some sign of an end to this dreadful war! Maybe when it is over we shall be able to experiment a little? Go to the best sales and study up the pedigrees and records of the Friesian herds as my father did with the Ayrshires. Maybe we shall build up a new herd, together . . .?'

'Do you know, Kirsty MacFarlane, you're a wonderful wife! And I know you'll be a wonderful mother too.'

As the summer passed Kirsty continued to do most of her usual tasks with Rhoda to help with the heavier work. They had mutually agreed that the girl would never be fit to work without supervision but as time passed she had proved herself a strong and willing helper, especially in the fields. So the turnip hoeing was finished, the hay was mowed and rowed and eventually gathered into the lofts and ricks.

Then came the harvest, by far the largest they had ever had at Fairlyden, even without the extra acres from the two Strathtod holdings over the burn.

'At least the new bridge the soldiers erected will allow us to cart some of the corn over the burn back to Fairlyden.' James decided. 'It will be more convenient for the thrashing in the winter.' This was true but it was easier to plan than to proceed. Day after day the rain prevented them getting any harvest in at all. Stooks grew green with sprouting corn as they stood in the fields for weeks on end.

'The situation is becoming desperate,' James muttered anxiously at the end of a particularly wet day in October. 'The crops are wasting and we havena even put the binder on to Westhill yet.'

'Unless the ground drys up I dinna see how even a tractor

could pull it up there,' Kirsty fretted.

'Well, there's no use worrying,' Beth consoled them. 'Ye've done your best and even the soldiers and older bairns frae the school have given their help and support, but no man can control the weather. We can only pray to God for mercy.'

So as the autumn of nineteen hundred and forty-two passed, the harvest was snatched in bit by bit whenever there was the faintest chance of a few dry hours. It was the same throughout Southwest Scotland and many other parts of Britain, but the knowledge brought little comfort to Kirsty and James. The yields were low and the quality poor. At the end of October there were still fields of bedraggled stooks sitting in rain-soaked fields. Fairlyden was more fortunate than many farms, especially in view of the extra acres. The corn on Westhill was all that remained to be gathered in.

'It is barely worth the effort o' harvesting,' James lamented bitterly. 'I should never have complied with Steel's instructions. It's been a waste o' seed and all the effort we put into cultivating it.'

'Ye're right, laddie,' Beth sympathised, 'but the weather hasna helped either.'

'It's a good job Steel has been relieved o' his work with the War Agricultural Executive Committee anyway!' James growled 'Or I wouldna have left him in doubt o' our opinion o' him.'

Two weeks later even the corn on Westhill was almost cleared. Kirsty's baby was due at the end of January and her condition was now apparent. James worried continuously about her working but they needed her help. She was the most expert at building the sheaves on to the carts.

'It isna such hard work, James,' she insisted, 'so don't worry about me. Rhoda forks the sheaves quite slowly. It would be a different matter if the crop was heavy and I had forkers sending up sheaves frae both sides o' the cart!'

'Even so you will take care?' James urged anxiously before he went to speak to Rhoda and Albert.

'Don't forget there are two open drains running all the way down Westhill on the remaining stretch,' he instructed. 'See that the horses dinna get too close. Take the waggons up empty and fill them on the way down. Are you listening, Rhoda.'

'Aye.'

'Ach, naebody wi' any sense wad be letting the horses cross

o'er the drains, Mr MacFarlane,' Albert chuckled. 'Rhoda and me'll soon fill the carts, if Jane and Mistress MacFarlane can load them.'

'Right, Albert. Just use the horses to bring the waggons down to the gate. I'll meet you there and cart them home with the tractor. It's too far frae Westhill to the steading for the horses. Paddy and I will stack in the yard, with Mrs Fairly's help.'

This team effort worked well despite the distance from the farmsteading, but by the end of the third afternoon in succession Kirsty was heartily sick of the Westhill ground with its humps and hollows and gut-jerking jolts. She suspected Rhoda allowed the horse to make its own way from stook to stook as they did on the lower, flatter fields, instead of guiding it. But at least she did not complain about having the heaviest work forking up the sheaves all day. It was the last waggon of the day and Kirsty lay down thankfully on top of the load of corn. She stretched out her weary limbs and closed her eyes.

'This load is not too full. I'll ride all the way home on it,' she called to Rhoda.

Deadly tired from her toil, and lulled by the swaying of the waggon, she failed to notice the increasing speed as the horse headed homeward. She was almost asleep when the cart gave its first sickening lurch. The horse whinnied in fear. Rhoda screamed. Kirsty clung to the sheaves on top of the waggon load but they began to slide. The cart jerked again. The whole load catapulted to the ground. Kirsty slid with it, groping blindly, smothered by the suffocating sheaves. There was a wrenching, tearing sound and another whinny from the terrified horse as the cart turned over. 'Rhoda must have let the horse cross the open ditch.' It was Kirsty's last coherent thought as darkness descended on her.

Kirsty tried hard to lift her heavy eyelids but leaden weights were pressing them down. The effort was too great and she sank back again into the long dark tunnel which had no beginning and no end, where pain ebbed and flowed bringing fire and ice. Sometimes she thought there were voices but they were always far away; she could not hear the words; she cried out to them to come closer, to help her out of the black abyss of pain and terror.

Then the day came when she prised her eyes open at last. She did not know where she was. She turned her head with a great effort and saw the figure of a man kneeling, his head level with hers, his face gaunt and white, his eyes dark-ringed and haunted as he stared at her. 'Kirsty?' He whispered her name hoarsely, incredulously. She tried to say his name but no sound came. 'Kirsty . . . Oh, my love . . . my only love . . . It's me, James.'

Again she tried to form the word but the effort was too great and she allowed her heavy lids to fall. When she opened them again it could have been moments later – or hours. The man's head was bowed. Tears were running down his drawn cheeks. One dropped on to her hand where it lay limp on the coverlet, but she felt it.

'Ja-mie . . .? He looked up at the thread of sound. She tried to smile. She felt him take her hand in his and hold it against his cheek gently as though the very bones were made of fragile glass which might shatter if he breathed on them. Her fingers curled ever so slightly against his unshaven cheek.

'Does she recognise ye this time, laddie?' Beth's voice was low, weary and desperately anxious. Kirsty knew it was her mother. She tried to raise her head from the pillow but the effort was too great and she fell back exhausted.

The next time she wakened James was still beside her bed but he was sitting in a low chair this time and she saw he had shaved the stubble from his cheeks, but they were still lined with weariness and his eyes were red-rimmed.

'Kirsty?'

'Hello . . . Jamie . . .' She smiled at him. His mouth, usually so firm, stubborn even, trembled, but his eyes lit with a love which was almost worshipping in its intensity. 'Lucy, Kirsty has wakened . . .' he called softly, his gaze never leaving her face. 'She really does know me.'

Lucy Kildougan moved into Kirsty's line of vision and she was glad she did not need to move her head because the whole room seemed to go round when she made the slightest turn; everything was such an effort.

'Aah, ma lamb . . .' Lucy's voice wobbled tremulously.

'Where am I?'

'Safe in your ain bedroom, lassie. Aah, but it's grand tae have ye back.' Now Lucy's voice choked. 'I'll tell your mother. I'll bring some clear soup. Must feed ye . . .' she muttered as she went silently to the door.

Kirsty's gaze was caught by the shadows flickering and dancing on the walls. Her eyes moved back to James. 'Is it night time?' Her brow puckered like a bewildered child's and her voice was low so that he had to bend to catch her words. 'Why is there a fire?'

'You – you've been ill, Kirsty.' He shuddered and pressed his eyes tightly shut as though by doing so he could blot out the memory of the past ten days. 'Very ill. But you are going to be all right now, my love . . .' He lifted her hand and cradled it against his heart as he fell to his knees beside her bed. 'My only love. I don't know what I should have done if . . .' He closed his eyes again briefly and when he opened them Kirsty saw the shimmer of tears in them. The door opened and Kirsty lifted her eyes to see her mother standing in the doorway. She looked almost fearful. Kirsty smiled at her. Beth caught her breath. She smiled back, though tears were rolling silently down her pale haggard face. Then she came closer, laying a hand on James's shoulder as she stood beside the bed looking down at them both. Her smile widened, encompassing them in its radiance.

'Ye really are better this time . . .' she breathed. She clasped her hands together. 'Thank you, God. Thank you for answering my prayers.' James bowed his head as though joining her in prayer.

'The doctor said we should give ye some beef tea as soon as ye could take it – just a teaspoonful at a time. Dinna move, lassie, but tell me if ye'll try just a sip or two . . .?'

'I'll try. Thank you, Mother.' Her brow creased in a frown as Beth left them alone again. 'Jamie? What's wrong with me? Why am I in bed? I can't remember how I got here?'

'There was . . . You've had an accident. We'll talk about it later when you are stronger, Kirsty . . .' He was relieved to hear Beth come in with a small tray holding a feeding cup with a spout like a teapot.

'Ye should have some rest now, James,' Beth advised. 'Ye look all in yourself and we canna do with two o' ye ill.'

'But I dinna . . .'

'Ye've hardly left Kirsty's bedside since the accident. Ye're worn out, laddie.' Beth's tone was firm. 'Now get some sleep in the spare bedroom. Lucy is filling a stone pig for ye and making some hot milk.'

James nodded. 'No use arguing with your mother when she makes up her mind,' he grinned shakily down at Kirsty, then he bent his head and kissed her tenderly on her temple.

Kirsty managed only a few sips of beef tea before exhaustion claimed her once more but gradually she managed to stay awake longer; always there was her mother or James or Lucy at her side. Then came the day James had dreaded.

'I have a vague memory of falling from a cart . . .' she said clearly one afternoon when she wakened from a deep but natural sleep. 'It was a waggon . . . we were loading corn.' Her eyes widened and she put up a tentative hand and touched her brow where a green and yellow bruise still lingered. 'Rhoda was there . . . the drain! The drain, Jamie! She let the horse . . .'

'Hush, Kirsty, my love, hush,' James urged anxiously. 'The doctor said you were not to have any excitement. You shouldna force yourself to remember until you are stronger,' he pleaded.

'B — but I do remember!' Her eyes dilated and she gripped his arm. 'Rhoda . . .'

'She has gone.' James's voice was curt. His lips were tight and set.

'Gone? Gone where?'

'Away to another farm.'

'But why?'

'We dinna need her any longer. The harvest is finished.' I thought she had killed you, he wanted to shout. He had been unable to bear the sight of the girl when he realised what had happened to his beloved wife, but deep down he had blamed himself for allowing Kirsty to load the waggons, however late the harvest, however desperate the situation. The supervisor had come that same evening and taken Rhoda away, afraid he might injure her in his distraught state. He shuddered.

'Jamie?' Kirsty's voice was low, tense, her eyes fixed on him, watching the emotions chasing each other across his lean face – fear, anger, and something else . . . remorse . . .? She frowned.

'Dinna try to think, Kirsty,' he pleaded softly.

'It's our bairn, isn't it? Isn't it, Jamie?' Her voice rose. 'He's . . .? Is he – dead?' She stared at him. 'Tell me! Jamie, tell me!' She clutched his arm, her eyes wild.

He nodded and bowed his head, unable to look upon her ravaged face. He swallowed convulsively.

'Try not to think of it . . .' he urged hoarsely.

'Not think of it!' Her voice was high, indignant, hurt and angry. 'He was your son too!'

'I know, my love, I know . . . But you are my wife and you matter more to me than anything in the world. The accident caused a miscarriage. Kirsty, you have been so ill, so very ill.

384

I-I thought you were going to die. Now nothing matters except that you have been spared.'

'Our bairn matters. I wanted it. I wanted to give you a son . . .' Kirsty's lips trembled and weak tears filled her eyes and rolled down her pale cheeks. She sank back against the pillow. 'Our son . . . is dead . . .'

'He . . . it never lived, my dear . . .' James tried to take her hand but she resisted and turned her face to the wall.

'Oh God, why?' she uttered with a sob. 'Leave me. Please . . .' Her voice shook. 'I need to be alone.'

James looked at her helplessly. He wanted to take her in his arms and comfort her, share her grief, even weep with her — but she was rejecting him. Doctor Broombank had warned him the loss of the baby might affect her badly. He had hoped Kirsty would have time to regain her strength a little before her memory fully returned. He longed to tell her there would be other babies later . . . But even that comfort was denied him. He bowed his head, remembering his glimpse of the blood-soaked sheets, the doctor's words.

'Your wife has lost a great deal of blood, Mr MacFarlane, but if she lives until morning there is a chance she will survive.' He had been too shocked to listen further. Later when Kirsty had regained consciousness the doctor had warned him the loss of the child might hinder her recovery. What was it he had said . . . 'Usually after a miscarriage, I would recommend another bairn as soon as nature allows, but this was not a normal case. I'm sorry to have to tell you this, but I believe it will be impossible for your wife to conceive another child. Her internal injuries were extremely serious.

Forty-Four

The spring of nineteen hundred and forty-three was approaching rapidly before Kirsty regained any semblance of her former robust health. She was easily tired and fatigue made her depressed and irritable, but there was too much work to be done to dwell on her personal misfortunes. When the German U-boats sank twenty-one merchant ships in March it seemed that Britain's wartime situation was growing even more desperate.

'We canna let them beat us, Kirsty,' James declared, gritting his teeth. 'I'll see that Fairlyden and the land we have in our care is the most productive in the Southwest, but I canna do it without your help. Three hundred and thirty-five acres is a lot o' land and there's no word o' getting another tractor yet.' Kirsty nodded, but her smile was wan. In her heart she knew she had to put the past behind her and face the future, just as her brother Luke was doing. Indeed, although he mentioned no real details of his work in London, it was clear from his letters that he had worked himself into a position of some importance and Luke had never been one to boast about his abilities. If anything he had always made light of his achievements. His visits were rare and invariably short.

Joey Little visited his parents in the Fairlyden cottage whenever he got the slightest opportunity, often travelling for more hours than he was able to spend at home.

'I have a feeling he comes to see Jane as much as he comes to see his mother and father – or anyone else,' Beth teased after one of his flying visits. Jane blushed prettily; it was true they did spend much of their precious free time together, despite Jane's earlier reserve towards all young men in uniform.

Every household seemed to have some connection with men in the services and there was nothing for it but to go on farming and producing as much food as it was possible to produce with the meagre rations which were now allowed for the cattle, pigs and hens and the shortage of imported fertilisers.

Avary Hall, the former home of the Guillymans, had been taken over by the government and as the year advanced prisoners of war were brought there and housed in hastily erected huts in the grounds. These men were expected to work in the surrounding district under supervision. James needed all the labour he could get now that he had so much land in his care, especially since new machinery was so difficult to obtain. It was largely thanks to the additional help of the prisoners that another difficult harvest was snatched in at Fairlyden. Many of the men were Italians; they appeared to enjoy working in the open air and cheerfully helped the women and children gather potatoes on most of the farms around Muircumwell.

Some of the prisoners spent their spare time weaving straw baskets and Kirsty was presented with four to gather in the eggs. One man carved a beautiful wooden doll for four-year-old Irene McGuire and he promised to make her a cradle for Christmas since it seemed likely he would be far from his own home and family.

Looking at the little wooden doll with its moving arms and legs and the dainty scraps of clothes which Lucy had made, Kirsty yearned for another baby.

'It's a year since I lost our own babe,' she sighed, looking at James with wide troubled eyes. His heart sank.

'You were very ill, dearest Kirsty. Doctor Broombank . . .'

'Doctor Broombank? What did he say?' she asked sharply, but James had neither the heart nor the courage to repeat the doctor's verdict in full.

'Er . . . he said it would take time to recover completely . . .' he prevaricated unhappily.

'Surely a year should be ample time?' James looked into her strained face with loving eyes, but Kirsty saw only the pain in their depths and did not realise the pain was for her. Of course James wanted a child as much as she did. All farmers wanted sons of their own – laddies who followed them around, learned to work with them, young men who would take over the land they had toiled to win and improve.

'If I canna give you a bairn I'm no use to you, Jamie . . .'

'Oh, Kirsty! How can you say that? I love you! I canna live without you.'

'Of course you can live without me – and you would still have your heart's desire! You have Fairlyden now, whether I'm alive or dead!'

'Kirsty!' James's face went white at the bitterness in her

voice. He understood her disappointment at not conceiving a child, but she had almost accused him of marrying her to gain Fairlyden. 'You are my heart's desire. Surely you canna believe—'

'Oh, James,' Kirsty's voice was brittle. 'I know you wanted to marry me – but things would probably have been different if I had lived in a cottage without—'

'That's enough, Kirsty!' James's eyes flashed angrily. He pushed himself out of his chair, his own weariness forgotten. 'I did not marry you to gain Fairlyden! I did not need Fairlyden! One day I shall prove that to you – when this bloody war is over!'

'Jamie! Aah . . . I'm . . .' But he had already passed through the door, just managing not to slam it behind him. He did not hear Kirsty's anguished whisper. 'I'm sorry . . . so sorry . . . I didna mean that . . .'

Relations were strained for some weeks between James and Kirsty after her unjust accusation, however veiled or unintentional it had been. She was careful not to mention her craving for a child again but as each month passed she waited tensely; a son for James had become her dearest wish. Now she could appreciate Lucy's and Paddy's terrible disappointment because they had never had a child of their own and she even understood Lucy's over-indulgence of young Irene McGuire.

'Do you still want to adopt Irene when the war is over, Lucy? she asked one afternoon when Lucy was down at Fairlyden helping Beth with the spring cleaning. They were beating the carpet which James and Paddy had helped to hang over a stout rope slung between two trees in the garden.

'Of course we dae!' Lucy barely paused. 'She's like our very ain bairn.'

'Oh Lucy . . .' Kirsty's voice was full of concern and sympathy. 'I wouldn't like to see you hurt, if Irene has to go back to her father . . .'

'It wad break my heart, I'm telling ye.' She beat the carpet with extra vigour as though she was relieving her anger against Josh McGuire. 'We've never heard a word frae him! He never even sent her a wee present at Christmas!' Lucy choked over the cloud of dust her efforts had extracted from the bedroom carpet. 'We ken he's still alive though.' She paused to catch her breath. 'Paddy enquired about adopting her when she had to start school. The headmistress registered her as Irene Kildougan but the authorities canna do anything official without McGuire's permission and we still get money for keeping her as an evacuee.'

Kirsty had had her twenty-seventh birthday in January. Supposing she and James never had another child? She pondered the question of Irene McGuire's adoption. Could she ever adopt a child and love it as her own like Lucy and Paddy? Could James? It was true she had grown very fond of poor Lenny, and now he was dead. She shook her head. Adoption was such a serious step – and yet there would probably be hundreds of children orphaned by this dreadful war.

In the past year it had been impossible to provide even the basic ration of two pints of milk per week in some areas, especially during the winter. Consequently government officials were now urging all dairy farmers to produce more milk wherever possible especially in the winter.

'We have a fine bunch o' heifers to sell, Kirsty,' James announced with pride one evening as they studied the milk records together and prepared pedigrees and information in readiness for a forthcoming sale of Ayrshire cattle.

'Yes, it's an ill wind if it doesna blow some good, I suppose,' Kirsty agreed with a sigh. 'There will be great demand as milk has been so scarce. The prices should be good.'

James laid an affectionate arm around her shoulders. 'Your father would have been pleased with our efforts to keep the Fairlyden herd so near the top of the market, but most of our success is thanks to you. I've been too busy ploughing and cultivating the extra land to grow more corn and potatoes.'

Kirsty leaned her head against his shoulder. 'My father would have been pleased just to know you were his son-in-law, and that you're back at Fairlyden, Jamie. I'm sorry I've been so horrid, and short-tempered, and miserable to you, all these months.'

'You've been through hell, Kirsty. I understand that. I know how much you wanted our baby. I wanted it too and I blame myself for the accident. I should never have let you work so hard, or load the waggons with Rhoda. I've died a thousand deaths just remembering that day.'

'It was an accident, Jamie. It certainly wasna your fault. Anyway,' Kirsty's tone grew resolute, 'I keep telling myself we have so much to be thankful for when you consider all the thousands of men and women who have lost their families, their homes – everything. Luke says the devastation is dreadful in London and the people are so brave and stoical.'

'Yes, we should never grumble,' James agreed fervently. 'We have each other.'

'And there seems to be some hope of winning the war at last now that the Allied Forces have landed in Europe.'

'There is always hope,' James stated emphatically. 'For everything. But I know what you mean, my love, and it would be wonderful for everyone if there was an end to the war in sight.' He turned her face towards him and kissed her lips tenderly. Suddenly, without warning all the old passionate desire flared between them, as it had done in the days before Kirsty's illness. The weakness and depression which had swamped her ecstatic loving had gone. She clung to him now with a fervour which surprised and delighted James.

'Come, my love,' he whispered softly. 'There will be time enough tomorrow to attend to the business of pedigrees and paperwork. Now is the time for loving.' Without waiting for an answer he picked her up in his arms and Kirsty trembled at the naked desire which made his greeny-grey eyes seem almost black in their intensity.

That summer night of nineteen hundred and forty-four was the beginning of a new life and a new loving for Kirsty and James. They had reached out past the troubles and grief which life had thrust at them; they had found each other again – not with the all-consuming desire of their youthful passion, but with a mature and deeper love.

Almost a year later, in May nineteen hundred and forty-five, came the long awaited news that the war in Europe was over. When Beth heard the announcement on the radio she burst into tears of relief. It was true that the war with Japan still raged, but now the end really was in sight. Later in the day she went with Kirsty and James to the Muircumwell Store to rejoice with Anna and Lizzie and many of the other local people from the village.

In his letter a few days later Luke briefly mentioned some of the dreadful atrocities which were being discovered in the Nazi prison camps. 'I am convinced at last,' he had written, 'that we had to fight for the freedom of the world, but it grieves me that so many people have had to die so that we might live in peace. When the war with Japan is over, and all the administration involved with demobilisation is complete, I intend to do whatever is necessary to be a true servant of God. My resolve has been strengthened rather than weakened during these years of war, but first I must give what assistance I can to those who search for loved ones. Many of them will search in vain, I fear, and it makes me feel ashamed of my helplessness in the face of their great need.'

Five days later came the unbelievable news that Luke had been killed by an unexploded bomb while going about his daily work in the streets of London. Everyone at Fairlyden was stunned.

Beth was too unselfish to allow her personal grief to mar the joy of others; she knew she was not alone in her loss. There were many loved ones who would never return. Even in the parish of Muircumwell she knew there were few families who had not lost a husband, a father or a son, an uncle, nephew or cousin. Beth's faith in God was her salvation now, as it had been when Logan died. She knew in her heart that Luke would not have wished her to grieve for him and she prayed fervently for strength to carry on.

At Mains of Muir Emma remembered the pain of loss she had felt over Cameron's death, and would always feel deep in her own heart; she proved a great comfort to Beth and Kirsty. Billy Fairly's letters also expressed a rare compassion and understanding and Beth regretted that he was so far away across the ocean. 'I salute sincerely all the men and women who have worked and fought, suffered and died, to free the world of tyranny,' he had written, 'and I pray they will be rewarded as they deserve with peace on earth and glory in heaven.'

Forty-Five

'There's to be a general election on the fifth of July,' James remarked to Paddy one afternoon during the milking. 'I shouldna think there'll be any doubt who will win though, after all Mr Churchill has done to keep up our spirits and help us triumph over Hitler's tyranny.'

'Ach now, and you never can be sure,' Paddy responded with a twinkle, though in his heart he was convinced Mr Churchill would lead the Tories to victory.

A few days later Paddy danced a jig across the farmyard waving a piece of paper in his hand and singing at the top of his voice. 'Paddy Kildougan is not caring who wins the election . . . Let them all heckle and shout and promise heaven on earth! We have got our bit of heaven right here!'

'What ever has got into you so early in the morning, Paddy Kildougan?' Kirsty asked, smiling widely in response to the little Irishman's own irrepressible grin. Lucy came hurrying out of the cottage after him, laughing and crying at the same time.

'It's the adoption, Miss Kirsty! Irene is our very ain bairn! Och, there am I calling ye Miss Kirsty in my excitement!' Lucy blushed. 'And your ain husband standing there beside ye.'

'Oh, Lucy! It doesna matter what you call me. I'm so happy for you, I really am!' Kirsty hugged her warmly. 'I must go and tell Mother your good news.'

The result of the general election came as a surprise to James and to thousands like him when at last the votes of members of the armed forces had all been counted.

'We can only hope Mr Attlee will have the strength and wisdom needed to make Great Britain truly great again,' Beth murmured with a troubled frown. 'He has many plans for what he calls a "Welfare State". It all sounds very praiseworthy, but where is the money to come frae with so much spent on weapons and all the debts we owe to America?'

'Taxes?' Kirsty suggested glumly.

'However he intends to pay for it, I imagine his first priority must still be to fill peoples' bellies,' James said decisively. 'We can only wait and see how he means to do it, and whether the Labour party will keep the promises made by the Coalition government. I hope they remember it doesna suddenly mean there will be plenty to eat just because the war in Europe has ended. The Japanese are still fighting and there's more than those in Great Britain with empty larders.'

'Then we shall just have to go on producing as much food as we can at home – just as we have been doing during the war,' Kirsty shrugged philosophically.

'A lot will depend on the Ministry of Food. It has control of supplies and prices, but I believe you're right, Kirsty. You were certainly right about the need for more milk!'

'Mmm . . . we canna grumble!' Kirsty grinned up at him with something of her old mischievous smile. 'And the more milk they want the greater will be the demand for good dairy cattle and Fairlyden is ready to oblige, don't you think, Jamie?'

'Indeed I do, thanks to you thinking ahead and refusing to give in to the likes o' Steel.' James agreed. 'We're making a nice little profit out of the heifer sales already.'

'Yes. Father would never have believed Fairlyden heifers would average five hundred guineas at a public auction.'

'He would certainly never have dreamed of an Ayrshire bull reaching a record of three thousand, two hundred guineas!' Beth exclaimed. 'Not even one from Mr Drummond's famous herd. It's more than the price o' a good house!'

'Well, we shall be humbly delighted if we can rear a few more bulls like our own Fairlyden Noble Hero!' Kirsty smiled.

'Logan would have been so happy and truly proud of you both,' Beth sighed. 'I'm sure he thought o' ye as a son, even when ye were a laddie, Jamie, and I ken it was his dearest wish to see ye back at Fairlyden.'

James nodded. 'I thought it was the most cruel blow imaginable when I knew Nithanvale was to be taken over by the government, but it's strange how life's pathways are mapped out for us.'

When Beth left them alone to attend to her cooking Kirsty turned to James and her eyes were no longer filled with happiness. James's heart sank. He knew the reason for those troubled shadows.

'Do you think you could learn to regard another man's son as your own, Jamie?' she asked softly.

'Another man's son?' He frowned. 'What other man? Who are you talking about, Kirsty?'

'Nobody in particular, but I've begun to despair o' giving you a child o' your own . . .'

'I know, I know, my love . . .' James's voice was gruff as he moved across the room and took her in his arms. Kirsty's eyes filled with tears but she blinked them away determinedly.

'So you have given up hope too?'

'Doctor Broombank warned me that it might prove impossible to have more bairns after the accident,' he admitted reluctantly. 'Oh, Kirsty . . . When I saw you, all I cared about was that your life should be spared – and you are all I care about now. Believe me!'

Kirsty nodded. 'I do believe you, because I love you too – more than life itself.' Her voice was husky. 'But do you think we should adopt a child, like Lucy and Paddy have adopted Irene? We could bring him up as our own. If we go on making progress, now that the war is almost finished, we should have so much to offer him . . .' she went on eagerly. 'Maybe we could even have two – a boy and a girl!'

'Hey, steady on!' James chuckled at her enthusiasm. 'This needs thinking about.' He remembered his mother's doubts and fears that young Irene would bring the Kildougans as much heartbreak as happiness – but that was if they continued to spoil her. He also remembered their joy when the adoption papers arrived.

'I'm sure there will be children who need love and a home and family,' Kirsty persisted.

'You are probably right, but I need time to get used to the idea . . .' James mused. 'I certainly think we should wait until the war with Japan is truly over. Who knows what might happen yet?'

Kirsty nodded agreement. She had planted the seed in James's mind. She knew he would consider it carefully and she would abide by his decision.

'The Japanese have really surrendered!' Kirsty announced after listening to an announcement on the wireless one morning in August. She frowned. 'Apparently the Americans dropped two atomic bombs to make them submit. I don't know what sort o' bombs they are but it sounds as though they have caused terrible destruction.'

The main reaction was relief that the war was completely

over at last, and joy at Prime Minister Attlee's announcement that there would be two days' holiday. In Muircumwell, as in the towns and villages all over Britain, victory celebrations were hastily finalised.

'I've sold more o' Lizzie's stock o' Union Jacks than I've sold ounces o' sugar,' Anna MacFarlane chuckled when Beth called in at the shop.

'That's because we had more flags than sugar to sell!' Lizzie muttered dryly. 'There's a committee organising a tea party and a bonfire for the village, Mrs Fairly. Mrs Turner was wondering if ye'd play the piano for some games and singing in the Mackenzie Hall afterwards?' She looked at Beth uncertainly. 'She didna like tae ask ye herself – you losing Master Luke and all. And Master Cameron frae the Mains.' Lizzie shook her head sadly. 'Not everybody will be rejoicing.'

'I will play the piano for the celebrations,' Beth said quietly. 'Ye may tell Mrs Turner, Lizzie.'

'Thank ye,' Lizzie said warmly. 'The committee will be relieved. There's awfy few musical folks i' the parish these days. I dinna ken who else they would have asked if ye'd refused tae help. Even the school teacher canna play the piano! There's naebody near hand tae teach any o' the bairns.'

'Is there any word o' Joey Little being demobbed,' Anna interrupted her sister.

'Oh yes, Jane had a letter two days ago,' Beth smiled. 'He expects to be released within the next two months – maybe sooner.'

'Will there be a job for him at Fairlyden?'

'James can find him plenty o' work, as I'm sure ye'll ken, Anna!' Beth smiled. 'In fact I suspect it will not be long before we see Joe and Jane getting married. James plans to offer them the house at Burnside – that is if he can continue renting the land frae Strathtod Estate.'

'And what would happen tae Mrs Brown then?'

'She has put her name down for one o' the new prefabricated houses.'

'Och, that's right,' Lizzie nodded, 'the council are putting them up on the wee bit o' land behind the smiddy.'

'That'll be fine all round then! Joe is a good laddie,' Anna said warmly, 'And I reckon Jane will make him a good wife – even though she wasna used tae country life when she first came.'

* * *

Both Kirsty and Beth helped with the large tea parties for the Muircumwell children and there was a great air of jubilation everywhere. James and Paddy had helped to cart wood and an assortment of materials to make a massive bonfire behind the village, but as Kirsty and James stood together later that evening watching the magnificent display of shooting stars, Catherine wheels, Roman candles and rockets, Kirsty could not deny the emptiness which filled her heart. She watched parents with their excited children, eyes aglow with wonder, and a terrible depression weighed down on her.

'The display is almost over.' James spoke close to her ear. 'Shall we go home now?' She nodded, suddenly unable to speak for the lump in her throat. James always understood exactly how she felt. He always had, even when they were children.

James was a considerate lover, but that night when he took her in his arms and kissed her, she knew he was being more than loving. More than anything else in the world he wanted her to be happy. Kirsty recognised that much of her own happiness lay in making her husband happy too and in her heart she knew the child she craved was Jamie's own child. She wanted more than a pretty infant to mother, to play with and even indulge. She wanted a child who was part of them both – a son, or a daughter, who would grow up with them, develop, become a person with traits, and even funny little foibles, inherited from each of them, to grow up into a worthwhile human being with character and compassion, with strength and a purpose in life . . .

However low her spirits it would have been impossible for Kirsty not to respond to James's tender and exquisite lovemaking. The events of the long busy day were forgotten as they created their own rainbow of stars, and soared to the pinnacle of heaven in each other's arms.

'We shall never forget the victory celebrations,' she murmured happily before she drifted into a dreamless sleep. At her side James lay awake pondering whether he was being selfish in not wanting to share Kirsty with any child who was not a part of them.

Once the victory celebrations were over it was essential to settle down to work again and at Fairlyden that meant the harvest, rapidly followed by the potato gathering, the turnip lifting and the bringing in of the cattle for the winter.

'I'm glad Joe was released earlier than he expected. Already I wonder how we ever managed without him,' James remarked to Alex Fairly and his younger son, Paul. The traditional Sunday gatherings between The Mains and Fairlyden had never completely ceased but they had become less regular during the last few years. Even now the rationing of petrol and food was still as big a problem as it had been at any time during the war; the stocks of food were simply not available anywhere. In the kitchen Emma, Beth and Kirsty discussed the queues which the townswomen had to suffer.

'Maybe we dinna get oranges or bananas the minute they arrive in the country,' Emma mused, 'but at least we dinna have the frustration o' queuing for hours only to be told they're all finished just when we reach the counter. I always think Lizzie Whiteley does her best to allocate things fairly.'

'What was it Uncle Alex wanted to discuss so urgently with Jamie, Aunt Emma?' Kirsty asked, changing the subject from the eternal food shortages.

'Aah, yes. Alex hopes to persuade that husband o' yours to join the National Farmers' Union, Kirsty. He believes James is just the type o' man needed to put the case o' the local farmers to the area committees and so on.'

'James?' Kirsty stared at her aunt. 'But he doesna even go to the meetings now. He never has time.'

'Well, maybe he will make time now that Joe Little is back frae the army and there should be more labour about soon – though some say a lot o' the men will never return to farm work.'

'But what could Jamie do exactly?'

'Alex says it is important that a fair picture o' every area, and every branch o' farming, should be put before the government. They have agreed to continue reviewing prices and supplies every year in February so it's essential to get the facts right for the sake o' the farming industry and for the good o' the country.' Paul already goes to the local meetings. It was his idea to persuade James to go too. He's been to college and got his education, but he also knows what real farming is about. Some o' these government officials dinna listen to ordinary farmers.'

'But Jamie is an ordinary farmer, Aunt Emma!'

'No he isna – though he can still talk to his ain kind. He knows what he's talking about and how to put it into words.

Alex thinks he's done well since the war started – managing all that extra land at Strathtod as well as Fairlyden. By the way, is the owner o' Strathtod going to keep James as a tenant now the war is over?'

'We hope he will, but the old laird died some time ago and the son is still in the RAF. We only have contact through the factor.'

'Ach well, Kirsty, you go through to the other room and help your Uncle persuade James to join the NFU. I'll help your mother finish the dinner dishes. Is that all right, Beth?'

'Of course,' Beth smiled at them both, 'though I dinna think Alex needs much help when it comes to persuading anyone.'

'I'm not so sure about that . . .' Emma frowned. 'He's been a bit shocked since we got the letter frae America with the news o' his brother's death.'

'But Alex knew Billy was ill . . . In his last letter to me he said he had seen enough of this world and its troubles. I felt he was more than ready to die. Of course he hadna been in good health for a long time, and he was so far away frae his own kith and kin,' Beth added sadly.

Emma nodded. 'I know, and I agree, Beth. It's just that it makes Alex remember his own age. He was sixty-two last week – a year older than Billy.'

'Aye, I'm forgetting we're into November already,' Beth sighed.

It was a couple of weeks after Alex Fairly's visit that the farming papers reported the desperate situation caused by a worldwide shortage of food.

'Mr Tom Williams, the new Minister of Agriculture, says the Labour Government intends to continue guaranteeing prices and markets for the main commodities,' James reflected, studying the reports intently. 'But that's because they are desperate for food at the present time and they're afraid the prices might get out o' control and cause a civil war instead of a world war. They intend to impose controls to ensure efficiency and regulate the wages for the farm workers. In Scotland we're to have two sets of controlling committees . . . Umph, so much for our "free world",' he grunted, then continued reading. 'These committees will direct the cropping and the dispossession of owners and tenants from land that is not managed efficiently . . .'

'At least we dinna need to worry this time. No one can say you aren't efficient, Jamie.'

'I hope they canna! But I think your Uncle Alex is right, Kirsty. There will be some tough negotiating to do – not so much at the present time while the Government needs farmers to produce as much as we can to keep starvation at bay – but later, when the world readjusts to the changes the war has brought about . . . It would be criminal to allow the land to become derelict again as it did after the last war, especially after the toil and effort we have had, and are still having, to bring the soil back to fertility. Anyway, who knows what sort o' demands Russia will make? Maybe Mr Boyd-Orr has the right idea when he speaks of having one big organisation to control food and agriculture throughout the world. It would be fine if we could have one massive larder for the whole world so that no nation ever goes hungry and nothing goes to waste either . . .' He grinned. 'They would need women like you and your mother to organise it though, for I'm sure the politicians canna do it.'

'Is that what you might call a pie in the sky, Jamie?' Kirsty chuckled.

'I suppose it is a bit unlikely, especially when we hear so much about the cruelties inflicted during the war – not to mention the present bickering of the victors!'

'So, will you do as Uncle Alex suggested and join the National Farmers' Union?'

'I don't know. I dinna want to attend too many meetings – not at the present time anyway.' He smiled conspiratorially at her. She grinned back and got up from her own chair to sit on his lap.

'You dinna need to worry about me, Jamie.'

He cradled her against his chest and allowed his chin to rest on her soft hair. 'I shall always worry about you, my—' He broke off hurriedly and Kirsty scrambled back to her own chair with flushed cheeks at the sound of Jane Bennet and Beth coming from the kitchen.

Beth looked sharply from one to the other and smiled.

'Jane tells me that she and Joe plan to marry in the summer if ye can give them Mrs Brown's house by then, James.' Her smile widened. 'And I do believe it is time I used some o' the money your Uncle Billy left me and bought a house o' my own – in the village.'

'Oh, Mother! You canna do that!' Kirsty was aghast.

'Indeed no!' James declared in a shocked voice. 'This was your home long before it was mine.' His face had paled. 'I never considered the situation before. You always made me feel so welcome.'

'And welcome ye've always been, laddie,' Beth said warmly. 'But I got a letter this morning frae Billy Fairly's lawyers in America.' Jane tactfully excused herself and Beth went on. 'I havena had a chance to tell ye about it until now. He had far more money than we could ever have imagined! He's left five thousand pounds to your Uncle Alex, Kirsty, and the same to your Aunt Ellen. He hadna left anything to Sadie, it seems, but he must have relented after she was widowed because the lawyer found a letter for her amongst his papers and a draft equivalent to a thousand pounds. He's left everything else to me . . .' Beth finished bemusedly, still finding it hard to believe. Her cheeks were pink as she looked from Kirsty to Jamie and back again. 'I dinna ken what he must have had in American dollars but the lawyer says I shall receive between fourteen and fifteen thousand pounds!'

'Oh, Mother!' Kirsty was astonished.

'That's a fortune,' James said quietly. 'But I'm sure Kirsty's Uncle Billy knew you deserve it. You have my sincere congratulations.'

'Oh yes, frae both of us!' Kirsty exclaimed, recovering from the initial shock. She went to Beth and hugged her tightly.

'I canna imagine what Aunt Sadie will say if she ever finds out, but you do deserve some good fortune, Mother. No wonder you are thinking of buying a modern little house all of your own – and just when we shall be needing your help and advice too.'

'Och, I'm only buying a house o' my own because it's time you two had a bit o' privacy. And when Jane moves out ye'll—' She stopped suddenly and stared at the young couple in front of her, noticing their bright eyes and happy smiles. 'What do ye mean, Kirsty? Just when you are needing my help and advice?'

Kirsty's cheeks flushed prettily as she met her husband's loving gaze. James gave a little nod in response to her silent question.

'We're going to make you a grandmother after all . . .' she whispered huskily.

'A grandmother! Oh, Kirsty! My lassie! Can it be true? Is it possible? O-oh . . .' She enfolded Kirsty in her arms, laughing with joy despite the two fugitive tears escaping down her cheeks. Then she turned and hugged James too. 'This means more to me than all the money in the world!' she breathed.

'And to us too,' James assured her.

'There's no doubt about it? Are ye well enough, Kirsty? I never even suspected . . .'

'You'd better calm down, Mother, or you'll have a heart attack!' Kirsty chuckled. 'The baby is not due until May, but Doctor Broombank assures me there is no doubt and I'm in perfect health.'

'What an eventful year this has been,' Beth murmured softly, thinking of the son she had lost and the grandchild she was to gain. 'God is indeed merciful.'

Forty-Six

Early in the New Year James was summoned to an interview with Sebastian Christie-Hall, the man who had inherited the Strathtod Estate.

'Well? Aren't you going to tell me why Flight-Lieutenant Christie-Hall – or whatever his title is – wanted to see you?' Kirsty demanded eventually, frustrated by his silent preoccupation.

'He wanted to warn me not to make any longterm plans. He intends to sell the Strathtod Estate – probably in a few months' time. He's a very nice fellow, but he made it plain there's no way we shall be able to keep on renting the land at Burnside, or at Strathwood.'

'Oh.' Kirsty frowned. 'I know you'll be a bit disappointed when you were just getting the soil into better condition but it will not make any difference to the number of cows we are able to keep at Fairlyden, will it? After all you were only asked to take over the land to make sure more of it could be ploughed for corn.'

'That's true.' James shrugged. 'No, I dinna think it should make much difference to the size of our herd, but the more cereals we can grow the better we can feed the cows. There'll certainly not be any imported feeding-stuff for some time to come.'

'The need for cereals seems to be greater than ever – at least if the bread is anything to go by! It's blacker than it's been all through the war.' Kirsty grimaced. 'We're supposed to believe it's better for us, but it doesn't taste better.'

'I hope you're not going short of anything you need for your own good health, Kirsty?' James asked anxiously, returning all his attention to her welfare.

'No, of course I'm not,' she laughed gently. 'Just look at the size of me and I've ages to wait yet. If Mother had her way she would wrap me up in cotton wool, but I really do need to take some exercise.'

'Just so long as you're careful. I couldna bear it if anything happened to you. You know that . . .' He moved across the room and cupped her face gently in his hands. He kissed her tenderly.

'Oh, I shall be glad when the waiting is over!' Kirsty sighed, 'I'm sure cows dinna have such problems and they exercise all day.'

'Maybe, but you're more precious than a whole herd o' cows, my love. Has Doctor Broombank persuaded you to go into the nursing home to have the baby yet?'

'Yes, he has! He was here this morning.' Kirsty gave an exaggerated sigh. 'Though I still canna see why he thinks it's necessary.'

'Aah, that is a relief!'

'Not to me it isna, James MacFarlane! It will only cost you a lot of money for nothing. In my opinion all babies should be born in their own homes! I've only agreed to go to stop you and Mother worrying so much. By the way, did Mother tell you what she plans to do with some of Uncle Billy's money?'

'Apart from building on two extra rooms, you mean – when building materials become available again, that is?'

'You knew she was going to start giving music lessons to some of the local children?'

'Yes. Aunt Lizzie thinks it's a splendid idea. So do I, as a matter of fact, so long as it isna too tiring for her.'

'Mmm, I agree, but she is also going to set aside a sum of money for a music scholarship to be awarded to any Muircumwell bairn with genuine musical talent who canna afford to study. Apparently that's what Grandfather Bradshaw once did for her in a smaller way, though she never knew about it until years later.'

It was on the last day of April, or rather during the night, that Kirsty felt the first severe pain. The baby was not supposed to be due for at least another three weeks but when the second spasm came she knew there was no mistake. James had been away all day on business and he had been deadly tired when he returned. Now she thought of it, he had never mentioned what sort of business he had been attending. She frowned thoughtfully but another spasm made her catch her breath. When it passed she wakened James. Instantly he flew into a panic and it took her several minutes to calm him and assure him she was all right.

'For a man who has seen so many births you surprise me,

404

James MacFarlane,' she said with mock severity.'

'That is completely different. We have to drive to the nursing home and it's the middle of the night . . .'

The pain returned. When it eased Kirsty whispered, 'I wish I hadna promised to go, Jamie. I'd feel much better here with you.' In answer James took her in his arms and kissed her gently, then almost before she knew it he was bundling her into the Morris and Beth was telephoning Doctor Broombank to let him know they were on their way to the nursing home so that he could be there too, as arranged.

It was evening when James crept into the room where Kirsty lay in the neat white bed, tired, but smiling with happiness at the sight of her husband.

'You look far more tired than I feel, Jamie!' she greeted softly.

'This has been the longest day of my life – and the most surprising!' Kirsty grinned up at him before he bent his head and kissed her with tender reverence.

'I saw a woman on my way in.' He spoke in hushed tones as though afraid to speak normally. 'She says I can only stay five minutes because you are very tired and you need to rest.'

'That's Mrs Langby – the owner and matron of this establishment,' Kirsty grimaced. 'Actually she is very nice – but she has taken away my babies and I'm so impatient for you to see them . . .'

'Twin sons! I still canna believe it. You could have knocked me down with a feather when Doctor Broombank came all the way to Fairlyden in person to tell us. He looked as proud as though he had produced them himself.'

Kirsty blushed and James thought how pretty and how modest she was despite her recent ordeal. 'He was wonderful!' she said softly.

'Hey, if he wasna getting middle-aged I'd be jealous of him,' James twinkled.

'You'll never need to be jealous of anyone, Jamie – not even your own sons – I promise.'

A few minutes later Mrs Langby bustled in and hustled him away, insisting that Kirsty must rest now.

'I shall keep your laddies in my own room tonight,' she informed them both, 'but if ye're here at two-thirty tomorrow you may see them. Prompt, remember.' James nodded as meekly as a schoolboy and Kirsty wanted to giggle, but suddenly she was too tired to do more than stifle a huge yawn and whisper goodbye.

The following afternoon both James and Beth arrived at the nursing home at two-thirty on the dot and were shown into Kirsty's room. Seconds later Mrs Langby arrived with two tightly swathed white bundles and placed them both in the large wooden crib which had been installed beside the bed. 'Here we are – the MacFarlane boys!' she announced like a conjuror about to perform an amazing feat. 'Identical, they are! Two fine laddies, even if I do say so myself. Now don't tire my patient,' she added sternly and swept out of the room, much to the relief of its occupants. Immediately Beth moved to the crib, James beside her. They stared in awe at the two tiny faces with their tightly clenched fists and button noses.

'They're beautiful . . .' Beth breathed tremulously. 'I canna wait to have ye all back home at Fairlyden, lassie.'

Kirsty smiled and looked at James; he had not spoken a word. He swallowed hard and his eyes were suspiciously bright as they met her own.

'It's a miracle.' His voice was deep and husky.

'What names will you give them?' Beth asked. 'These MacFarlane laddies . . .'

'We considered various names for a boy or a girl, but not for two at a time! What do you think about Logan James, Mother?' Beth nodded vigorously, delighted at the thought of another young Logan at Fairlyden. 'And the second one?'

'Nicholas Luke?' James suggested, but this time Beth frowned, considering.

'Nicholas . . . That'll be for my ain father? Aye, I like that. But Luke . . .' She sighed. 'He was a good laddie, but he was never a farmer . . . Ye'll be wanting both o' your laddies to follow in your footsteps – another generation for Fairlyden!'

'They will make their own decisions in life,' James said gravely. 'At least they will if they have their mother's determined character.' He grinned at his wife. She shook her fist at him playfully.

'Just you wait until I'm on my feet again. You needna think you can bully me just because I shall have three MacFarlane males to deal with – and all of them proud and stubborn as only MacFarlanes can be, no doubt! Anyway, what about Nicholas Alexander? Or Nicholas Crispin perhaps?'

'Such a big mouthful for a tiny scrap,' Beth murmured

406

softly. 'But I know your Grandfather Bradshaw would have been proud to have had another Crispin – and none o' us could have stayed at Fairlyden if it hadna been for him . . .'

'Nicholas Crispin and Logan James it is then,' Kirsty announced proudly.

'It's just as well ye concluded that business with Mr Christie-Hall so successfully, James, now ye'll have two sons to provide for.'

'What business? What have you been up to, Jamie, while I'm imprisoned in this place?' Kirsty teased.

'I bought another farm.'

'You *what*?' Her smiled changed to consternation when she heard her husband's reply.

'I didna tell you before because I didna want to worry you and I wanted it to be a surprise if it all worked out. Strathtod Estate has been sold. Most o' the farms have gone to existing tenants. Sebastian Christie-Hall wanted the Burnside and Strathwood holdings for two of his ex RAF friends who have a fancy to try farming as they have both been invalided out of the forces. He told me about them the first time we met. The Tower House is to be demolished, so I offered for Strathtod Home Farm and now it is ours, Kirsty.' He grinned triumphantly down at her shocked face.

'Oh, Jamie . . .' Kirsty chewed her lip. He looked so pleased with himself, but her own heart sank. 'However shall we afford it?' she whispered hoarsely. 'I mean . . . I know the heifers have sold well, and we have quite a bit o' money in the bank now . . . b-but the Strathtod Home Farm! It must be nearly three hundred acres.'

'Three hundred and ten to be exact.' James was smiling broadly. He moved back to the bedside and took her hand gently in his. 'I didna mean to alarm you, Kirsty. Remember when Nithanvale was sold, I told you I had invested most o' the money in Government Savings Schemes as part o' the war effort.'

'I remember you told me, just after we were married, but . . .'

'But you never asked how much, and it was all tied up in the war effort anyway. There wasn't quite enough to buy the Home Farm, but with the money we had frae the heifer sales we can pay for it outright.

'I can scarcely believe it!'

'It will be some time before we can make any improvements of course,' James added cautiously, 'but I'm sure you will be pleased when you see it. It has a good house too and Joe Little will make a reliable foreman when he has Jane for a wife . . .' He broke off and looked anxiously into Kirsty's face. 'I did it for you, my love,' he whispered softly, 'For us – the MacFarlanes.' He glanced at the sleeping infants. Kirsty smiled radiantly and followed his gaze, then she looked up at her mother.

'Things have come full circle,' Beth said quietly. 'Fairlyden was once part o' Strathtod, Kirsty. Your Great Grandfather Bradshaw owned it for a time. Your Great Grandfather Logan was factor there too. If they're looking down on us I'm sure they'll be happy to know there's another generation ready to carry on. I only hope Rabbie Burn's prophecy will prove true in the bairns' lifetime.

> 'Then let us pray that come it may,
> As come it will for a' that,
> That sense and worth, o'er a' the earth,
> May bear the gree, and a' that.
> For a' that, and a' that,
> It's coming yet for a' that,
> That man to man, the warld o'er,
> Shall brothers be for a' that.

'I'll leave ye alone for a wee while now, before the matron comes to send us out again.'

The door closed softly behind Beth and Kirsty gazed at James with loving eyes. 'I love you, Jamie – father of my sons . . .'